ELEKA:
THE HIDDEN KINGDOM

LEAGUE OF SUPERNATURAL ASSASSINS

By

J.E. Taylor

Eleka: The Hidden Kingdom © 2023 J.E. Taylor

Cover Art by SLM Creations

BOOK ONE:

THE WITCH ASSASSIN

An assassin tasked with taking out a mythical fae king...

In a realm that doesn't exist...

Mya's mission is to get in, obtain the fae king's DNA, and get out.

It should be easy with her gifts, except when does anything ever go as planned?

But failing in her line of work is a death sentence, and nothing in her training prepared her for Tavin Zorander—the most powerful Elvren to ever exist. After all, it's his family's magic that's kept his kingdom cloaked from the prying eyes of the universe for centuries.

When she finds herself at the mercy of the fae king, Mya has a choice to make.

Does she use her darkest power, thus compromising her mission, or should she surrender to Tavin's desires and put his entire kingdom at risk?

THE WITCH ASSASSIN
CHAPTER ONE

MY LUNGS BURNED AS I ran toward the section of Ireland where Earth's portal to Icarus resided. Multiple footfalls followed, echoing in the deep night. I had too far to go to escape, and their drunken slurs were getting closer.

My luck had run out when I'd crossed in front of a pub at the same time these drunken assholes had spilled out the door. I didn't have time to pull my weapons from the ether before one of them grabbed my shirt, tearing it as he tried to grope me. I planted my knee in his groin and slipped past another hand, hoping that was enough to stop them.

But it only made them more savage and determined after a night of drinking and probably reminiscing about imagined conquests.

I tucked the vial of blood I had gotten from my last job into the pocket in my bra. If I lost it, the Director would have me beaten within a breath of life. He wouldn't give a damn that a drunken crowd of men were trying to accost me. He would only care that I had finally failed one of his impossible missions.

A hand grabbed at my shoulder, tilting me off-balance, and I tumbled to the ground. The men surrounded me, mocking me and laughing as they circled like a pack of rabid wolves.

I didn't have my normal assassin outfit on that was sleek like a second skin and covered me from ankle to neck. Here on earth, I only had this skirt and thin shirt.

And now that I was on the ground, the skirt had slid up, giving the drunks a good view of my ass, feeding their frenzy.

I rolled onto my back, trying to straighten myself out, but their eyes lingered, flashing with lust. Alcohol from their breaths hung on the air strong enough to make me gag, even from six feet above me.

The man I'd kneed started unzipping his pants.

"Hold her, boys, while I make her regret hitting my family jewels." He grinned.

Anger flared inside of me before anyone so much as touched me. I should have attacked in front of the bar. I bared my teeth at them in a hiss, but it didn't stop them. Hands grabbed my shoulders, trying to pin me to the hard ground.

I did the only logical thing a soul eater like me could do. I ripped their souls, along with every ounce of their life force, from them, swallowing their essence with a snarl. Their souls filled me more than the adrenaline pumping through my veins, making my muscles buzz with an extra boost of power.

I rolled, avoiding their crashing bodies, and climbed to my feet, feeling the euphoria of devouring their crooked souls. I licked my lips in satisfaction and stalked off into the woods, straightening out this unpleasant outfit. I could not wait to get back home and get into something more comfortable.

But that wouldn't happen until after I reported to the Director. Which about on par with entertaining a group of drunks.

I wasn't looking forward to it at all. I dreaded interacting with him, especially when I had extra information from a job. He didn't instill loyalty from his league by being benevolent. Instead, he ruled us with fear that had been conditioned into us from birth.

Sometimes, I thought he put an obedient gene in the mix of our DNA because I had never heard of anyone disobeying him. The fear of being made an example of lived in our hearts and minds, staunching rebellion in its tracks.

Of course, none of us ever talked about dissent. That was akin to mutiny, and even though most of us had a haunted look in our eyes, one that mirrored what I saw in my own eyes every night, we never spoke about our unrest.

We never talked about disobedience because we saw the ramifications. There had been a few assassins in my lifetime who had not met their deadlines, and they were dragged back to Icarus and publicly tortured to death.

We knew the cost of failure.

Just like we never spoke about how we came into existence. Some assassins were engineered. Some like me had real parents, versus test tubes as incubators, but we all had been manipulated with various strains of DNA.

So, we focused on learning and training and surviving and interacted more as competitors than comrades.

I was lucky. I had no family for the Director to lean on to keep me in line like some of the others. I couldn't imagine the fear of failure if someone else's well-being was on the line. My insides squeezed at the thought.

I glanced around, getting my bearings. I had miles to go to get to the portal, and teleporting, or what we called zapping to other places within a realm, wasn't possible. Not when I'd need all my energy to make it back.

The thought of walking that far raked my nerves, but the blood sacrifice the damn portals required made me slow my pace, conserving the energy infusion from those drunks.

I hadn't heard the others complain about the sacrifice portals' requirements, but for me, the portal wouldn't let me pass without at least a pint of blood.

Maybe it was the fact that I usually conjured a portal wherever I was, and perhaps that made it require more of a blood sacrifice to get back to Icarus. But even with normal portals, I found them to be greedy bitches when I wanted to go home where the League of Supernatural Assassins' compound resided, and my dorm room and pet snake awaited me.

Perhaps bypassing the compound's outer portal was why it demanded more blood from me than others. Everyone else jumped to the portal outside the compound to reach their destinations, but I just jumped to and from the compound.

The why didn't matter. Every trip home was the same.

I shook my head, dismissing the thought. I waved my hand, conjuring my own portal home with a fraction of the energy that it would have taken to zap to the normal portal placed in some random field near a bluff overlooking the ocean.

I pulled a blade from the ether and took a deep breath before slicing my wrist. I swiped my blood across the portal, and it opened, sucking me in and then spitting me out in the portal room at the complex.

The room was barren, and I startled, holding my wrist to my chest. The Director's guards weren't here. Someone always monitored the portal room to sign us out and sign us back in.

I blinked and headed toward the door, hoping my wrist would mend by the time I got to the Director's office.

In the halls, there was pandemonium. People ran as if the world was on fire, and no one even spared me a glance. Ava, the Director's mate, didn't even acknowledge me as we passed in the hall to his office. She looked just as harried as the rest of the people in the complex.

I didn't stop to ask what was going on, not with the exhaustion setting in from the blood loss. I just headed to the Director's office to deliver the sample and the extra information I had obtained on this latest mission.

Dread seeped into my skin with each step I took.

THE WITCH ASSASSIN
CHAPTER TWO

I T SEEMED WHILE I was away, someone had finally rebelled and destroyed the UV field that spanned over the compound and kept the night walkers like the Director safe.

Which explained the absolute chaos in the hallways and the darkness the Director's office was plunged in. Metal barriers encased all the Director's windows, but that wasn't what unnerved me.

"I want to know who the fuck destroyed my protections!" the Director yelled into the phone with barely contained fury.

His voice rang through the room, making me flinch.

I stood in front of his desk waiting for him to get off the phone as I refrained from rubbing my sweaty palms on my thighs. If I showed any sign of weakness while he blasted whoever was on the other end of the line, he would pounce.

My chances of getting out of his office unscathed diminished with every second he growled into the phone.

I had nothing to do with the destruction of the UV field over the compound, but that didn't matter. I was here. A body to be smashed if he couldn't get his anger in check.

His salt-and-pepper hair stood on end from too many hand-rakes, making him look more like a mad scientist than the Director of the League of Supernatural Assassins.

He slammed the phone into the cradle and turned his gray, snakelike eyes to me. His hands fisted, and I twitched, waiting for him to give a nod to his guards who hid in the shadows to beat me to within an inch of my life for his entertainment.

He regarded me for a moment, smoothed his hair, and masked all that fury I had witnessed, turning his expression into the cold and calculating one I was used to.

This was his normal state. It was when he displayed emotion that a shit storm was imminent.

"What do you have for me?"

The edge in his voice sent a shiver of fear through me.

I swallowed hard, pulled out a vial of blood from my bra, and put it on his desk. "Here's the DNA from the seer hiding out on Earth. Unfortunately, she did not see me coming."

I suppressed the smirk that wanted to surface from my bad pun and focused on the Director's cross look. He did not find me amusing. He picked up the blood, rolling it between his fingers before he pocketed it. He leaned back in his chair and gave me a curt nod.

My shoulders relaxed.

My specialty was getting DNA from unwilling royal lines, and sometimes, I had the bonus of being allowed to kill them if I chose. I embraced killing the way the Director embraced beating us into submission.

After all, it was part of my DNA. I was a demon-witch hybrid and a special demon breed at that. I existed on the essence of souls, otherwise known as a soul eater.

And in a pinch, I had the kiss of death at my disposal, but I couldn't deploy that on my targets until I obtained their DNA, because the moment I employed the kiss of death, my victims turned to ash.

I shifted my weight, unsure of whether I should repeat the information the seer gave me as she begged for her life. I did not know how to approach the situation with the Director's current mood. She had dropped a few juicy tidbits while trying to bargain for her life, but it wasn't enough to save her.

I focused back on the Director and his narrowing eyes. Normally, I dropped the DNA and headed to my room to clean up and attend to my pet snake.

"You have more for me?"

I swallowed hard. If I didn't give him the information now and opted to do it later, he surely would have me beaten for not divulging the information when I first arrived.

It was a no-win situation, so I forged on. "Yes. The seer mentioned Eleka is not what it seems. It holds blood you covet. Fae blood."

The Director slammed his palm on his desk, flashing his fangs. "Wrong! Eleka is a dead world. It has been since before I was born!"

Dead. Right. At least that's what we were taught in all our history lessons throughout school. I even read about explorers who had been tasked with searching for Eleka, but no one ever returned. It was as if it were a massive black hole that screamed death to anyone who ventured there.

He nodded to the guards. His elite shadow demon guards were loyal to a fault. But I guess you have to be once you take a blood oath to obey the Director's every order.

I licked my lips and continued, "She said it was a glamour created by an ancient and supreme Elvren clan."

I started to shake as the guards approached, towering over me like rabid beasts with smiles that broadcast pain was coming. I could take them, but I was not allowed to use my skills against the Director's guards. That was an immediate death sentence, and I liked living.

The Director's hand went up, and the guards stopped.

"She said ancient and supreme Elvren clan?" His eyes sparkled with interest, like this information had made him forget that he had a disaster on his hands with the UV shield gone.

"Yes, sir." I flicked my gaze to the guards and then back to the Director.

He slowly ran his fingers over the line of his jaw and chin as if determining whether it was worth not having his brutes beat me.

I schooled my features. If I showed any sign of fear, he'd sic them on me.

After a moment, he waved them back into the shadows.

"Go to your quarters and wait for my summons." He dismissed me.

I didn't need to be told twice. I turned and headed to the solace of a hot shower and my boa constrictor.

I didn't slow my stride until I was halfway across the complex, and I knew the Director's people were no longer focused on me. Only then did I allow my muscles the release of tension.

I hated being afraid and feeling helpless. I was a demon seed, after all. I could syphon energy from the souls around me, and in a pinch, deplete them into cardiac arrest. Yet every time I faced the Director, I felt like a child being scolded.

Exhaustion pummeled my muscles, making each step even more onerous than the last. I just wanted a shower and my bed. The trip back to

Icarus through the portal had left me off, like it always did. The only thing that seemed to abate the jaunt home was a good night's sleep in my own comfy bed with my snake wrapped around me.

My wrist throbbed, and I glanced at the healing scar. The portal from Earth seemed to be a bit greedier this time. Thankfully, we were engineered to heal pretty quickly in comparison to the non-supernatural beings of the different realms. Even so, most of the other assassins never had open wounds when they exited the portals like I did.

Sometimes, the guards in the portal bay slapped on a bandage so I wasn't openly bleeding when I stepped into the Director's office. Every once in a while, I would end up in the medical bay to be stitched up before they allowed me into the Director's office.

Which was a good thing, because getting close to a night walker with an open wound could be deadly.

I turned down the corridor leading to my sparsely furnished dorm.

I didn't require much. Not with the nomadic lives we led in the League of Supernatural Assassins. But a comfortable bed was a must. If I could have fit a king-size bed in my unit, you bet I'd have one covered in satin and silk.

But there was only room for a double bed in this little dormitory room that the company provided for us, and that was pushing it. Most of my co-assassins only had a single bed in their dorm room.

I pressed my fingers to the scanner at my door, and the whoosh of the electronics came to life. A moment later, my door swung open, and I stepped into my tiny abode.

When it clicked closed behind me, I headed toward the bathroom, stripping my clothing as I went. I didn't care that the ultraviolet protection had been compromised outside my window or that any one of a half-dozen assassins could peer in to see me strut my stuff.

Because of my mother, I had a curvy human form that blended in on Earth and pleased men on most of the realms the Director sent me for my missions. Looking this way made my job easier. All I needed to do was bat my eyelashes and smile demurely while sticking out my chest to get close enough to get my victim's DNA.

Even the women reacted to me as if I let out pheromones when I chose to flirt. No one expected that I was capable of soul-syphoning. I didn't have to use glamours like some of the other assassins who had stronger traits of non-human DNA, like horns or wings or canine teeth like the Director. Nope, I looked human even with a high dose of demon blood running amok in my system.

I did not care who saw my naked form. Especially since I just wanted a damn shower.

I turned the water on, and it sputtered cold water at me. I danced out of the spray, cursing at the spigot.

This wasn't like the showers on Earth where hot water just poured out of the spout. Here, we had to wait for the heating unit to kick in. Until then, the water was cold as a frozen tundra.

I stuck my toe in, testing it this time. The cold bite had abated, but it had only achieved lukewarm status. Truthfully, I should have turned on the shower and then undressed and stepped in.

When the water hitting my toe landed in the higher warm zone, I stepped in. It still wasn't anywhere near scalding, so I rushed through washing my body, hoping it would dial up by the time I got to my hair.

Some things were just not meant to be. And a scorching shower here at the League of Supernatural Assassins' compound on Icarus just wasn't in the cards.

I had been spoiled on my last job on Earth's realm. It had taken a few days to track down the seer, and I'd stayed at a swanky hotel that had the most amazing walk-in shower and oversized bed.

I wondered if my next job would afford me the same luxury. Usually, the Director was stingy in his allowances. But where the seer was located on Earth made it necessary for me to stay in a more upscale place instead of a cheap hostel.

With my luck, he'd send me to the dead planet to validate what the seer had told me.

I sighed and turned the water off before toweling the wetness from my skin.

I approached Snape's tank as he slithered toward the glass where I stood. I conjured a mouse and dropped it into the boa constrictor's tank, smiling as he devoured the meal.

Looking beyond him at Icarus made me sigh. It was so different from the green lush of Ireland on Earth. Icarus was painted in brown and red hues and was rocky with patches of swaying wheat-like plants here and there. The only other prevailing color was the steel of the compound and surrounding structures.

I sighed and opened the tank, running my fingers over my boa's silky skin before stepping away.

My bed called, and I answered, crawling under the sheets without bothering with even a pair of undergarments. The soft pillow cradled my head, and my eyes fluttered closed as sleep captured me in her silky grip.

THE WITCH ASSASSIN
CHAPTER THREE

THE HARSH RING OF my coms pulled me out of sleep. Sun still streaked through my window, and I glanced at the clock. I had only been asleep for an hour at best. I jammed my finger into the button to answer the call, and a hologram materialized over my bed.

The Director's pinched face appeared, and he scanned me, his upper lip curled in disgust. "You are still in bed?"

"I've only been asleep for like an hour." My voice carried the scratchy quality of sleep.

"You arrived yesterday." His stern glare, as well as his words, pierced through me.

I blinked at him and glanced back at my clock as my sleep-ridden brain attempted to catch up. "I slept for more than a day?"

"Get dressed and get to my office." The hologram dissipated like a fog rolling out to sea.

I shot out of bed and quickly straightened out the rumpled covers into some semblance of order before stepping into the bathroom to wash the sleep off my face and scrub my teeth until they gleamed. With a flick of my hand, I conjured my standard black uniform, my weapons, and a pair of kick-ass boots.

I waved at my snake's tank, sending a half-dozen mice into the case with him. That would tide him over if I was sent on another mission today.

My clothes from the day before were still lying on the floor where I'd dropped them, and I tossed them into my hamper. I didn't want to return to a messy room. I didn't know how some of the others could leave their places in a state of disarray, but my neat ways were not shared by all the assassins.

My roommate at the training academy had been a slob, and it took everything I had not to suck every ounce of energy from her just to relieve me of my misery. I eventually got my own room, but I was sure it was just a safeguard once they realized that I fed off the energy of others.

As I maneuvered through the crowded halls, I absorbed energy from those souls around me. A little here from a fellow witch, a little there from a day walker, a little more from a shifter assassin, and several other assassins rushing around the compound.

I was replenished by the time I sauntered into the Director's office. The iron panels were still dropped over his windows to block out the sun, so his vampire ass didn't fry.

"Eleka." He glanced at the papers on his desk with an exaggerated frown.

His sharp gaze nailed me.

I waited for more.

"It seems the portal to Eleka has a problem."

"We have a portal to a dead world?" I asked before I had the sense to not let the question slip past my lips.

"Yes. We have portals to all the realms." He leaned back in his chair and crossed his arms, studying me with narrowed eyes. "But you already knew that."

I just shrugged. I did know, but my brain apparently hadn't awoken yet.

Besides, portals weren't really a worry of mine. If I couldn't find one to quickly escape, I conjured them. It was my little secret, and for some reason, I was never inclined to tell the Director about this handy power of mine.

I just took the fastest way home from a job despite the dangers they beat into me. The more blood I offered, the more the portal seemed to behave for me. The only time it got hairy was if I was depleted of energy and required to give a larger sum of blood.

He raised an eyebrow.

I guess he did expect a response. "What's the issue?"

"The first assassin we sent never came back. The second thankfully had the ability to levitate but couldn't breathe. He was able to get back to the portal and pass through, but he said the first assassin was dead at the bottom of a ravine. Stuck like a pig to a stalagmite. The portal seems to be in a cave of some sort and set at the edge of an interior cliff." He pursed his lips in a contemplative manner, but there was an edge to it.

"And?" I didn't understand what he wanted from me.

"And no one has been able to confirm your seer's claim that the world is alive." He tapped his index fingers together, pushed his chair back, and stood to pace the floor like a caged lion.

His guards stiffened, waiting for an order to let out their aggression.

"Perhaps your seer was seeking revenge for her own impending death."

I slowly shook my head. The seer had been trying to bargain for her life by offering me something she thought would stay her execution. The way she blurted it out wasn't calculated, and her soul certainly didn't give any indication she was lying when I devoured it.

"No. She thought the information would save her."

He slowed his pace, glared at me, and nodded toward his guards with one finger raised.

Arms flexed all around the room, anxious to deliver a beating, but only one of his guards stepped forward and threw a punch that hit my stomach with enough might to lift me off my feet and force all the air in my chest out.

"Souls don't lie," I hissed out as I slammed down on my knees.

His pinched lips terrified me, but he jerked his head to the side, and the guard stepped back into the shadows.

"One of our assassins has already died." His sneer said enough to jolt me.

I climbed to my feet, swallowed my fear of the Director, and forced myself to digest his words. In most of the worlds we traveled to, the portals weren't death traps. Some were in caves, but nothing set to kill on entry like he'd described. That tickled my curiosity.

"When was the last time someone tried to get to Eleka?" I asked.

The slow narrowing of his eyes made me squirm. I was sure this time he was going to prescribe a bone-breaking beating now. A beating that I prayed wouldn't come.

My stomach throbbed. I'd rather take my chances in a land of no air and deadly drops.

"Could the fae have moved the portal?" I asked.

Hell, if what the seer told me were true, the fae on Eleka could do miraculous things like keep their world cloaked. Moving a portal, even one anchored with magic, could easily be done.

This time, he stopped and stared at me. Possibility danced in his grey eyes. "And what of the lack of air?"

"Did the assassin have any signs of a space vacuum? Dry eyes? Freezing mouth? Seizing of his lungs?" If Eleka was a dead realm drifting in space, then at least one of those things would have affected him.

At least in theory, anyway.

The Director narrowed his eyes and shook his head.

My lips tilted into a semi grin. "If it's an enclosed cave, magic can make it seem like there's no air."

"Or it's a dead realm."

I nodded but kept my mouth closed. I'd learned the hard way not to test the Director. My arm still ached from time to time from where it had nearly been torn in two. The scar still remained, white and jagged. A stark reminder not to be a smart-ass, or pry into the Director's things, including my own personnel file.

He studied me and worried his bottom lip between his teeth as he resumed pacing.

When he stopped again, he pointed at me. "You have a week."

I blinked at him, trying to catch up. Instead, I just repeated his last two words. "A week?"

"Yes. A week. If the realm is real, that is all I'm giving you to get me royal fae blood. If it's a dead world, then I guess you'll have to conjure a week's worth of air." He crossed his arms, trying to be intimidating.

It worked.

My eyes widened. "You're sending me to my death?"

"Would you rather me have you beaten to within an inch of your life and then toss you into the portal?" He waved at his more-than-eager guards, and a sadistic smile crept onto his face.

I pulled my arm against me and scanned the guards with a shake of my head.

Gulping down my fear, I muttered, "No, sir."

He gave me a curt nod. "Dismissed."

He turned his back on me and crossed behind his desk.

I didn't wait for him to sit or level that cold, calculating look that always seemed to rile up the demon inside of me. I turned and stalked out of his office, heading toward the portal and uncertainty.

What if the world was truly dead?

What if it wasn't?

Either way, I was fucked.

THE WITCH ASSASSIN
CHAPTER FOUR

I WALKED INSTEAD OF just zapping myself to the portal, like most of the assassins in this building would do, ignoring the hot sensation in my stomach.

This wasn't going to be an easy assignment, and walking afforded me the chance to feed my soul from the crowded hallways. I weaved between the assassins and guards traveling from place to place, syphoning energy.

Species didn't matter. As a soul eater, anything with a soul could fuel me. If Eleka were truly dead, I would need all the energy I could withstand to make it a week in limbo.

The supply room was on the way, and I stopped to grab some items I might need if the world was as desolate as we thought. Medical supplies, bandages, and a sleeping bag went into a backpack.

I paused and closed my eyes, conjuring two items I would need in the first few seconds before I could get my bearings. An oxygen mask and tank. Then I pulled my hoverboard from my private ether.

I had no intention of dying on entry. I didn't have the magic to levitate, but I certainly had tools that would do it for me, like my hoverboard.

Of course, I hadn't used this thing in a few years, but I used to be a terror in these hallways on the thing, zooming around and annoying my comrades. I smiled at the thought as I stared down at the swirling colors embedded in the enamel. I had saved monthly allowances for years to buy this thing, and I was so thrilled when I finally was able to get it.

The Director wasn't so pleased though, and neither were my teachers. But instead of letting them confiscate the thing, I sent it off to my private ether for safe keeping.

I ran my hand over the smooth surface and then muttered a magical spell over the items that would let me retrieve them at will, no matter where I was. Then I sent them into my private ether again.

The only things allowed through the portal were things that fit into the protective body suit we wore through the portals or were attached to our bodies. While technically I could wear the backpack, I didn't want to be restricted by it.

I made sure I had all my knives and killing stars in place before I left the supply room and crossed to the portal room.

The guard's gaze met mine with wariness that made me pause. And it wasn't because I was a soul eater.

"Where are you headed?" Cameron, one of the Director's regular portal guards, asked.

His voice, usually deep and calming, held a stitch of nerves. His eyes were as dark as his skin, and he stood stoically on the side of the room. He usually looked bored, but not today. It was as if today had left him on edge.

"Eleka."

The air shifted, and a portal appeared.

His eyes darted to me. Normally, they programmed the portals, opening the one that spit us out on the surface of Eleka where we would then transfer to another portal to get to our final destination.

But being that I had blood of a portal guardian, I could bypass the process and go straight from the building to my destination.

Heat prickled over my skin, and I fisted my hands, controlling the tremors that wanted to surface.

I met his gaze, schooling my features to one of boredom so he wouldn't see the nerves threatening to make my limbs shake. "Don't worry, Cam. I'll send back the dead assassin to let you know I've gotten through, okay?"

When I had control, I reached my hand out with my finger extended.

Cameron stepped closer and dragged a blade across the pad of my pointer finger. He waved me toward the swirling air, and I made a diagonal stripe across the entrance with my bloody finger.

The vortex opened, accepting my blood. It sucked me inside, and I had to keep my wits about me because the moment this thing spit me out, I needed that hoverboard powered up and under my feet.

The chill of the portal seeped in through my suit, and I clamped my teeth together to stop them from chattering. I focused on the tiny white dot in the distance. That was my goal, and if my eyes drifted to the jagged edges surrounding me, my mind might just throw me off course, too.

According to the notes I'd read in my file, I was the only one the Director ever infused with portal guardian DNA. I tended to think the untimely death of the last portal guardian had something to do with that. He didn't have a reservoir of blood to tap anymore.

Anyhow, I was thankful for this manifestation of power. It had saved my ass more times than I cared to admit.

Getting caught snooping through his files had led to one of the worst beatings I had ever gotten, but he had left me in his office alone, with unlocked cabinets, for long enough to discover some hard truths about the assassin program.

It's how I found out that all of us assassins were infused with DNA that allowed us to travel through a portal. There were less than a handful of beings who could naturally travel through these hellish wormholes, and the Director needed a way to get us through them without relying on other untrustworthy beings to escort us.

Especially after some of the disasters that the early program had suffered.

I had been left long enough to uncover the evolution of the assassin program. The contents of that file had been engrossing enough to occupy all my attention to the point I hadn't heard the Director return.

Honestly, the information I gained in that file-snooping session had been worth the beating.

I aimed purposely toward the exit point as the white dot expanded with every second. Thankfully, I knew what was on the other side, and as the opening widened, I tempered my need to pull my things from my ether.

Too soon, and I would tumble about in the portal like a child's plaything, and it would spit what was left of me out without warning. Too late, and gravity would suck me down to my death.

My heart clanged in my chest, and I fisted my hands so I wouldn't jump ahead of myself. The more pressing of the two dangers was the fall. The lack of air would be secondary, unless it was indicative of a planet with no atmosphere. Then, I had a maximum of fifteen seconds before I'd pass out from lack of oxygen to the brain.

If it was truly a dead planet, it would kill much quicker than most people realized. Suffocation by space was swift.

The end of the portal was within reach, and beyond it revealed a dark void about as inviting as being summoned to the Director's office.

I took a deep breath, blowing the air out of my lungs as I stepped out of the portal, conjuring my hoverboard under my feet.

Magic in the cave bombarded me, sliding over my skin like an electric eel, stinging every inch of me as I teetered over the abyss. My eyes didn't feel like the moisture was being sucked out, and my mouth did not feel frozen like they would in a space vacuum.

I pulled the oxygen mask from the ether as soon as I was stable on the hoverboard.

The portal blinked out, plunging me into darkness before I finished fitting the oxygen mask over my face. I muttered a light spell to illuminate the cave. A quick glance behind me showed a small outcrop in the wall where the portal had dumped me out. The floor of the cavern was indeed littered with deadly stalagmites.

We weren't the only ones trying to get onto Eleka either.

Quite a few dead bodies in various stages of decomposition lay pierced on the spikes. I recognized the freshest death in the same suit I had on and steered my hoverboard lower until I could pry her from the spike. With her dead weight over my shoulder, I maneuvered the board back to the ledge. As I got closer, the portal materialized on its own without me willing it back into play.

Using some of the tacky blood still surrounding the hole in her body, I swiped my hand across the portal opening, hoping it was enough. I waited, holding my breath. When the portal widened, dropping its glossy front, I tossed the dead assassin inside and zoomed away so I wouldn't be sucked in with her by accident or knocked off the hoverboard if the portal spit her back out on this side.

The portal popped out of existence again, and I sighed. It had accepted her and would drop her onto the ground of the main portal in Icarus.

Well, at least that was the theory, but I'd never tested a portal's destination with a dead body before. I didn't know whether a dead body would sail through or if it would just hover in the portal until someone came along.

I guess I'd find out in a week at the latest. If this wasn't a dead world, I'd be able to see after I got my sample. Otherwise, I was stuck here to wither away for a week, because if I set foot back at the compound before the time elapsed without royal fae blood, I'd be the one hemorrhaging on the Director's office floor.

I wiped the remainder of the blood still staining my hand on my thigh. Then I spun around, taking a more studied look at my surroundings.

The only resting place in this cavern was on the shelf where the portal existed. Everywhere else, jagged walls met my gaze. I guided the board to the wall and raked my fingers over the stone. With a grimace, I pulled my fingers back and stared as blood welled from new cuts.

I wiped my fingers in the same place I had wiped the rest of the dead assassin's blood, ignoring the twinge in the back of my mind telling me it probably wasn't sanitary.

My gaze fell on the other dead bodies. Bodies didn't decay without oxygen. Without oxygen, they would become dry husks.

But these bodies were in various states of decay, and I could almost smell it through my oxygen mask.

I glanced back at the ledge, wondering if I could get into the alcove behind where the portal was without activating it. Then I'd have half a chance at analyzing the magic draped over this cavern. I tried to get close at a few angles, but every time, the portal appeared and blocked me.

Instead of harping on it, I decided to study the cavern in more detail to see if I was overlooking some way out in my haste to get this slithering magic away from my skin. It was weighing me down like a two-ton boulder.

After what felt like hours scouring the cavern, I had yet to find an opening. The only area I had not investigated was the damn ledge.

I willed the light brighter as I approached from the front. The ledge itself was rectangle-shaped with one side lined with a solid wall to where the portal appeared, blocking all access to the ledge as if it was a defense mechanism that triggered automatically.

I moved back a little, and the portal faded. But maybe if I circled around to the wall farthest from the outcrop and hugged it as I approached, I could get onto the ledge without triggering the portal.

I studied the sharp edges of the wall to the side, discouraging any attempt at reaching the ledge in that manner.

I'd get bloody, but it seemed like the only way, and even if the portal appeared, I might be able to squeeze behind it. If not—I glanced down at the spikes rising from the floor, waiting for more reckless souls—I might be bloody enough for the portal to accept me back without spitting me to my death.

I took a good look at the wall as I steered in that direction and noted there were no stains on the edges. No one else had attempted what I was thinking.

I let out a laugh which fell flat in the oxygen mask. I would bet no one else had lived long enough to try this insane plan.

As I closed in on the wall, the magic in the cave changed from that stinging, scratchy sensation that I'd ignored when I first arrived to that of a blaze burning my skin, alerting me that this had to be the way to get out of this godforsaken cavern. Otherwise, it wouldn't be protected with such repelling magic.

No dead realm would be protected with this kind of repellant. If anyone had lived long enough to get to this point, they would have forged on because all the signs of a vacuum in space were not present. It was not freezing in this dark cavern.

I called on the demon part of me, the one that had no issue with burning, and drank it in as if the spell had a soul of its own.

I navigated the board so it was parallel to the wall, scraping the edge as I went along. Gritting my teeth against the shards as they dragged across my arm, I pushed forward until the front of the hoverboard hit the ledge.

The portal hadn't activated.

I grinned in the oxygen mask, despite my torn arm and the magic still pounding through me, trying to raise my internal alarms with false tricks that would send me away from the ledge. I jumped off the board onto solid ground and dropped to my knees, wheezing with the effort to withstand the magical repellant pummeling me. I summoned my backpack and slipped it on as I sucked breath after breath of clean oxygen through my mask.

I forced myself to my feet and focused on where the jagged wall met the smooth wall lining the far edge of the ledge. I was sure that was where this magical barrier from hell ended. While my demon side reveled in the burning sensation of the magic, my human-witch side shuddered with every step.

I leaned into it as if battling a brutal wind. The energy I expended was not fully replenished by my demon half, and I doubted I would be able to push through another magical barrier this strong without feeding.

And the souls in this cave had long since moved along.

My thoughts kept betraying me with ludicrous what-if scenarios such as what if this was it? What if it was only a corner? Or worse, what if I broke through the magic only to find a desolate world and another drop to certain death?

I was near enough to find out, and my heart decided now was the time to hit in triple beats and send a rush of adrenaline through me.

Pain tore from the inside out as I forced my way through the magical barrier, and my cry echoed around me.

And then I fell into a pit of blackness.

THE WITCH ASSASSIN
CHAPTER FIVE

AWARENESS SCRAPED INTO MY brain. Hard coolness caressed my cheek, and my breathing came in short bursts like there wasn't enough oxygen.

That shocked me awake. I must have passed out when I'd breached the cave's magical barrier.

I sat up, dizzy from the motion, and adjusted my mask. That didn't help. I glanced at the oxygen meter on the canister, and it read empty.

Damn. I closed my eyes, retrieving a full oxygen tank, and switched it out before sending the empty one into the ether. A moment later, fresh oxygen filled my lungs.

I rubbed my eyes and then looked around. A shaft of light came from the far end of this cavern, but it wasn't enough to make out more than just shadows. I conjured more, enough to light up this cave as if the sun blessed the darkness.

My eyes adjusted to the sudden brightness. I blinked at the lone skeleton lying face down in the center of the room.

My arm throbbed, and I glanced at it, wincing at the amount of blood still seeping through the fabric. With how long I had blacked out, I would have thought the cuts would have healed.

I slipped my backpack off my shoulders and peeled off my shirt, then attended to the wounds with the salve and bandages inside the pack.

Uncertainty rattled through me as I finished my patch job. I closed my eyes, letting the air settle over me.

With a deep breath in, I detected the magic slowly caressing my skin. It was different than where the portal had been. Almost intoxicating.

I pulled the mask away for a moment and tried to inhale, but air pulled out of my lungs instead. I snapped the breathing mask back on and opened my eyes, feeling foggy, as if all I wanted to do was sleep.

My gaze landed on the skeleton. Torn fabric fluttered in a breeze I wasn't close enough to feel. But there was no skin left on the bones. It had fully decomposed, which meant air was present, just suppressed by the magic spell cast on this hellhole.

I glanced toward the natural light in the far corner. If this was truly a fae realm, I couldn't step out in a torn black assassin outfit. I would be immediately killed. I needed clothes that would fit in and hide my weapons.

I conjured clothing that resembled what I saw of fae in the different realms I had been to, along with holders for my weapons, before I stripped down and stuffed my outfit, along with the ruined shirt, into my pack. I sent it to the ether and then dressed in the flowing skirt and the loose shirt that dipped at the top to show my cleavage.

The Elvren I had encountered were obsessed with sexual escapades, and I hoped this realm was no different. This outfit would give them enough of a view to divert attention, and all I needed was a moment of distraction to escape.

The sleeves of this shirt ended in elastic so I could maneuver easily to get to my blades strapped to each forearm. My boots carried slots for my knives, and my bra held the sharp stars that, if thrown hard enough, could travel through flesh as effectively as a bullet.

I stood, and my stomach tightened. What if this truly was a dead planet, and all these magical signatures were warnings left by whoever inhabited this realm before it succumbed to death?

If this world were truly dead, it would be freezing enough to kill within a few minutes. The absence of the frigidness of space made my feet move toward the light.

With a wave of my hand, the illumination I had conjured disappeared. I sucked in a deep breath of cleansing oxygen, and the fog in my brain cleared a little.

If it were a dead planet, there would be no need for magic to make anyone think there was no air. Whoever cast this spell had fallen short. They didn't know the actual science of a vacuum in space.

It was something I had been fascinated with and knew the dangers more than most because of my studies on the subject. I had a space traveler phase when I was little after we learned about the realms and the different solar systems and planets within each realm. At the time, all I wanted to do was drive a ship through space.

That didn't last long before the Director squashed that dream by laying my reality on me.

This was my destiny. To collect rare DNA for him in his quest for a perfect army. There was no other option. It was this or death.

I shook my wandering thoughts out of my head and carefully picked my way across the rocky terrain, avoiding the lone body on the ground. With the magic still gently caressing me in a dangerous seduction, one that made me want to give up and just sleep, I wondered what other magical gotchas were lying in wait for me to trip on.

I closed my eyes and pushed my senses farther out, inspecting for any changes in the magic. When I glanced up, the area of light I had been trudging toward didn't seem any closer. However, when I looked back, the skeleton was far enough from me to give me a proper gauge of my progress. I had crossed a great deal of the distance.

"Deflect."

Nothing happened, which meant the magic was infused in the surrounding rock and wasn't aimed directly at me.

I kept moving, ignoring the optical illusion of not getting anywhere along with total exhaustion pressing down on me. It was just another ruse to protect whatever was outside of this cave.

The closer I seemed to get to that shaft of light, the more the magic pressed down on me. And the more my eyelids sank.

I shook it off. Obviously, only one body got past the original room, and this magic had either suffocated them or they'd succumbed to the order to lie down and sleep until they withered away and died.

That wasn't going to happen to me. I justified my actions with logic. Logic and the knowledge I had accumulated as a child with wild dreams beyond what I had been bred for.

This was not a dead world. My teeth weren't chattering from bone-chilling cold. My eyes didn't feel dry being exposed like they would in a space vacuum. Still, an iota of respect for whoever conjured this magic flitted through me like a band of butterflies.

I took a deep breath of clean oxygen, and my mind cleared. Blinking, I stood before a solid wall of rock. It was as if that elongated view had finally snapped into reality. The magic felt different here, as if the sleep portion of the spell had been left behind.

The sliver of light was now to my right, and I stuck my hand into the rays, holding my breath against a burn that did not come. Another telltale sign that this was not a dead realm.

If it had been dead, that light would have scorched my hand. With more sureness than I had felt since before I woke this morning, I slid along the wall, certain there was a way to get around this rock.

If not, this was a wild goose chase. And I would have to figure out how to survive for a week in this cavern before I went back to a substantial beating. The Director would punish me for my failure.

I glanced back at the body, wondering if the same things running through my head had also fluttered through theirs before their last breath.

My focus swiveled back to the opening as my skin prickled in the same way it had when I tried to breach the exit of the cave where the portal was. The magic pushed at me, making me want to run back the way I'd come, and I gritted my teeth, forcing my way through it.

The stronger the magic, the more certain I was that this was the proper way.

A lesser witch would have given up. Hell, any other species would have succumbed, especially if they didn't understand magic.

I let a huff of a laugh escape. It got trapped in the oxygen mask, and I lamented that perhaps I was crazy the way my associate assassins said I was.

I won every challenge put to us, and this was no different.

The stakes were the same. Death or victory.

I liked to think I was allergic to failure. I mean, I'd gotten away with more than others. Hell, I had the double bed in my dorm room, something that was overlooked on inspections and never mentioned by the Director. He seemed to enjoy the stories of my ruthlessness and prowess in the hunt.

Although my mouth was more likely to get me a beating than anything else. It had a few times, and my arm still ached from being broken by the Director's guards.

I shook my thoughts away and sidled up to what looked like an indent in the wall where the spell seemed to be at its apex. I forced myself around the corner and into the shining light.

Magic squeezed my abdomen painfully, and the bright sunlight blinded me. I shuffled step by step, and the invisible wall I'd hit seemed to elongate. It snapped, and I fell to the ground, gasping in my oxygen mask.

Whatever magic had weighed me down was no longer stabbing my skin. I pulled the oxygen mask away and breathed in without looking at my surroundings. Sweet, clean air filtered in, and I stripped the oxygen off before sending it to the ether in case I needed it.

I blinked, and shadows crowded over me. I slowly looked up at a line of swords pointing at me. Beyond them was a scene so beautiful that I wondered if I had died trying to get out of the cave.

Windswept grass swayed. Trees of different colors reached for the bright sunshine. Mountains in the distance dotted the landscape around an endless ocean.

Eleka wasn't dead. It was by far the most stunning realm that I'd ever visited.

But I wouldn't have time to explore it.

I focused on the danger before me. Slowly, I climbed to my feet, keeping my hands in view as I inhaled their essence, strengthening myself enough to stand steady. They tasted like a little slice of heaven. Sweet and pure.

"Who are you?" the tallest of the bunch snapped.

His eyes were the color of a purple sunset, and the tips of his sharp ears poked through a mane of blond hair that seemed to shift in the breeze.

"Mya," I answered, trying to draw my stare away from the group of men who looked more like gods carved from stone. "Who are you?"

I flipped my hair over my shoulder and stood tall, pretending to blend in. But even my natural beauty didn't compare to these men.

They were hotter than anyone I'd ever encountered. Broad shoulders, cut abs on full display under the open shirts they wore, and thighs built for speed and power. Thick hair, the kind women loved to run their fingers through, covered their heads. Their sharp cheekbones and supple lips pressed together bloomed heat in my core.

"Deflect," I muttered to myself.

There was nothing I hated more than sensual magic, and these asshats were pounding me with it.

They blinked, and the swords dropped a hair.

After a shake of the tallest guard's head, his sword came back up, and his eyes narrowed. "We are the king's guard, and you are trespassing."

He grabbed my arm, yanking me forward amidst the blades. None of the guards flinched or moved their weapons away. If I chose to fight, I would be run through in an instant. Stripping them of their souls crossed my mind, but they were the royal guard.

They would bring me to the king, and then I'd get my sample for the Director.

I stood down and let them manhandle me. I did, however, syphon more energy from them. The jaunts through the cave of doom had really taxed me. I needed to replenish, and the six guards surrounding me didn't necessarily need all their energy.

As they pulled me through the manicured grounds surrounding the dark mountain that the portal cave was in, I studied my surroundings. My outfit was quite far off from the fae who lived here compared to those I had seen on Earth. While I looked like a flower child, the people wandering the streets in the distance looked like goddesses carved right out of Greek fables. I was sorely underdressed.

However, those outfits wouldn't hide a weapon at all. Not with the high slits and the halter tops leaving their backs wide open and their arms uncovered.

"Where am I?" I asked as they nearly dragged me along.

I played innocent because anything else would get me killed. I kept looking around, widening my eyes as I took it all in, making myself look as innocent and awed as I could.

They walked without comment.

Around the bend, the castle glistened, reaching into the clouds like a lonely sentinel. It cascaded out into tentacles across the land, and they marched me toward the nearest squat building at the end of the cascading arms of the castle.

Once inside the building, the lead guard grabbed my hands and bound my wrists behind me in metal cuffs. Then he swung me around and gripped my shirt, tearing it off my body. Leaving me only in my bra and skirt. The guards still surrounded me with their blades nearly touching my skin.

"Again. Who are you?" he asked as he ripped off my weapons.

I tightened my jaw, glaring at him as I pulled a little more energy from him, watching as bags of exhaustion appeared under his eyes. "I told you. My name is Mya."

His hand wrapped around my throat, squeezing. He tore my skirt, baring the rest of my weapons.

"Why do you have assassin's weapons?" His bright, violet eyes bore into me. "And how the hell did you get through our magical barriers?"

His voice was more of a growl now.

I didn't speak. I just looked right through him, even when he slapped me to try to get a rise out of me. Without my clothes, there wasn't anything I could do to hide the weapons I'd brought, and they were stripped from me. All except the ones tucked snugly into my bra, but with my hands clasped behind my back, they were useless to me.

He grabbed my face after they took off my shoes. "Where did you come from?"

The urge to rip his soul right out and feast on the power took hold, but I took a deep breath, putting the urge away. If I did that, I'd never get close to the king.

"Ireland," I answered. It was the last portal I'd crossed through before this one. "And as far as the weapons, I'm a woman. I'm not interested in being at a man's mercy."

His eyebrow cocked. "You have all that for self-defense?" He pointed at the pile of weapons on the chair.

I mimicked his raised eyebrow. "Have you ever had a group of drunk Irishmen chasing after you?"

He let go of my face and nearly threw me into the cell. "If you won't talk to me, I'm sure the prince will be able to pry open that mind of yours."

The cell door slammed closed, and they filed out the door. None of the other cells in this building were occupied.

I closed my eyes, willing my backpack to me.

Nothing happened. My eyes flew open, and I snarled. This cell had a magical dampener on it. I couldn't conjure anything in here.

Fuck. I had less than a week left in this place and no way to access my magic while sequestered in this cell.

A jailed assassin was just as dead as a failed assassin.

I huffed. I'd have to take them all down the next time they took me out of here. That was the only way to escape.

Otherwise, I was doomed.

THE WITCH ASSASSIN
CHAPTER SIX

AS THE LIGHT WANED, I started to shiver, which didn't help my sore wrists as the metal continued to rub them raw. The clasp holding the cuffs was too close together to get over my hips.

I had tried quite a few times, but it wasn't going to happen. Not without breaking my wrist. So, I huddled in a little ball on the bare cot in the corner, trying to keep as much heat as possible.

The soft whisper of footsteps had me squinting out into the room beyond the bars. I caught sight of movement that matched the footfalls, and the form that came closer made me straighten.

My heart leapt into my throat, throbbing. And my damn teeth kept chattering from the bone-chilling cold raking over my skin.

Blue eyes, the color of the lightest aquamarine stone, cut through the darkness, and a gleam of gold sat atop his head. He was taller than the guards and cut from the sleekest stone.

Broad and hard. Dangerously beautiful.

His dark hair fell down his shoulders in wild curls. This god-like creature stopped in front of my cell and crossed his arms, stretching the fabric of his shirt over his well-formed chest.

His heavy sigh felt like a warm breeze. "The least they could have done is unclasp your wrists."

His voice dripped like honey, caressing me, and I shivered even more, trying to staunch the incessant clacking of my teeth. I didn't speak, afraid of what would tumble out of my mouth.

His magic seemed to work in this cell. It made me want to spill all my secrets and drop to my knees before him. I resisted and remained in the spot where I had planted my feet.

He beckoned me forward with his finger.

I wasn't falling for this game. I stood my ground, not moving.

His eyebrows rose. "Do you not want those shackles off?"

I blinked at him, processing his words. "Why would you do that?"

He waved at the bars. "You're no threat to me inside this cage."

I huffed and glanced around. If he released me, I'd have access to the throwing stars stowed in my bra. Instead of refusing his shortsightedness, I approached the bars and turned, offering him my wrists.

"Nice try. Stick your hands through the bars."

I glanced over my shoulder at him. His eyes hardened as he stared at me, waiting. I shuffled back against the metal and tilted so I could get both hands between the bars.

He grabbed hold of the shackles and yanked me against the bar. One hand snaked through and grasped my throat.

"Who are you?" he rasped as if it was his throat being squeezed.

"Mya," I hissed and pulled on his spirit, needing more energy.

But the blast of pain that shot back caused me to cry out, nearly yanking the strength from my bones. The magic of the cell seemed to protect him from my soul syphoning.

His grip on my throat loosened, and he took in a deep breath, pulling his hands away. The click of shackles followed, and the metal fell away from both wrists. Where his fingers touched mine still burned, sending heat up through me and right to my core.

I yanked my hands in and spun, freeing a killing star as I turned. I launched it at the fae royalty before me. It sailed between the bars and sliced his arm. Mine stung in the same place his now bled.

His reaction was immediate. He yanked the cell door open and crossed the distance, grabbing me and slamming me against the wall. His power overwhelmed me, making my breath come in quick, panicked bursts.

The bra I had on was ripped from my body, and then he was gone, followed by the clang of the door closing.

I turned, still shaking with one less garment on my body. I covered my chest and watched as he pulled the stars out one by one. His breath came in pants just as hard as mine.

With nimble fingers, he found the small vial that I was supposed to fill with royal blood and palmed it as he inspected the rest of the garment. When he seemed satisfied that there weren't any other dangers in the fabric, he tossed the bra back inside for me.

I picked it up and put it back on. Modesty wasn't the reason, either. The fabric of my bra offered an iota of warmth to my breasts. If it had been warmer in the cell block, I would have gone without it, but at this point, any material was helpful.

"Mya," he said and paused as if a shiver had ripped up his back.

He pulled his shirt tighter around him and focused on me.

The sound of my name on his supple lips sent an unnatural thrill through me.

"What kind of magic is this?" The growl in my voice caused the prince to return a glare that made me gulp.

He ignored my question and held the vial up between his fingers. "What is this?"

I pressed my lips together. I needed that vial back. If not, my entire mission was defunct.

I dropped my gaze to the discarded stars far out of my reach and then at his bleeding arm. "It's to capture blood of any creatures I found on this dead world to see their makeup."

The words fell from my lips, shoveling a little bullshit in with the truth.

He laughed and glanced at the stars on the ground and the array of weapons on the table out in the main room. "You're one of those famed assassins from Icarus, aren't you?"

He stuck the vial into his pocket.

My stomach plummeted, but I covered it up by scrunching my brow. "Icarus? What's that?"

He turned to the side, giving me his fine profile and gold-tipped ear. The crown lay behind it, and it struck me as odd. I'd never seen a fae with golden-tipped ears. He delivered a haughty side-eye my way and stalked off without a word.

"Can I at least have a blanket?" I called after him.

He waved his hand, and the air sparkled, leading from him to where I stood. A blanket materialized just outside the cell. Within reach.

I stared at it and then at his backside just before the door shut, leaving me in the dark cell. A chill radiated around me, and I pulled the blanket through the bars and wrapped the fabric around my shoulders.

I headed back to the cot and stretched out, wrapped like a burrito, and analyzed the situation. I wasn't getting out of here easily. I'd have to wait until the door opened to try to make a break for it. Then I'd be able to feast on the souls around me, but the magic in this cell was as suppressing as I'd ever felt before.

Deflection didn't work. My magic didn't work. My soul syphon didn't work. I closed my eyes and attempted to transfer myself somewhere else on this planet. But that didn't work either.

My arm throbbed, and I pulled it from the blanket and took a closer look at it in this dank cell. A clear scrape marred my skin in the exact location I had sent that star clawing against the prince's skin.

He bled, but I hadn't. Although my skin felt as raw as an open wound.

My head throbbed from trying to syphon his energy, inhibiting my ability to think clearly. I needed this pounding to go away so I could devise a plan. I needed to eat, and I needed to get out of this magic suppressing cell. But my migraine persisted, drowning out coherent though in a tribal beat.

THE WITCH ASSASSIN
CHAPTER SEVEN

A CLATTER ON MY floor made me jump up.
The covers pooled around my feet as I stared
at my hoverboard.

The prince stood outside my cell clad in black
pants that looked like they had been painted on
his muscular form. His shirt hung open, and the
edges were frayed like that particular shirt had
been through so many washings that it was
nearly threadbare. His gaze pierced mine.

"There's no other sign of you in that cavern. No torn clothing or anything hinting at those bandages." He pointed at the patch job on my arm. "What are you?"

I jutted my chin out and tried to syphon some energy from him. A wave of dizziness hit as pain drilled through my head. This kind of magic was detrimental to my existence, and I nearly dropped to the floor. As it was, I sat down hard on the cot.

"Deflect," I whispered and tried again.

The same acute cranial pressure accosted me, and I closed my eyes. I could not get around whatever protected the prince from my powers.

I blinked the tilt of the room away and shook my head, wondering just what I could admit to without putting my life more in danger than it already was.

"I'm a witch." I looked up at him and twirled my finger. "And the dampening spell in here is pretty strong. Otherwise, I'd be dressed in something more than my underwear."

He held his palm to his temple as if a headache had formed. He smiled at me in such a way that heat flushed me. "And I bet you'd have all of your weapons as well."

I rolled my eyes, not fearing this man the way I did the Director. After all, he had given me a blanket the night before and hadn't cracked my cranium when I assaulted him with the killing star.

"My men tell me you said the weapons were to fend off drunk Irishmen."

His voice rolled over me like satin, and I clenched my thighs together.

"And?"

He laughed in a soft and secret way that had me pulling the blanket around me before he caught sight of my hardening nipples. Being this exposed was a problem, especially when my body was reacting sexually to the fae royalty outside my cage.

"What kind of magic are you slinging at me?" I snapped, clasping the blanket tighter.

He shook his head. "I do not *sling* magic." He waved at the cell bars in front of him. "The dampening spell doesn't allow for my magic to penetrate your prison, just as it does not allow yours to manifest."

The door in the hall opened, and the guards who'd initially brought me into the cell strolled in, looking as refreshed as ever. It was enough to make me ravenous.

Before I could stop myself, I pulled at their souls, expecting the same debilitating pain as when I'd tried to use my demon magic against the prince.

However, the opposite happened. Energy infused in my skin, and they as a group seemed to slow just a bit. Enough for my mind to stall and my gaze to jump to the prince.

The biggest guard headed toward the cage, and the prince opened the door, allowing him access.

"You've got nowhere to hide, little girl." The guard sauntered in as if he were in no danger at all.

Well, they had all guessed what I was, but I was sure they'd never encountered one of us. Otherwise, they never would have approached me with so much confidence.

After all, I had a blanket in my hand, and the gods knew that was akin to giving me a weapon. It could suffocate him.

I let him get almost an arm's length away, and then I twirled the blanket up and around him, yanking the ends closest to me. I twisted away, pulling the blanket taut, and used it to pull him forward while I ducked low and tossed him over my hip.

Before I could deal a fatal blow, arms grabbed me, pulling me off the guard. I reacted, turning into the new assailant, and jutted my hip out, pulling him over me.

Except this one didn't just fall; he pulled me with him and rolled, pinning me beneath him.

I stared up into the prince's angry eyes as he slammed my wrists to the ground next to my head. His crown had fallen near where we lay, and both our breaths labored. Having him laid out on me melted my core, making me long for him to take me in violent thrusts.

His cheeks reddened, and his lips thinned into a tight line as he stared down at me.

"You are going to tell me everything." His hair tickled my neck.

"Bullshit." It slipped out before I could stop it.

The blaze in my blood apparently didn't allow for my brain to clamp down on a response.

"Move, Tavin," one of the guards growled.

The prince glanced at the swords aimed in our direction, and then farther up at the guards.

"I need information before we end her." He released my wrists and stood, moving away from the sharp edges.

He swiped his crown off the floor and stormed from the room without looking back.

The door to the building slammed, and I wondered what my chances would be. The cell stood open, and six swords pointed at me, each guard wary of my presence. I sucked in a breath, readying myself for destroying souls.

The guard on the floor untangled himself from the blanket and stood, pointing at me. "That's going to cost you."

He moved fast this time, and I had a choice—kill or step into the blades pointing at me. I might *still* end up perched on a blade.

I ducked below the man's swing and yanked, feeling the essence of his soul transfer from his body to me, infusing more power into my blood. He kept going, barreling into a couple of the guards' swords. His body didn't realize he was already dead.

Four guards got out of the cell and clanged the door closed, locking me in and leaving me at the mercy of the two living guards with their swords sticking into their dead friend.

Swords were not ideal in such a small space. Not for defensive purposes, at least, and based on what the prince had said before he left, he wanted me alive to question.

Instead of pulling the blade from the dead guard, the closest leapt over the heap of a man and shoved me into the wall.

I slammed into it face-first. A snapping sound followed, and I hissed in pain. I glanced over my shoulder in time to see a whip snap again, slicing through my flesh.

My anger rose, and before he could hit me a third time, I tore his soul right out of him, breathing it in as he collapsed on the floor as if someone had ripped his spine out.

My gaze landed on the third guard trying to get his sword out of the dead man. He let go of the sword and grabbed the dagger at his side.

Before he could get it loose, the door to the building clanged open, and the prince stumbled in.

I lunged for the guard. He brought the knife out and jabbed forward. I spun to the side, but the knife tore through my hip.

"Stop!" the prince bellowed, limping forward as he held his leg in the same place mine was bleeding.

He slipped inside my cage, crossing over the dead, took hold of my arms, and slammed me into the wall.

We both winced.

"Get out!" he bellowed over his shoulder and then returned his focus to me.

His gaze dropped down to the cut in my thigh.

"Your Highness?" a guard asked by the door.

The prince glanced his way and shook his head. "This stays between us."

The guard nodded and disappeared down the hall.

"What did you do to me?" He slammed me against the wall again.

Fire lit up my insides. "Me? I did nothing. What protection spell did you invoke, Tavin?"

I used the name the guard had earlier, and the reaction was immediate.

His pupils bloomed until there was only a small ring of blue surrounding the black. He growled between his teeth and clasped both wrists in one hand, raising my arms above my head.

"What kind of witch are you that you can kill with the suppressions in this cell?" With his free hand, he pointed at the dead bodies on the ground.

"I'm a conjuring witch," I said, jutting my chin out.

"Bullshit," he replied with venom. "That is not all you are." His gaze dropped between us where my pebbled nipples were pressed against his chest. "You are going to tell me all your secrets, or you are going to experience pain like you've never envisioned."

I tried to push him back a step with my body, but he was unyielding and hard. All of him was hard, including his dick pressed against my abdomen. Just the thought of him being stiff near me flushed my skin like being doused in fire.

"I'm not afraid of pain," I snarled up at him.

His lip tilted as if a smile wanted to sneak by him, but he caught it before it formed.

His eyes narrowed. "Maybe I'll fuck the answers out of you, then, Mya."

My mouth dropped open, and then I started struggling in earnest. I kicked at his shins, and an echo of pain flashed in mine. Then I turned and bit his arm, whining when mine throbbed in the exact same spot.

He growled through clenched teeth and clamped his free hand on my throat again, squeezing.

"What are you?" His words wheezed.

"None of your fucking business!" I pushed off with all my might and only knocked him back an inch, but it was enough to give my knee room.

I used it, raising it quick enough to slam into the prince's crown jewels.

His face went red, but he didn't let go of me. He held me fast to the wall, but his posture bent with his discomfort.

Agony spiraled through me from low in my groin, rushing the breath right out of my lungs, mirroring the prince.

"What the fuck, Tavin?"

His eyes focused on me. He removed his hand from my throat and leaned in, biting into the spot where my shoulder and neck connected. He winced and pulled away fully as his hand shot to the same spot on his neck. His eyes widened, and he nearly tripped over the bodies in a bid to get out of the cell.

"This cannot be," he whispered and then shut me in the cell before he backed all the way out of the building, as if I had just rained down the seven seals of hell.

THE WITCH ASSASSIN
CHAPTER EIGHT

I WAITED FOR SOMEONE to come claim the dead bodies. Their presence crawled under my skin.

The cell hadn't affected my soul-eating abilities after all. Only the prince seemed immune.

Ignoring the tug in the center of my chest at the thought of the prince, I got up and crossed to the bodies, wondering if I could dispose of them with my kiss of death in this cell.

With the magical suppressions here, I wasn't sure this would work, but the moment my lips pressed to the back of the first guard's head, and I called forth the kiss of death, his form crumbled. The second followed suit, and all that was left were their weapons, which I considered hiding, but there would be no easy way to retrieve them quickly, so I leaned them on the cot and waited for the next guard to approach me.

With the dead taken care of, my brain returned to Tavin. I stretched out on the cot, mulling over everything that had happened since I was thrown in this cell. I had my demon magic, despite the suppression spell in here. But it didn't work on Tavin.

I dropped my gaze to the ashes. Would the kiss of death work on Tavin?

I shivered and swallowed hard at the thought. I glanced at the scratch on my arm representing the spot that had been torn on Tavin's arm by my weapon and my wrist where it looked like teeth marks in the exact spot I'd bitten Tavin.

I didn't know what kind of magic he was using, but with the echo of all of Tavin's ailments in my skin, if I used the kiss of death on him, it would probably render me just as dead.

It was as if all my magic just bounced off him and slammed home into me. It wasn't just magic though, and it only happened with the prince, so he had to have some serious mojo protecting him.

Except I couldn't sense his power at all. But I could sense the suppression magic in this jail cell like a wet blanket spread over me. I shivered.

The door squeaked open, and a pretty fae with lavender hair stepped inside with a tray of food. She crossed to the cell, eyed the weapons inside and the piles of ash before she continued to an opening near the end of the cot. She slid the tray through the opening and paused as she scanned my scantily clad form.

I studied her from my vantage point and pulled in a little of her energy, even if I was already full from the two souls I had already reaped. Neither of us said a word.

She extended her hand to the side, and a slip materialized in her grip. Without a word, she slid it over one of the rails and headed out the door.

"Thank you," I said, and she waved a hand in the air in acknowledgement before she left the building.

I picked up the slip and marveled at the satiny feel of the fabric before I slid it on. The food was a nice gesture, but I didn't need it. Not with the guard's souls feeding my appetite and the handmaiden's contribution of energy.

But the cup caught my attention. I took a whiff of the drink, and my mouth watered at the citrus scent.

If I didn't know better, I would have thought someone had picked my brain because citrusy food and drinks were my weakness. I would expend the extra energy needed to digest on such things as orange juice or lemonade, or anything similar. I was pretty sure this was a coincidence, because if someone had been in my head far enough to pull out my favorite type of drink, I would have felt that kind of violation.

I took a tentative sip, and the flavors bloomed in my mouth in such a sweet and tart mix that I closed my eyes, savoring it before I emptied the rest of the contents into my mouth. I would have drunk an entire gallon of this sweet nectar if it had been left for me.

I set the cup back on the tray next to the uneaten food. The taste lingered on my tongue, and I licked the last drops from my lower lip.

It took a moment for the liquid to hit my stomach, and then a bloom of heat enveloped me like that one time I actually had nectar, a drink that was like the strongest shot of alcohol to us assassins.

I stared at the cup, blinking as my vision tripled. My muscles went loose, and I plopped down on the cot. I moved my gaze to the drink. If that was actually nectar, the cup was large enough to put down a rogue dragon.

"Shit." I tried to shake my head to clear it, but that just served to make me even woozier.

The door opened, and four guards, along with the prince, entered the building. The prince's face distorted, but he was still the prettiest thing in the room.

"My, you're pretty," I slurred and fell sideways on the cot.

He slowed, eyeing the weapons on the cot and the dust on the ground. His jaw jumped, and his eyes landed on me. He unlocked the cell and swung the door open.

"Bring her to the interrogation room," he ordered.

He kept walking to the far end of the building before he pushed buttons on the wall, and a door opened.

The guards stripped me of my undergarments but left the slip on and then dragged me into the room where the prince had disappeared to. I didn't get a good look at the room because my eyelids kept drooping.

I no longer had any access to my magic, witch or demon, with whatever they'd drugged me with, so principally, I knew it hadn't been nectar. Although this feeling of being a wet noodle certainly did mimic my nectar-drinking expedition. I should have known better, but the citrus scent had driven me to drink their potion.

Damn that weakness of mine.

Cool metal surrounded my wrist, and I blinked my eyes open in time to see them secure both my wrists. My ankles came next, and I didn't so much as kick out.

I hadn't fought at all. That went against all my training, everything ingrained in me since I'd taken my first step. I had never submitted even after being drugged. Which had happened a time or two, but I had yanked those souls out and wandered around until my bearings returned enough to complete the mission.

This was unheard of, and my skin heated with panic.

When they stepped away, I was splayed out like a giant X.

What the hell?

One of the guards pressed something against my side.

"Don..." Tavin didn't get the full word out before the guard depressed the trigger.

My muscles seized, and I gasped as electricity zoomed through me. Pain did not register like it should have, but the electric shock certainly cleared my head. The room came into clear focus, and my gaze dropped to Tavin on the ground as if he had been the one electrocuted. His body jerked a few times as his glare moved beyond my face.

The shock stopped just as quickly as it had started, and the guards scrambled to Tavin, helping him off the floor.

"Don't use any of the normal methods," Tavin hissed through a clenched jaw. He wiped sweat from his forehead. "It seems this *thing* is my spirit mate." He waved at me in disgust. "You harm her, you harm me."

The guard's mouths dropped open in unison, and their eyes widened. I was sure I looked exactly like them as my brain tried to make sense of his words. I had never heard the term "spirit mate."

"Are you sure it's not a spell?" the guard who'd zapped me asked.

He was the one who had caught my attention at the cave entrance. Blond and built with lavender eyes.

"Yes. I'm sure. If it was some sort of spell, it wouldn't have worked in her cell." Tavin straightened himself out, squaring his shoulders as his gaze pinned to me.

He stared at me in such a way that I tried to shift my weight to free myself. I had no idea what he had in mind, and underneath his ire was something that made me gulp.

"But she clearly has access to some sort of magic. She killed Zephyr and Lyre," the guard still holding the Taser said.

"Yes. But that wasn't magic. Now was it, Mya?" Tavin stepped close and tilted my chin so I had to stare up at him. "What are you?"

His voice fell over me like honey, making me want to tell him all my secrets.

"I told you what I am," I said, still keeping my wits about me even though my voice sounded distant as I rode the wave of whatever they had given me. I couldn't pull energy from anyone to build up my defenses against him. "What did you give me?"

He ran his fingertips over my cheek, sending heat through every inch of my body.

"An elixir that muzzles whatever powers you harbor for the next twenty-four hours." He smiled, but it didn't reach his eyes. "And if I don't get answers in that time, I'll force you to drink more before you can access whatever powers you do have."

The sudden rush of adrenaline that had come with the electric shock sputtered out, and my eyelids drooped.

"I'd like to see you try," I managed to say.

If he hadn't been holding my head up, I was sure my chin would be against my chest. My body felt like liquid that I had no control over, and I sagged in the chains.

"Mya," he sighed and leaned into my ear. "Did you know you can die from too much pleasure?"

His whisper sent a rash of goose bumps over my skin, and my brain cleared enough for me to pull back and meet his gaze.

His finger drew down my neck to the edge of the slip covering my breasts. Heat traveled from his finger right to my core. He traced the hem as his eyes twinkled.

He stepped away and took a seat, crossing his arms and his ankles as he grinned. He gave the guard with the Taser a nod.

"Oh, hell no," I said as he stepped in back of me and unzipped his pants.

He pressed against my back, and his hands wandered. My heart pumped hard in my chest. I had never given myself to a man. My breathing shortened into quick pants of panic.

"What are you?" the prince asked in a voice so reasonable that I thought I'd scream.

I growled as the bastard behind me kissed the side of my throat and raised the edge of the slip so he could touch me where I had never been touched before, and in full view of the prince. Even though I was chained, there was no way I was going to let them have their fun with me.

Just like those assholes in Ireland. My virginity was not theirs to take.

Anger blossomed in my chest, and I turned and kissed the bastard's cheek, pushing the kiss of death from the well of my soul.

The bastard gasped and then flaked away to ash. I smiled at the prince, pleased I still had access to my deadliest power despite the drugs muzzling the rest of me.

Tavin's wide blue eyes shot to mine, and he stood, clenching and unclenching his fists.

No one moved. They all stared at me as if I had opened the portal to hell.

"Go." Tavin's order was accompanied by a shaking finger pointing at the door.

He didn't break eye contact with me. The guards fled the room before they had a chance to react to another death in their ranks.

"But Your Majesty…"

Tavin looked away. "I'll be fine. Close the door behind you." He focused back on me as the door latched closed. His expression was guarded as he studied me. "What are you?"

He lashed out, gripping my throat and pulling me close, but his grip was nothing more than slight pressure.

My lips tilted up as I stared into his furious blue eyes. "I am not to be trifled with. Let me go."

There was no fear in the prince's eyes as he stared down at me. Just a spark of hunger that echoed in my blood.

"Would you do that to me, I wonder?" His free hand traveled down the satin covering me, tickling my skin. "Would you kill your spirit mate?"

"What the hell is a spirit mate?" I said, but it lacked the venom I meant to put into it.

His touch distracted me, and the heat it bloomed was traitorous.

His eyebrows rose, but he didn't answer my question. Instead, he stepped away and reached for a wand that was on the table in the back of the room. He waved it over my form. It started dinging when he ran it over my shoulder blade.

He grabbed a pen and did the scan again, stopping when it made that hideous loud noise. Pressure of the pen marked the spot on my back, and then he tossed the items onto the table.

"From what my father taught me when I was little, there was a certain realm that churned out assassins like butter. Mixing DNA from several species to make the perfect killing machine. One that can be controlled and manipulated into conforming. Except they did not educate them in the ways of those around them or even the DNA within them. And they were said to carry a tracking device so the head of the organization could find them anywhere." He pushed his thumb on the spot. "Am I wrong to assume you are one of them?" His body pressed against mine. "Am I wrong to assume you are one of those abominations?"

He dared to lick the side of my throat. I turned and glared at him, but my heart was already galloping in my chest, and my core had tightened in anticipation of his touch.

His hands fell to my sides, his fingers brushing the edges of my breasts, sending tingles through me. "Am I wrong?"

His whisper in my ear nearly undid me.

"No." I jerked in his grip and gritted my teeth, trying to get my mind back in my control, but his hands had begun wandering, demanding I spill my secrets.

His tongue dragged up and over my cheek. He forced my head back and pressed his mouth to mine. I moaned from the sensation.

"Damn you," I whispered under the pressure of his soft lips.

His free hand dipped down my abdomen, pulling the silk up until his fingers found my flesh. He slowly circled my clit before running his finger through my folds in such a way that my mind stalled. A low, growling groan came from his throat, and he forced his tongue into my mouth, tangling with mine in a decadent dance that left me wanting.

My body lost all rigidness, becoming pliant under his expert stroke.

"What were your parents?" he whispered, still manipulating me with both his tongue and his fingers.

Before I had the sense to stop it, the words tumbled out. "A powerful human witch and a demon prince."

Tavin pulled away so fast, I thought he had been struck by something. My body still tingled with his touch, and he stepped in front of me with an expression that could only be categorized as filled with hate.

"A demon spawn," he hissed. "My spirit mate is a fucking demon spawn?"

I blinked some clarity back into my mind, which was difficult with the way my body felt. I craved his touch so much that I couldn't understand it. But anger welled up inside me.

"And mine is an arrogant asshole fae prince who thinks he is better than everyone else," I snarled back at him, still unsure what the hell a spirit mate was.

He took another step back, and it was more effective than a slap.

The horror and bitterness on his face made me want to cover myself up and curl into a ball. I ignored the burn of it and decided that the truth might just set me free.

"I need your blood in that vial. Then I'll be out of your hair."

His face contorted in disgust. "So your boss can use it to breed more monsters like you?" He waved his hand at me. "I think not."

"I was not a product of science." I stood tall, lifting my chin in defiance.

But that wasn't totally true. I was infused with DNA outside my birth parents. It was how I could call portals to me wherever I was.

"Were your parents soulmates, or were they forced to...to produce you?" he snapped back at me.

I lifted my shoulder in a shrug. I knew my parents were taken from their respective homelands, but I never had the opportunity to talk to them before they were destroyed.

"Did you even know them?" he asked.

This time, there was less of a bite to his words, as if he couldn't fathom not knowing his parents.

I shook my head.

"Then how do you know what you speak is truth?"

His challenge was clear, and I recoiled. I blinked at him and opened my mouth to speak but closed it just as fast. The Director had told me that I was different than most of the others. I did have fleeting memories of my mother holding me, but none of my father. And I had seen enough births of creatures in my time to understand what those memories were.

"I remember my mother holding me."

It was his turn to blink as if he had stepped into a plume of smoke. His hands fisted and opened repeatedly. "But there are others who were scientifically created, correct?"

I clenched my jaw. I did not want to answer that question. It would mean I'd have to physically take the blood from the prince or the king, and right now, my odds of even making it out of this jail alive were slim. The answer would make those odds dwindle to nothing.

"What does spirit mate mean?"

He moved swiftly to the spot in front of me, his form shaking with barely reserved anger. "Answer me!"

A wave of his heady power fell over me.

I shook my head. "Not until you answer me," I wheezed out, denying his command.

My skin burned against it, almost like pushing through the magic where the portal was, and I pulled my demon blood to the surface as protection. The heat dulled in response.

"A spirit mate is the other half of your soul." He growled out the words as if it physically hurt him to speak them.

I jerked back, trying to pull away from him. I was intimately familiar with the soul. It's what I survived on. And to think that what I feasted on was only half a soul was ludicrous. It provided too much power on its own.

I shook my head. "That's not possible."

His lips formed a slow smile. "This is part of the education you lack, Mya." His fingers ran along my chin until he held it firmly and tilted my head up. "They don't sully your commitment to the cause with truths like spirit mates. That would taint their control over you."

"Bullshit." I yanked my face from his grip.

He grabbed both sides of my face, trapping me. "You will never get royal blood to bring home to your master. You will never again set foot in his presence. You leaving my world puts it in danger, and I will not allow that to happen. Understand? My world must remain dead to the rest of the realms, especially Elbeeon."

His teeth clacked closed on whatever else he was going to say.

He was a fool.

"They'll know. When my time is up, they will know I am no longer locked in your hellish portal room."

His smile turned sour. "Yes. That." He glanced at the wand and then back at me with a sigh. "That's a complication that I cannot avoid. My father would kill you on sight." He huffed a laugh and stepped toward the table where he had flung the beeping wand. He picked it up and showed it to me. "This little doohickey of his finds your filthy chips. He dealt with your kind when we lived on Elbeeon."

He put the wand down. "That was before the war when his people relocated here. To the rest of the realms, they mysteriously disappeared, and no one could find a trace of us. We like it that way. If I had my druthers, I'd kill you myself, but with whatever this is between us, it would probably put me in my grave, too." He picked up a scalpel from the table and approached me. "And if you choose to kill me, it will likely render the same results."

He moved behind me and put his hand gently on my shoulder. "Although, I have never heard that a soul bond could form before an actual soul binding ritual." He huffed. "All this is a damned mind fuck."

I turned my head to look at him. "I still don't understand."

He sighed. "Enough procrastinating. This is going to hurt like hell."

He met my gaze and then focused on my back with a resolved grimace.

Searing pain gripped my back, and I gasped as the blade continued to slice through flesh and muscle.

"Fucking hell," he groaned with a voice laced with as much pain riddling my back.

He pressed his forehead to my shoulder with a bellow that matched the one coming from my mouth. The blade dug farther into my flesh.

"What are you doing?" I cried, trying to pull in the chains holding me so I could curl with agony.

"Getting your tracking chip out." He gagged, and the blade dropped to the ground.

His fingers wormed inside, ripping muscle and skin as they dug behind my shoulder blade.

I screamed along with him, and then sagged the second he pulled away. His breath labored as hard as mine. Hot paths flowed down my back, and I hung my head forward as blood dripped onto the ground, making perfect circles as it splattered.

He stumbled to the chair and dropped a piece of metal on the table before he collapsed in the seat.

I couldn't decide if he was pale or green, and I probably looked just as weary as he did. My back throbbed.

"Are you okay, Your Highness?" The question came from the door behind me.

The prince lifted his gaze to mine, and he slowly nodded. "Can you get me the healing salve and some water?" he whispered with a shaky voice.

His hands rested on the arms of the chair, and my blood dripped from his fingertips like slow, streaming tears.

He rose and crossed to the table where a towel lay. With his back to me, he wiped the blood from his fingers. A stain marred the back of his shirt, slowly spreading on the fabric.

"You're bleeding," I said. My voice was as hoarse as his.

He stiffened and turned toward me, and his hands paused on the blood-smeared towel. "Where? My shoulder?"

"Yes. Near your shoulder blade."

He uttered a high-pitched laugh and went back to cleaning his hands.

His guard came in with a pitcher of water and a jar that looked like wax. He halted a few steps in, his gaze zeroed in on the spreading blood on the prince's back.

"Did she stab you, Your Highness?" His question filled with an edge of anger as his glare rested on me.

"No." He dropped the towel and peeled off his shirt, hissing as the material ripped from the cut. "Put some salve on it, and then leave us," he said without turning.

He gripped the table as the guard put the pitcher on it and unscrewed the jar. The guard applied a liberal amount of the goop on the cut on the prince's back.

Coolness tingled in the same spot on mine.

The prince put his hand out, and the guard set the jar in his hand. "That will be all, Galen."

The guard scuttled out without a word, but the look he gave me promised there would be retribution.

Tavin took a handful of the salve, crossed to me, and slathered it on my back. That cool sensation magnified.

Then he returned to the table, cleaned off his hand, and poured a glass of water. With a shaking hand, he brought it to his lips and emptied the glass in one continuous gulp. Then he refilled and offered me the water by way of pressing the edge to my lip and tilting enough to wash water into my mouth and over my face.

I swallowed, and he pulled the cup away without an apology for dousing me with most of the glass.

He put the glass down next to the metal he had pulled from my back. I stared at the gouge in his back.

"Does mine look as bad as yours?" I couldn't pull my eyes away from it.

"I'm sure yours is worse. I had to dig for the chip."

His rough voice made my breath hitch, and he glanced back at me.

"What am I to do with you?" he whispered, more to himself than to me.

"They are going to be coming for me," I said.

He dropped the chip into the remaining water and left it there. He faced me, and I got a clear look at his cut abs, pecs, and shoulders that made me forget the throb in my back.

He put his hands on his hips and looked at the ground before he crossed and crouched down. A couple taps, and the ankle cuffs let go. When he stood, his tousled hair draped across his forehead. He ran his hand through it, pushing it back so he could see me.

I stared back, waiting for the worst, but all he did was smile.

Then he thumped his fingers on my forehead, and a dark curtain fell over my eyes.

THE WITCH ASSASSIN
CHAPTER NINE

M Y HEAD POUNDED LIKE someone had put an ice pick in it. I groaned, covering my head as I pulled the sheets over me.

That's when I blinked. My fingers slid along the sheets, and I rolled onto my stomach. The bed was larger than that thin cot in the jail.

I jerked into a sitting position and bounced my gaze around the room before dropping it to the satin draped over my legs. This bedroom was more luxurious than anything I had stayed in, even Earth's five-star hotels. A black camisole and matching shorts slid with my movements.

The prince stared out the window and lifted a glass to his lips, sipping it like this was normal. A bandage stood out against his tanned skin, along with a couple bruises that I hadn't noticed before. He turned enough so I could see his profile.

"I figured a sabbatical at my summer cottage was in order after the fiasco at the jail." His blue-eyed gaze pierced through me. "It would at least give me time to figure out what the fuck to do with you before my father finds out and takes matters into his own hands." He moved to a tea set in the corner and poured me a cup before crossing and offering it to me. "It will help with the headache."

I pointed at the bruise on his face before I took the cup from him. "What happened?"

"I knocked us out." He chuckled. "I honestly didn't think I was going to go down with you, but I did, and I guess I hit the chair." He wiped his face. "My guards had specific instructions to dispose of your chip in the cave and then bring us here."

"Where is here?"

"As far away from my father's court as possible."

"Why didn't you just throw me in the cave with my chip?"

His lips tilted in a smile, and he reached for the nightstand next to the bed and picked up a book before handing it to me. "You can read Elvren, correct?"

"Yes." The Director had made sure we were educated enough to read all the realms' dialects. It came in handy when one wanted to find out secrets. Diaries held the most telling of things, especially when people thought they were hidden. "Why?"

"That explains spirit mates. It explains the bond that ties us together and what happens when it is severed. For some reason, we are inexplicably bound together without having to go through a bonding ceremony. The only thing we lack is the marking." He waved to the book and then left me in this spacious bed with the softest sheets in the entire universe of realms.

I had to prop myself on my side because my back flared every time I put pressure on it. The book was intriguing, to say the least. I knew about bonded mates by way of the Director and his mate, Ava. Bonding made them vulnerable. None of us ever wanted to put our lives in another's hands. It was frowned upon.

And now I was saddled with a prince who I needed a blood sample from before I went back to the compound.

I read about the different mate statuses, and the rarest by far were spirit mates. The books said these were two halves of a single soul. Most beings went through multiple lifetimes without ever finding their spirit mate.

The sun had moved through the sky when he returned with a tray of food. "I don't know what you eat."

"I survive on the essence of souls around me," I said with a cocky tilt of my head.

His little O of shock made me smirk.

"You're a soul sucker?" His voice cracked as he put the tray down on one of the side tables.

"Soul eater. Yes. It's why I had my own room at the compound. I used to constantly tire my roommates." I flipped the page and began reading the next tidbit of information on soul bonding. "And I can't tap your soul for energy. Doing so hurts."

I scanned the next set of words and finally looked up when I realized he hadn't moved.

His eyes narrowed. "You tried?"

I nodded. "At first I thought the spell you had on the jail cell was inhibiting me, but then your guards came in, and I syphoned some energy. Then I thought you had some sort of protective spell." I waved at the book. "Which all makes sense regarding spirit mates." I sighed and closed the book before I found my feet. "I devoured those two souls before you drugged me."

I stood and stretched, reaching for the ceiling and arching my back with it. My shoulder tweaked, but I ignored it. I was not used to lounging in bed. I closed my eyes and reached farther.

Hands landed on my waist, and my eyes flew open. I tensed at the look of interest on Tavin's face.

I reacted, twisting in his grip, and rolled him over my hip onto the ground. I took a step toward the door, and in a blink, I was laid out on my stomach with him straddling my back. His knees squeezed my sides as his grip on the back of my neck held me in place.

I tried bucking him, but he held on.

"Yield."

His growl tickled my ear. I jerked my head back, but he was quicker and moved away from my attempted headbutt.

"Do I need to knock you out again?"

I brought my feet back, hitting him in the lower back with my heels. The echo of discomfort slammed into my back at the same time.

"Stop it, Mya."

I glared over my shoulder at him. "Not when you have that look in your eyes."

His lips spread into a full smile, and my heart squeezed in my chest. "What look is that?"

"I'm not here to get laid. I'm here to get your blood and go home."

He let go of my neck and settled back, still keeping me on the floor. "You can never leave Eleka."

There was no arrogance to his tone. It was soft, as if he knew about being plucked out of a place he loved.

"I need to go back. I need to make sure my pet is set free and not barbequed."

"You have a pet?" He moved to the side and stood, moving far enough away so I couldn't tag him.

I climbed to my feet warily. "A boa constrictor that I found on Earth."

His brow creased. "A boa constrictor? Like a snake?"

"Yes."

He smirked, and his eyes sparkled in a way that had me crossing my arms over my chest. "Most women are afraid of snakes."

"I'm not afraid of anything." Well, except the Director and his goons, but I wasn't about to admit that to this man.

He cocked his manicured eyebrow at me. "You seem skittish around me."

"Well, with that thing pointed at me, can you blame me?" I pointed at his cock which had been standing at attention ever since I'd gotten out of bed.

Now, he actually grinned. "My cock makes you nervous?"

He stepped closer.

"If you want a kick to the groin, keep coming," I warned and stepped into form.

Even though any blow I made would echo in my own body, I wasn't about to let him take advantage of me.

"I thought you assassins used any trick to get close to your targets. Including sex."

His purr was enough to ignite more than anger in me.

"I'm a soul eater. Do you really think I need to spread my legs to get close to my target?"

His smile fell, and he blinked as his mouth slowly opened. "Have you ever?"

He waved toward his hard member clad in soft-looking sweats.

I straightened and flipped my hair back, and then I saw the room behind him. His question was instantly lost at the sight of his magnificent shower.

I crossed toward it, bypassing the prince. This shower alone was bigger than my entire dorm at the complex. It was perhaps bigger than the jail cell I had been sequestered in. I undressed and stepped inside.

"You don't seem to be modest in any way." He leaned against the door.

"Don't assume that my lack of modesty is an invitation. I'll punch your junk if you get near me," I said and turned on the water.

Hot mist surrounded me, raining from above and pulsing from the sides. It was as if I had stepped into heaven. I think I actually moaned.

"Is it men you don't like?" he asked, still trying to figure me out.

I ignored him and ran my hands through my hair, letting the water soak into my dark locks. Normally, I wasn't turned on by anyone, or at least it had never crossed my mind before.

I knew men reacted to me. Hell, I had been chased by a group of drunk Irishmen. That hadn't gone so well for them. But then this fae prince had stepped in front of my cell, and now, all I could think about was running my tongue over his body.

"So that's it. You don't like men. You like women?"

I smiled. I liked that he didn't have me all figured out. I liked the doubt flickering in his eyes.

I turned my back to him, reaching for the soaps on the shelf. The one I settled on was a citrus blend that made me think of the sweet drink that had drugged me. I ran it over my body and my hair, basking in the scent.

I put it back on the shelf and turned to rinse.

Tavin stood at the shower entrance, gripping the sides. "Answer me."

Power rolled with the demand.

"No."

He blinked, stepped into the shower still dressed, and grabbed me by my upper arms, yanking me to him. "Answer me."

I glared up at him, annoyed that he was now in my personal space. "I did answer."

He slammed me against the wall where a spigot pulsed into my lower back. His mouth captured mine, tangling his tongue with mine long enough to make my muscles quake.

When I brought my knee up, he blocked it with his hip and then pressed against me with all his weight. His hands moved from my arms to my breasts, gently caressing as he kissed me.

He broke the kiss and stared at me, his cheeks blooming red from more than just the heat of the shower.

"No one has ever done this?" He lowered his head and took my nipple into his mouth.

I ran my hands into his hair and gripped, pulling him away despite the heat filling me. "No."

No one had ever touched me the way he'd dared to, and it burned in equal shares of anger and desire.

He spun me so my front faced the wall and pressed into me, running his hand down my stomach like he had while I was chained.

I reached down and grabbed his wrist as my heart galloped away.

"No," I whispered with as much ferocity as I could muster.

I was not interested in more of a soul bond than we already had.

His forehead pressed on the base of my neck, and his hands moved to my waist. "Fuck."

His whisper was followed by a breeze of cold air. I glanced back in time to see him strip his sweats and slap them over the side wall before he left the washroom. I got a full view of his perfectly round ass that was as pale as the moonlight.

The prince did not sunbathe in the buff. I smiled and turned back to the shower, letting it pulse over me until I nearly fell asleep standing. Then I turned off the dials, wrapped myself in a towel, and searched the drawers. I finally found a brush and worked the knots out of my hair.

I stepped into the room, debating on what to wear today. The prince sat in one of the side chairs, fully dressed, with his elbows on the armrests and his fingers steepled.

"You don't always kill with your soul-eater thing?" His fingers tapped together.

"No. I used to walk the halls of the complex and take a little here and there, and that would refresh me." I closed my eyes and conjured my normal assassin attire, dropping the towel as the cloth draped across my skin.

It wasn't quite as soft or luxurious as the slip or the night clothing had been, but it was what I was used to.

Irritation raked across his features, and he waved his hand. My clothing morphed into a light dress and fancy lace-up sandals.

I cocked an eyebrow and redressed myself again.

He slowly stood, glaring at me. This time when he waved, a collar and handcuffs accompanied the skimpy outfit, securing my wrists behind me. A chain attached to the collar, and he yanked it, pulling me a step forward.

His lips twitched as his gaze caressed my body. "That's more like the submissive whores I drag through town."

"I can still land a kick." I closed my eyes and wished for my clothing again, except neither the collar nor the cuffs disappeared.

"You cannot wear that in this town," he snapped.

The next outfit draped over my shoulders, and I glanced down at the soft shirt with laces loosely crisscrossed across my chest. The material went down mid-thigh, and while it was more comfortable than the last outfit, it still left me partially exposed.

"That will do," he said, pulling me forward by the chain. "We can walk to the shore, and you can feed on the people of the village. But you cannot feed on my guards. That will leave us vulnerable. Understand?"

I clenched my teeth. The idea that he was portraying me as one of his whores burned.

"No." I'd rather starve.

"If my father thinks I'm here sowing my wild oats, he will leave me be. This is the way to do that. I am known for this sort of behavior." His cheeks flushed, and he glanced out the window.

"Are you blushing?" I laughed, forgetting my place for a moment.

He didn't seem like the type to blush, but there he was, red-cheeked as if the admission embarrassed him in some way.

His gaze jumped back to mine. "You will leave my guards alone?"

I pressed my lips together and straightened my back. I wasn't about to agree to that. If they were all I had access to, they would be part of my meal.

"I cannot have you hurting them. You've already stripped me of three of them, and I still have no idea how I am going to explain their disappearances." He pulled me closer as he spoke and then clasped my face. "So, either you go hungry, or you agree to my terms."

I ripped myself out of his grip. "Fine. But all agreements are null and void if anyone touches me."

I didn't want to be a free-for-all for the men in this place. Especially if Tavin treated me like a common whore.

He nodded.

"That includes you," I challenged.

"I will touch you as I see fit to keep up this farce." His finger traced the edge of my shirt down to the top of my breasts to bring his point home. Then he curled his hand into a fist and stepped back. "You will walk a step behind and keep your head bowed so your hair covers your ears."

This was such crap. "I am submissive to no one."

He closed his eyes, and his nostrils flared. I could almost feel the rage building inside him.

He grabbed my chin, forcing his fingers into my cheeks hard enough for me to open my mouth. Before my brain caught up, he dumped a small cup of liquid into my mouth and clamped it closed.

I swallowed the sweetness and glared at him. It was the same type of cocktail I had drunk in jail. The one that made me pliant so I lacked the energy to fight back and dampened my ability to syphon souls.

I narrowed my eyes at him. "Oh, great. You gave me the same shit you did back at the jail. Now I will go hungry, asshole."

"This doesn't have the magic suppressor in it." He slammed the glass down on the table to make his point. "It will only make you a little more...compliant."

"Oh." I didn't know what to make of that.

The smile that spread across his lips didn't match the anger in his eyes. "You will be submissive to me today, and you will follow the rules."

"Or what?" I asked as my muscles loosened from the drink.

"Or I will tie you to my bed and have my way with you." He cocked a suggestive eyebrow at me.

I remembered the feel of his fingers when I was tied up and unwillingly shivered. "Then I'll have to use the kiss of death on you. Consequences be damned."

Fire flared in his eyes, and he spun on his heel, yanking me forward by the chain.

I stumbled and caught myself. If I fell, I had nothing to stop my face from smashing into the marble below my feet.

I glanced around as he cut through the bungalow. It was more like a mansion with breezy accents and soft colors. The walls were lined with shelves of books and crystal figurines, and the windows had sheers billowing in the light breeze. It looked just as gorgeous as the prince himself.

On the table near the front door sat a picnic basket, and he grabbed it on the way out. The door opened without the use of his hands, and the guard I'd seen at the jail stepped in, taking the basket from him.

"You remember Galen," Tavin said, pointing at the guard with the basket. "This is Shayne, and his brother Rayne, and the last of my surviving guards, Tomack." He glared at me. "Do not harm them, understand?"

I stared him down, unwilling to concede to his rule over me.

His gaze sharpened and his jaw tightened before he faced forward and led the procession out of the house.

THE WITCH ASSASSIN
CHAPTER TEN

I THOUGHT ABOUT SYPHONING energy from the four guards surrounding us, but Tavin shot me a warning glare before we had a chance to clear the outside stairway and reach the road.

My eyes widened at the vision beyond Tavin. The small coastal town was something out of a painting, colored in soft pastels with an ocean in the distance that matched the color of Tavin's eyes.

The entire atmosphere carried almost a lavender shade only broken by shafts of golden rays. The only view I'd had of Eleka had been a quick march from the portal to the jail building, and its beauty had greatly impressed me despite my concerns with staying alive to meet one of the royal subjects who would provide the sample I was sent to collect. This put that view to shame.

Energy pulsed in the air, and I breathed it in, careful not to syphon it from those in close proximity. Trying to pull from Tavin would render me with such a headache that I might fall on my face, and his guards were off-limits if I knew what was good for me.

But the rest of the town was a plentiful buffet. People scurried through the streets with their daily activities.

I sighed, feeling the energy merge with me, fueling me. Just like walking through the halls of the compound, or any other place I ever visited, I inhaled essences like air, pulling a little in at a time until I had my fill.

Tavin glanced back at me, and his steps faltered. He let out a grumble.

"Head down," he muttered and faced forward.

He took a meandering route through the market, stopping at several of the tables and smiling as the vendors bowed at the sight of him. He waved it away.

At one of the tables, a dagger caught my gaze. It had jewels on the smooth handle, and the blade glistened in the sunshine.

Tavin caught me looking at it and stopped at the table. He picked it up and glanced sideways at me.

"Do you have a leg holder for this as well?" he asked the vendor.

The man behind the table reached behind him and then held out a soft leather scabbard that the knife slid into. Tavin pulled a coin from his pocket and handed it over before he crouched down and affixed the knife to my upper thigh. His knuckles brushed my core as he stood.

I wanted to wipe the smirk he wore from his face, but having a weapon actually made me feel a little better about this little parade through town, even though I couldn't reach it with my wrists bound.

When we finally reached the beach, we hung back while Galen spread a blanket on the sand and placed the basket on it. The guards fanned out around us and faced inland as Tavin led me to the blanket.

"Kneel facing the ocean."

I did as he said, glancing at the people dotting the beach in the distance. They all took notice that the prince was on the beach with them. Some pointed, and the women fanned themselves as if swooning over him.

He knelt behind me and reached forward, pushing my knees wider before settling his thighs against mine. "Are you full?"

"I can still reach the knife and stab you in the balls."

He chuckled in my ear with his hands on my knees, pushing them wider before he nuzzled my neck. His fingers slid up my leg that had the thigh holster. He unclipped it and set it out of sight behind him.

"I usually fuck on the beach," he whispered in my ear.

My body tensed, and I glared over my shoulder at him.

"Don't worry. I won't defile your virginity here unless you make a scene." He sucked on my earlobe before biting down on it. "But I will settle for making you moan."

His hand slid between my legs.

"I will kill your guards."

His hand stalled right at the apex of my thighs, brushing the spot that nearly had me melting against him. He teased me with his fingers, pushing the envelope as he dragged his finger against my folds. His other hand pinched my breast through the fabric.

"Then I will muzzle your power and let anyone who wants to fuck you have you here on the beach."

I started at his words. The drink he had given me back at the bungalow might stifle my willpower, but I'd proved to him at the jail that nothing he did inhibited my demon powers. I didn't know if he was capable of nullifying my demon side or not, now that he knew what I was.

And truthfully, the idea of anyone other than him pawing at me disgusted me.

"Then I will kill everyone who dares to touch me."

He didn't seem deterred by my words. His fingers continued their quest, gentle and prodding, which was far from his wrathful tone in my ear.

I had never been touched before he did in the jail, and this heat inside me felt as foreign as the collar around my throat. I didn't know how to act or what to do. Panic filled me, and my breath quickened into ragged pants.

"Relax," he whispered in my ear. "Just let yourself enjoy this."

My body wound so tight I barely felt his hand. He glanced at me, but he didn't stop his sensual ministrations of my clit and my folds. The small smile on his face revved up the rebel in me, and if my hands weren't clasped behind my back, I would have knocked his hands away.

"Please tell me you've at least had a man's hand down your pants before."

I shook my head. I was a virgin in all things beyond a kiss. That was my fatal blow, so I knew how to make someone want to take me somewhere private just by kissing.

"Bless the gods. You are so fucking wet." He slid his fingers between my folds and dipped them inside me. "And so tight."

His voice shook, and he bit my shoulder through the shirt. His thumb swirled on my clit in the same slow pace his fingers slid inside me. His other hand slipped into the shirt, and he cupped my breast, brushing his fingers across my nipples, which were already hard enough to draw attention. His cock dug into the small of my back.

Suddenly, the air shifted around us, shimmering, blocking my ability to see anything but the water in front of us.

"Did you do that?"

"Yes. I don't feel like sharing this." His breath fluttered over my throat. He moved, pushing me down on my back as he knelt between my legs, pulling them wide. "It has been a very long time since I tasted virgin pussy."

I tried to get my leg so I could kick him away, but he wound his arms around my thighs and dove under my oversized shirt like a man hell-bent on his goal.

Good lord, his tongue was even better than his fingers.

"Mya," he whispered, his breath teasing, and then his tongue filled me before returning to the sensitive bud that blanked out all arguments from my brain. "Come for me, you sweet little demon."

My body tingled, and my last coherent thought before my body betrayed me was no wonder the Director forbade sex for his top assassins. This was like being shot into another stratosphere. Lights flashed behind my eyelids as I broke apart, moaning Tavin's name.

He moaned against me as if he was sharing in my pleasure.

His fingers replaced his tongue, and they kept up the slow, penetrating pace as he rose to his knees, freeing my thighs from his grip. He crawled up me and took my mouth like an enemy attack with my juices still on his tongue.

Tavin pulled me into a sitting position. Our tongues mingled as relentlessly as his fingers still working me. My brain-stall faded, and I gasped for air the moment he broke the kiss. His pants pooled around his knees, freeing his cock from the fabric. He pulled his fingers from between my legs and slid them into his mouth, sucking my juices from his digits.

When he threaded his hand into my hair, moving me toward his massive erection, I snarled, "I will bite you."

His lips tilted into a smile. "You might find you enjoy it," he purred. "Just like you seemed to enjoy coming for me."

He did not understand. If he put his cock into my mouth, I would bite the damn thing off.

"Be shortsighted and see what happens." I stuck out my chin with a glare.

He weighed my words with the look on my face and must have seen something that made him let go of my hair. A flash of annoyance rolled over his eyes like a distant storm. Then the privacy barrier dissolved as he stood and stepped out of his pants.

The attention of those closest to us riveted in his direction, and he glanced around. When his gaze landed on a woman a few meters away, her hungry gaze spurred him to head her way.

Even before he stepped in front of her, she was on her knees and licking her lips. I did not know the customs of this world, but the willingness to suck the prince irked me. When the woman's lips slid over the head of his cock, he glanced at me with a fuck-you smile of his own.

He made sure I had a full view of her sucking him.

Something inside me broke at the sight. Fury filled me. How dare she touch him!

I acted before I could regain my senses. I didn't even have a name for the rage that consumed me, and I yanked that bitch's soul right from her body.

One minute, she was sliding her lips up and down his shaft, and the next, she collapsed onto the sand with her dead eyes staring at the sky. And damn if her soul didn't taste particularly sweet.

His head snapped in my direction, and his mouth dropped open as he stumbled away from the fae's dead form. The barrier erected around us immediately, separating us from the rest of the crowd.

"What the fuck?" Tavin pointed at the dead woman.

I had no logical response. I gazed at the dead body and then back at him and his still-hard member. A smug smile crossed my lips at the same time my conditioned mind balked at my impulsiveness. I didn't quite understand the darkness this prince stirred in my soul.

Sure, the book I'd read explained the connection, but it went against everything I had trained for all my life. I had killed that woman out of spite. I had defied my training and acted on pure emotion.

Tavin marched to me and grabbed my hair, tilting my head back. "Why did you do that?"

I shrugged, trying to school my features while confusion at my actions muddled my thought process.

He pulled me higher on my knees. His glare pierced through me. "Why, Mya?"

I tried to yank out of his hold, but his grip on my hair was too tight.

"Are you getting possessive?" His words were wrapped in a growl. "Is that what happened?"

I pressed my lips together, refusing to put a name to what had come over me.

His eyes narrowed into accusing slits. "Were you jealous?"

"Fuck you, Tavin." I ground my teeth together, shooting daggers from my eyes.

He growled as he ran his hand over his shaft in swift motions. "You don't want anyone else to get me off? Is that it?"

His eyes turned wild, almost feral as he jerked himself. He yanked my head back, and I cried out as semen shot out of his cock. It covered my face and seeped into my hair in hot pulses until he finally stopped stroking himself.

"You can wear my cum on the walk home." He put on his pants, gathered the knife and the blanket, and shoved them into the basket.

He dropped the barrier and pulled me to my feet, jerking me by the chain as he started toward the bungalow on the hill.

He didn't even glance at his guards as he sauntered by. But they certainly did a double take at me.

I kept my head bowed, but it was impossible to hide the liquid that slid down my skin and dripped onto my shirt.

The only time he glanced back at me was when some of his semen slid into my mouth, and I spit. I didn't want his jizz in my mouth,

125

even if it did taste like something decadent and taboo.

The picnic basket ended up on the same table it had been when we went to leave. None of the guards followed us inside. The prince didn't let up until we were in the bedroom, and he latched the chain to a notch on the bed. He undid one wrist, yanked my arms above my head, and clamped it closed again before he waved my clothing away.

His silence unnerved me enough for my body to shake. He pushed me onto the bed and then left me in the bedroom, naked and bound to his bed with his cum drying on my face and hair. His shadow moved back and forth in the adjoining room, and then he bellowed long and loud.

Silence fell again, and the only indication that I knew he was still here was the heavy presence of his annoyance.

MY ARMS ACHED, AND I tried to curl them under me, but I couldn't bring them down far enough to be comfortable. At some point, I must have dozed because a sheet now covered me.

Warmth radiated from the other side of me, and I turned my head, blinking at the nest of dark hair on the pillow next to mine. Tavin was a stomach sleeper, and he gripped the pillow like a life float with his head turned away from me.

Rage roared back into my muscles, and I kicked him in the thigh, clenching my teeth against the flare of pain that resounded in my leg.

He jerked up onto his elbows and turned his sleepy, confused eyes my way.

I kicked again. "Get out of my bed."

I pushed against him with my feet, sliding him toward the far edge.

He grabbed my feet. "This is *my* bed. If you don't like it, you can sleep somewhere else." He shoved my legs away and settled back onto his pillow. "And if you kick me again, you are not going to like what happens."

I considered kicking him again just to be defiant. Instead, I said, "At least release me from these shackles so I can get some decent rest."

He looked at my wrists and then at me. "So you can get my blood and leave? That's a hard pass."

He settled in again.

I stared at the back of his head and his bare shoulders. The sheet settled near sexy dimples in his lower back. I had to tear my gaze away before I did something I would forever regret.

He turned his head and regarded me with sleepy eyes. "Why did you kill that woman today?"

"I didn't like..." I turned my gaze away from him and shut my mouth before the rest of the words tumbled out.

What I had done was born of emotion, not cool or calculated, which was what I normally was, but the prince had scrambled my brain like no other ever had.

"I probably would have done the same if anyone touched you." His eyes closed, and he sighed, falling into the soft cadence of sleep.

All his severe lines softened in slumber, and his words diminished my anger but brought another part of me roaring to life.

The one that wanted his mouth between my legs again, making me quiver with a foreign heat that washed my duty away like a tidal wave. I closed my eyes, forcing the memory away. The Director would slaughter me for thoughts like this.

My treasonous feelings betrayed me as my eyes opened back up to cascade over what was visible of his form. Tavin was a death sentence waiting to happen.

If I didn't get his blood and get back to the compound, who knows what the Director would send to this world as punishment?

THE WITCH ASSASSIN
CHAPTER ELEVEN

I BLINKED MY EYES open to brightness streaking through the windows. The binds on my wrists lay open, and the shower was running.

I rubbed my chafed wrists and glanced at the bathroom. While I would love a shower, this was probably the only time I'd be able to slip out of this building and find my way back to the portal.

I willed clothes onto my body that would more than fit in on this oasis, based on the traipse through town yesterday, and tiptoed through the bungalow. My gaze landed on the picnic basket, and I stalled, glancing back toward the bedroom.

The shower still ran, so I rummaged around for the leather holder with the dagger and found it. It took a moment to strap on my thigh, and then I swung open the front door.

I slid toward the opening and was thrown back onto the floor as if I had hit a wall of electricity.

The shower turned off, and Tavin came running out with a towel draped around his waist.

"Figures. I leave you alone for a second, and you get yourself in trouble."

I pulled the knife out and turned, facing him. "You can't keep me locked up forever."

He crossed to me and stood in my personal space, dripping water from his dark locks down onto my face. "Why not?" He glanced at our surroundings. "Is this not luxurious enough for you?"

I blinked up at him and started to laugh. "This is more luxury than I'm used to. The jail cell was more in line with my dorm at the compound, except it was close to double the size. I have a job to do, and if I don't do it, there are dire consequences."

His eyebrows rose. "You confuse me."

I still held the knife at the ready. I could cut him and get the blood, but I wouldn't be able to get out the door with whatever barrier had knocked me on my ass. "Yeah, well, we're even in that respect."

"Go shower and then we can discuss our situation." He had the audacity to turn his back on me and head toward the bedroom as if I wasn't at all a danger to him.

The bear of it was, I really wasn't. Any pain I inflicted on him, I would feel, and it just didn't seem to be worth it until there was a solid opportunity to slip out.

"Why won't you let me go?"

"Because that puts this entire realm in danger." He didn't even glance back as he diverted to his chest of drawers for clothing.

I continued to the bathroom and peeled off the clothing I had conjured. They seemed to be the best option for the day, even if we were just chilling at this bungalow. I could pilfer his library and learn as much as I could about this faction living in the shadows of the universe.

My brain was still focused on the task I was sent here to do, but I was fast becoming used to this shower. Hot water poured out on demand, and the various spouts massaged my body in such a way that I could see myself settling for this above the Director and his minimalist requirements for us.

I had been in palaces and homes of presidents. I had seen opulence, but I had never been pampered like this. Even chained to the bed was more comfortable than some of the predicaments I'd had to deal with.

And without my tracker, the Director would never know I had gotten out of that cave. However, if they sent someone as smart as I was in to retrieve my body, they would only find the chip and know something was up.

I hadn't told anyone how I planned to navigate the cave though, and I thought the demon half of me was the only way I'd gotten through that magic. I didn't know if another assassin had demon blood. They certainly didn't have the blood of a prince of hell, but regular demon blood...I couldn't rule that out.

I washed with the same citrusy soap as I had before and then just stood under the spray until my muscles were as loose as they'd ever been. Only then did I turn off the water, dry myself, dress, and head out to the living quarters.

A servant stood with his hands clasped behind his back. "I am Alvin. The prince's house master. He asked that I bring you to him once you have finished dressing."

"Thank you," I said.

I always treated the help with respect wherever I went. They were the ones who made the worlds run, regardless of what the dictators and royalty thought. I was tempted to pull a sip of energy from him, but I refrained. I still had plenty of reserves after killing that woman and ingesting her soul.

I followed him up a winding set of stairs and paused at the top. The view was even more spectacular than it had been on the front steps.

Tavin sat on a chair facing the ocean with his back to me. He had a tablet in his hands and a stack of books on the table next to him. A large pitcher and two glasses sat on the coffee table in front of him, along with at least a dozen other books.

Alvin left me to make my way across the rooftop veranda and I headed for the chair next to Tavin. I wanted the same breathtaking view he had.

He didn't look up from the tablet until after I took a seat. When he turned off the computer, he rubbed his face.

"We've been monitoring the portal."

I kept my gaze on the horizon. "And?"

"There are three more dead bodies."

"The fall?"

His lips twitched into a smirk. "Two of them. The third suffocated. None of them breached the second cave." He glanced at me. "That skeleton and you are the only two who got through. But you were the only one to think to bring oxygen tanks. How did you get those through the portal?"

I held my hand out, called my backpack from the ether, and tossed it to Tavin. "I conjure things, and I can store something just beyond wherever I am and retrieve it at will."

"And you were the only one to think to bring a hoverboard."

"I had a heads-up. One of ours had natural levitation skills but couldn't breathe and was able to jump back into the portal before they died. Otherwise, I probably would be dead on one of those nasty spikes, too."

"But the fact remains. You are the only one who made it through to the outer cave and burst through the barrier we had up." He stared at me. "Why?"

"Because I am damn good at my job."

"You steal DNA so your boss can make more monsters to do his bidding. That's not a job to be proud of, demon." His stare beat down on me.

"Oh, and acting all sanctimonious and thinking the people you rule over are beneath you is?"

"I do not—"

"You walked across that beach acting like you deserved to get sucked off. That isn't putting the people first. That's using them like toys that you can just discard after you've satisfied your libido or ego or whatever." I gripped the arms of the chair tightly. "You expect everyone to kneel down before you because of who your father is. What have you done for your people?"

"I hide them from those who would want to ruin us, or enslave us." He waved at the sky. "This is my magic. My power at play here. I keep them safe from vicious sleazeballs like you." He leaned toward me. "Your prowess didn't get you through those barriers, demon. Your connection to me did." He picked up one of the books and tossed it to me. "Your demon heritage may have helped get you out of the portal pit, but it wouldn't have gotten you through the outer barrier. That one is set to kill anyone without Elvren blood."

"I don't have Elvren blood."

"No. You're just a spirit mate to one of the most powerful Elvren to have ever lived." He pressed his lips together for a moment. "And what baffles the fuck out of me is why you would want to go back to a life where your every move and every thought are controlled."

"And how is it any different here? You've taken what you wanted and kept me tied up most of the time. At least there I am trusted to come and go as I please between jobs."

"So, you can just go to any realm you want at any time?"

"Well, no. I can go anywhere in the compound, though."

His point started to sink in.

"The compound where your place is half the size of our jail cells?"

I ignored him and stared out at the sun glinting on the ocean surface, looking like a web of diamonds on a sea-blue background. "I'm not free to come and go here."

"That is correct. On close inspection, you are not Elvren. Yesterday, having you keep your head down and your hair over your ears was necessary to keep the charade going. Otherwise, your life would be in danger."

"From who?"

"We are warrior fae, sweet demon. We kill what we don't understand. And trust me when I tell you, they will not understand you." He pointed at me, and I wanted to snap his finger in two.

I leaned back in the chair, digesting his words. "This world is not a secret. A seer told me it existed." I chewed on my lower lip and then glanced at him. "She said an ancient and supreme Elvren clan lived on Eleka. How would she know unless there's some sort of breach here?"

"A seer who spoke to you." He lowered his chin and stared at me through his thick lashes.

"Stop playing games and speak plainly." I was tired of this conversation.

"You. A seer told you."

"Yes." And then it clicked.

Seers weren't omnipotent. They were influenced by those around them, and I had been there. I'd triggered the vision.

"Oh," I whispered and planted my hand on my face.

"Can your boss find that seer?" Tavin asked.

"No. She was my mark, and my marks never survive. Normally," I added, because he was as much a mark as she was.

He tapped his index fingers as he leaned back in the seat.

"What's going on in that pretty head of yours?" I asked.

My question caught him off guard, and he let out a full laugh, giving me a side-eye. "I'm thinking your boss could think that seer set you up, and perhaps that will work in our favor."

"It won't work. He voiced the same thought, and I shot it down. If I don't show up at the compound on the seventh day, he will send his army after me. He knows I'll survive. I do that as well as I do my job, and he won't be willing to forfeit me to the unknown."

I was sure of it. The way he kept me under his thumb, he didn't want to lose me as an asset.

"Does he have light Elvren blood?"

"No. He does not have royal Elvren blood."

That was the one thing the Director was adamant about. The thing he coveted the most.

"I'm not talking about royal blood. I am talking about commoner Elvren who hail from light fae. They would be able to breach the outer portal."

I didn't know the answer. I thought the Director only shot for the most powerful blood, so I wasn't sure he thought to take a simpleton's blood. He sure hadn't asked me to collect it for him.

"I don't know. It's not something he's asked of me, but I am not the only assassin out there. There's a whole complex full of trained assassins, and I can't vouch for anyone else's jobs."

He continued tapping his fingers.

"If I go back..."

"You will be killed."

"Not necessarily."

"I took your tracker out. You will be killed."

"Can you get it back, and I can have it in my pocket when I arrive?"

He tilted his head in a nod. "Then what?"

"Then I forget you ever existed." I couldn't believe that had tumbled from my mouth.

I would have to do a fair amount of lying, and I had never been good at that. If the Director suspected I was hiding something, I would be tortured until he was either satisfied I was telling the truth or I was dead.

He scanned the horizon. "And seal our fates."

He shook his head, stood, and crossed to the far railing.

I followed him. "What do you mean, seal our fates? Your world would be safe."

"No, it wouldn't be safe. Our clan fled to survive the war on Elbeeon. If the dark Elvren on Elbeeon found out where we were hiding, they wouldn't stop until this realm was stomped out of existence." He pointed at the array of books behind us. "Everything you'd ever want to know about spirit mates and then some are in those books. Read them, and then talk to me about deserting my side or putting yourself in harm's way."

EACH BOOK I SCOURED left my heart pounding in my throat. Spirit mates, as the first book he gave me the other day had alluded to, were as rare as the Hope Diamond. A once-in-a-millennium type thing.

And according to the lore, once spirit mates attach, separation would kill them both.

I wiped my hand down my face and glanced at Tavin still staring out at the ocean. The sun had transitioned through the sky, and I closed the last book.

If Tavin died, the protection he afforded this world would die with him. If the warnings happened to be bullshit, and being separated didn't kill us, the Director just might kill me to prove a point to the other assassins.

And we would be in the same place.

The pain transfer was evidence of the spirit melding. The damage had already been done to us. Here on Eleka, the only danger was Tavin's father. If he got even a whiff of who I was, my life would be forfeited, thus taking Tavin with me.

God, this was such a mess. I wondered exactly what that seer had seen to send me on this path. Was it my death? My imprisonment? Or something else entirely that I'd missed because I was too hell-bent on finishing the job and getting home.

Tavin glanced back at me as if he sensed the turmoil brewing inside me.

As prisons go, this one really wasn't that bad. But it did burn that what little freedoms I'd had were now gone. I was bound to the prince, and from the unseemly gleam in his eyes, he knew he was inexplicably bound to me, too.

Fated mates could reject the mating bond and choose someone else. Soulmates who went through the mating ritual would wither and die if separated from their mates. In that way, they were similar to spirit mates.

But the differences were much more morbid. Spirit mates were bound by the bond in ways that no other pairing was. They didn't need the mating ritual to be connected. Separation was at best debilitating pain, and at worst, death.

The other notable difference was when spirit mates went through the mating ritual, their powers became transferable and accessible at will afterwards.

I would *never* share the power I held.

In the wrong hands, my power could conquer the realms.

THE WITCH ASSASSIN
CHAPTER TWELVE

"NOW DO YOU UNDERSTAND our predicament?" Tavin asked as I approached him at the wall.

"That we're screwed?"

He laughed. "That's a good way of putting it." He glanced at me. "I always thought I'd find my soulmate here on Eleka."

He scanned the horizon then headed back to the chairs and gathered the books.

I didn't take offense to his comment. Most beings naturally migrate to a member of their own species.

I picked up the last two books and followed him inside. Instead of heading down to the living area, he stopped on the second floor and entered a large room with books lining the walls. Comfortable chairs with lights hanging over them dotted the floor between a center table with chairs that had books strewn over the top of the fine-grained wood.

"Is this a room I can explore?" I crossed to the opposite side of the table.

Tavin glanced at me as he placed the books in his arms onto the table. "You can explore any of the rooms in this bungalow. You just can't go outside without me."

"I'm not going outside on a leash again. That was demeaning." I dropped my books with a bang that resounded through the room.

His lips curved. "You didn't like being my sex toy?"

I crossed my arms and glared at him. "No. I'm not here for your pleasure."

"Prisoner, pleasure. What's the difference?" He stalked toward me.

I shifted my stance and brought my hands up into loose fists. "I will kick your ass if you try anything."

His face broke out in a grin.

His grin widened as I stripped the thigh holder of the dagger he'd bought and pointed the sharp blade at him. I tracked him as he moved around the table.

"If you can nick me with that knife, I'll yield." He nearly glided across the floor with fluid motion that screamed of grace and ruthlessness.

I didn't wait for him to attack. I went on the offensive, and he blocked all my motions. Not one of my maneuvers caught him, either. When I went straight at him, intending to impale his stomach, he caught my wrist and wrenched the knife from my hand, throwing it across the room where it clattered across the floor.

His grip was tighter than a vise, and he pulled me flush against him. I attempted to break his grip and throw him. While he fell, though, he pulled me with him and rolled on top of me, pinning me in place.

Tavin's hair framed my face, tickling the edges of my throat as his smile grew. His eyes sparkled as if this was a game to him.

"Has anyone ever told you that you are incredibly beautiful for a demon?"

I rolled my eyes and tried to buck him off. "Maybe this is my glamour."

His smile slipped, and he recoiled as if I were a hideous, horned being.

I laughed. His reaction was worth the lie. It seemed to cool the sudden heat licking at my skin.

His eyes narrowed. "This is no glamour."

He leaned forward, grabbed the top hem of my shirt, and dragged it down over my breast. Then he took my hard nipple into his mouth, running his tongue over the sensitive flesh, teasing me with his touch.

Damn it, why hadn't I put a bra on this morning? I stared at the ceiling, trying my best not to react, but all I could think of was that mouth between my legs on the beach and how intense his emotions had been.

"Stop."

"You didn't stab me with that knife." With his teeth, he lowered the shirt more, gaining access to my other breast.

I growled and started struggling underneath him, trying to free a leg from underneath his. He wrapped his feet under each ankle and spread his legs, moving mine along with his. When he settled back down, his hips pressed into mine through our clothing.

I bent my knee and tried to roll us, but he remained in place, sucking my breasts and leaving me squirming under him, which just caused more friction between us.

I conjured a knife in my hand and lashed out, cutting both of us.

He hissed and sat up on his knees, staring at the cut on the edge of his thumb.

I sat up and pressed the blade to his throat, glaring at him.

He grabbed a handful of my hair and pulled me to his lips, despite the blade pressing against the flesh of his neck.

I had the urge to simultaneously slit his throat and stick my tongue into his mouth. I followed the second urge, pulling the blade away from him so I didn't follow through on the first part of my instincts.

Admittedly, Tavin knew how to kiss. He was better at it than anyone who I'd coerced before.

His free hand slid between my thighs, and I tried to pull away from the kiss, but he held me tight, pillaging my mouth with purpose.

"You're supposed to yield," I mumbled around his tongue.

His lips pulled into a grin, but he didn't stop the kiss until he was ready.

Then he met my gaze and nodded toward the knife in my hand. "That is not the knife I gave you."

His fingers continued to rub the apex of my legs through the material of my skirt.

"Fucking fae," I muttered under my breath, but that seemed to bring a gleam to Tavin's eyes, which were nearly full pupil with very little iris showing.

"Do you want me to stop?" He tilted his head in question.

I opened my mouth to say yes, but his fingers were sending heat signals through my abdomen and stalling my voice. I cleared my throat and nodded.

"Yes," I forced out of my mouth, even though my body was sending a resounding *no*.

His hand stilled, and I dropped the knife on the ground and gripped his face, pulling him back to my mouth, crushing his lips in a kiss that was meant to consume.

This time when he laid me down, I didn't fight him at all, giving in to the need raking through my form. It was as foreign as this bungalow's opulence.

He broke the kiss and put his forehead against mine. "I should not have started this."

His pained groan snaked through me.

The fact he'd stopped on his own nearly pulled a whine from my lips.

"Why not?" I didn't recognize the husky quality of my voice.

"My body is compelled to claim you."

I stiffened underneath him and met his hooded gaze.

"And I can see you are not ready for this."

I narrowed my eyes at him. "You were gung ho on violating me in the jail and again on the beach. Why the sudden concern for me now?"

His lips tilted in a smile. "Perhaps I've become fond of you, my sweet little demon."

He climbed to his feet and offered me his bloody hand.

I accepted it and let him pull me to my feet. Our cuts rubbed together, and heat jolted through my veins. He stared at our joined skin clasped together before he lifted his gaze. Feral need pounded through me directly from where our blood blended.

"Fuck it," he whispered and had me in his arms, slamming me into a wall of books as he tore at my clothing.

The mix of our blood turned him into a beast, a savage with only one goal.

"Tavin," I hissed as his mouth dropped to my throat.

I tried to push him away now that panic had replaced the heat sizzling my skin.

He reached down, lifted each of my thighs, and pressed against me as he sucked on the side of my throat. His hips rubbed through my clothing, hitting my most sensitive spots and numbing my mind in a way that alarmed me. Clothing still separated us, so there was a part of his brain that still worked enough for him not to wave the fabric away.

His low groan against my skin sent a wave of delight through my muddled thoughts. He ground his hips harder into me in frantic circles that I couldn't help but match. I leaned my head back, giving him more access to my throat.

"Sir?" A loud voice rang through the library.

Tavin dropped my legs and shot back a step, putting his arms out wide as if he hadn't been ravaging me at all.

Thankfully, I caught myself before I plummeted to the ground.

Tavin stared at me with his chest heaving before he wiped his face.

Without turning, he asked, "What?"

His tone was as terse as I'd ever heard it. Whatever the reason for the interruption, it was obviously unwelcomed.

I fixed my shirt so my breasts were no longer hanging out, but the fabric did nothing to hide my pebbled nipples. My cheeks were hot, and I was sure I was just as flushed as Tavin.

"There's a situation that requires your attention," his butler said.

Tavin's gaze tore away from me, and he nodded, adjusting his pants before he sauntered away.

He stopped at the door and looked back. "Feel free to..."

He waved at the books and then his gaze slid down my body and back before he disappeared from view.

I sagged against the wall. "What in the hell?"

I glanced down at my bloody hand, still feeling the fire of his blood tingling through me. On shaking legs, I started looking at the titles on the shelves with a hint of an idea raging in my head.

It wasn't until my gaze landed on the title *Blood Oaths and Blood Bonds, A Historical Commentary* that it stopped and refocused back on that book. I slid it off the shelf, curious to see if this volume contained any clue of what had just happened between us.

I took it with me and escaped down to the garden courtyard outside the bedroom and living area in search of both nature and lighting.

"What do you mean there's been a breach?" Tavin's angry hiss pulled my attention even before I could open the book I'd retrieved.

I leaned closer to the open window, eavesdropping on the conversation, the book in my hand forgotten.

"It seems another assassin has come through the portal."

I wished I was in the room to see the guard's reaction because his tone was downright deadly. I wondered who got through that hellish portal and if they were in the jail cell that the guards had put me in.

"And?"

"The queen is dead."

THE WITCH ASSASSIN
CHAPTER THIRTEEN

RAW PAIN CLENCHED MY gut and I folded over. It felt as if someone had just stabbed me. Or Tavin.

In a blink, I was up and moving, my protective instinct flaring enough for me to ignore the brutal assault on my insides. I slid into the living area, ready to defend against another attack.

But Tavin stood stoically as if the pain lancing through me was not real. His gaze jumped to mine before he focused on the guard again.

"And the king?" His voice was steady, belying the turmoil pummeling my insides.

"He wants to know what this means." The guard pulled something out of his pocket, along with a piece of paper, and handed both to Tavin.

I recognized what he handed Tavin. My tracker.

Damn them. The Director had not waited the full week before coming for me, and based on the fact that someone got through the barriers, he did have assassins with fae blood.

"What does it say?" I asked.

Tavin stared at me before dropping his gaze to the paper. His jaw clenched.

"They want you back or they will keep sending assassins until the royal family is dead and chaos has erupted throughout the realm." He glanced up at his guard. "Did you catch the assassin?"

"No, sir, we did not."

Tavin crumpled the letter and closed his eyes. "Tell my father I will be back momentarily. I'll help plan the funeral and ensure we stop any further attack from Icarus."

He wiped his face, tracking blood from his cut hand down his cheek.

"Are you okay, sir?" The guard's concern was evident, and he glanced at me as if I were the enemy.

He wasn't that far off. If it wouldn't kill me, I would be taking Tavin's blood and getting out of here. The softness growing inside me needed to be eradicated. Since when had I cared for anything other than my snake?

"Yes, I am fine. Tell my father I will explain things when I get there." He pocketed the note and chip and dismissed the guard with a nod. As soon as we were alone, he turned to me. "What do you think you were doing?"

"I thought you were hurt." I held the book to my chest as if it could protect me from the livid fae standing in the room. "I thought you had been stabbed, and I came to defend us."

His stare never wavered, and the muscles in his jaw relaxed enough that they didn't stand out in stark relief like they had before. "To defend *us*?"

I nodded. "I felt your pain. I thought you had been stabbed."

He nodded and schooled his features into a neutral blend of sorrow and aggravation. "The news of my mother's death felt like that." His voice softened, and his brow creased. "But that was emotional anguish, not physical harm." His questioning lilt implored me for answers that I didn't have. His gaze dropped to the book clutched in my arms.

I turned it so he could read the title.

When his eyes lifted to mine, my heart slammed in my chest at the shock that hit.

He shook his head as if too many thoughts crowded his brain. "I don't have time to analyze this. We have to go. Now."

He waved a hand at me, and my clothing altered into something more suited for a formal meeting. Silk and satin ruffles fell from my waist and swayed as I walked. The fitted bodice left my arms and shoulders exposed. It was quite extravagant and very uncomfortable given what I was used to wearing. Even the bandage now donning my hand seemed like overkill.

He waved down his body, changing into royal garb as if we were taking a meeting with the king on arrival. He was handsome in his daily attire, but dressed to the hilt with a golden sword hanging at his hip was nothing short of stunning. The only thing marring the look was his bandaged hand.

He headed toward the door, and I followed, feeling the familiar weight of the dagger on my thigh. I reached him at the same time the rest of his guards did as if he had sounded some sort of silent alarm, and they flanked us, two in front and two in back.

Tavin grabbed my hand. One instant, we were walking out of the beautiful bungalow, and the next, we entered the formal throne room. Royal guards lined the walls, and all eyes fell on us.

Hostility radiated in the air as if they were just as on edge as the rest of us. I guessed I could understand. If the Director had been assassinated, I thought we would be very much on edge as his agents.

An older fae sat on the throne. His sharp eyes tracked us, and the only difference between Tavin and the man on the throne, apart from age, was that his eyes were emerald as opposed to Tavin's aquamarine eyes. The strong build and square jaw, along with the silky chestnut hair, were the same. Tavin obviously got his exceptional looks from his father.

The empty seat next to him brought a heavy pang in the middle of my chest. A glance at Tavin told me that's where his eyes had roamed. He still held my hand, and when I tried to pull it away, he clamped down painfully. He must've sensed my need to flee.

The king's eyes landed on me, and they narrowed with such hatred that my throat constricted. I again tried to pull my hand out of

Tavin's grip, but he kept hold as if his life depended on it.

"What happened?" Tavin asked in a soft and respectful tone.

The king continued to glare at me. "An assassin killed the queen while I was entertaining ideas for a new structure in Talica with a crew of engineers. The coward slit her throat and left a note pinned to her chest with her own dagger."

Tavin hung his head, giving me a side-eye, but he did not release me.

"Is that the reason my wife is dead?" The king pointed at me, venom lacing every word.

At the same time, guards from around the room moved closer to where we stood with their hands on the hilts of their swords.

Tavin nodded. "Mya. My spirt mate."

All motion stopped, and King Zorander's eyes widened before his brow dropped again.

"Spirit mates don't exist," he growled.

"And yet when Mya is cut, I feel her pain, and if it's deep enough, I bleed along with her and vice versa."

I inhaled deeply, sucking in some energy from the souls around me, weakening them as I powered up. My heart fluttered at the thought that I might need to battle my way out of a death sentence.

Tavin untangled our hands and put his palm up expectantly to me.

I arched an eyebrow in his direction.

"The dagger."

My eyes narrowed, but I lifted up the hem of the dress, riffling through the layers to find the hilt of the knife. I yanked it from the holder and handed it to him blade first. He flipped it in his hand so his fingers held the handle and then stabbed me right below my clavicle.

I gasped. "What the fuck?"

Pain spiraled from the spot outward, and it screamed worse when Tavin pulled the knife out. I glared at him, but while the spot he'd stabbed hurt like hell, there was nothing behind it to cause any lasting damage.

He handed me back the knife and then winced as he slid his royal jacket off his shoulders. A red stain spread over his white dress shirt from a matching location near his shoulder. He unbuttoned his shirt, showing a bleeding puncture wound.

I stared at the bloody knife in my hand and then back at him as my skin burned with anger at his audacity. "You stabbed me."

"Yes," he said while buttoning up his shirt again.

The warning glance he shot me said for me to simmer the hell down. He looked back up at the king as blood freely ran from the punctures in our skin.

King Zorander gripped the chair arms so hard his knuckles were pale white. "So, if I kill her, I kill you."

Tavin nodded and dropped his gaze to the floor. "Yes. And if she leaves, we both die."

"And if I chain her in the dungeon until she rots?"

"Then I probably can go as far as the garden before the separation affects me." He glanced at me. "I tested out the separation distance last night to see how far I could go before being incapacitated." He shook his head. "I couldn't even get to the main road outside the bungalow."

My jaw dropped open as his gaze flashed to mine.

"You should have told me the moment she arrived." The king's glare felt like ice flowing over my skin.

"You would have killed me," I said, lifting my chin. "And they still would have sent more assassins. So instead of just losing your wife, you would have lost your son, too. The Director is relentless. He will not stop until he gets what he wants, especially since he now knows this place exists. Even with your wife's royal DNA at his disposal, he will keep coming for me."

King Zorander sneered at me. "And you would happily go back."

I opened my mouth to speak and then closed it when turmoil churned my stomach. I dropped my gaze to the floor and then slid it to Tavin. Up until that moment, if anyone had asked if I wanted to go back, I would have said yes. But the fae next to me had gotten under my skin enough for me to hesitate.

I turned my attention back to the king, confused by all these emotions accosting me. "It would harm Tavin."

My brow creased and I wondered what the hell was wrong with me.

"And that would bother you?" King Zorander leaned forward, studying me.

165

I stared at the ground, finding it would bother me a great deal. "Yes."

He nodded to the guards surrounding us. "Take them to the whipping post. My son's oversight cannot go unpunished."

Tavin's guards took our arms, and their fear radiated off them when their eyes landed on me. I tensed, ready to defend myself.

"Don't," Tavin whispered, meeting my gaze. "I'll be fine."

"I'm not letting them harm you," I said, but I yielded and let them march us out to the courtyard.

The guards stripped Tavin of his shirt and clasped his hands in the shackles at the top of the post.

"Ten lashes," King Zorander announced.

They positioned me where I could see Tavin's face and not his back. The first crack of the whip hit, and pain bloomed in my back. Both Tavin and I arched and groaned.

Then my attention darted to the man holding the whip.

"Don't, Mya," Tavin said through clenched teeth.

I looked back at him, mystified at his stubbornness. Instead of yanking the man's soul from his body like I wanted to, I fed off it. I would leave that bastard so drained that it would take him weeks to get his strength back.

The second crack ripped through Tavin's skin, leaving the same welt on my back. I called upon my demon side, pulling it to the surface. That part of me dulled pain.

I pulled in more energy, feeding that part of me as Tavin and I stared at each other. He didn't have the benefit of my heritage to protect him.

The next lashing hit. He winced but didn't speak. The hits were getting weaker as I tired out the owner of the whip. They still smarted, but it was more of a burn rather than skin tearing open.

After seven strikes, the man traded the long whip for something that looked like a cat-o'-nine-tails with barbs at the end of the knotted cords. He stepped close to the prince and struck with that hideous thing.

Both Tavin and I yelped as the barbs gouged Tavin's back. Tavin closed his eyes and pressed his forehead against the pole, waiting for the next strike.

I, on the other hand, had had enough. My back felt like a thousand claws had raked across it. As the torturer raised the handle for another strike, I yanked, devouring the bastard's soul.

He fell back with his arm cocked and hit the floor hard.

Tavin's eyes flashed, and silence fell over the courtyard.

The hands holding my arms shook. Tavin's guards had to know what had just happened. They knew I was responsible for the death, but they also knew I did it to protect their prince. They remained as quiet as Tavin.

"What the..." King Zorander hurried over to his dead worker and pressed his fingers to the man's throat. His gaze rose to Tavin and then moved to me. "What are you?" he hissed.

"She has the power to kill everyone in this room," Tavin said, his voice filled with the agony scraping his back.

The king's eyes narrowed. "What is she?"

"She feasts on soul energy. And if cornered, she can yank the soul right out of a body, killing instantly." Tavin glanced at me. "I guess the barbed whip pushed her over that edge."

"I couldn't let him hit you with that thing again," I mumbled as wetness leaked from the corners of my eyes and tracked down my cheeks.

He turned back to his father. "I understand why the Director wants her back. This power is more dangerous than anything we have at our disposal."

The king reached for the barbed whip. "You still have two more lashes."

Tavin's eyes widened and jumped to me.

Fear gripped my heart, but it wasn't mine. It was Tavin's, and it had nothing to do with physical harm. He didn't want me to hurt his father.

"Please don't," he whispered just as the whip connected with his back.

We both bowed with the pain. The second shot quickly followed, peeling a scream from my lips.

King Zorander dropped the whip, glared at me, and snapped, "Take her to the dungeon. And take my son to the medical suite."

"No." Tavin straightened, wincing. "She goes where I go."

His father glared at him. "Take them both to the dungeon," he snarled and turned away, marching toward the door. "Separate cells."

THE WITCH ASSASSIN
CHAPTER FOURTEEN

"SAME CELL," TAVIN SAID as they pushed me into one and tried to lead him to another.

"You heard what your father said," Galen, his closest guard, said.

Tavin glared at him. "Same. Cell."

"I can't. Not if I want to live." He tried to push Tavin away from the entrance to my cell.

"Same cell. If you want to live," I said.

If Tavin hadn't insisted, I wouldn't have laid down the threat.

Galen stared at me and then at Tavin.

"You heard the lady." Tavin gave him a tight smirk.

Galen let go of Tavin, letting him enter my cell. He reached into his pocket and handed Tavin the same jar of healing salve that he had given him not so long ago in a different jail and then slammed the door closed.

"Tell my father I coerced you with my magic. He'll go easy if he thinks you had no choice."

Galen nodded and glanced at the other three guards, herding them out, leaving us in the dank cell. This one had no amenities the way the jail had, only a hard, damp floor and a bucket in the corner. It was probably meant for the worst of the kingdom's criminals.

Tavin unscrewed the jar and applied salve to the puncture wound on his chest before he turned to me. He waved at me, and his brow scrunched in frustration as his magic failed in the warded cell.

"Take the dress off so I can attend to your wounds."

"Let me get your back first," I said, approaching him, eyeing the torn skin seeping blood down to his waistline where the cloth soaked it in.

I thought he was going to argue with me, but he just handed over the salve and turned, putting his head against the bars.

"How many times have you been whipped?" I asked softly as I applied the magical healing goop.

Coolness layered over the burn in my back. After I finished covering his wounds, I applied some to the puncture near my collarbone and then handed him the jar.

"Enough to know how essential this is." He lifted the salve and twirled his finger, indicating for me to turn around.

The zipper scraped along my skin as Tavin dragged it down as gently as he could.

With the clasps undone, the dress fell from my shoulders. I didn't bother covering up as I laid the dress out on the ground, fanning the skirt enough so that more than one person could use it as a buffer to the damp ground underneath.

I gave him my back, and he layered my cuts with the salve, blossoming that cooling sensation.

"You shouldn't have killed that guard. He was only doing his job."

I glanced back at him. "I should've done it sooner. Then maybe all we would've had were single whip marks and not shredded skin."

Tavin screwed the cap on the jar, slid it into his pants pocket, and then wiped his hands off on the fabric before turning me toward him and cupping my face.

"You protected me." His thumb dragged softly across my bottom lip.

When he leaned forward to kiss me, I panicked. "I was protecting myself."

His low chuckle sent tingles down my spine. "You keep telling yourself that."

He closed the distance, pressing his lips softly to mine. It wasn't possessive like the last time he'd kissed me. This was gentle and much more intimate.

Despite my injuries, heat flushed my skin.

"You gave me energy to endure the beating," he said against my lips. "And I think I felt that guard's soul pass into me, too."

I tried to pull away, but he held me in place and used my protest to tangle his tongue with mine in an exquisitely slow dance, melting something inside me even more than he already had.

When he broke the kiss, he just stared into my eyes for a moment before releasing me.

"Rest." He nodded at my dress spread out on the floor.

I didn't need to be told twice. I stretched out on my stomach, leaving some fabric for him, and pointed to the spot next to me. "You need rest, too."

He didn't argue. He lay down and folded his arms, wincing at the pull of his muscles, but settled in with his face in my direction.

Silence blanketed us.

"Regretting my existence?" I asked, intimidated by his piercing gaze and the look on his face like he was trying to solve a complex problem.

One side of his lips quirked up in a half smile. "I should. But I don't."

His eyes closed, and his breathing fell into that steady flow of sleep.

I studied him as he slept, and I finally closed my eyes, succumbing to the exhaustion of wounds mending.

"I SAID SEPARATE CELLS!" King Zorander's booming voice echoed in the dungeon.

Tavin turned his head away from me and rested it back on his arms. "I coerced them," he mumbled in a voice laden with sleep.

I gazed at Tavin's back and wondered if mine was healing as fast as his. The torn skin had mended enough to not be seeping blood anymore, but it still looked angry and raw.

I pushed myself up onto one arm and glared at the king. "You did this to your own son? What kind of father are you?"

His green-eyed glare matched the tightening of his jaw. "I'm the kind of father who leverages an opportunity to teach his son a hard lesson."

I scoffed and climbed to my feet, slamming my fists into my hips.

"Leave it be, Mya." Tavin's voice sounded much more awake now that I was judging his father.

His father's gaze traveled the length of my body. "I see why you're fucking her."

"He's not fucking me," I snapped before Tavin could get a response in.

He stood and handed me my dress before turning to his father. "We have not mated."

"Perhaps I should make her my concubine," his father said with a mean smile as he kept leering at me.

"No." Both Tavin and I spoke at the same time.

"You forfeited your right to have a say the minute you hid her existence from me. That mistake allowed for your mother's death." His voice was downright menacing. "If I choose to bed the vile thing, I will, even if I have to drug her to make her compliant."

Tavin's hands curled into fists, and the turmoil inside him echoed inside of me.

"The only one I will allow to touch me in any manner is Tavin." I held the dress to my chest and stuck my chin out. "Anyone else who dares will die." I stared down King Zorander. "Even you, Your Highness."

Tavin met my gaze with both a warning and something else blazing in his eyes. "Drugs don't work on that specific power of hers." He looked back at his father. "The suppressing magic of these cells doesn't diminish that either."

I took a deep inhale, pulling power from the king and his guards, feasting enough to clear the webs of healing haze from my head.

Tavin shook his head at me, and I stopped pulling energy. He looked more refreshed though, like my powering up had also powered him up.

Damn it. I wished I'd had a chance to read that book I grabbed at the bungalow. That could've explained this weird dynamic between us now.

His father still stared at me, weighing Tavin's words. "Bring Tavin to his quarters." He glanced at the guards. "Use force if you have to."

"She comes with me." Tavin stepped back, pressing into me.

"No. She stays here until I have made my decision on what to do with her." His father's words were unyielding.

"Go, Tavin."

He gazed at me as I still held the dress to my skin.

"Please don't hurt my father," he whispered to me.

"I can't make that promise, Tavin. If he attempts what he insinuated..." I shook my head. "I will do what's necessary."

His aggravation raked over me, along with resignation. He couldn't control me where anyone else was concerned, and he knew it.

"If you kill the king, I will be forced to execute you for the crime."

"So be it." The same type of pain that lanced through me when he heard about his mother nearly doubled me over, but I stayed standing tall, just like he had.

He turned and allowed the guards to take him from my cell, leaving me with only the king blocking the open cell and a feeling of utter helplessness.

THE WITCH ASSASSIN
CHAPTER FIFTEEN

KING ZORANDER STARED DOWN the hallway, waiting until Tavin was out of the dungeons before he turned to me. He scrutinized me, measuring me with his gaze as his face remained impassive.

"Tell me about the threat to my kingdom," he said in a conversational voice as if he hadn't just threatened to use me at his pleasure.

I blinked. "I'm not a threat. I mean, when I stepped through the portal, I was but..."

He held up his hand, silencing me. "My son is alive, and most of his guards are as well. If you were a true threat, I am sure there would be a path of dead bodies back to the portal." He crossed his arms. "Tell me about the threat."

I took a breath. "They know you exist now. And since my chip was discarded without being inside my body, they assume you are somehow holding me as a prisoner. At least that's what I would assume. The Director doesn't believe we're capable of deserting on our own accord."

"Arrogant fuck."

I let out a laugh at the king's slight. "He is. And he uses every possible pressure point to keep us in line. If he figured out that fae blood got that assassin through the gate, he'll keep sending those with fae blood through. They won't just have fae blood though. It will be bred with vampires, wolves, dragons, or something else entirely."

"So, to stop them from actually getting through, we have to look for additional DNA attributes."

I nodded.

He scanned me again. "Come with me."

I remained in place, just staring at him.

"My son trusts you. Am I wrong on that?"

I laughed at him. "He made it so I couldn't leave the bungalow. He doesn't trust me."

The king smiled. "That sounds like my son."

The fondness in his voice caught me off guard.

"Why did you have him whipped?"

"Because he put the kingdom in jeopardy. And I was angry. His actions allowed for another assassin to slip through our defenses, and my soulmate paid the price." He sighed deeply. "His mother would not be pleased with my actions."

I did not know what to think of this man. There was a warmness in him that reminded me of Tavin, along with steel grit that reminded me of the Director. A bloom of fear settled into my lower belly. This man had a ruthless streak, and I should not underestimate him. I swallowed hard.

"Why did you threaten to..." I waved at the cell door as if that would finish my sentence.

He smiled in a way that made me want to put on the soiled dress I held. "I wanted to see your reaction. I knew it would piss off my son, but your reaction was more important. If you were a gold digger on top of being an assassin, you wouldn't have acted so violently opposed to sleeping with a king."

I let out another nervous laugh.

"So back to my question. Can I trust you?"

"Can I trust you not to do anything that will get you killed?" I replied back.

"I have no interest in bedding you. I have no interest in sex whatsoever now that my wife—my queen—is dead. I hope you never have to feel this utter emptiness." He stepped back and waved to the hallway, inviting me to join him.

"We can't experience it. Spirit mates don't wither away like soulmates do. They die together when life is severed from one or the other," I said before I had the sense to shut my mouth.

One look, and that hardness returned. He just gave me a curt nod as I stepped into the hallway, still holding the dress to my chest.

He waved his hand, and the dress disappeared, replaced by a slip like the one they'd given me in the jail. The satiny feel clouded my brain for a second because all my mind could focus on were Tavin's hands. I shook my head and kept pace with the king.

I could not believe King Zorander trusted an assassin enough to walk side by side without protection. I slowed and stared at him as he took a couple steps before he noticed I wasn't at his side.

He turned, his gaze shadowed.

"You're being reckless." It wasn't a question.

His eyebrows arched, and his mouth popped open. Utter surprise registered in every feature before he locked it down. "What makes you say that?"

"You're walking in a remote area without escort with a known assassin. You're being reckless, sir." I crossed my arms, staring him down. "On purpose." And then for good measure, I added, "Your wife would be pissed at that."

A genuine smile found his lips, and although sadness still reigned in his eyes, a little mirth worked its way in. And holy hell, did Tavin look like his father.

"A smart assassin at that." He turned his back on me and kept walking.

I caught up to him and kept pace, thinking over Tavin's reactions and the king's words. "You've had him beaten before."

The king nodded.

My protective reflex bristled. "Why?"

"For lying. For stealing. For being negligent." He paused. "For being insensitive to those around him. It will make him a more just and empathetic king when the time comes." He shook his head. "But today was harsher. And I meant it to be even though I know he is mourning the loss nearly as much as I am."

"You beat him to keep him in line," I said.

That was precisely what the Director did, and it left a sour taste in my mouth.

"No. It is a lesson for him to learn. Not a control mechanism."

"What kind of lesson was today?" I snapped as he reached for the door leading out of the dungeon.

"That keeping vital information from those who need it can result in those you care about dying." He glanced at me. "And being near you in the dungeon just muddied my point, but being separated from you... That will slam it home."

"Would you have killed me if he had told you about me?"

King Zorander nodded. "And I would have thrown your body on one of the spikes to serve my purpose. They would assume the world was as barren as we project it to be."

"You would have lost your son."

The king pressed his lips into a thin line and gave me a curt nod. "That assumes you wouldn't kill me first." He slid his gaze to mine. "And you would have, prior to whatever this is with my son happened. If my guards had found you, things would have worked out differently."

I nodded. "Yes."

The thought of never finding Tavin clenched my chest.

"Honest and smart and beautiful and deadly." He chuckled. "If I were Tavin's age, I would have jumped all in, too."

His hand wrapped around my upper arm, entering what looked like the residence part of the castle. The king took the stairway leading to the upper floor and brought me into a room with a beautiful fae laid out on a pedestal.

He pushed me forward. "That is my wife."

That righteous anger surfaced.

I walked to her, studying her fine features. Features that also echoed Tavin. The high cheekbones and supple lips came from his mother. The two had blended well, and their only child was just as beautiful as they were.

I never saw my victims dead for long. Usually, I turned them to ashes. It was harder to pin a murder if there wasn't a body.

The queen, even in death, carried an air that I would have recognized because her son had that same impact. It was humbling.

"She's quite beautiful," I said, still studying her.

"Was." The king's tight voice interrupted my reverie. "She *was* quite beautiful. Now she is gone."

"Ah, but her essence still radiates, even without her soul anchoring her to her body." I smiled and glanced his way. "She had a pure soul. One that would light up the realms if she were to travel on diplomatic business like so many other royalties do."

A wisp of a smile graced his lips. "She used to enthrall entire courts before we took refuge here." He ran his finger down her arm. "Tavin has some of that bedazzling aura, too."

I nodded. I saw hints of it. "If he could just let go of the arrogant asshole side of him, he would be unstoppable."

"Oh, that's me, honey." King Zorander grinned at me. "And that side will never go away."

"He's not always an asshole. After all, he is the one protecting the gate, right?" I asked, trying to move the subject away from Tavin.

My heart hammered just a little harder at the thought of him.

The king nodded, still running his fingers over his dead wife's arms. "We helped, but his powers have multiplied over the years, and it doesn't tax him like it used to run us down." He pulled his hand away from the queen and focused on me. "Tavin is a force to be reckoned with. Which means if you are the other half of his soul, you are just as daunting."

"Why would you assume that?" I glanced away from the queen.

"Because spirit mates are rare and powerful combinations. Ones that bring massive change with them. Sometimes that change is for the greater good; sometimes it is just the opposite. Realms have fallen to spirit mates."

I swallowed hard. "I wouldn't say I'm as powerful as your son, sir. He has successfully made this world all but invisible for decades."

"Centuries," the king corrected me. "And yet you came."

"That was a seer's doing. She was trying to barter for her life in exchange for telling me something she thought I would value more."

"Did it save her?" His voice carried darkness with it as if the mood in the room had shifted.

I shook my head, and my cheeks heated. "I stupidly thought she was offering me something the Director would want. But I now think she was seeing my future." I sighed. "I wish I would've let her live to expand on it more because I likely would never have set foot here had I known."

He crossed the room and grabbed my wrist, dragging me between two pillars. I was so stunned by his actions that I didn't react quickly enough to him slapping a shackle on my wrist. It bit into my skin, and before my brain registered, he had my other wrist shackled as well.

Tavin's father was a walking contradiction, and I didn't know how much was grief and how much was just plain crazy. He pulled a syringe from his pocket and stabbed it into my outstretched arm, depressing the liquid into my veins.

He yanked the needle out and then grabbed my chin, prying my jaws open just to dump a cup of the sweet nectar that nullified my witch magic down my throat. He clamped my mouth shut and tipped my head back forcing me to swallow just before my veins started burning like they were on fire.

I screamed. My knees buckled under me, but the way I was pinned, I couldn't fall into a ball on the floor.

The king wrapped his hand around my throat, squeezing. Darkness played in his eyes like an eternal void.

I had been a fool to trust him. Tears leaked from the corners of my eyes. My lungs burned. He had played me so well, using my only vulnerability against me.

The door to the room burst open, and a red-faced Tavin stood there. He tried to draw a breath as hard as I was trying, but his father's hand prevented either of us from getting the air we survived on.

The king released his hold on my throat, and Tavin fell to his knees, sucking in air.

I hung from my arms as I pulled air into my lungs as well.

"Do not harm her," Tavin wheezed. "Or I will pull all our protections, leaving us vulnerable for anyone to invade."

"What did you give me?" I wheezed.

My veins still felt like lava flowed through them, and it hurt like a mother.

"It nullifies demon magic for a spell. Just as the drink nullifies almost everything else." He waved to me and gazed at Tavin. "Compliant, or at least unable to kill for an hour or so. Just long enough for me to violate the demon bitch."

King Zorander circled around behind me as Tavin stood.

Tavin's gaze landed on his mother, and all the color in his face bled out.

The king ripped my slip and ice filled every last one of my cells. "What are you doing?"

My panic laden words grabbed Tavin's attention from his dead mother. Rage flushed his features.

"Don't you fucking sully the queen's memory in that manner." His growl echoed through the room as he stalked in our direction.

Murder reflected in his eyes, and the level of his rage pumping through our bond was drifting into the irrational zone.

My mind moved at lightning speed, trying to make sense of all this, and then it clicked. "Tavin, he wants to die. Your father wants you to kill him."

That was the only logical explanation for what he was doing. His absolute recklessness made sense, as did drugging me, so I couldn't kill him and be executed for treason, taking Tavin with me. The prince wouldn't be persecuted in the same manner as I would. The king also knew I was his son's spirit mate. Violating me would push Tavin over the edge.

"I didn't harm him when he freed me from the prison, so..."

His father clamped his hand over my mouth. "Shut up, slut."

His voice shook as he pressed against me, like he didn't quite believe what he was doing either.

"Dad, she's never been with a man." Tavin's tone softened, as did some of his rage. "Please don't do this. Don't shatter her innocence in the hope that I will kill you. My god, don't shatter her innocence in the same room as my mother's corpse." Tavin waved at the dead body behind him as he approached me from the front. "Don't try to manipulate me in that manner. This time, I will not do your bidding. I will not take your life, and as much as it will pain her, Mya won't either. So, you'll be doing this only to hate yourself more for not being able to see the damned future." He took a breath and reached out, peeling his father's hand from my mouth. "Don't use how I feel about this woman for your own selfish means."

The king's head pressed against the back of mine. "Damn it. Why did you have to have so much of your mother in you?"

Sobs broke out.

Tavin glanced at me and then moved under my arm, leading his father away. Then he returned, and without a word, he unlocked me and picked me up in his arms. He stopped beside his mother and leaned down to give her a kiss on her forehead.

Sorrow ate at me. I remained quiet as he carried me down the stairs into an equally large living area. He didn't stop until he was next to his oversized bed. Only then did he put me on my feet and wrapped his arms around me, careful not to hit the spots on my back that still hurt.

He held on with his forehead on my shoulder. His emotions slammed into me like a blunt hammer.

He shook against me, and on instinct, I wrapped my arms around him, pulling him closer, trying to appease the pain running rampant through him. He lowered to his knees, pressing his forehead to my stomach. I ran my fingers through his hair, not knowing what to do with this level of vulnerability.

He looked up at me with tear-streaked cheeks and licked his lips. He tried on a smile but failed miserably. "I'm sorry."

I palmed his cheek. "Why are *you* sorry?"

He stood, waved his pants away, took my mouth with his, and fell onto the bed on top of me. His hips met mine with a thrust that yanked a pained scream from me as he did just what he'd asked his father not to do.

He pulled away from my lips, still seated deep inside me. "Because I need you."

"Of all the dirty…"

He crushed my lips again, silencing my rant as he began to move his hips, making my pain transition into something feral and hot. I arched, picking my back off the mattress so I could enjoy this without the constant rub of irritation of my cuts against the sheets.

Tavin rolled, pulling me on top of him, keeping his kiss going as he gently guided my hips. Each slow swirl sent tingles low into my belly, building like my body had on the beach when his mouth had been on me. He moved his hand between us, finding my clit with his thumb, and circled in opposition to my hips.

I broke away from his mouth and closed my eyes.

"Look at me, my sweet little demon." His voice held a challenging command.

I opened my eyes, taking him in as if for the first time. Seeing down to the purity of his soul. His yin to my yang. I could see where together we were whole.

These sensations frightened me because I could get lost in them forever.

His cheeks still glistened with tears, and I gave in, leaning down, licking them, savoring the salty taste. I moved to his mouth, ravaging it with my tongue as he tried to keep up with what he had awakened in me.

I moved with him, tilting my head back with the sweet pressure of him. His mouth latched onto my breast, sending more of those insane tingles right to my pussy stretching around him. I met his hooded gaze, his mouth parted just enough to let his breath rush in and out in time with mine.

He rolled and took control. Kissing my throat and my breasts as his hips pounded into me, heightening my pleasure until I finally came undone, crying out his name as my body squeezed him, milking his cock until he hissed my name with his own release.

Instead of collapsing on top of me, he rolled me on top of him and embraced me, kissing my forehead as he ran his fingers through my hair.

"Damn you, Tavin," I whispered and turned my head away from him, but I didn't move.

I let him hold me and run his fingers through my hair as he twitched inside of me.

He kissed the top of my head, but he made no excuses for his actions as if apologizing to me up front was enough. "The shower here is even more amazing than at the bungalow."

My head shot up, and I stared down at him, cocking my eyebrow.

He pointed beyond the end of the bed.

I was off him and scrambling across the room. His musical laughter followed me.

THE WITCH ASSASSIN
CHAPTER SIXTEEN

NOW THIS WAS JUST obscene.

I gawked at the sheer number of body sprays, along with the massive rain shower above and multiple handheld units hanging from the walls. I flipped them all on and stood in the center, letting the hot water pulse away the grime from my back and what stress was left in my muscles.

The air changed, and I opened my eyes to Tavin standing right in front of me.

"I can still land a kick," I said, glaring up at him for invading my space in the shower.

This was my only sanctuary, and while I had warmed up to the idea of Tavin, having him impose on my shower irritated me.

He smiled and ran his hands through my hair, planting the kind of kiss that could lead back to the bedroom, silencing my pending tirade. But then he turned me and poured a sensational-smelling shampoo into my hair. He used his fingers to lather up my hair as I tilted my head.

His touch turned me to rubber, heating me more than the shower did. When my hair was squeaky clean, he picked up a citrus bar and ran it over my body, avoiding the cuts on my back.

He dropped to his knees before me, cleaning my privates so gently that heat bloomed like a garden of roses in the springtime. He soaped up one leg, had me rinse, and then did the other. Then he handed me the soap before he hooked my leg over his shoulder and licked me in a long, slow stroke.

"Tavin," I said, trying to warn him, but he just squinted up at me in the water spray and smiled, pulling me closer.

His mouth latched onto my sensitive bud, flicking his tongue while he sucked. It was just as sensational as it was on the beach, but this time, it was just us and all the pulses of the water.

My orgasm was quick and violent as I moaned his name. He continued as I settled back down, enjoying his sexual ministrations.

I soaped up his hair like he had done to mine, pushing it away from his face as he tickled me with his tongue. Rinsing until his locks ran clean between my fingers.

My muscles quivered under his touch until Tavin kissed his way up my torso and found my lips. He took my hand that held the soap and put it against his chest, helping me to clean him. Then he turned, giving me his back to wash. I gently ran the soap around the raw scrapes and then down to his perfect ass.

I dropped to my knees and soaped up his legs. Before I could rise, he turned toward me. I glanced up at him as I washed the front of each thigh.

He captured my hand, moved it along his hard member, soaping himself up, then took the soap from me, and wrapped my fingers around him. He moved my hand slowly along his velvety skin. When he rubbed the tip against my lips, I pulled away.

"I will bite," I said, but I didn't move away when he did it again as curiosity flared.

He smiled down at me and repeated the motion as he tucked a wet strand of my hair behind my ear. "I want your lips around my cock. And then I will do whatever pleases you until you are satiated."

His voice was soft and sensual, and the implications of his words actually made me wetter than I could imagine. I licked my lips and kept eye contact as I slid his tip into my mouth and tasted every inch of him with my tongue.

Citrus and salt and warm water played against my taste buds, and he slowly guided himself deeper into the cavern of my mouth.

"Mya," he whispered and tightened his grip on my hair. His eyes flashed with such intensity that I almost stopped. "Don't stop." He shook his head and moved his hips deeper and then out until just his tip was between my lips. "Swallow all of me." He pushed himself into my mouth until I gagged, pulling back a little before doing it again. "Swallow."

I did as he asked, sucking and swallowing, breathing and drooling all over his shaft. My eyes watered.

"Oh fuck, Mya," he groaned as both his hands framed the sides of my head.

His hips pulsed deeper and harder with each pass until he was fucking my face.

"Rub my balls," he demanded.

I reached up to the sac between his legs and massaged it gently. His deep grumble of satisfaction was my reward, followed by a deep push as his muscles tightened, and then he flooded my mouth with his manly essence, pulling out enough to douse my face with what was left. I swallowed the combination of cum and water and tilted my face up at him.

He lifted me to my feet, kissed me, and then searched my gaze, tracing my lips with his fingers. "You didn't totally hate that, did you?"

I wavered my hand in a so-so gesture and then smirked. I actually liked the power I held over him, along with the fact that I could probably get anything I wanted in return for sucking him off.

His smug grin surfaced, but then it faded. Intensity replaced it. "What is your pleasure?"

"Honestly?"

He nodded.

"About three days of solid sleep."

He tilted his head back and laughed, pulling me against him. "If that's truly what you want, then I guess I need to deliver, don't I?"

I smiled against his chest. Then the melancholy hit as if the past however long we had been in the shower was only a reprieve from reality, and now it was coming with the force of a hurricane.

"But first..." He kissed the top of my head and laid his cheek on it, squeezing me tighter. "I have to bury my mother."

THE WITCH ASSASSIN
CHAPTER SEVENTEEN

M Y WISH FOR THREE days of sleep was a
pipe dream. Especially with a queen's
funeral at hand, and Tavin insisted that I be by
his side for her funeral.

The outfit that I wore had been conjured by
the royal seamstress, and while she did actually
sew, for this occasion she created my outfit with
magic. It was eye-opening, especially since Tavin
did it effortlessly, but the seamstress struggled
enough to break out in a sweat before something
suitable appeared on my form.

It took three tries to get Tavin's approval. The two other tries were beautiful, but not what Tavin wanted.

His father looked even more haggard than when we'd last seen him. Tavin brought him over to me.

"Mya," King Zorander said, dropping his gaze to the ground in front of me.

I reached out and took his hand, much to his surprise. "You were grieving."

For some reason, that seemed like the most appropriate thing to say regarding his actions. But they formed a lump in my throat. I blinked the mist from my eyes, wondering at what exact moment this emotional mess inside me was set free. This was one of the times I hated that Tavin broke down all the walls I'd built around my heart for the past twenty-five years.

He squeezed my hands and nodded, pressing his lips together in a tight smile. The apology was right there in his gaze.

I didn't need the words, so I squeezed back and then stepped into place by Tavin's side. The glass case that held the queen radiated in the sunlight. Her royal dress was dainty and more stunning than anything I had ever seen, and it made that lump in my throat larger.

I cleared my throat and looked out at the crowd gathering for the funeral. It seemed like all of Eleka came out to pay their respects to the queen, and I stiffened.

This would be the type of situation that the Director would take advantage of. The grieving wouldn't be hyperaware of their surroundings. Especially with the continuing line of mourners offering condolences to the king and prince.

My stomach plummeted at the thought, and my mind started shuffling through all the spells I had been taught in the league. What could I do to protect Tavin and his father if there were assassins in the crowd?

I tugged on Tavin's hand, scanning and rescanning the masses waiting for their own viewing of their queen.

"What?" he whispered in my ear.

"Can you put an invisible protective bubble around you and your father? One like you had over the door at the bungalow?"

He glanced down at me and then out at the crowd.

"This is a perfect opportunity for an assassination attempt. Blood is no longer their goal." I gazed up at him. "No one should be allowed to approach the two of you."

Tavin leaned over to Galen, whispered in his ear, and then he did the same to his father. He received a nod of ascent.

Tavin took my hand and blew a slow stream of air out of his mouth. The air around us crackled and then settled. It took me a moment to realize I was inside his protective bubble, and my heart swelled.

With so many people here, there was enough energy to keep a steady stream filling me without stripping anyone of their strength. It was like strolling through the compound, or in a park on a national holiday, or a special concert venue. It sharpened my mind and my senses.

I concentrated on the crowd as opposed to the service. As people started filing forward, the lower level of guards kept people back far enough from the king to keep him safe, but I knew the Director's assassins didn't necessarily need to touch the king to kill him.

As far as I knew, I was the only one who could yank a soul though. But others could stop his heart or make his head explode. Which was why I kept scanning.

Then I saw her. A fae, based on her pointy ears, but something else as well.

The eyes were the wrong color for this world. Plus, I recalled seeing her in the halls, except her hair was black back then, not wispy blonde like today. I squinted and caught a hint of dark hair under the glamour she wore.

Her gaze met mine, and her eyes widened.

Suddenly, the fact she was here to harm my prince bled into my consciousness, creating a burning anger that consumed me. I yanked with vicious intent and inhaled, absorbing her soul. The infusion gave me a heady rush.

She collapsed, dead on the spot. The commotion as people moved back made Tavin glance at me. But even with taking her soul, my discomfort grew as if she were not alone. I didn't know what type of arsenal the Director would send or what their instructions were. If he knew I was here by choice and not by force, would he stop?

If he knew I had found my spirit mate, would he yield?

As if answering from beyond, the queen's body exploded.

The blast hit our protective bubble and then bounced outwards, taking out the first row of mourners in the process. It was powerful enough to send us on our asses.

King Zorander bellowed from his knees. Tavin stared at the mess that had been his mother with his mouth hanging open. My ears rang, and

I was far enough away to have been thrown out of Tavin's protection.

I glanced at the crowd and zeroed in on a man. And it all clicked. The assassin who had killed her had put a device like our tracking chips in her. One that could be blown as necessary.

That bastard stood with the detonator in his hand, smiling like a damn fool.

I growled, and his gaze moved to mine just before he collapsed without his soul. The quick kills left me unsatisfied, even though I received their energy.

The Director's message was loud and clear. He would keep coming unless...

A sharp pain gripped my side, and I glanced down at my unharmed skin. I swiveled to Tavin and found the killing star sticking out of his tailored suit. His angry gaze was focused on the crowd, and then an infusion of energy hit me.

Tavin had torn that soul out. He ripped the blade out of his skin as pandemonium continued around us.

Another knife hurled through the air, but that one hit Tavin's protective barrier that he'd put back up to protect both himself and his father, bouncing the knife to the ground.

An arm wrapped around me, yanking me farther away, and a blade scratched my throat. The arm was clad in one of our assassin suits.

Tavin's gaze jumped to me as whoever had me dragged me backwards. Tavin roared, his eyes flashing almost white.

The body holding me went limp, and then Tavin was at my side.

I scanned the crowd as panic I had been holding at bay crashed down. I couldn't yank innocent souls. My mind whirled, focusing on my training. My magic. I had been trained in spells, and as rusty as I was, I knew how to target those with ill intent.

"Keep me safe, Tavin," I whispered.

He nodded.

I spread my hands palms up. "As flame lights shadows, and truth ends fears, open locked thoughts to my mind's willing ears. Target only those whose thoughts run afoul by lighting up their darkened souls."

I prayed I'd spun the spell correctly. It was one of the few I'd done flawlessly when I had been in school.

One scan of the crowd highlighted four souls with ill intent. Without overthinking, I ripped all four souls from their bodies. The rush of soul power hit.

I repeated the incantation, and there were no others that stood out. "I think we're good."

Tavin surveyed the crowd, and he nodded. His lips pressed into a tight line, and the rage inside him simmered under the surface like a poison.

We crossed to his father, and I helped the king to his feet, holding the shaking and sobbing man as he stared at the desecration of his wife's body.

The fury in Tavin bled into me, and I had to stomp down the feeling of lashing out unjustly.

Tavin cleared his throat. "Good people of Eleka," he roared over the din. Silencing the pandemonium. "We are no longer hidden from the realms. It seems Icarus knows of our existence and believes my spirit mate belongs to them." He glanced at me holding his father. "They are wrong, and I will stop this madness. I give you my word that they will pay dearly for this slight against our queen, even if I have to bring the fight to them."

THE WITCH ASSASSIN
CHAPTER EIGHTEEN

TAVIN PACED LIKE A caged lion as I sat next to his father on the couch in the living quarters. Guards flanked the room and the hall leading to where we sat.

"We need to fortify the magic around the portal," King Zorander said, speaking for the first time since we'd escaped the tragic fiasco of his wife's funeral.

Tavin nodded but kept pacing.

"How exactly does your magic to the portal work?" I asked.

"Fae blood will allow the user to step out onto the ledge and then get through the veil to the outer cavern without issue. They can breathe in the caverns. Those without fae blood exit the other way." His smile told me exactly what he had done to keep Eleka safe. The portal was purposely a death trap to non-fae. "In other words, the way the portal faces is contingent upon the blood of the user. And they cannot breathe in the caverns, nor can they exit to our world."

"Shut that down," King Zorander said. "Set a trap outside the outer cavern to trap those who get through regardless of their blood makeup. Only royal blood can let them into our world."

I shook my head. "They got the queen's blood when they killed her. You cannot rely on royal blood to be the safety card anymore."

The king gazed at me and then dropped his face into his palm with a groan of discontent. "Then it needs to be a combination of Tavin's blood and yours," he said from behind his hand.

"If something should happen to us, this world would be stranded," I said. "If you ever needed help from another realm, there would be no way in."

The king met my gaze and slowly nodded. "I can live with that."

"Fine." Tavin marched to the window, and his magic bloomed, covering the room with a suffocating heat. Then it dissipated to a dull hum. He turned with a dark smirk. "The outer cage carries the nullifying magic from the dungeon as well, so most assassins will be vulnerable." He glanced at me. "I could add that nifty spell you invoked, too."

"What spell is that?" his father asked.

"She cast a spell to tell her who was the enemy and who were allies in the crowd today."

King Zorander's eyebrows shot up and his gaze darted to me.

"I couldn't rightfully wipe out the entire crowd," I mumbled, picking at my nail. "Besides, it's a basic spell that all of us witches in the league learn. I just happened to be better at it than most."

I shrugged a single shoulder.

King Zorander looked at his son. "An assassin with a moral compass?" He smirked and pointed his thumb in my direction. "She's a true enigma."

Tavin nodded. "Equal parts light and dark, just like me."

"We need to send a message back to the Director using the bodies of the dead assassins." I met Tavin's gaze and worried my lower lip between my teeth. "It might not be enough to stop him, though."

A servant came in and set a tray down on the table.

He turned to leave, and my senses tingled.

Tavin reached for one of the drinks, but I put my hand out, stopping him. My eyes were still glued to the servant's back. The guard went to open the door.

I didn't want the servant leaving, and his next step hit a barrier that knocked him on his ass, dazing him. He climbed to his feet slowly.

Tavin's eyes widened, and he glanced at me, but whatever shock filtered through us was quickly put aside.

"Why don't you have the first drink?" he said to the servant as the man turned in our direction.

I took the opportunity to drain him of strength, leaving him just enough to stand but not enough to struggle.

"What did you do to me?" he asked as he swayed on his feet.

I tapped my lips. "Or we could send a live assassin back with a message."

I pointed at the man just as he reached into his coat and pulled out a blade.

"Drink," the servant commanded.

I felt the compelling need to drink. Tavin and his father reached for the glasses.

"Deflect." I pushed the magic back at the assassin and knocked the glass out of the king's hand, holding him against the couch so he couldn't follow through on the mind controller's order.

Tavin had stopped reaching the moment the word escaped my mouth, and he glared at the assassin. That was all it took. His fury snapped.

The assassin collapsed, dead.

Tavin's gaze moved to the guards in the room. "Bring everyone from this palace into the throne room. No one comes in or leaves without my say."

Thankfully, the spell died with the assassin, and whatever compelled the king had vaporized with the assassin's death.

Tavin and I stared at each other. He had used my powers, and I had used his. My skin chilled at the thought of someone else with the dark powers I possessed. I was sure Tavin was just as hesitant, especially since I didn't understand the extent of his powers.

"No one is getting past that outer trap now. And anyone who identifies as foe will be instantaneously turned to ash the moment they touch the bars I have erected around the entrance."

I gasped. "You infused the kiss of death into those bars?"

His smile said it all, and I shivered. "Only for those with ill intent to the crown. And only you and I can pass through the gate."

King Zorander glanced between the two of us. "Kiss of death?"

Tavin snorted a laugh and nodded. "I figured out the spirit mate thing pretty quickly, and I thought she might have made the connection, too. So, I thought we could fuck the answers out of her instead. At least that way I could derive some pleasure from the torture session, instead of sharing in the agony. She didn't agree with our methods. We thought she was at our mercy, but that wasn't the case. She couldn't access the soul-stealing magic, but she sure as hell could deliver a deadly kiss that turns her enemy to ash. She annihilated Clay just as he began fondling her."

The king let out a long, low whistle. "He was always a bit of a whore that way."

"Not anymore." I let my gaze bore into Tavin. "His whoring days are over. Right, Tavin?"

A knock interrupted us, and Galen stuck his head inside. "The staff is waiting for you, sir."

Tavin glanced at me. "Can you cast the spell from here?"

I nodded. I thought I could, at least, and when he waved me on, I recounted the spell, modifying it to manifest in this building only.

"As flame lights shadows, and truth ends fears, from tower to dungeon, make it clear, open locked thoughts to my mind's willing ear. Target only those whose thoughts run afoul by lighting up their darkened souls." I raised my hands and then brought them down to my sides, pushing the spell outward to every recess of the building we stood in.

"Your Highness." I waved toward the door.

He nodded. "Why don't you start calling me something less formal?"

"Sir?" I raised my eyebrows as he stood.

"My friends and closest guards call me Cal. It would please me if Tavin's mate would call me that as well." He threaded my hand through his elbow and walked ahead of Tavin with me on his arm.

"Only in private," Tavin said as he followed behind.

When we got to the area behind the thrones, the king handed me off to Tavin and straightened his back. His gaze hardened, and he glanced at us with a nod.

Galen opened the door for him and let us pass before he closed it and stationed himself in front of the exit.

The king took his throne, and Tavin and I stood beside him, leaving the queen's chair empty. We still had the queen's coagulated blood splattered on us, so I was sure we were a sight to behold.

Six people in this room had their souls lit up. One gave me pause, and her eyes widened at the sight of me next to the prince.

Tavin gripped my hand tighter as he seemed to categorize the staff as well.

He inhaled and then whispered a command. "Sleep."

He waved his hand over the room, and the true Elvren collapsed, including the king and guards behind us, leaving the six outside forces left standing.

That was a really handy talent to have. It was similar to that forehead tap that had knocked me out, but this was a mass command. Those that remained standing were shocked by the display.

I held up my hand and stepped forward, blocking the king and Tavin. "If you attack, you die. It's that simple. And whatever lies the Director told you, I am not being held against my will. I'm here by choice." I looked at my former roommate. "I would prefer not to kill you." I addressed her directly and then moved my gaze over the rest. "But I will if you don't yield."

A knife sailed toward us and clanged against the force field Tavin and I held around us, and that assassin crumpled to the ground without so much as a twitch from me. Tavin took the initiative, and it made an impression.

"Ask the Director about soulmates. Better yet, do your own homework. Find out about the things that the Director has kept from us all our lives."

A few of them exchanged looks like there had been rumblings about such things.

My throat constricted as if something was strangling me. "Deflect," I hissed and faced my palms outward.

The assassin clawing her throat went down a moment later, leaving four, including my roommate. The fact that the magic got through the barrier concerned me, but I didn't let it show.

I reached my hand to the side, and Tavin's fingers laced through mine.

"She may not wish to kill you, but I have no qualms with it." His voice carried the malice pounding through me.

He placed his free hand on my shoulder and moved flush against me. We both now protected the sleeping king behind us.

"Hanna, step forward," I said and pointed to the empty space before me.

As she moved, I yanked the souls of the others, feasting and strengthening my reserves. She was dangerous, but I was always faster and physically stronger than she was. She knew my fighting style. She knew I didn't fight fair when lives hung in the balance. I fed off her essence as well, tiring her the way I used to when we lived together.

Annoyance flashed over her features. "Why should I believe you over the Director?" she snapped as she stepped to the spot and stopped.

"The prince is my spirit mate. I don't wish to leave his side, and if the Director keeps sending assassins, his numbers will continue to dwindle. If he doesn't stop, we will be forced to bring our brand of nightmare to him."

She cocked her head. "Mates like Treya found?"

A deep crease appeared between her eyes.

I blinked. "Treya found her mate?"

This was the first I'd heard of another assassin falling into the same circumstance. Sure, assassins bonded from time to time, but that was rare, and it was usually paired assassins that went that route. Mates, soul or spirt or fated, weren't a regular occurrence in our business.

"Where have you been?"

"Collecting DNA for the Director until I came here. When did this happen?"

"Treya was the one who took down the UV field."

No wonder the Director was mad as hell the last time I saw him. He had lost his top agent. Which put me in that coveted spot.

"Do not come any closer, or I will yank your soul right out of your body," Tavin hissed from behind me.

I hadn't thought twice about Hanna moving closer. Nor had I noticed that her hand had snuck behind her back. The wall between us sizzled with renewed power.

Hanna stepped back, and her hand came into view, along with the deadly blade she gripped. She muttered a swear and flung the knife. It hit the barrier and slung back at her. Impaling in her abdomen.

I moved to go to her, but Tavin held me in place.

"It's not just royalty who are targets. You are one as well. The Director said to kill you if you were not willing to come back," Hanna hissed before she went limp.

Her soul tasted bittersweet.

THE WITCH ASSASSIN
CHAPTER NINETEEN

I SAT ON THE couch in Tavin's room. He had the guards collect all the bodies of the assassins and brought them near the portal.

They reported back that there was a significant amount of ash in the outer room, signaling that the Director was still sending assassins to their deaths. He was burning through assassins like a sugar freak devouring a box of chocolates.

"He knows what you can do," Tavin said from his station by the window.

"He knows I can conjure and feed off soul energy. And he knows I have the kiss of death at my disposal. But he never knew I could devour souls. I mean, up until those drunks in Ireland, I had only yanked my targets' souls out before I took their blood. Ireland was the first time I yanked multiple souls out at the same time."

He turned and raised an eyebrow. "So that story about defending yourself against drunk Irishmen was true?"

"Yes. Except I didn't use knives to defend myself. I went straight for the big guns."

The way his lips tilted and his eyes sparkled fanned a burning flame inside me.

"So how did you get close to your targets?"

"Flirting."

His smile faded, replaced by a scowl. He moved his gaze back to the scene outside, which looked more like a striking painting than a sunset. The colors mixed vibrant pastels and darker hues as if forecasting the end of a storm.

A foreign emotion crawled up my spine. It felt a little like what had raged through me when I saw that other woman on the beach take him into her mouth.

And I realized it was Tavin's emotions. Not mine.

"Are you jealous?"

He looked to his side and then back out the window, unwilling to meet my gaze.

"Why?"

This time, he did spin around with a full glare. "You flirted with strangers."

"And?"

He pressed his lips together against speaking.

I laughed, grasping at the utter ridiculousness of the situation. He was jealous of me flirting with others since I had never turned on the charm for him. Not even once in our short but heated relationship.

I stood and pulled that card from my deck of assets, licking my lips as I approached him, using my hips to sway the skirt adorning my form.

He blinked and recoiled. His eyes widened as I approached him. When I stood in front of him, I ran my finger underneath his chin.

"Are you feeling a little left out?" I batted my eyelashes and smiled demurely. "Do you think we can find somewhere a little less...populated to continue this conversation?"

"And that worked?" he asked, but his voice cracked, betraying him.

I smiled up at him and ran my hands down the front of his pants. His hardness pressed into my palm.

"I say it worked just fine." I dropped the act and went to turn away.

He grabbed me and slammed me against the wall, kissing me with such force, I gasped.

"And then what happens?" he demanded against my lips.

"Then I yank a soul, slice a vein, get my blood, and then use the kiss of death to get rid of the evidence. It only takes a moment, and most of the time, I was in shadowed areas. I operated fast and efficiently in situations like this, but most of the time, the poor souls grabbed my hand and took me to a more private setting. Then I would subdue and silence my targets, get the blood, and engage the kiss of death." I pulled away from Tavin's lips and palmed his cheek. "If you want my sultry side, just ask."

"There's something disingenuous about it." He searched my eyes. "It isn't you."

"You like my abrasive, argumentative self better?" I found it hard to believe he'd take a pass on my seductive qualities.

"I like the real you. Headstrong and smart are far sexier to me than that fake slinky crap. Although a little role-playing sometimes might be fun." A smile toyed on his luscious lips.

"I'll think about it after we get through this shit storm." I gazed out the window, taking in the sunset.

The full spectrum of the rainbow painted the sky as the last of the sun's rays lit up the heavens above. It was surreal.

"It's over. No one can get in now."

My gaze snapped to Tavin's. "Don't be so naïve. The Director is a brilliant scientist and has a bonded mate who is a strong witch. They will figure out a way through your defenses sooner or later."

"He has a bonded mate?" Tavin asked with a single eyebrow cocked in contemplation.

"Yes." I could see the wheels in his mind turning.

Tavin chewed on the inside of his lip for a moment. "Interesting. I wouldn't think a man like him would actually acquiesce to something that could leave him vulnerable like that."

"Oh. It wasn't done out of love. It was done for a purpose. He wanted to leverage her power, and she wanted immortality."

"Still. It makes them vulnerable in the same way we are vulnerable."

"Oh." My eyes widened. "If one dies, so does the other?"

"Yes. The bonding ritual strings lives together. Entwining destinies." He smirked.

Things started snapping together in my brain. "Your parents never bonded."

"No. That would have made the kingdom much more vulnerable." He sighed. "If we had just been soulmates or fated mates, I would have destroyed you before any attachments were made. But what we are is so much more complicated. So much more powerful."

"So much more dangerous to your kingdom." I couldn't help but point that out.

If either one of us was taken down, the entire kingdom would suffer.

He slowly nodded. "Is he the top of the food chain in the organization?"

"Excuse me?" His question threw me. It wasn't anything I had ever thought about before.

"Does the Director answer to anyone?"

"I, uh...I don't know." I never considered that he might report to someone, especially after the jobs he'd had us take on that usually left realms in chaos.

But his purpose was getting DNA of species he didn't already have to make more assassins who questioned less. The scientifically created creatures were more in line with automated computers. They took orders and didn't deviate, most of the time to their detriment.

"He's a scientist." I shrugged.

Tavin started pacing and tapping his fingers in front of him. "If I had an army of trained assassins, would I be using their skill to extract more DNA, or would I be conquering worlds?"

"He has an army at his disposal, too."

Tavin stopped and stared at me, digesting my words before he went back to pacing. "And he isn't conquering worlds? He's just harvesting DNA for his scientific projects?"

"I think he's using the army to protect his scientific projects."

"To what purpose?"

"To make the perfect killer."

"But for whom?" he pushed.

The Director was narcissistic enough to do it for himself, but Tavin had a point. The Director wasn't someone to do things just because it seemed impossible. He'd have to have someone to flaunt it to. He wasn't a war machine either, but what he was trying to accomplish could be used in that way.

"I think we have to assume he isn't at the top," I said slowly. "I would hate to think there's someone pulling the strings, but that would make his bonding with Ava make more sense. It leaves him less vulnerable."

His lips tilted into that adoring smile. "Then killing him might potentially make things worse."

I turned my attention out the window, catching the last bits of color before night swept in.

Tavin's statement burned under my skin. Could we all be pawns in some dangerous game that none of us understood?

"Yeah. He's not willing to wage all-out war with the realms, but whoever is pushing the buttons might not be so squirmy about it."

"Then our play is to threaten his mate. Trade her safety for ours."

I spun towards him, unsure if that was the right move. "I don't know, Tavin. There is no real love between the two, and she's powerful."

"But killing her would kill him. He knows that."

"An idle threat without some teeth behind it won't work. She can defend herself quite well, and he'd bet on her getting away."

"What if we drug her and I have a blade to her throat as we issue our ultimatum?"

Tavin was bold. An actual pending death threat was something the Director would pay very close attention to. But we'd have to contend with the entire complex in that case.

"And what about his guards?"

He snorted a laugh. "Rip their souls out. Display the power we have and the lack of vulnerability between the two of us."

His answer seemed so simple, but I knew what the Director's guards were capable of. I'd seen them tear assassins apart at the drop of a hat.

"What if there are more than just a handful?"

Tavin crossed to me and palmed my cheek. "You do recognize that if you had wanted to, you could have killed everyone at my mother's funeral, right?" His thumb caressed my lips. "You are capable of much more than you realize."

I blinked up at him and bit my lip. I had such debilitating fear of those guards. Fear that had been bred into me since I could think on my own. It was why I never lashed out at them for fear of what the Director would do.

Realization hit, and I took a faltering step back. I started to chuckle because I could have taken them down without breaking a sweat, just not with my fists and knives like I had been trained to do. The thought of me being afraid was so absurd that laughter bubbled out of me, ramping up into near hysterics at the lunacy.

Tavin smirked. "Something funny?"

"You mean I didn't have to get the shit kicked out of me when I mouthed off?" Spit flew from my mouth as I pushed out the words through the laughter.

I leaned over with my hands on my knees, guffawing. I thought I even snorted a few times.

When I finally gained control over my faculties, I continued. "The fear of death was put into us at a young age. It was expressly forbidden to use our powers against the Director's guards."

I grinned up at Tavin as if he had stripped away the last veil of hypocrisy.

He flashed an irresistible smile at me. "Those rules do not apply to you any longer, and that obviously scares the hell out of the Director. Otherwise, he wouldn't bother with sending precious resources after you."

"I don't know why the dickhead is so obsessed with getting me back. He'd use any excuse to have his goons beat the crap out of me," I muttered.

Tavin raised an eyebrow.

"He never got his hands dirty. But he did like to watch his guards terrorize us."

Tavin glowered, and white-hot anger flashed within me. "At least when I dole out punishments, it's me doing the beating."

I huffed at him. "You were willing to have your guards fuck the answers out of me."

His mouth dropped open and then snapped shut as he moved into my personal space. "That's because I could not keep my mind straight around you. And it's probably a good thing because you disintegrated one of my best fighters."

I smiled. "I didn't do that to you, though."

He pulled me against him. "No, you didn't."

His mouth claimed mine in that possessive way that instantly made my panties wet.

"I can still land a kick," I whispered against his lips.

"Do your worst."

His tongue tickled mine after his daring words, making me stall for a moment. I pulled him closer, deepening the kiss as I slowly turned my hips.

Then I pulled away and grinned as I yanked him off balance and flipped him on his back in the middle of the floor. "That's really not my worst."

My feet were swept out from underneath me before I could step away. I yelped as my ass hit the floor. My teeth clacked down on my tongue hard enough to draw blood.

"Ouch." I touched the side of my tongue, and my fingers came away with a red tint. "You made me bleed."

Tavin rolled onto his hands and knees, grinning at me as if he considered this rough game foreplay. He crawled toward me, slowly, looking every bit the predator he was. The gleam in his eyes promised I'd pay for knocking him down.

I couldn't get up fast enough.

He caught me and dropped me onto my back, crawling on top of me only to pin me to the floor. "Sweet demon, you play some dangerous games."

His husky voice layered over me, and my heart sped up in my chest.

"I need a clear mind if we're going to make a plan that isn't shit."

He grinned down at me. "Then you shouldn't have thrown down the gauntlet." He nipped my throat in a playful manner that tickled and tingled at the same time. "Now you're going to have to be punished to the fullest."

His fingers caught on my buttons. The shredding of fabric made me look down at my ruined top and his now unobstructed view of my breasts.

"Tavin," I hissed, but that didn't stop him from taking my breast into his mouth.

His eyes sparkled with mirth as he moved from one breast to the other and then continued lower.

"We need to figure out how we're going to..." My words turned to a low moan as his hand started rubbing the spot between my legs that shut off my brain. "If I had discovered sexual

237

pleasure before you, I would have sucked as an assassin."

Tavin chuckled and waved the rest of my clothing away. "I doubt that. I'm just superbly skilled at making women come."

His mouth dropped to the spot his fingers were coaxing just to prove his point.

THE WITCH ASSASSIN
CHAPTER TWENTY

DAZED AT THE INTENSITY between us, I stared at the ceiling as Tavin uncoupled from me and headed into the bathroom to clean up.

I didn't bother following him yet. I needed a few minutes to get my bearings after having my mind blown so many times I couldn't see straight.

"Mya?"

I blinked my eyes open and stared at Tavin. He was already dressed and buttoning up his shirt. His wet hair slicked back from his face.

"Did you fall asleep?" He chuckled.

I sat up and rubbed my face. "I believe I may have."

A satisfied grin passed over his lips. "Go clean up. I left some clothes for you on the bed."

Heat brushed my cheeks, and I stood from the mess of discarded clothing and headed to the bedroom. My euphoria faded. I had left us utterly vulnerable by basically passing out from exhaustion.

Tavin had tired me out, and that was saying a lot considering I had devoured my share of souls earlier. I might need a stroll through the kingdom before we attempted anything close to what Tavin had suggested earlier.

After a quick shower, I dragged a comb through my hair and dressed in what Tavin had left for me. The shirt was another one of his, but this time, there were comfortable leather pants instead of nothing for my legs. The pants had several weapons in holders, and I smiled at the familiar weight. My ruby-handled dagger hung from my hip.

He also left a belt for me to clasp around the shirt. When I glanced in the mirror, I smiled. I looked like a clean pirate. I guess if we were breaking into the complex, this look would turn heads.

Tavin waited for me in a chair with a book in his hand. He gazed at me, slowly closed the book, and set it down on the table. The same look he had when he'd crawled across the floor to me blazed in his eyes.

"No." I pointed at him. "Wipe that look off your face. We need to properly plan this suicide mission, or it will be just that, and I am not too keen on dying."

The heat in his eyes didn't diminish, but he schooled his features and gave me a nod. He stood and held his hand out.

I crossed to him and took it without overthinking it, following him out the door of his quarters. The four guards I had become familiar with since arriving in this realm snapped to attention.

"Situation room," Tavin barked and then looked at Galen. "Go grab my father, please."

Galen nodded and hurried off to retrieve the king. The rest of the guys fell into step around us, two behind and one in front with his hand on the hilt of his sword. Every member of the guard, as well as the staff, were on high alert, snapping to attention at the sight of royalty.

Tavin's sleep command had saved them from the unpleasantries in the throne room. Most we passed looked refreshed, as if Tavin had also given them sorely needed rest.

The situation room consisted of a large table in the center of the room with a map of Eleka etched into the wood. I stared at the map, trying to get a sense of where we were on the grain. They didn't have one of those nifty "You are here" signs like those I had seen in the massive markets in other realms.

Tavin flipped on a light and pointed it to the side of a mountain that overlooked a mass of water, and then he took a seat, waiting for his father to arrive.

"The portal cavern." He jutted his chin at the illuminated spot on the map.

"Where were we before?"

He pointed to the southernmost point on the map. He was right; it seemed to be as far away from the central kingdom as one could get.

Galen brought King Zorander into the situation room. The king glanced at me and then Tavin, waving his hand in my direction without a word.

"Mya has experience in stealth missions. We haven't planned something like this since we escaped to Eleka." Tavin crossed his arms and stood tall.

Everything about his stance screamed challenge.

King Zorander's gaze pierced into me. "How many missions have you successfully planned and executed?"

"A little more than fifty missions over the last seven years."

"And how many failed?"

I held up one finger. "Just this one, sir. I didn't anticipate Tavin because we were not educated about the different types of mates that may be out there. The compound conveniently left that out of their curriculum."

"What exactly did they teach you?" King Zorander leaned forward, as did most of the guards.

"They groomed us to be competitive to a fault. There were no true allies. War tactics, strategy, how to remain invisible in plain sight. Written and spoken languages across all realms. How to win in an impossible situation." I shrugged. "How to take down multiple attackers. How to get into difficult places. How to survive."

The king rolls his eyes, unimpressed. "Well, the last dozen or so assassins failed miserably."

I smiled. "I was second best. And it seems the top assassin turned on the Director as well." I exchanged a glance with Tavin. "Or so Hanna said just before I yanked her soul out."

"If you never failed, why did the Director have you beaten?" Tavin asked.

"You've experienced my mouthiness enough to understand it."

Tavin snorted a laugh. "But even with your sarcasm, that isn't cause for a beating."

"Well, my internal editor is defunct, and he liked to make me regret speaking." My comment provokes some barely concealed smirks around the room.

The Director didn't always have a valid reason for having me beaten or any of the others. We could sneeze and send him into a tirade that left us in the medical unit.

I pointed at Tavin. "Can we get on with discussing what's running through your head instead of dissecting my past?"

Everyone in the room focused on Tavin.

He nodded. "Mya pointed out that even with the beefed-up security around the portal, the Director will never stop sending his people to take us down. That includes Mya." He looked around the room. "While you all were sleeping in the throne room, the assassin that Mya knew said the Director wanted Mya dead if she didn't agree to come back."

"And he won't stop. He'll figure out how to bypass the extra security just like he figured out how to bypass the existing security." I survey the room. "The Director is a night walker and a brilliant scientist. He's mated to an extremely powerful witch, so he has a lot of brain power and magic at his disposal."

"So," Tavin stated, "I suggested we convince him that coming after us is not in his best interest."

"How?" the king asked as if he already knew the answer.

"Threaten his mate."

"We can do that without crossing realms," his father argued.

"Unfortunately, we can't," I said. "The Director will not take a message sent through a portal as valid. We have to show her vulnerable and at our mercy for him to be convinced enough to make a blood pact."

"A blood pact?" Tavin asked.

"It's the only way to guarantee he leaves us alone. Without it, he's not bound by his word."

In other words, I didn't trust the Director's word to be worth a damn.

But with a blood pact, he couldn't double-cross us.

"Telling the Director that Tavin is your spirit mate won't do it?" the king asked.

"I'm not releasing that information to the Director." That was like asking for them to keep sending people to kill us. "He'd use that against us. One death takes down two people. Uh-uh. No way."

"And royalty at that," Tavin added, shaking his head. "That information is not to be distributed beyond our borders. Our people can know so that they will accept Mya as my queen when the time comes, but the world beyond is to be left clueless."

Tavin ran his hand through his hair.

"You are aware that you do not have to take her as your queen," the king said.

The disdain in his look said enough. Even with Tavin's acceptance of me, it would be difficult for this realm to accept me, especially if the king couldn't.

Tavin laughed. "If anyone touches her, they will die by my hand. So yes. I am making her my queen. And I will give her my mark so our world knows she is mine, and mine alone."

I cocked my eyebrow and crossed my arms. "No one owns me, Tavin."

"I own you just as surely as you own me. So, stop with this cocky bullshit." His eyes drilled into me. "Neither of us is the sharing kind." He glared pointedly at his father. "Now back to the plan."

"Well?" his father prompted.

"Mya and I go to Icarus, find the Director's mate, and hold a knife to her throat as we issue our threat."

"And I enter into a blood pact with him," I added.

Even though we'd fully cleared that part out before we came into the situation room, I knew it was the only way to win this battle of wills.

I gazed at the king and then back at Tavin. "First off, we can't go in there as ourselves. That would set too many alarms off." I chewed on my lip, remembering some of the classes at the complex. "Elvren have the ability to glamour themselves, right?"

Tavin rolled his eyes and waved his hand. The likeness of Galen stood where Tavin had been a moment before. With another wave, he returned to his original form.

"How about me? Can you do both of us at the same time?"

"You do know I've glamoured this world for nearly a century, right?" Tavin asked with sarcasm lacing his words.

With a wave, an icky layer fell over me, settling on my skin in such a way as to make me itch.

I stared at Tavin and then at my massive hands. "Did you turn me into Galen, too?"

Tavin waved his hand and grinned.

"Fine, but instead of one of your guards, you'll have to conjure up a couple of the dead assassins instead. Hanna is the logical choice for me, and probably Ramik, because he's the only male one whose name I remember."

"Okay, we go dressed as them..."

I put my hand up to stop him. "We'll need their blood so the portal thinks it's actually them. That way, their return will be catalogued." I chewed my bottom lip some more. "Assuming we can dupe a portal."

He was quiet for a moment and then offered a nod.

"Now, I can call a portal from wherever we need to jump from, whether that's his office or his home."

"Wait a second. You can call portals?" Tavin's eyebrows rose, and he glanced at his father before returning his gaze to mine.

I nodded, and my brow furrowed. "How did you get your people here?"

From what I knew of portal travel, they either had to be guided by one of the species who can travel freely through the gates, or the gate had to be spelled by a portal guardian. As far as I was aware, the Director at one time had the only portal guardian in existence under his thumb, but last I heard, he had died before he could contribute any more DNA to the Director's science experiments.

King Zorander sighed. "We made a deal with a druid witch. Her freedom for ours. She came with us to Eleka and charmed the portal. It is her magic that makes the portal face toward safety for light fae, and to a death drop for any other species. The rest of the cavern magic is ours."

"Tavin will have to hold my hand going through the portals. I have the DNA that will allow us to freely travel through any portal."

"Does anyone else have that skill?" the king asked.

"All of the Director's assassins can freely travel through any portal."

"Which answers the question of why there were so many assassins here, but that is not what I was asking. I'm questioning your ability to call a portal to you from anywhere," he said. "Which I'd like to see with my own eyes."

The skepticism on his face burned under my skin.

"I'm going to need a little energy." I met Tavin's gaze and got a nod.

I inhaled, pulling some energy from the guards. Then I turned, focusing on one of the more benign portals, willing it into existence. Although, I truly hoped no one was traveling from Earth at this very moment. That would be too hard to explain.

The portal faded into existence, emitting rolling blue smoke around it, mixed with the normal black tendrils that seemed to depict every standard portal I'd ever seen.

Everyone gasped.

"Where does that one go?" the king asked.

"Earth." I waved it away quickly because we didn't need a surprise, whether an assassin or one of the other species who traveled freely.

It was always a risk playing with portal access, but I had yet to run into an issue. I didn't want to push that luck though.

I turned back to the wide-eyed king. "And to answer your question, beyond a portal guard, no, I don't think any other of the Director's people can do this."

"Which is another valuable reason for the Director to keep you under his thumb." Tavin's gaze remained on the spot behind me. When he finally looked at me, he added, "And you'll have to hold my hand on the way back so the portal knows which way to face when we get here. How many others have that DNA?"

"We all have some infusion of the species who can freely roam through portals. But I'm not sure if we each get one type or if we get combinations to be sure we can go through portals. Druids, dragons, and fallen angels can be part of our DNA signature. I'm the only one with portal guardian DNA, though. At least, that's what I read in my file."

My cheeks burned red. I had peeked once at my file when the Director had to address an urgent matter in the building. That memo had given me a chill because he had noted that I hadn't shown the ability of a portal guardian except for being able to move through them.

"Just be grateful I have one of the handier talents because of it," I asked.

"You could have dragon DNA?" Galen asked.

"Possibly. I was naturally born from a witch and one of the demon princes of hell, and then the Director added at least the DNA from a portal guardian to the mix." I shrugged. "I can't breathe fire, and I don't have barbequed angel wings, so if I got some of that shit in my bloodstream, it isn't prominent by any means. All of this is beside the point. We've got the plan down for getting to Icarus. But then we need to get from the portal room to the Director's apartment."

"Why the apartment and not his office?" Tavin asked.

"Because we have a better chance of subduing Ava at the apartment than at the office. It's always a crap shoot whether she'll be at the office or not. And if we get to their apartment early enough in the morning, we'll catch them by surprise." At least that was my thought. "But we need something like that drink you gave me to nullify her magic, and then we only need to watch out for any defensive moves."

"I have something better. Something that will lock her in her skin but not have her able to move or access her magic." The king grinned. "It's more powerful than the demon suppression I gave you."

I glared at him. "We likely won't be able to get close enough to jab her with a needle."

We would have seconds at best before she tossed her magic at us.

"We have darts that are small enough to fit in straws," Tavin said. "Usually, we use them for big game, but with some modifications, I can have something that hides in my hand."

"And Tavin never misses." The king beamed.

A couple of the guards nodded in agreement.

"I'd suggest backup just in case," I said because I was pragmatic and usually had an alternate plan in place before I even took off on a job.

"Like the killing stars in your bra?" Tavin challenged.

"Exactly. How long does the tranquilizer last?" I didn't want to talk about how poorly I'd executed this job.

I had not factored in the type of connection Tavin and I carried. That was a sucker punch I never saw coming.

"Twenty-four hours."

I nodded. "Then all we do is wait for the Director." I smiled. "That could work. But what if he comes in with his full guard?"

Tavin rolled his eyes. "Then we yank their souls out and get on with the negotiations."

My mind whirled at all that could go wrong. "And what if they get shots off before they die?"

Tavin blinked. He hadn't considered heavy artillery. That was clear in his initial look of shock and his even further slow response.

"They carry firearms," I said. "Not just swords and knives like the League of Supernatural Assassins."

They were all expert shots, but I kept that piece of intel quiet. I didn't want to completely freak out Tavin or his father. Their faces already showed enough angst.

"Bullets tear through bodies much quicker than a steel sword," I pushed because I didn't know if this realm had anything that would deflect a bullet.

At least Earth in all its infancy had Kevlar, and I had yet to see anything remotely like a firearm on any of the guards on Eleka.

"We don't have anything that can withstand a bullet," the king said softly.

The look in his eyes confirmed that he knew of the weapons I spoke of, and from his expression, he utterly despised them.

I sighed. "Well, we better pray they aren't holding their weapons at the ready, and we yank souls out before they can point those things at us."

"And if he doesn't go for the deal?" the king asked.

Tavin and I exchanged a glance. "Then we kill them both," we said at the same time.

"And destroy the log of anyone going to Eleka," I added.

That way, this place would fall into obscurity again.

"What else could go wrong?" King Zorander asked.

I blew air out. "The portal could reject us violently, and we fall to our death. The guards in the portal room don't believe we are Hanna and Ramik and try to kill us on sight. We zap into the Director's apartment, and he is there, and Ava gets the drop on us. I zap us into the wrong apartment altogether."

I sighed and ran my hand through my damp hair. "We could be shot. I can't call the portal we need to the Director's apartment, and we have to try to make our way through the complex back to the portal room with hostile forces chasing us."

I looked at the king and then around the room. "Basically, a whole shit ton can go wrong."

"In the event the plan goes sideways, I'd like Galen, Shayne, Tomack, and Rayne, along with our healers, waiting for us outside the portal," Tavin said.

The king nodded. "I don't know that I'm comfortable with this."

Tavin let out a soft chuckle. "Then I guess we'll need to execute flawlessly."

THE WITCH ASSASSIN
CHAPTER TWENTY-ONE

"WAY TO PUT THE pressure on," I muttered as we entered the prince's wing in the castle.

The tables in the sitting room were covered with pastries that filled the air with decadent scents, and my mouth watered.

Tavin crossed ahead of me and took a seat on the couch in front of the newly delivered spread of food.

He eyed the delectable trays and then looked up at me. "Do you think it's poisoned?"

"Do I look like a poison connoisseur?" I was exhausted after all the planning and stress of the day.

I needed energy just as much as he did, and pigging out on these treats would only deplete me of even more energy.

His brow lowered into a glower. "Galen," he called.

Galen came in quickly with his hand on the hilt of his sword, his gaze bouncing around at the shadows, looking for whatever had caused the warning in Tavin's tone. "Yes, sir?"

"Can you find the cook? I need someone to test the food." He rubbed his face.

This was not his normal, and it was taking its toll on him. They had lived so long in relative peace in this realm, and neither he nor his staff was used to this level of distress.

Galen looked at the spread and took a step closer, reaching for the nearest pastry.

Tavin put his hand out palm first. "No. The cook. If it is poisoned, I don't want to lose my closest friend."

Galen's cheeks flushed before he bowed. "Yes, sir." His voice sounded clipped as he spun on his heel and headed out of the room.

I collapsed in the seat next to Tavin. "I think you may have upset Galen."

Tavin let his lip curl into a shadow of a smile. "It's his job to keep me safe. So, yes, I'm sure my order annoyed him."

"I'm sorry for being bitchy about not being a poison connoisseur before, but I'm exhausted, and hungry, too."

"I thought with all the souls today, you'd be set." He cocked his head, studying me.

"It was akin to an adrenaline rush, immediate infusion of power, and then when the danger was mitigated, it evaporated. Normally, it would be enough, but I expended a lot of magic, too, so it wasn't enough to sustain me for very long." I leaned back in the cushions and closed my eyes for a moment.

He took my hand and kissed my palm.

I peeled my eyes open and looked at him. "When I'm not stressed, that kind of infusion would keep me going for days. But the whole fighting for my life thing just drains it that much faster."

"Once I get something in my system, we'll take a stroll through the market. We have to go to the cavern anyway. I need to see what this Ramik looks like so I can do a decent job with the glamour."

"Power up and then sleep. Sounds like a plan." I smiled.

If I thought beyond this evening, my stomach clenched. Thinking about our pending mission tomorrow left me feeling unhinged. Going after the Director was against all the years of programming that they had beaten into me, and I swept the thoughts away so I didn't burn through what little energy I had left.

"Power up, and you sleep while I get the tranquilizer ready, along with the delivery method, then maybe I'll get a couple hours of shut-eye before we jump into this mission in time for the sun to rise on Icarus." His expression remained stoic, but unease reflected in his eyes as well as through our bond.

Galen walked in before I could respond. He waved the cook forward.

"Is this not to your satisfaction, sir?" The cook stepped forward, dressed in white with a chef's hat hiding his white hair, which was secured at the nape of his neck.

His uniform was immaculate, which made my eyes narrow. He should at least have some smear of food on his clothing.

Tavin looked at the spread. "It looks very appetizing. However..."

He pressed his lips together and closed his eyes.

"We're worried it may be poisoned, considering more than half a dozen assassins infiltrated the castle today," I said, taking the burden from Tavin.

The cook's eyes widened in understanding. Without being asked, he reached out and snatched a pastry from the middle of the display and devoured it. Once he was done swallowing the food, he said, "I dumped everything that had been prepared and prepped prior to your bringing us to the throne room into the garbage. The idea that someone may have wanted to cause harm to you, or your father, angered me enough to waste the food." He glanced at me and then looked back to Tavin. "It pained me to do it, but none of the kitchen staff were willing to risk it, sir."

Tavin nodded. "Thank you, Monroe."

"Sir. Your safety matters to the staff here. Just as it matters a great deal to all of Eleka." He sighed. "I do offer my sincere apologies that this is not a proper meal. It was all I could prepare in the small allotment of time I had left."

I laughed, and he turned to me as if I'd committed a great sin.

"This is a magnificent spread." I waved at what he'd prepared.

"It is worthy of a picnic, not a prince," Monroe said, looking down his nose at me.

"She's right, Monroe. This is more than adequate." Tavin straightened and delved into the pastries before him. One bite, and he closed his eyes as if savoring the flavor. "It's magnificent, Monroe."

The cook beamed, revealing a row of crooked teeth before he schooled his features. "Thank you, Your Highness." He scanned the table. "If it will ease your mind, I can try everything before you do."

"That's not necessary, Monroe." Tavin looked over at the window and the painted sky beyond. "However, since you mentioned a picnic, I think that just might be what the doctor ordered. Fresh air, ocean breezes, and a nice meal on the bluff."

"I will pack you a basket." Monroe clapped his hands together. "Should I leave this here for you for after your walk?" He indicated the food on the table.

"Do you have enough in the kitchen for a basket?"

"Not as much as this, but yes, we have enough for a light picnic for two." He smiled.

"Then, yes, leave this here. We can graze on it later."

"Very well, sir."

As soon as he left, Tavin turned to Galen and the other guards waiting outside our door and waved to the spread. "Feel free to eat something before we go for our stroll."

They hit the table like a group of hungry wolves. Tavin picked at a few things but waited for Monroe to come back with the picnic basket before he snatched one of the sweet-looking desserts and scarfed it whole.

"You can have more when we get back. Monroe will throw a hissy if he sees you eating my food," Tavin said quietly as footsteps approached the door.

The guards all turned, blocking the view of the pastries as we walked to the door. They fell in formation around us, and Galen opened the door, intercepting Monroe before he got to the room. Rayne closed the door behind us, sparing Monroe the scene of a prematurely picked-over buffet.

Tavin's security detail flanked us in the normal two in front, two in back formation as we headed out of the castle. Outside of the funeral this morning, I got my first unobstructed view of the countryside. It was much more winding and populated down to a grassy knoll overlooking the tumultuous ocean. Pastel flowers dotted the whitewashed walkways, softening the landscape. Wide windows adorned the buildings lining the road, and as we left the castle proper, the scent of baked goods drifted in the air.

My mouth watered at the decadent smell. My shirt and leathers seemed out of place in all the wispy dresses I caught sight of on the women, but it made me fit in with the men. It was an odd dichotomy that made everyone turn our way to check out the prince's procession. This was a more pleasant walk than the last time Tavin had tried out a picnic.

I guessed here, he didn't flaunt his conquests with the townspeople like he had at the bungalow. I traveled as his equal, inhaling the essence of the city, along with the soul energy pulsing through the place. The market was active, even in the evening, and people parted, allowing the prince and his consort to look at the wares.

Vendors brought things out into the crowd for me. Clothing fit for royalty as opposed to a warrior. I smiled politely and touched the fabric. In a couple cases, that was all it took for me to change my mind about the look of the clothing. The fabric itself felt like air.

I glanced at Tavin, raising an eyebrow. He nodded and smiled his approval at the things I ultimately picked out. The vendor scurried away with the items that would be packaged up and appear as if by magic in Tavin's rooms.

We moved on, and there were enough people that I wouldn't tire any single person out with my gluttony. I feasted, bolstering up my energy stores until I was overflowing with it.

When we were finally sitting on the blanket on the bluff, enjoying the pounding of the ocean against the rocks below, Tavin dove into the picnic basket, savoring each bite the way I had savored the soul energy through town.

"Can you eat anything?" he asked with half a bite still between his fingers.

"I have, but it's best to reserve my energy for the mission. Digesting actual food burns through some of the energy I've collected. And I don't want to syphon any more from the kingdom's people."

He took a swipe of the cream filling and held his finger out. "Trust me. It's worth the energy expenditure."

Citrus wafted from his finger, and my mouth watered.

He grinned. "You love all things citrus."

Tavin had pegged that right. I pulled his finger close and lightly licked the confection. A burst of orange and lemon and lime mingled on my tongue in a symphony of flavor.

"Oh my." I put his whole finger into my mouth and sucked the cream off it, closing my eyes as my taste buds danced with the sweet taste.

Tavin slowly pulled his finger from between my lips.

I opened my eyes to his gaze, intense like I had lit his libido. "Put that idea away. We need to conserve our strength."

"You suck my finger like that and then cut me off?" He popped the rest of the pastry into his mouth but didn't make a move to strip me down and fuck me on this bluff like he wanted to.

I could see it in his eyes.

"After. And if you get a bowl of that filling, I'll lick it off every inch of you until there's nothing left." I would suck that for days on end.

Nodding, he dropped onto his back and stared at the sky. "I will collect on that raincheck after we get back."

He smiled and reached into the basket for another pastry. This time, he slowly licked the cream out, using his tongue in such a way as to create a bit of heat between us.

I understood the effect me sucking his finger had on him. I fanned myself and turned my attention to the water. We let the silence drift on the air, broken only by the roar of the ocean.

"Do you think we can pull this off?" Tavin asked quietly.

The serious expression carved into his handsome features made me think before I let some asinine comment tumble from my lips. Tavin's gaze moved from the water to me.

"I've pulled off some hairy jobs in my lifetime. And looking at this one without any emotions involved, it should be easy, even if a few of the clusterfucks happen. But I've been conditioned to fear the Director and his guards. That's the real wild card."

Tavin sat up and pulled me against him. He kissed my temple and stared at the crashing waves without comment.

"If I hesitate because my mind freezes, we could die." I hadn't wanted to disclose my weakness, but it was very important for Tavin to understand the absolute mind fuck that the Director was to me.

"I've never truly been in a war situation. We've had squabbles, but there really hasn't been danger to the crown until you arrived and brought the storm with you." He kissed the back of my head.

I tightened against him.

"Relax. I'm not blaming you. But it's true. I didn't have the sense at the funeral to set out any protections. But you did. I'm rusty, and I was too young to fight in the war before we sought asylum here." He sighed and reached for another pastry. "I may be from a warrior Elvren clan, but I've never truly had to be a warrior until today."

I glanced at him. "You've bested me three times. And you're worried about your fighting skills?"

He looked at the backs of his guards and then returned his gaze to mine and nodded.

"You know how many assassins have actually brought me to the ground in all my years?" I cocked an eyebrow at him.

He shook his head. "How many?"

"One. And I'm still waiting for a rematch. But seeing as Treya apparently bailed out of the league before I came to Eleka, that rematch will probably never happen." I palmed his cheek and ran my thumb over his cheekbone, trying to erase the unease filling his face.

His lips tilted into a little smile. "Thanks for saying that."

"I'm not kidding, Tavin. If you think I am, pitch your guards against me and see who's left standing." I waved at the four sentinels guarding us.

Tavin eyed his men. Every single one of them stared back at us, and there was not a relaxed muscle in the bunch.

He turned back to me. "Without weapons?"

I nodded. I could take them without weapons easily. And I really wanted Tavin to understand he had superior skills, even to mine.

"Fine. I want to see this. I'll take your swords." He pointed to the spot next to him. "And I'm serious. No weapons, or you'll have to deal with me."

He waved to the open grass. I stood and crossed to the middle of the field, glancing at the distance to the bluff before nodding at the guards.

They looked to Tavin again as if waiting for him to tell them he was kidding.

"You're going to let us hit her?" Galen asked as he started in my direction.

"Yes." Tavin stretched out on his side with his head propped on his hand and continued eating pastries from the basket. "Just try not to break any bones or knock anyone unconscious."

His gaze was on me when he said that last part. I didn't know who that directive was for, but I planned on whooping ass, and if I shattered a bone or two, all the better.

"Once you are on the ground, you're out," Tavin said loud enough for everyone to hear.

The guards surrounded me, grinning like fools as if they had been given a gift. I certainly knew Galen wanted to school me, especially since I'd drawn the prince's blood with my throwing stars on that first day.

They stopped the same distance away on the north, south, east, and west sides. They seemed to be communicating with each other silently as I stood with my arms loose and shifted my weight from foot to foot.

It had been a while since I was in a fight that wasn't to the death or to the point of unconsciousness, and my heart pounded in my chest, relishing the adrenaline rush.

Instead of waiting for an attack, I took the initiative, darting toward Galen. I shot my fist out at the last second and connected with his stomach as I ducked under his swing. The air rushed out of him, and I twirled, kicking the backs of his knees, sending him sprawling on the ground before spinning away from one of the twin's attempts to grab me.

I grinned, trying to sweep their feet from under them. But one of the twins got his arm around my neck. Stupid move on his part. I shifted my hip toward him and gripped his arm as I flipped him over my hip. Then I ducked out of his grip as he landed on the ground on his back with an "oof."

That was two out of commission according to the prince's rules. I spun to face the other two. I needed them lined up, not separated like they were, because they were coming at me as two units, splitting my attention.

I stepped toward the other twin and launched a spin kick, catching him in the chest. The blow knocked him off his feet. He tumbled over and crouched as if he were going to join in again.

"You're out, Rayne," Tavin said.

I had no idea how he could tell the twins apart, but my focus was on Tomack. He was larger than the other three and reminded me of the lavender-eyed guard I'd turned to dust for attempting to touch me.

Tomack circled, keeping his distance as the other three crawled to where the prince was now sitting at attention. Tomack's hands were clenched into fists, and his eyes were alert.

I stepped in and threw a punch, but he parried, knocking it away and delivering a punch of his own.

I moved, but his knuckles grazed my cheek. I used his motion against him, grabbing his arm and yanking it, making him move too fast. I stuck my foot out, and Tomack stumbled on it.

He didn't fall though. If he hadn't put on the brakes, he'd sail right off the bluff.

I darted at him, hooking my arm in his and spinning him back toward the prince. Tomack couldn't catch himself this time. He sprawled on his stomach on the ground.

I sidestepped away from the drop and then stopped, out of breath. Tomack rolled and stared at me with wide eyes. He looked toward the drop a few feet behind me and then gave me a nod of acknowledgement.

I nodded back, ignoring the sensation of eyes on me.

Tavin stood in a stance I recognized. He wanted some of this action, if only to prove to himself that he could take me down. He waved me in with an impish look that stole my breath. I walked forward until I was just out of his reach.

"I can still land a kick." I smiled, energized by this entire ordeal.

My words produced a smirk.

"You seem to always say that, but you've never landed a kick yet."

I opened my mouth to argue.

"The knee in the jail cell doesn't count." He pointed at me and then narrowed his eyes in a challenge. "Take your best shot, demon."

My heart clamored in my chest, pounding hard enough for me to have difficulty catching my breath. I was turned on by the idea of grappling with Tavin until one of us yielded.

The guards had resumed their posts, but instead of having their backs to us, they faced us with intense interest. I had bested them in such a quick timeframe, I was sure their egos were a bit bruised. But my action to save Tomack from a devastating fall must've raised their level of respect for me.

I was sure they expected me to school Tavin in the same way I'd schooled them.

Instead of initiating, I found myself on the defense as Tavin launched his attack. His fist caught my shoulder, spinning me, and then he was on me, but I ducked out of his arms with a jab into his midsection with my elbow.

Blow for blow, we parried and deflected hits, the shadow of each one echoing through my form, until I started feeling fatigued.

I stepped in and grabbed his shirt, falling backwards with the intention of flipping him over my head, but he closed the distance between us, not allowing my feet to reach his thighs. He caught my wrists and landed flat on me, knocking the air from my chest.

He pinned my wrists to the ground above my head. "You let me do that," he grumbled.

"No, I didn't." I hadn't anticipated him closing the distance.

Or falling on me with his full weight. I licked my lips, trying to rein in my lust. I couldn't afford another sexual encounter with Tavin. Not if I hoped to have my wits about me in the morning.

"I was supposed to throw you over my head with that move, but you countered it."

He grinned. "I forced myself closer to you. You couldn't get the leverage without a little distance." He leaned down and nipped my lower lip. "You are fast. I'll give you that."

Then the nip turned into more as he kissed me in earnest.

I squirmed under him.

He cut the kiss and sighed. "I know. I know. You need to reserve your energy for tomorrow."

He rolled his eyes and stood, offering me a hand. I let him help me to my feet, and then he led me back to the blanket and started packing up what was left of the picnic.

His guards still faced us, their eyes wide with what they'd witnessed. I sported some bruises on my exposed skin, and so did Tavin. Most of them were in the same locations on our cheeks and arms where we'd tagged each other or blocked attempted punches.

Their shoulders tensed as if our little display of nearly equal power unnerved them. The prince was stronger and more agile than his well-trained guards, and I didn't think they expected me to be a near-even match for Tavin.

That knowledge seemed to seep into their consciousnesses, and I could see the what-ifs in their eyes as they followed our every move. After all, they were the ones who'd brought me into the kingdom's jail instead of killing me at the portal cave.

I stopped in front of them as Tavin packed up the leftovers. "You didn't cause the trouble here on Eleka. I did. And I'm going to fix it."

They shifted their feet and dropped their gazes with half-hearted nods.

Tavin stepped to my side and handed Galen the picnic basket.

"We need to detour to the cave," he said.

Galen led the way, and I used the walk to gather more energy from the people we passed, replenishing all I had lost fighting. When we arrived, the bodies of the dead were laid out in a line outside the entrance.

I walked down the row, stopped in front of Ramik, and pointed. "He's a little more bloated than normal."

Tavin waved his hand, and he flickered into Ramik. Shorter, slighter, with thinning hair, just like the corpse in front of us, but without the plumpness of death sticking to him.

"Perfect. Now do me."

Another wave, and that same change of skin layered over me, causing me to shiver. I took slow breaths, calming the need to itch the glamour off.

He waved the illusion away. "Put the bodies in the outer cavern."

I pointed at Ramik and Hanna. "But not these two. I don't want someone coming in and deciding to collect the bodies and have our cover blown to bits for tomorrow."

"As the lady wishes," Tavin said.

He and Galen traded a nod before the four guards dragged bodies in one by one. Tavin released them from the cave each round until only the two we were using for our identities were left outside of the portal cavern.

"Their chips are in the front pockets of their shirts." He smiled at me. "We should have those on us when we go, too. It may help with fooling the portal. We can destroy them before we come back."

I hadn't thought about using the tracking chips to our advantage. It was a smart move. "I'm glad you're on my team."

Tavin slung his arm over my shoulder. "Let's get back so you can rest, and I can figure out the tranquilizer situation."

THE WITCH ASSASSIN
CHAPTER TWENTY-TWO

TAVIN GRABBED ONE OF the pastries as he followed me to the bedroom. He changed into loungewear and dropped a kiss on my forehead after I stripped and curled up under the covers.

"Hopefully this doesn't take me long." He moved the hair from my brow.

"I'll see you sometime before dawn." I yawned through the words.

I didn't even remember Tavin leaving the room.

MY EYES OPENED TO dark shadows casting over the halls of the complex. Tavin followed behind me, and the warmth of his hand swallowed my palm, giving me a certainty that nothing would go wrong.

I had more energy and more sureness flowing through me than I'd ever felt on an assignment just from having Tavin with me. I felt invincible.

The maze of hallways seemed endless, making my steps sluggish. We rounded a corner, only to find another long hallway in front of us vacant of any doors.

Around the next corner, we found ourselves in the Director's office, suddenly surrounded. Gunfire echoed in my ears, leaving them ringing. I spun to see Tavin's body jerk with each bullet as it tore through his flesh.

He fell in slow motion. I slammed into the ground at the same time. His bounce splattered blood all the way across the floor until it almost hit me. Tavin reached for me.

I willed my limbs to move toward Tavin, but I couldn't move. I could hardly bring air into my lungs, and the wet sound of breaths wheezing from bullet holes layered over the last of the ringing shots.

The Director stood over me, laughing as I writhed in agony at his feet.

Hot branding irons punctured through my abdomen and chest, matching Tavin's bullet holes. I stared at Tavin's outstretched hand, unable to get to him. Unable to whisk him to safety. Hot tears leaked from my eyes.

"This is your hell, my little demon. I've trapped your soul and made it so you relive this moment for the rest of eternity."

The horror of his words raked sharp claws over every inch of my skin. Tavin's eyes begged for help. Help I couldn't give.

My chest squeezed against the anguish, overpowering the pain. When his eyes glazed over with death, my heart seized. Darkness started to descend.

Gunshots broke through the veil of nothingness, replaying the horrid scene again. I screamed in frustration.

"Mya!"

Tavin's voice echoed in my head, and I blinked my eyes open, expecting to see him bleeding on the floor. Instead, shadows surrounded us, and the warmth of his hands clasping my shoulders settled my clanging heart. Tremors still rattled through my bones.

He pulled me against his bare chest and whispered, "Shhh" in my ear.

Only then did I realize I had been in the throes of a terrible nightmare. One that clung to me with grim determination, much like I was clinging to Tavin. But with his arms around me and his continued placations in my ear, I finally drew in a breath and pulled away.

"I'm fine," I mumbled under my breath, shaken by the fact that a dream about Tavin's death could affect me this way.

He smoothed my hair back and hooked his finger under my jaw, making me meet his gaze. "It's normal to have nightmares about what we are attempting to do."

I pulled my face from his soft grip. "Not for me."

Oh, I'd had nightmares before; that wasn't new. But I'd never had anything with such an emotional punch.

"You've never had a nightmare?" His skepticism bled through his words, but the way he crossed his arms and scoffed at me brought it home.

I rolled my eyes at him. "I've had nightmares. Just not like that. You died in my nightmare."

His arms slowly uncrossed, and his brow creased.

"I've never dreamed about anyone else's death." I blinked and then started to chuckle. "Well, not by anyone's hand but mine, anyway. And it never had that kind of impact on me."

His teeth flashed in the dark, as if he knew it was about him, but he didn't say anything right away.

Then he stretched out on his back. "Get some more sleep. We only have a couple hours before we have to get up and get moving."

He pulled me down onto his shoulder, tucking me against his side as if that could ward off bad dreams.

I soaked in his warmth, but, thankfully, sleep didn't pull me into dream depths again. When a buzzing came from the other side of the bed, Tavin stirred.

He groaned and rubbed his face, echoing my sentiments of crawling out of the warm sheets into the still dark morning. If it had been light out, I'd feel better. The passage of time here seemed to be in line with Icarus. At least I hoped like hell it was.

I wanted to attack when the Director least expected it. First thing after Ava woke seemed best. She wouldn't be at her sharpest, which was what we were hoping for.

After the nightmare I'd had, there was no way I was going to suggest the Director's office anyway, even if we had to wait all day for the Director to come back to the apartment.

"How long will Ava be out from the tranquilizer?" I climbed out of bed.

Tavin stretched. "A little longer than twenty-four hours. That should give us a good window of time in the event we have to wait."

"You don't have time to linger in the shower," Tavin called after me as he rolled out of bed himself.

I grunted. I wanted to be fresh and loose, not half asleep with my muscles aching, and a shower would allow for that, even a quick one in the bliss of his washroom amenities. All I wanted at the moment was that fresh citrus scent surrounding me and a little distance from that horrid nightmare that still hung to my consciousness.

Halfway through the shower, Tavin stepped into my space, moving me out of the direct stream.

"What are you doing?" I demanded, glaring up at him as I pushed him back so I could stay in the heart of the shower.

"You had your turn. Now you need to share. I'm not pushing you out of the shower, am I?" His brow knit in irritation.

I grumbled but yielded and stepped to the side, enjoying one of the side pulses of water on my lower back as he lathered up and rinsed. Then everything turned off before I was ready.

I opened my mouth to protest, but I got a finger in my face and a glare to go with it. His foul mood softened my response. He offered me a towel, and I took the peace offering, drying off the water from my skin before I wrapped the towel around me and squeezed the excess moisture from my hair.

I took more time than normal brushing and then braiding my hair to keep it out of my face. I needed an unobstructed view today, and my hair had a tendency to get in my eyes if I turned quickly.

"What do you suggest we wear?" Tavin asked when I walked into the bedroom.

I nibbled on my lower lip and waved at him, conjuring the standard assassin outfit that the men wore. The pants fit without hugging every inch of him, but they did allude to his magnificent physique. The black T-shirt, on the other hand, showed off his chiseled chest and cut abs like a second skin. I also waved the normal utility belt adorned with knives and other sharp objects meant to be thrown at the enemy onto him.

The only things difficult to hide were his ears. Even if I pulled his long, dark hair back into a man-bun of sorts, his ears would still poke through, but with the glamour he was going to don, it didn't matter.

Once I was satisfied with his look, I waved my assassin outfit on. It moved with me, giving me the freedom of motion that I was used to, and it had all the weapons I was accustomed to as well, with one addition—the knife Tavin had given me. That was strapped around my thigh in a sleek black holder instead of the one he got for it.

Tavin's gaze slowly caressed me from the top of my head all the way to my toes and back. It was slow enough to braise my cheeks with heat. When his eyes landed back on mine, he grinned.

"I never fully appreciated that outfit on you until right now. You are a damn sexy femme fatale." He crossed the distance and planted a kiss on my lips. "And I am so looking forward to getting you alone with that sweet cream filling after this."

I forgot about my side comment about the decadent filling of one of the cook's pastries.

Images of what I would do to him erased all the snapshots of the nightmare, and I smiled back, pushing him toward the door. I wanted this over as quickly as possible, too.

As we walked out of the castle, the brightening dawn ate through my desire replacing it with the daunting task of finishing this fast. I needed to be sharp, focused on the task and not on what might happen after.

I turned my mind away from the idea of Tavin's touch and centered everything toward taking down Ava and then issuing our ultimatum.

Tavin squeezed my hand as we crossed into the cavern. I expected my lungs to close, but I guess touching him gave me the ability to breathe and not feel that oppressive magic when I'd first entered this barren cave.

More recent bodies dotted the floor, all suffocated from the magic. My heart thundered. What if we ran into another assassin?

The answer was easy. We would tear their soul out on sight.

I had Hanna's chip tucked into my pocket and her blood coating my right hand. Tavin had the chip from Ramik in his pocket and his left had coated with Ramik's blood. We stepped through the barrier onto the ledge in the far cave. Death hung on the air in here as well.

More bodies lay scattered over the ground, impaled.

How many assassins had the Director sent before someone got through?

Tavin closed his eyes, letting the glamour of Hanna fall over me and Ramik fall over him. I blinked and then gazed at him, scrunching up my nose.

"You don't like this view?" Tavin asked, waving at his new form.

"Not particularly."

He scanned me and nodded. "Same here. I much prefer Mya."

Now for the difficult part. Fooling the portal that materialized before us.

THE WITCH ASSASSIN
CHAPTER TWENTY-THREE

I HAD PRACTICED PULLING portals to where I was at least a dozen times in the castle and making them disappear just as fast. I would tap that skill once we got the Director's assent that he would forever leave us be. It was our escape, and it was a unique part of my makeup. One that the Director had programmed into me with portal guardian blood.

But fooling a portal into thinking you were someone else based on glamour and blood? I didn't think that was possible. But here we were, trying it anyway. My hand was soaked in Hanna's blood, and Tavin's was doused in Ramik's as we stood outside the portal on the ledge.

With our hands clasped together, each of us raised our blood-soaked fingers and swiped the portal. I had the destination in mind, the one right in the center of the complex. The moment we stepped out, we'd have to start acting or yank souls.

The portal opened, and we were pulled in together, side by side. I kept my nerves in check and pretended as if I belonged. Tavin was wound just as tight on the inside, but he projected sureness as well.

When we stepped out into the portal room at the complex, it was empty, which was very strange.

Tavin looked at me as if he could read my confusion.

I thought the Director had it manned at all times. Then I heard the sounds of a toilet flushing.

I didn't want to get caught in the room, and I didn't want to wander the halls of the compound. Instead, I pulled Tavin with me, zapping us directly into my room. It looked exactly like I'd left it, except Snape looked a little sluggish in his cage.

Tavin let out a soft laugh. "She has a heart," he whispered.

I smiled and unclasped his hand before crossing to the tank that held my snake. I opened the top of the case and took a moment to pet him before I set him on the bed.

I conjured two dozen mice, and he lunged, swallowing one in a single bite.

Tavin shifted as a mouse ran over his foot. His expression of disgust nearly threw me into a fit of laughter. But we didn't have time for appreciating the humor of the moment.

"Happy hunting," I whispered to the snake.

With him not locked away, I knew he'd follow these mice wherever they led him. Under the bed, into the walls, and eventually out to freedom. Knowing the snake was free made me feel so much better.

I turned to Tavin, ready to finish the job we'd come here to do. This hadn't been part of the plan, but by the amused look in his eyes, he understood my digressing.

Now for a bigger hurdle. If the timing was wrong, we'd be screwed.

I reached for his hand, and he threaded his fingers through mine before giving me a reassuring squeeze.

"Relax," Tavin whispered and pulled a small straw from his pocket.

Inside was the only dart we had to subdue Ava before she used her magic.

Instead of harping on the what-ifs circling my mind, I focused on the Director's home in the subterranean floors, where the night walkers lived. I prayed Ava lived in the same apartment structure. If not, this was a fool's errand.

The pull gripped us, and I opened my eyes to an apartment that would rival the bungalow in opulence. Instead of a window with a beach view, a mural painted on the wall depicted nearly the same type of natural beauty that Eleka held.

Tavin nodded toward a room to our right.

The sound of a running shower came from that room. But we didn't know if it was the Director or Ava, and we were not anywhere inconspicuous.

"Oh."

We spun in the direction of the voice from behind us. Ava stood with her coffee cup clutched in her hand. A swinging door behind her swished closed.

"Ava," I said and forced a smile.

Tavin covered his mouth with his fist and coughed in her direction.

"We've just gotten back from Eleka and needed to speak with the Director," I said, remaining in character.

The dart Tavin shot under the cover of his cough lodged into the side of her neck. I moved toward her just as she started to collapse, catching the cup while Tavin grabbed her and folded her into the chair facing the bedroom.

It all happened so quickly and flawlessly that my eyes were as wide as Ava's. Whatever Tavin had given her had fully incapacitated her to the point she couldn't speak, but her eyes moved, and she understood just how precariously close to death she was.

Tavin stripped our glamours, yanked out the dart, and pocketed it. He pulled one of the knives out of its holder and placed it against her throat, holding her hair so she faced the bedroom.

"Freeze..."

No sooner had the order slipped out of someone's mouth than a thump hit the floor near where I assumed the kitchen was. Ava's personal guard lay dead on the floor almost in the same spot Ava had been hit with the tranquilizer.

I glanced at Tavin, and he just shrugged.

Ignoring the dead man in the room, I moved in front of Ava and squatted. "Whether you survive today or not is based on the Director."

The water went off in the room behind me.

I stepped next to Tavin and slid my arm through his elbow. Touching him calmed my nerves.

"Ava?" The Director came sliding out of the bedroom only in a pair of slacks as if he had somehow been alerted to the danger.

I guessed there could be some level of silent communication between the two of them, or at least the emotional connection like Tavin and I had. Her fear could have sent him into the room with us with that alarmed look on his face.

His chest was so white that he looked like he could almost be made of stone. His eyes widened at the sight of the knife against Ava's throat, and then they darted between me and Tavin.

He put his hands out, splaying his fingers. "Don't hurt her."

Tavin's rage zipped through me.

"You had my mother killed," he hissed, barely containing the beast running amok inside him.

"Tavin," I whispered without taking my eyes off the Director.

This wasn't the script we'd talked about.

The Director had the audacity to grin. "And I got confirmation that your world exists, along with royal fae blood."

"My mother was a commoner. She did not harbor royal blood," Tavin growled, and the Director's smug smile fell.

A crease appeared between his eyes as they dropped to Ava. He probably expected her to get them out of this. When she didn't so much as move a muscle beyond her bulging eyes, the Director blinked a couple times.

"What did you do to my mate?" His voice cracked.

Tavin's jaw tightened, and he leveled the kind of smile at him that would normally make anyone lose their bladder.

"Guards!" the Director yelled.

The door burst open. Bodies flowed in. Both guns and knives were drawn.

I yanked at the same time Tavin did. Every last guard fell to the ground, but not before pain bloomed in my hip and a gun report echoed through the room.

Tavin's jaw was tight, but I didn't see anywhere that he could've been hit and bleeding. Then I dropped my gaze to my leg. A knife stuck out from my flesh, and relief swept through me. That was the only spot that hurt.

Ava grunted. I stepped closer to the chair. Her arm was bloody, and the fabric of the chair arm was splattered with her blood. She wasn't going to die from that wound. I wasn't going to die either.

Tavin's raw anger bloomed in my center.

Before he lost his shit, I said, "Here's the deal. You make a blood promise with me that you will back the fuck off, and no one from this compound, along with no one remotely associated with the League of Supernatural Assassins, will ever set foot on Eleka again. No assassins. No word of its existence to dignitaries. Nothing and no one is to know. Otherwise, we will end Ava. Thus ending you."

The Director's eyes were still glued to Ava. His face turned a shade of red I had never seen on him before. I didn't think it was possible for a night walker to turn that color, but here we were.

He glanced at the dead guards and then back at me. "I'll agree, if you agree to return to the League of Supernatural Assassins."

Tavin laughed. "No. She belongs with us. Agree to the terms or die."

He pressed the knife harder against Ava's throat. A line of blood bubbled around the edge, adding more wounds to the Director's mate.

Ava squeaked, her eyes as wide as saucers. Death frightened her. After all, she'd bonded with a night walker just for immortality.

The Director ran his hand through his wet hair and growled at me, his fangs more pronounced than usual. "Then send back my other assassins."

"They're all dead." I crossed my arms. "Just like your elite guards."

I waved toward the dead on his apartment floor.

His eyes narrowed. "I see you've fully embraced your demon side."

His gaze moved to Tavin as if looking for shock.

"The prince knows what I am. Stop playing games. Agree to the terms, or you'll find out just how painful death can be."

His eyes darkened, and his face scrunched in fury. "Fine."

I yanked the knife from my leg and limped to the Director, keeping my good side facing him. I held my hand out for his palm. He obliged with an angry hiss. His glare was deadly enough to nearly make me shake uncontrollably, but with all my preconceived notions torn away, the Director didn't frighten me to inaction or peeing my pants anymore.

I dragged the blade against his palm, then mine, and slapped my open cut against his. "Do you promise to uphold your end of the deal?"

He clenched his teeth and then relented. "I will not send anyone from the compound, or anyone related to the compound, to Eleka ever again, and I will not divulge that Eleka is anything but what the realms believe it is to any visiting dignitary in exchange for my mate's life."

"Or any dignitary that you visit, or anyone else for that matter," Tavin added.

"And I will not divulge Eleka's true nature to anyone here or abroad," the Director growled.

Satisfied, I nodded and backed away. There was no way I would ever turn my back on him in the state of near irrational anger he was projecting.

"But if you ever set foot on any other realm, I'll make sure you pay dearly." His furious smile shook me to the core. "And you still need to make it through this building to the portal room."

I stopped next to Tavin. He hadn't removed the knife from Ava's throat. His need for vengeance pounded in my muscles.

"He'll never stop coming after us if you renege on the deal," I whisper.

Tavin's low snarl rocked the room, but he pulled the knife away, letting go of Ava. She slowly collapsed onto her side.

The Director took a step in her direction but stopped when Tavin pointed his knife at him.

"I have her blood. I can get to her from anywhere. If you renege on leaving my kingdom alone, and that includes Mya, I will make sure Ava's death is painful, and you will feel every bit of it." He sheathed his blade. "And with the blood pact with Mya, we will know if you break the deal."

"As far as this,"—I waved at her limp form—"she'll be back to her old self in a little less than twenty-four hours."

He sneered at me. "The minute you leave, I will sound the alarm. Good luck getting to the portal alive."

I grinned and then waved my hand. "Thanks for the portal guardian blood, you coldhearted dick."

A portal opened in front of me. I handed the knife to Tavin. He sliced his hand and sheathed the blade before we clasped our uncut hands.

The Director's eyes nearly popped out of his head.

We swiped our blood on the opening, and the portal sucked us in. The Director's yell of rage followed.

I slammed the portal closed behind us, thankful it didn't require me nearly bleeding out to accept us. Pain rippled through me, and I glanced at my leg. The damn portal actually had required more, and my blood pumped at a higher-than-normal rate, satisfying the portal's greed.

"Greedy little bitch," I muttered and almost lost sight of our exit. "Fuck."

Tavin swept me off my feet, holding me close as we sped to the other side of the portal on his will alone. The minute his feet hit the ground in the cavern, he ran in a limping gait through the caverns and through his own hellish cage meant to stop those with ill intent.

He tripped once he made it outside the death cage but caught himself before we both went sprawling on the ground. Galen steadied him, along with his other guards.

"Healing salve," Tavin hissed through his teeth. "Her leg."

My legs dropped from his arm, and I tried to stand. The world spun. I guessed the number of souls I'd ingested in the Director's apartment had given me enough of a power kick for me to not recognize a serious cut. Now, the energy, along with a significant amount of my blood, was gone.

"Double fuck," I whispered, and my eyes rolled back.

I collapsed. Pain flared along my ribs as if a boulder had landed on me, and someone shouted directions, but it sounded far away.

Heat engulfed my leg, fading to a chill that saturated my bones.

And then the nothingness swallowed me.

THE WITCH ASSASSIN
CHAPTER TWENTY-FOUR

WARMTH WRAPPED AROUND ME, and I snuggled into it. Softness brushed my temple, making my eyes flutter open. My body hurt as if I had been through a blender and came out a lot worse for wear.

I groaned.

"Shhh, my sweet little demon," Tavin whispered in my ear.

I blinked the haze out of my eyes and glanced around Tavin's bedroom and down at the arms holding me. Tavin had me against his chest in a hold that could only be categorized as a death grip.

"Ease up, fella," I breathed out.

Even though his hold loosened, my chest still felt constricted, like I couldn't draw a deep breath.

I gazed down at the wrap binding my torso. "What the..."

"When you passed out, I passed out," Tavin said. "I guess my face is harder than it looks. I broke a couple of your ribs."

I couldn't help my snicker, but my chuckle evaporated at the black and blue highlighting his forehead and the side of his face.

"I guess my ribs must be pretty nasty if that's how *you* look." I slid my fingertips over the mark his fall had left.

Even bruised, my prince was still a stunning sight.

He gently kissed my cheek. "We still need rest."

"I need energy." Yet I cuddled into him further, taking his warmth and using it to stave off the shivers.

"I know, but you lost a lot of blood, and the cut on your leg was deep. It's still aching enough for me not to let you limp through the kingdom."

"I heal fast." While I enjoyed being in his arms, I did not want to be coddled.

I tried to move out of his grip, but he held fast.

"Do I need to tie you to the bed?"

I glared at him. "If you so much as try…"

He pushed me onto my back, and his lips crushed down on mine, cutting off my warning. He pulled away just as fast, and his face formed a stern hardness. "Rest."

His command irked me, but I really didn't want to be bound to the bed again. Not with the depth of intensity flashing in Tavin's eyes promising to act if I didn't obey. I settled back down with a nod, giving him my back.

"Just for another hour or so," I mumbled.

Well, that hour turned into half a dozen hours, and this time when I woke, I was alone in the bed, the windows were dark, and the shower was running in the bathroom.

My energy reserves were almost empty. I barely had the strength to stand. Damn Tavin for insisting I rest. Now I'd be lucky to stumble out onto the street.

Hell, if an assassin tried to attack, I didn't know if I'd have enough energy to yank their soul out. I shuffled across the floor to the bathroom as the water turned off. Tavin stepped out with a towel wrapped around his waist. The dark circles under his eyes mimicked just how lethargic I felt.

His gaze wandered to the door as though he sensed me standing there. The smile that formed in greeting was forced as if he didn't have the energy to tilt his lips up at the corners. "We have to get you out into a place where people are, don't we?"

"Yes. And you need food."

His stomach growled in answer. "I can wait. I don't think you can."

I raised an eyebrow and leaned my weight on the doorjamb. "I told you before I needed energy."

Talking sapped more of my reserves, just as standing did, but I was enjoying the view, bruises and all.

"And you needed rest, too." He slid on his clothing and towel-dried his hair, then ran his

306

fingers through it to get it into some semblance of order.

"Do you have restaurants in the kingdom?" I asked, thinking about all those that I'd passed in the cities I frequented over the years.

He nodded and glanced out the window. "Although the only things open at this time of night are the taverns."

"That'll do. But I need something that will cover me a little more than just these bandages."

He waved his hand, and a light, airy dress covered me. One that would fit in with the people of his realm.

The fabric caressed my skin and flowed like silk. Thankfully, he didn't make it too long. The skirt reached my mid-calf, and the footwear was more sensible than the spiky heels I had seen on some of the more well-dressed women. These were flat with leather straps that crisscrossed over my feet and wound around my ankles.

He crossed and offered me his elbow. I slid my arm through his, thankful for the support. I wasn't sure I'd be able to make the trek without some help.

"If you need to feed in the castle, just take a little. Not enough to affect the guards, okay?"

I glanced up at him with wide eyes.

"I know I told you my men were off-limits, but I think we will both end up face-planting on the street if you don't get sustenance now."

Without answering, I gazed forward as we approached the door to his suite, nervous at the prospect of taking too much energy from those in the immediate vicinity. Limiting my pull of energy when I was this hungry was difficult. Usually, the first person I encountered was left almost catatonic on their feet. They recovered, but only after a good long nap.

I couldn't do that to his guards, not when their protection was critical to our survival.

If anyone wanted to do us harm, there was little we could do about it. The only things between us and someone with nefarious intent were his guards.

I hesitated, stopping our forward progress. "I would rather not have your guards be the first people we see."

Tavin glanced at the door with his brow creased.

"I'm literally on the verge of collapse. When I'm like this, I tend to syphon more than usual. It's like giving a starving man a pile of steak." I prayed he'd understand.

His eyes widened, and then he murmured, "Ah" before he maneuvered me to a chair. Then he slipped through the door and whispered to the guards in the hallway.

A few minutes later, the door opened, and a handful of servants brought trays of food into the room. The infusion of energy was immediate and nearly overwhelming. I forced myself to stop when the last servant swayed with a tray balanced on his shoulder.

Tavin rescued the platter before the servant lost control over it. He smiled at the four men.

"Why don't you go rest now," he said.

They formed tired smiles and shuttled out of the room in a near-zombie state.

As soon as the door closed, Tavin looked at me. "Thank you for the warning."

He snatched one of those pastries with the citrus filling and pushed it into his mouth, then he moaned a little as he swallowed. He grabbed a handful and waved for me to follow him as he ventured out of the room, popping the pastries into his mouth one after the other.

The guards created a barrier around us as we headed out of the castle and into the near-deserted streets of the kingdom. Those who saw us paused, gawking and blinking like they had never seen the prince out for a stroll on the streets before.

"Why do they stare?" I whispered as I syphoned energy from all we passed, avoiding taking it from the four guards.

Galen glanced over his shoulder. "They've never seen the prince with a black eye."

His lips twitched into a smirk as he looked forward.

The bruise stretched from Tavin's forehead to his cheekbone, varying with different purple tones, some angrier than others.

"And to think, I wasn't even conscious when it happened." I touched my aching ribs.

Tavin's lips twitched, and then he reschooled his features. His gaze kept surveying the street, just like his guards.

Tension lived on the air as if the darkness had yet to be done with us. But I guessed after the last week of horrific events, everyone here had the right to be tense. Their peaceful existence had gone to hell in a blink, all because a seer had told me this was where the most powerful fae lived.

What if the Director had sent me here first? I would have been the one impaled on the razor-sharp stalagmites, and I would never know the draw of my mate or the feel of his mouth on mine.

But then again, his mother would be alive, and no one else would have breached the cave. Unless they had fae blood like the other assassins.

I shuddered. That would mean Tavin would probably be dead, too.

Tavin steered me toward a dark pub that vibrated with a bass beat. Inside was packed with fae, drinking, dancing, and having a good time. The energy level was through the roof, and I soaked enough in to feel like myself again as we crossed to the bar.

Tavin helped me into an empty seat and stood behind me with his guards at his back in a semicircle, facing out like this was the most natural thing in the world, but from the sudden quiet rolling through the club, I knew Tavin didn't do this often.

The bartender hurried over with eyes wider than the saucers on the shelf behind her.

"Y-your Royal Highness," she stuttered and then curtsied. "What can I get you?"

She ignored me completely.

He held up two fingers. "Your best nectar."

I spun the chair to face him and raised my eyebrows. I hadn't had nectar since I'd turned sixteen and a few assassins took me out and put a drop in my drink.

My memories of that night were hazy at best, so my eyes widened as two shot glasses full of the sweet potion slid across the polished wood in my direction.

I turned to Tavin with wide eyes as he held the shot, waiting for me to pick mine up. He cocked his eyebrow, and his lips twitched into a smile that promised things I couldn't comprehend. I glanced around us and sighed at the taut backs facing us and the patrons gawking at their prince.

Tavin leaned close. "I dare you, my sweet little demon."

My eyes narrowed, and I swiped the glass off the counter, sucking in a little more energy from around me because I had a feeling I would need it.

Tavin clicked his glass to mine and drained his in one gulp, then slammed the glass on the counter.

God help me, I did the same. The moment it hit my stomach, an unfamiliar warmth spread through me like fire. My limbs felt heavy, enough so when he ordered another round, I shook my head at him.

"Do you want me passed out cold?" I asked him.

His eyebrows rose as he looked at the drinks that had just been delivered.

"As it is, you may have to carry me home." I gripped the edge of the bar to settle the sudden swirl in my head.

"You can't handle nectar?" He reached for the second shot like he had no reaction to the potent drink.

I chuckled, tempted to take the second glass, but I knew with what I'd already drunk, I might black out. A drop of the stuff had nearly dropped me to the floor, and I had just taken a damn shot. How many drops were in that glass? Even so, my hand drifted to the second shot almost against my will.

"Are you trying to get me drunk and take advantage of me?"

He grinned and downed his drink.

My skin prickled. I stared at the drink in my hand as a feeling of being watched settled over me. I slowly set the drink down and stared at it, assessing my reaction. I muttered the same incantation that I had at the queen's funeral and then slowly turned my chair around, scanning the crowd. My gaze caught a disturbance in the air on the other side of the room.

I slid my gaze to Tavin. He stiffened as he glanced in the direction I had seen the disturbance.

There were assassins who could cloak themselves, becoming invisible.

My jaw tightened, and I took my drink, facing Tavin. Out of the corner of my eye, that same disturbance floated closer. Tavin looked at me, and his eyes clouded with irritation. He sensed the anomaly, too.

I took his hand and squeezed before I closed my eyes, zeroing in on the soul that my magic illuminated. Their intent was even clearer, and before they got within striking distance of the guards, I yanked, devouring the soul and giving myself an extra infusion of energy.

The body shimmered as it fell, knocking into patrons and making them spill drinks. When the assassin hit the floor, her body was in full view, like she'd just appeared out of nowhere.

Again, I recognized her, but I didn't know her name, just the number the Director had assigned her.

I always preferred a name to the numbers we were assigned. I could still hear my mother whispering mine in my ear. Perhaps the human witch side of me was more prevalent because I always inserted names in my head for the others

I lived and worked with as opposed to their numbers. It used to drive the Director bonkers.

People rushed toward the girl but stopped short at the knife still clenched in her hand that had been as glamoured as she had been. The blade glared in the colored lights blinking overhead to the beat of the music.

Their gazes darted up to our little group as understanding settled on the room, stilling everyone, even the guards.

Tavin and I scanned the crowd again, looking for any other disturbance or sign that there was intent to harm the prince or me. My magic still blanketed the space, but no one else was highlighted by it.

"He didn't keep his end of the bargain," Tavin growled, his fists curling tightly.

I huffed and shook my head. "There was plenty of time between the day of the queen's funeral and when you put up that barrier to slip at least one or two more in. I wouldn't jump so quickly to think the Director screwed us."

I glanced at the thin line still visible on my palm where we had traded the oath. It had not signaled a double-cross by the Director.

"I don't get the sense that he broke his word." I raised my palm to Tavin. "And I'd know the moment he screwed us."

Tavin took my shot, downed it, and then took my arm. "You good?" he asked as the tension weaved its way through him.

"Is there a way to get word out that whoever may still be on Eleka is permanently here? The portal is no longer accessible?"

He raked his bottom lip between his teeth as his arm wrapped around my waist, pulling me against him. "Spread the word. If there are any other assassins hiding in plain sight, they are stranded here. Their means to get home have been permanently blocked."

He let that settle even as alarm spread over the crowd's face and their eyes darted over the other patrons.

"Are we not hidden, Your Highness?" one of the older patrons asked, his face a mask of horror at the thought.

"We are still hidden, Harrod," he said to the old man. "And the breach in security has been taken care of. Although, there still may be a few souls that slipped through before I could fix the situation."

"Is that what happened?" He pointed to the prince's face.

Tavin's stiff features softened, and he gave the older gentleman a nod.

"If you notice any strangers who do not seem to know our traditions, please inform the king's guard. Do not take matters into your own hands." He escorted me out of the tavern with the four guards surrounding us.

Before the door closed on us, I syphoned another serving of energy from the crowd, enough to satisfy me and leave the people a tad more tired than they had been. Tired enough to call it a night.

I glanced back as people filtered out after us, as if our departure had signaled the evening was over.

The journey back to the castle was much tenser than the walk to the tavern. More people were out, and with a silent threat hanging over us, our muscles wound tight as we waited for another gauntlet to fall.

THE WITCH ASSASSIN
CHAPTER TWENTY-FIVE

THE MINUTE WE ENTERED the castle, Tavin headed for his father's rooms. We found the king lounging in his living room with a platter of pastries and a book in his hand.

Tavin ran his hand through his hair as his father's gaze rose from the words on the page.

"I just wanted to be sure you and your guards were on alert. There may be stragglers from the portal still here," Tavin said.

The king cocked his head as his gaze moved between the two of us.

"We went to Milly's Tavern, and Mya detected and annihilated an assassin there."

The king marked his page and set the book aside, giving us his full attention as he seemed to formulate his thoughts. "Your mission failed?"

Tavin glanced at me and shook his head. "There have been no other breaches since I put up the outer barrier. But as Mya pointed out, there was a period of time between the queen's death and when I put the extra magic in place, enough for one or two more to slip through."

"But you don't know." He straightened.

Tavin shook his head. "No. We don't."

"The Director hasn't broken our deal. Besides, he's a coward, and regardless of how much I angered him, he isn't going to chance his existence for revenge." I knew we'd pissed him off, but both his and Ava's fears of dying were greater.

However, I had to wonder, if there was another assassin or two still here on Eleka, would the taste of freedom knowing they could never get back to Icarus change their mission?

Mine changed because of Tavin and his recognition of what we were. That we shared a soul, and if I killed him, I killed myself. It wasn't the lure of freedom or even love that had changed me. It was self-preservation.

The king nodded slowly. "I'll keep it under advisement. In the meantime, I'll raise the threat level here at the castle."

He picked up his book and returned to reading without a formal dismissal.

Tavin escorted me out, and we traversed the castle to his rooms. The moment we stepped inside, Tavin closed the door and leaned on it, sagging under the release of tension. When he turned, his gaze flitted beyond me to the buffet still laid out.

"There's nothing we can do about an assassin tonight." His piercing gaze shot through me before he cracked the door and whispered instructions that I couldn't make out.

As soon as the door clicked closed again, he crossed to the food and took a seat, then he picked at a little of this and a little of that.

With each bite, his grumbling stomach settled, and a healthy rose hue bloomed at his cheeks. His eyes brightened when he licked the remnants of the pastries off his fingers.

A knock on the door interrupted his grazing, and dimples appeared, along with a knowing smile. His eyes slashed from me to the door.

"Come in," Tavin said, leaning back in the seat.

Monroe entered with a large bowl in his hands. He set it on the table, bowed, and retreated without a word.

The barely concealed smirk on Tavin's face had me do a double-take at what was in the bowl. He stood, grabbing the dish in one hand and my hand in the other, pulling me toward the bedroom.

Citrus wafted from the bowl.

Tavin closed the bedroom door and clicked the lock before he turned to me. In that moment, his gaze became predatory and focused. "I believe you promised to lick this off every inch of me."

My mouth popped open, and I looked at the yellow custard. When my gaze rose, Tavin was already undressed and stretched out on the bed. "But don't use it all because I want to return the favor."

His grin set my skin on fire.

I had indeed said I would lick this particular dessert off every delectable inch of him. I dipped my finger into the confection and slid it between my lips, sucking the lemon filling off. The pudding sent tingles of tartness over my taste buds, along with a sweet aftertaste that made me want to tip the bowl to my lips and chug it down in one long gulp.

But a promise was a promise, and his intense stare had stirred more than my taste buds.

Tavin waved his hand, and my clothing disappeared, leaving me only in the bandages around my chest and thigh.

I sauntered over to the bed and crawled up while balancing the bowl on my hand until I straddled Tavin. Then I settled down on his stomach, latching my knees to his sides like a vise.

I licked what was left on my finger before I dipped it into the batter and brought it to his mouth, coating his lips before I slid my fingers between them. Tavin's tongue swirled around my digit, licking and sucking the cream.

He closed his eyes and groans.

I considered dumping the bowl on his chest and rubbing it over his skin from head to toe, but I wasn't sure I wanted to waste the custard like that. Instead, I set it aside where we couldn't knock it over and leaned forward, pulling my finger from his mouth.

Before he could lick the custard from his lips, I licked it off slowly, tasting the sweet-tart confection. Then I attacked his mouth as if kissing him was more than enough. Our tongues mingled, twirling in a slow dance as I reached for the bowl and dipped a few fingers in.

Breaking our kiss, I met his gaze before I sat back up. I rubbed my hands together and then ran my fingers down both sides of his throat, trailing custard in wide rows from his jawline down to his collarbones. I had the man's undivided attention as I slowly licked the lemon filling from my hands.

I shifted into his hard shaft, moving myself down a few inches and trapping his cock between us. Tavin's eyes closed, and a satisfied growl rumbled in his throat.

I licked each line up to his jaw, cleaning his skin and delighting in the taste of the lemon filling mixing with Tavin, who was like a large, delectable candy himself. Sweet and sin, all wrapped up in a chiseled chest that tapered to a thin V-shaped waist and strong hips that led to thighs that could trap me any day.

With a finger coated in custard, I traced his left ear and ran my tongue from the tip of gold down the side and then nibbled on his earlobe before I whispered his name and slid my tongue into his ear.

He shivered under me, trying to push his shoulder up to stop me. "That's not where I want your mouth," he said, keeping his hands on my thighs.

I flicked my gaze to his bright-blue eyes and smiled. This was my first true exploration of his body. I knew the mechanics of sex, and I knew he melted when I sucked his dick, but I didn't know what else he liked. Tonight was mine to find out what brought him to his knees.

He liked when I licked and sucked his neck. He lifted his chin and gave me more access to the spots he really enjoyed, and he basically purred. However, when I nipped his skin, that sexy growl of his came forth, making me wet with anticipation.

I kept moving down his body. Nipples and his belly button seemed to be spots that produced a satisfied purr.

It wasn't until I got to his inner thigh that his muscles reacted, tightening under my touch as his cock twitched. I sucked off his thigh until a red mark marred his skin. I turned my attention to his other thigh, marking him in the same way before I lathered his balls in the lemon custard.

His hands balled in the sheets, and he groaned as I took his ball sac in my mouth.

"Fuck, Mya." His breath quickened with that low rumble in his chest as I slathered his hard cock with the pudding.

I paused to lick the dessert from my palms before I took my tongue from the base of his shaft to the tip, swallowing the treat. I licked him clean and swirled a fingerful over his sensitive tip. Then I slipped him into my mouth and sucked, keeping my eyes on his hooded gaze.

He kept his hands gripping the sheets, letting me spoil him without taking control. I licked back down to his balls.

"Suck me, Mya," he said as I started to move down his legs.

I flicked my tongue over him before ignoring him and moving down his thigh to his knee.

He groaned in response, tilting his head back as if this was all too much. I went all the way down to his toes before moving to his other leg and worked my way back to his hard shaft.

His veins stood out, and the pattern of his breathing and clanging of the blood rushing through him echoed in me. I wanted to feel him inside me, but I focused on bringing him to the edge of reason. I slowly lowered my mouth over him, sucking more to get a rise out of him.

His hands captured my head, threading into my hair, pulling my mouth down his shaft while his hips pressed him deeper. His control burst as he fucked my mouth with frantic abandon, growling his satisfaction as I sucked as hard as I could.

With three deep thrusts, he lost it, sending his seed down my throat in a torrent. I sucked and swallowed until his grip released me.

He stared at the ceiling, catching his breath. Before I pulled fully away from him, he grabbed me, twisting until I lay with my back to the sheets where he had been. His eyes reflected his need to retaliate. To make me quiver under his touch the way I had to him.

With a wave of his hands, bindings clasped around my wrists and ankles, spreading me out into the same position as he had me in that first day in the lockup. But the restraints were soft leather instead of steel shackles.

"I want you undone and panting for me, needy like you've never experienced. Begging for me to take you. To fuck you." His fingers dipped into the cream, and he spread it over my lips before he stuck his fingers into my mouth for me to devour.

And then he brutalized my mouth, demanding more from me with a kiss than I could ever dream.

I moaned as he attacked my throat, holding my chin up so he could lick and nip to his heart's desire. By the time he moved down to my breasts, I was already panting.

"You are mine until the gods decide to rip us from this land."

His whispered words flushed over me like a binding promise, and then his teeth pierced my skin at the top of my cleavage. Branding me with his mark. It spiraled through me like a whirlwind engulfing me, heating me from the inside out.

He licked the wound before he moved onto my other breast. "Do you accept me in the same way?" he asked and then sucked the hard pebble of my nipple.

"Yes!" I cried out, arching into his mouth despite the binds stretching me.

That whirlwind surrounded us, drowning out my moan as he slid down to my belly button, avoiding my bandaged ribs.

He spread the custard on my abdomen and then licked it off in long, slow strokes the way I had done to him. His eyes never left mine, and his hint of dimples appeared, showing me his smug satisfaction at my whine.

I wanted him lower. Every nerve screamed for him to find the spot that drove me crazy, but all he did was skim over my core, teasing enough to make me growl. I understood the tension and irritation that had bloomed from him when I went down his leg instead of giving his cock the attention he craved. He did the same, ignoring my whispered pleas and instead lining my thigh with cream.

He flowed down, skipping over the bandage on my thigh to my calf and foot. His tongue sliding up my insole sent tingles of heat through me, and seeing him suck my toes nearly undid me. It was far more intense than a foot massage.

By the time he licked his way up my other leg, I was trembling. He spread the filling over my center and left a mound of it over my sensitive bud. Then he lifted my ass and licked from the back to the front so slowly that I thought I would lose my mind.

And when his mouth settled over my clit, sucking the pudding off, I pushed my hips into him, wanting more.

His tongue flicked me, and I let out a low moan in his name. His thumb pressed against my anus as his fingers slid into my dripping path.

The feeling of fullness pulled another cry from my lips. He relentlessly tongued my clit, fluttering his tongue back and forth, building the heat inside me.

I writhed against the bonds and both his fingers, and his mouth continued fucking me into oblivion. When the orgasm hit, my back arched, and my scream filled the room.

"You are my sweet little demon," he whispered against my core, pulling his hands away.

I whined again at the emptiness, but Tavin climbed up my body, kissing every inch of me. He waved the binds away and teased me as his shaft dragged across my opening, dipping in just enough to make my eyes roll back.

"Please, Tavin," I whispered, trying to pull him in with my hips.

"Please what, my sweet demon?" He stared down at me with the same intensity flowing through my blood.

"Please fuck me," I said, staring into his eyes.

He slowly grinned. "Mark me and I will."

"I already marked your thighs."

"No, Mya. Mark me where everyone can see that I belong to you."

His words settled into me, and a fierce possessiveness followed as he tilted his neck so I could access the spot where his shoulder began. The tender skin at the juncture beckoned me.

"Brand me as your mate." He swiped his finger into the bowl, taking a small amount of cream and wiping it where he wanted me to place my mark.

I stared at the lemon custard and then into his eyes. What I saw there made me lean forward and suck the pudding away before I clamped down with my teeth.

His hips thrust forward with a groan, sending me over the edge again. I licked the blood from his skin, moving my gaze to his.

"Mine." It was the only word I was able to utter as wind whipped around us, and his mouth claimed mine in a rough kiss that matched the fervor in which his hips pounded into me, claiming all of me.

Undoing me as I howled my pleasure.

By the time we finished, the bowl had been knocked off the bed, and the sheets had been balled up into an utter mess. Our marks were no longer bloody bites, but Elvren mate runes embedded in our skin like tattoos.

Tavin rolled onto his back, his chest huffing with exertion. He tucked me into the crook of his shoulder.

"That was world bending." His voice was rough and scratchy.

I traced my fingers across his chest and looked down at the floor at the last of the pudding splashed on the rug.

His gaze followed mine, and he let out a laugh. "Don't worry. We can get more of that any time you'd like."

"I know. It's just a waste flung on the floor like that." I brought my gaze back to his and let my lips tilt into a smile.

I swung my leg over him and twirled my hips, running my fingers down his chest as he jerked to life under me.

"You're going to kill me one day, Mya," he whispered and gripped my thighs, moving with me. "But damn, what a way to go that will be."

He sat up, and his hands moved to my face before he kissed me hard, demanding more.

I met his demands, and found my soul was finally at peace here in this hidden kingdom.

The End

Continue with THE ELVREN ASSASSIN on the next page!

BOOK TWO
THE ELVREN ASSASSIN

Mya is missing. And the Director wants her back. Or worse, dead.

Avery's mission was to find Mya, the lost assassin, who stepped through the portal to Eleka and disappeared. If Avery finds her, she must bring her home, or if Mya is unwilling to return, Avery must kill her.

But Mya was the only assassin at the complex who saw Avery as a person. She even gave her the name Avery instead of only the numbers issued to each assassin by the Director.

This is not a job she wants. But she's one of a handful of assassins with fae blood, and she has no choice but to follow the Director's orders. If she fails, her handler will pay the price.

And he has angel blood like she does, which makes him the closest thing to kin that she has.

Her only hope is to find Mya and convince her to come home. Or Avery will witness her handler's death before her own.

THE ELVREN ASSASSIN
CHAPTER ONE
Avery

THE DIRECTOR OF THE League of Supernatural Assassins paced in front of twenty of us, rattling on about our mission, but my mind was stuck on Mya. Mya, the best and most dedicated assassin in the league, was missing.

I refocused on the Director as he ran his hand through his white hair, stretching the ends until he looked like a mad scientist.

I smirked because he was a scientist, and we all thought he was madder than the crazy Ilyium who hunt us. Or so I'd been told.

I'd never left Icarus before. My training to fight and kill had been extensive, but it was something I had yet to put into practice. I fidgeted in my seat at the thought of an actual mission. My stomach flipped, and I glanced around at the other trainees being sent into the field.

The experienced assassins lined the front row, and the rest of us filled the seats behind. I recognized a few faces but not all of them, so I wondered what dorms they were from.

"You are here because we have found that the portal to Eleka reacts much more favorably to those with fae blood. You are to find Mya and bring her back." His gaze landed on the front row. "Those with more training will bring me back royal DNA."

"What if Mya is dead?" the assassin in the front asked.

"Then bring me her body. We found this in Eleka's portal room." He held up a chip. One that everyone in the room recognized. It looked like the chips the Director placed in each of our bodies to track us or to disable us if he so desired. "Her body wasn't there, so that tells me Eleka is not dead like we thought." He handed the chip to one of the assassins. "Be sure to send a message to the royal family."

He got a nod in return.

"If Mya is not being kept against her will, then she is your enemy. Understand?" He pointed at a girl in the front row. "I don't care if you shared a room at one time or not. She is the enemy if she is there willingly. Bring her back by force if you have to, or kill her and bring me her body."

He looked over the small crowd. "Understand?"

"Yes, sir!" we all said in unison.

He stared us down, and I tried not to shift in my seat when his gaze settled on me. "If you fail, you and your handlers will pay the price." That settled over the room like a wet blanket. "Be ready to go in twenty minutes."

His curt nod was our cue to leave, and the twenty assassins in the room made their way through the exit near the back.

I hurried to my room to change and gather my weapons. As I turned the corner, I drew up short at the sight of Ren, my handler.

Ren was at least a foot taller than I was, with black hair that fell in soft curls to beyond his shoulders, and he was all muscle. Believe me, I had a difficult time knocking him to the mat, no matter how hard he drilled me in training sessions.

He leaned against the wall next to my door with a scowl on his supple lips. It intensified upon seeing me.

"What's up?" I asked as I swiped my fingers across the door pad to my dorm.

The door swished open, and Ren remained silent. I paused in the doorway and met his sharp gaze.

"You missed your morning training." His crossed arms flexed under his shirt as if he were a breath away from striking something. Even his white wings rattled with tension.

"The Director called a bunch of us in to get ready for a mission." It surprised me he didn't know this already, but from the way his eyebrows shot up, this was probably breaking news to him.

His arms dropped, and his steel-blue eyes narrowed as if itching to call bullshit.

"If you don't believe me, go ask the Director yourself. I have to get ready to go."

Normally, I did not argue with him or cut him off or walk away like I was about to do. That usually ended with me on the ground and Ren lecturing me about appropriate behavior.

"Where are you going?"

"Eleka." I didn't have time to expand on the rest. If he needed to know the details, he'd have to talk to the Director.

"And if I fail, both of us will pay the price," I muttered as I stepped into my dormitory room to change into my battle clothing.

The shared closet that the half-dozen assassins who cohabited this room used wasn't nearly big enough for all our things. My section only had a couple of items. One being exactly what I needed. My battle gear for assignments was the same color as my hair and wings. Purple and blue hues graced the suit, and they shimmered as I pulled it from the hanger.

Ren hadn't left. He remained leaning against the doorway with his arms crossed in front of him and one ankle hooked over the other. While he looked like he didn't have a care in the world, his sharp gaze never left me. He reminded me of a hawk scouting the ground for his next meal.

Although on closer inspection, Ren's eyes held concern. I had seen that look when I lost a training battle and had been reduced to a bloody, broken mess. The same look he wore now was that same concern he had leveled at me as he'd picked me up and carried my battered form to his room to patch me up.

As handlers go, Ren wasn't bad. He seemed eager to teach me all the techniques that would someday save my ass in the field. But he also wasn't above beating me to reinforce his point when others were around.

"Eleka's a death sentence. Why would the Director send you there?" He framed his question in a thoughtful tone, as if his mind kept circling the information I had given him.

This was not his usual demanding bark.

Because the Director did not want to lose his best assassin. That much was clear. He'd rather see her dead than lose her to another realm. But I kept my thoughts to myself as I pulled on my clothing.

Ren chewed on his bottom lip, and his angelic wings spread out when he straightened his back. His soft down appendages always amazed me. He was said to have been bred from the fallen, but his wings hadn't turned black like all of the other fallen.

Angel blood connected us and made him family. While he shouldn't ever show preferential treatment, he seemed to have a soft spot for me. The rest of the compound saw him relentlessly pushing me, but no one, especially the Director or his cronies, saw this softer side. If they had, they'd have put him to death ten times over.

The angel blood mixed with my fae heritage made my magic easier to turn on. I could glamour anything with this connection. My only other gift was that the angel blood gave me both strength and speed that surpassed a mortal being. It also boosted my healing abilities beyond what the rest of the assassins were bred with. Even though I had a pair of wings, they were more ornamental than useful.

I shivered at the thought of Mya being alive. Talk about gifts. That assassin could suck the energy from someone to the point they fell into an exhausted slumber. She also could conjure things at will. Her magic was as impressive as her energy tapping, and those didn't even hold a candle to her deadly fighting skills.

I couldn't believe she'd been bested by anyone, much less a dead planet. Not with her skills. My heart clenched at the thought of hunting her.

"He wants Mya back," I said after I sheathed my swords and daggers in their holders.

I ran my hand through my long locks, finger combing the knots out before I swept my hair behind me and squared my shoulders.

Ren's eyes widened. "You're hunting, Mya?" His voice cracked with the question.

"That's the task. Bring her back dead or alive." My gut twisted. I would likely end up being the one dead, but I had to find her and talk some sense into her.

I was not going with the same "kill her" mentality that I saw in that room. Not with how she had treated me for all these years.

"Just don't do anything stupid," Ren said.

"I don't plan on it."

He grabbed me before I could slip past him and forced me to look at him. "I mean it. Mya is dangerous, and you don't have the same level of experience out in the field. So, use your head." He released me and wiped his face. "I'd rather deal with the whipping post than have you killed on this insane assignment."

"I will do my best not to get killed. Okay?"

He studied my gaze for longer than normal, as if he wanted to say more, but then he gave me a nod and stepped back.

I wasn't keen on a death mission, either. I had to at least try to reason with Mya.

Even if it put me in mortal danger.

THE ELVREN ASSASSIN
CHAPTER TWO
Avery

I STEPPED OUT OF my room, physically ready for my mission.

However, my mental state was not aligned, especially after Ren's concern. His strange behavior had me doubting my abilities and this mission even more than I was before.

Each step became heavier as I made my way down the sanitized hallway toward the portal room, which would dump us out on the barren surface of Icarus and the gateway to Eleka. It felt as if I would never grace these halls again once I slipped through that portal.

A shiver skittered up my spine, and I arched my back against it.

I slipped into the nearly full portal room and received a sour look from the Director.

"Good of you to join us, sixty-nine. You'll be paired with one-twenty-two for this mission." The Director's sharp gaze pinned on me as if he read my intentions to talk to Mya instead of using violence as we were programmed.

I pressed my lips together against the need to correct him. I had never truly been sixty-nine. Mya had dubbed me Avery early on, and it had stuck. Even Ren referred to me by name as opposed to just a number.

Instead of stewing on the Director's obvious dis, I looked at my mission partner.

One-twenty-two gave me the creeps. She could become invisible and attack without mercy. Her presence meant I could not reason with Mya. Not without ditching the girl. From what the Director was saying, those of us who had never been on missions before were not to leave the side of our partners. So, dumping this one would be as dangerous as confronting Mya.

I moved closer to one-twenty-two. It was hard to miss her in the room with her spiked neon-green hair and ember-colored eyes that stood out like a beacon on her pale skin. I sure hoped she would blend in where we were going because she stood out even amongst fae blood.

She cut a glare in my direction and faced forward stoically, as if I were beneath her.

My wings fluttered in response, but I kept my mouth closed.

"My guards have programmed the outer portal to take you to Eleka." The Director's voice boomed over the room. "Remember your mission. I want her back on Icarus within the next forty-eight hours, or else your handler will pay for your failure. I don't care if she is alive or dead. Understand?"

"Yes, sir," all of us responded in unison.

He nodded to the first group of assassins, and the morbid procession began moving through the portal.

"What can I call you?" I whispered to my unwanted partner.

She slashed her gaze to mine, and she scrunched her brow. "One-twenty-two."

"Your handler doesn't have a nickname for you?" I had heard my fair share of name substitutions over the years, and sometimes they were decent enough to stick. Thankfully,

Mya had taken care of that for me, and Ren seemed to take to it as well.

She pressed her lips together and looked forward, her cheeks reddening. "Lo calls me Em because my hair reminds him of emeralds. That is the name I use on jobs if I have to interact with others."

"I shall call you Em."

"Don't."

"I can't call you by a number while we're trying to blend in on another realm," I mumbled under my breath. "It would be too strange."

She rolled her eyes at me, just like Ren always did.

Ren said I had an innocence that shouldn't have survived this place. We were supposed to be fierce assassins with zero feelings. I think somehow I was defective in that way. I kept my expression neutral around the Director and his guards, and when training in the groups, but when Ren and I were one on one, I smiled and laughed between sparring sessions enough for him to chide me regularly.

"Fine," she growled as we stepped closer to the portal.

My heart jumped in my chest as the two assassins before us stepped into place in front of the portal. Each of them held out their hands, and one of the Director's portal guards slashed a blade across their palms.

We were next.

I stared in fascination as the two more senior assassins swiped their blood on the outer shell of the portal, and what looked like an empty space inside churned with black smoke.

The guard gave a curt nod, and they stepped forward, engulfed by the dark fog.

The quick view of inside that foggy space made my wings flutter. I had no idea how I was going to find the nerve to step inside that frightening tube.

I swallowed hard and stepped into place, trying to school my features.

"Palms," the guard demanded.

Em immediately put her hand out. I was a fraction of a second slower, and she cut me another glare as the guard's knife bit into my skin. I couldn't suppress my hiss fast enough.

Em wiped her hand on her side of the portal entry, and I followed suit on mine. That black swirl rolled in the center of the entrance before widening enough for both of us to step through.

My mouth dried, and before I could retreat, I swallowed whatever fear had blossomed in my stomach and entered the portal with Em. Sweat pooled at the base of my back and tingled on my forehead, and I struggled to remember Ren's lessons on portal jumping.

"Focus on the white dot in the distance. That is your destination." Ren's gaze jumped to his window and the night beyond as he explained what the portals were like. *"If you let your mind wander, you'll drift off course and get cut up by the portal. So, remember to concentrate on that expanding dot."*

I blinked and replayed Ren's lesson in my head along with the mantra that this was just a short jump to the surface outside the complex.

I nearly tumbled onto the rocky outcrop of Icarus's outer portal plateau.

The chill of the night seeped into my skin, and I shivered, rubbing my arms as I glanced around at our surroundings.

The training towers of Icarus rose high in the distance. And behind me, the main portal shimmered, waiting to swallow us into the unknown.

THE ELVREN ASSASSIN
CHAPTER THREE
Ren

I STARED AFTER AVERY with my pulse pounding. She wasn't ready to go up against Mya.

Hell, I'd successfully buffered her for the past year from any job in the field. Which was probably why the Director didn't give me any heads-up.

I'm still not sure how I was able to keep her from being sent on an assassination mission. Especially since I had been sent out on my first job the day after I turned eighteen.

Dread built in my stomach, and I headed back to my barren room before my composure cracked enough for anyone to see underneath my facade. My senses weren't off this morning, and I knew something was wrong when she didn't show for our sparring session. I had every right to panic at her absence, but it wasn't for the reasons I thought.

If she failed at this job... I closed my eyes and hung my head.

Twelve years ago, I had failed, and they made me watch as they beat my handler, Amara, to death. Afterward, they beat me unconscious. I thought I was following her to the great beyond, but no such luck.

When I had woken in the medical bay with my jaw wired shut, a cast on my arm, and bandages around my ribs keeping my wings tucked in, the Director sat stoically beside me, waiting.

Amara had taught me some secrets relating to purebred angels that I never divulged to the Director. Things like being able to borrow powers from others if they allowed it, as well as telepathically checking in on anyone I was close to. She had also taught me the perils of healing others. She said if I wasn't careful, I could expend all my energy, and that would be a fatal mistake.

But in the Director's eyes, she had failed to beat the empathy from me. She failed to make me an assassin, which was the very reason for creating me.

And my failure brought about her death. She had one other protégé I had yet to meet because she was far too young to include in the brutal sparring sessions I encountered.

That young protégé was now my problem in the same way I had been Amara's. I was the last of the pure angel-blooded assassins in this complex, and if I couldn't beat the empathy response out of my new protégé, a half breed at that, I could expect the same result as my handler.

I shivered and stared out the window at the distant portal, where my only assigned assassin would jump to a dead planet for her first assignment. The procession of assassins heading to Eleka had already started, and I squinted, trying to discern Avery in the group. I recognized a few of the assassins just by some of their more noticeable hair colors. When Avery's lavender hair shimmered into view, I sighed.

The kicker of it all was I loved that girl more than my own selfish existence.

From the first moment we were introduced, my heart tugged toward her like she was specifically made for me. It was such a strong reaction that it scared the living shit out of me. But here on Icarus, when the Director laid down the law, it was a death sentence to break it.

I had no recourse but to follow through with every heinous act of dominance, to breed fear so strong that Avery wouldn't rebel against an order. I pushed her, but she never grasped the ruthlessness the others around her did.

Damned empathy.

After I'd watched her beaten to the point of unconsciousness, I'd bring her back to my room, lock the door, and use my angel heritage to patch her up just enough so she could function. She hadn't let me do that the last few times because she woke to witness what healing did to me.

But pain is pain. Whether it was seeing her broken or feeling those same punishing hits while I fixed her, it didn't matter; the effect was devastating.

God help me, when she turned eighteen, I started teaching her ways to seduce a man because that was the only way she would ever get close enough to deliver a killing blow.

Perhaps if I painted all men as selfish pricks, she'd be able to take a life, regardless of her bleeding heart. Then I'd never have to put her through the agony of seeing someone she cared about gutted and beaten until all they were was a pulp of ripped flesh and broken bones.

It was expressly forbidden for handlers to have sex with their assassins. But I could not help myself. She didn't have a clue about sex, and to be honest, the only introduction to sex I'd ever had was on that one job that I royally screwed up on in so many ways. One of which was being seduced by my mark.

So, I taught Avery the things that undid me while on that first job. But I kept it as impersonal as I could. Framing it as a teaching lesson for her survival, instead of satisfying my fucking libido.

I instructed her what to do with her mouth and her hands, but I never touched her with mine in the way I ached to. I knew if I allowed myself to indulge in that, it would be my undoing. The Director would probably make me watch as they killed Avery instead of the other way around.

I wasn't proud of my behavior, but I wouldn't trade those private moments for anything in the universe.

Now I'd have to wait and see what fate would deliver next.

My death. Or hers.

THE ELVREN ASSASSIN
CHAPTER FOUR
Avery

EM CLEARED HER THROAT and pulled a blade from her belt. She put her hand out.

I stared at her upturned palm and then met her gaze.

"I need to draw blood again." Her foot tapped on the ground, as if she thought I was daft. The snide tone didn't help, either.

Heat filled my cheeks. "Oh."

I handed her my palm, and a second later, the sting of the blade cut into my skin. I hissed air through my teeth.

Em glared at me and did the same to her palm before she shoved me into place on the other side of the gateway entry. She swiped her palm on the entry, and it swirled open. She aimed a raised eyebrow in my direction.

I replicated the same action, and subsequently, the force of the vortex pulled me inside. Em moved next to me as we trudged toward the ever-widening dot. My heart lurched in my chest, and I prayed we wouldn't die on entry like the rumors at the compound suggested.

The portal spit us onto a narrow ledge, and I stumbled. Em grabbed my arm so I wouldn't teeter off to my death on the deadly spikes lining the floor.

The magic in the cavern pressed down on me as I looked around. Dead bodies impaled on the stalagmites at the opposite end of the ledge we perched on tightened my stomach. Something rust colored and pieces of black fabric peppered the wall to the side of the ledge, right up to the point where the ledge began.

I swallowed hard, trying to shake off the heaviness pushing down on me.

Em pulled me along beyond the wall, where there was a small space to slip through into a larger cavern with a dead, decayed body lying prone in the center of the floor.

The magic in this room was different, almost hypnotizing, but not oppressive like the first cavern. We made our way out of the cave, and I halted at the magnificent, lush view before me.

I had only ever seen the vast desert-like landscape of Icarus in muted shades of red and brown, and the pictures of other realms in the study books always seemed so muted. The greenness of our new surroundings, along with the blue of the water in the distance, left me stunned.

The sky was a conglomerate of blues, lavenders, yellows, and oranges that was just as unnerving as the rest of the color overload pummeling my senses.

Em didn't seem fazed by the change in scenery and ushered me away from the cave entrance.

I glimpsed one of the other assassins heading in the opposite direction and traded a glance with Em. "Shouldn't we be going that way?"

"No." Em grabbed my wrist and shimmered, fading to just an outline that I could barely make out. Her magic pulled me along as she continued farther from the portal toward a crowd in the distance. "We're going to the market to see if we can overhear anything about Mya."

As we neared the market, the different fragrances drifting around us made my mouth water. I recognized the scent of fresh bread and cookies and some of the more savory dishes, and all of them made my stomach groan so much that Em glared at me.

"It smells wonderful." I closed my eyes and inhaled, indulging in the mixture of scents filling the air.

My hunger bloomed, clawing at my insides. Breakfast seemed like eons ago, when it had only been a couple of hours.

The market was more of a large square lined with little partitions for each vendor. Tables lined the opening, and clothing, food, herbs, lotions, and weapons decorated the different tables. I had never seen anything like it, and my overloaded senses didn't know where to look.

Men in neutral tunics walked beside women in flowing dresses that shimmered in the warm sunshine. I could never see myself wearing something so elegant. I'd be more likely to wear pants and a tunic rather than a dress. Dresses were impractical for anything but show. In the world of assassins, pants that moved with us were preferred.

"Be quiet and watch where you are walking. No one can see us, and we certainly aren't here to sample the local cuisine," Em snapped.

"Why not? It's right here." I waved at the various vendors as we entered the market.

I had never seen such a variety of food in one place. My gaze bounced across the aisles until it landed on the weapons dealer, and I stopped, pointing.

"No," Em muttered between clenched teeth and tried to yank me away.

"That's the type of place Mya would check out," I said, even though it was pure baloney.

I had no idea what Mya would look at, but considering how deadly she was, weapons made sense.

Em huffed but moved closer to the dealer's cubicle.

"I heard the prince has a new whore," a man looking at a set of knives said to the dealer.

The large man behind the counter laughed. "Is that why he went to their beach castle? So his father wouldn't find him?"

The man inspecting a knife chuckled. "Probably. From what I understand, she's a beauty."

"Who is she?" The dealer pulled out a matching pair of knives to the one the man held.

"No one I spoke to recognized her, so she could be some hussy from the beach community that caught his eye." He chuckled. "You know how he is."

Em pulled me away and kept us moving. When we passed a vendor who had maps of Eleka, she pocketed one before the vendor noticed.

As soon as we were out of earshot, Em said, "We need to head to this beach community that those men were talking about."

"Why?"

"I bet the woman they were talking about is Mya. Getting close to a prince rather than the king or queen is a sneaky way to get DNA for the Director."

I sucked air between my teeth at the reminder of the Director's quest for unique DNA for making more experimental assassins. While I was thankful for my existence, this just wasn't natural. His quest to breed the perfect assassin was always going to fail as long as free will was in the equation.

Em found a quiet spot out of sight and opened the map. "This is where we are now." She pointed at our current location. "It looks like we need to get down here. Think you can zap that distance?"

If the map was correct, the spot we were aiming for was as far from this side of the realm as possible. I had only teleported from one place to another at the compound, not across an entire planet.

"I don't know," I admitted.

Em rolled her eyes and pulled out a small satchel. "My handler made this to help with zapping in the event your teleporting skills were just as lame as your magical skills." She peered down her nose at me. "I only have one of these, so if Mya isn't there, you will have to figure out how to zap from there back to here because I'm not walking."

She grabbed my wrist, shimmered out of sight, and in the following moment, the satchel hit the ground. The pull of zapping from one place to another assaulted my muscles.

Em kept hold of me, keeping me upright when I stumbled on the soft sand. The ocean view was glorious, but Em turned inland towards the castle towering on the hill above. She kept hold of my hand, keeping us invisible, and we moved toward the only place a prince would likely be.

We dodged people on the walking paths, and when we had the palace doors in sight, Mya and the prince, decked out in fine clothing, stepped outside.

But the shock of seeing her in such finery was nothing compared to the sight of their hands clasped.

Four guards surrounded them, and suddenly, they vanished.

Em released my hand, and I shimmered out of her invisibility spell.

"Damn it," she said from the spot next to me. "That was Mya, right?"

I nodded, and my chest constricted. She did not look like someone who was being held against her will.

Which meant Em was going on a hunting expedition and wouldn't stop until she delivered Mya's cold, dead body to the Director.

Unless I could find a way to stop her.

THE ELVREN ASSASSIN
CHAPTER FIVE
Avery

"WAIT HERE AND TRY not to look so conspicuous." Em's voice moved away from me toward the castle.

A moment later, the air in front of the castle crackled just before the ground near me, some twenty yards away from the door, crushed under the weight of an invisible object.

"Avery?" A strained voice broke the stillness.

I moved toward the voice. "Em?"

"Who else would it be?" Her exasperation filled the gap between us.

I zeroed in on the disturbed gravel to my right and crouched toward her voice, reaching out, hoping I'd connect to her invisible form.

A hand gripped my forearm, and I shimmered out of view. In the same invisible state, I could make out her form on the ground.

"What happened?"

"Force field." She waved at the palace and used my grip to ease herself into a sitting position. "We aren't getting into that fortress to wait for their return. We'll come back after I get something to eat to recover from that damn blast."

I helped her to her feet, and she wiped off her backside, mumbling under her breath.

"And we'll need glamours to mix in at the market." She pointedly looked at me and raised an eyebrow.

"Can't we remain invisible?"

She glared at me, and I blinked as we transformed back to solid forms on the street. Thankfully, no one was anywhere near us to witness our solidifying out of thin air and see us in clothing that did not seem to represent this realm.

"I can't hold it without sustenance," Em said. "So do your thing."

"Oh." I nodded.

I shut my eyes and concentrated on the women we'd seen at the market near the castle when we first arrived. Their airy outfits didn't hide much. Certainly not the weapons we had stashed on our bodies, but we weren't actually changing. I needed to create a believable glamour for both of us.

With a clear vision in my thoughts, I opened my eyes and waved at Em, covering her in deep violets and dark blues.

My clothing was similar, but my colors were of a softer palette that matched my wings—lavender and pale blue.

She scowled at me and rolled her shoulders as if the glamour were as itchy as mine. Glamours tended to do that, but she said nothing as she marched back toward the town we'd cut through to reach the palace from the beach.

As soon as we got to the more populated areas, wailing filled the air. It was a far cry from the hustle and chatter we'd encountered on the way to the palace.

Despair raked across my back, and I traded a glance with Em. She wore the same confused expression that encompassed my entire demeanor.

The vendors in the market were rolling up their wares. We stopped at the baker's shop as he boxed the goodies on his table.

"Excuse me, can we grab a few of those pastries before you close?" Em asked.

The baker raised his bleary gaze and waved to the remaining goods on the table. "Be my guest. These will not keep until after the queen's funeral." He sniffled.

I gasped as Em started tossing pastries in a box the baker handed her without any reaction to his words. "Funeral?"

"The queen was murdered today," he said and sighed as he watched Em stowing away a feast.

The baker's sorrow filled me, along with everyone else's within the vicinity, hitting my overactive empath button. I covered my mouth. Ren said this was the one thing that would be my downfall. No other assassin had this affliction, and from the side glance I got from Em, I needed to curb my response.

"How much do we owe you?" I asked when Em stepped closer to my side with a glare that could peel off my glamour if I let it.

She opened the box so he could see what she had grabbed.

He waved us away. "No charge."

"Thank you," I said as Em grabbed my wrist and pulled me away.

When we found a quiet place under a large tree with white flowers to dive into the box of goodies, Em said, "You looked almost as devastated as the baker back there."

I huffed. Explaining my empathy to someone programmed to have none was a waste of my breath.

"The entire town is grieving," I muttered and took a pastry.

"I guess that's why the prince and Mya left in formal clothing. We should get ourselves to that funeral. It's the perfect place to take Mya out," she said around a mouthful of food.

I ate quietly, trying to figure out a way to delay our arrival. I did not want to see Mya killed, but I couldn't very well say that to Em.

"Won't the rest of the assassins be there?" I asked.

She nodded.

"Why don't we take our time in the event they fail?" I took a bite of a delightful berry-filled pastry and closed my eyes at the explosion of sweet and tangy tastes that captured my tongue. "These are fantastic."

Em had her mouth so full of pastries that she didn't speak, but that little crease between her eyes told me she was considering what I'd said. Finally, she nodded and offered me the remaining pastry.

"Do you think she's being kept against her will?" she asked while I wolfed the last bite down.

She wiped the crumbs from her lips and leaned back against the tree.

"I'm not sure. They were holding hands, but that could be a control thing for the prince." I would like to think she hadn't turned her back on the league, but if she had even an ounce of aversion to the Director that I had, maybe she saw this place as an opportunity to escape his tyranny, especially since they removed her tracker.

But she had to know the Director wouldn't just let her fade away into the woodwork. The Director couldn't lose his number one and number two assassins in the same month. That would cause too much friction in the ranks.

Em nodded and stood. "Think you can zap back to where we were before?"

"I've only zapped the length of the compound." I chewed my bottom lip as her face turned almost feral, as if she were considering killing me instead of Mya.

"I told you I didn't want to walk. That could take weeks, and we only have forty-eight hours to get this done." She trudged to the road and started walking away from the ocean.

"Where are you going?" I scrambled after her while my mind jumped to Ren. I didn't want to contemplate what would happen to him if we didn't show until after the deadline.

"North." She waved the map at me and then shoved it into her back pocket.

"We can make intermittent hops." I wished my wings actually worked. If they were like Ren's, and not these decorative, wimpy things, I could easily fly us back to the portal and the main castle beyond.

"Does zapping across the compound tire you?" she asked with a side glare.

"Well..." I sent her an apologetic smile.

It did tire me, but according to Ren, I'd get used to it before I was sent on a mission. Neither of us planned for me to be out in the field so early, though. Otherwise, he would have pushed me on that as hard as he'd pushed combat training.

"We don't have a steady stream of food like at the compound. Out here, we either have to hunt and prepare food or steal it, and stealing would raise flags." Each footfall of hers was heavy enough for me to feel the tremors in the earth below her.

"Why wouldn't we just pay for it like we were going to back there?" I hooked my thumb over my shoulder to the town behind us.

Her lips pressed together, and she stared at me. "Do you have any money?"

I blinked at her. No one had given me coins before we left. I shook my head.

"Neither do I. I had no intention of paying for that food, and I nearly took off your head when you asked him how much." She scowled at me. "You are very lucky he gave it to us. Otherwise, I might have taken you down along with him."

Her brazenness rubbed my skin wrong.

"And what would you have told the Director?" After all, he had told the more senior assassins that they were responsible for those of us who had no fieldwork under our belts.

"I would have told him the truth. That you are useless in the field." She continued moving toward our destination. "Your handler has done you a disservice."

"What do you mean by that?" I grabbed her arm, spinning her toward me, unable to accept a slight to Ren.

"He has not beaten your softer side out of you. You were nearly crying back there." She waved toward the town.

"Angels are natural empaths. Some just know how to hide it better," I snapped.

"Neither the fae nor the druids have that issue." She jarred her arm from my grip. "The only thing I feel is related to body functions. Hot, cold, hungry, tired. There is no place for empathy in our job. That's what your handler missed in his teachings." She poked my chest and spun on her heels, continuing on her way north, but she stopped after a few paces. "And if you don't eradicate that, the Director will eliminate you."

"Ren has told me the same thing." I couldn't help defending him.

"You'd do well to listen."

I caught up to her. "Even if I think he's wrong?"

"We do not have the luxury of thinking for ourselves. We follow orders." She leveled a hard stare at me. "Otherwise, we die. It's that simple."

Em was the same as every other assassin branded with a number versus a name. She was programmed to be this way. So was I, but it didn't take, not in the way it took with the rest of the assassins at the complex. Maybe it was the combination of fae and angel that allowed me to be stubborn and not programmable. After all, I came here with the hope I could convince Mya to leave with me.

If I couldn't convince her, I wasn't sure what I would do. I did not know if I could kill the only other assassin who seemed to have a sense of humanity.

Could I?

THE ELVREN ASSASSIN
CHAPTER SIX
Avery

WE WALKED IN SILENCE since there didn't seem like we had anything else to discuss. Em's hostility surrounded her, pelting me with each step we took.

The light had shifted during our walk, fading into night. Before all the light dwindled, Em pulled out the map and looked at a sign along the roadside. She pulled out a knife and punctured a hole in the map where we were and another where we wanted to be.

She also punctured a hole where we had been. We had not gone very far, even though we seemed to have been walking for a good part of the day.

I studied the distance and subsequently pointed to a spot on the map halfway between our current location and our intended destination. "I think I can make it here. Especially if we are zapping together."

It might tire me, but at this pace, I'd be uselessly exhausted if we walked the entire way, and our timeline would be blown to bits.

"Fine." She finally succumbed to reason and glanced at the map again before folding it up and sticking it back in her pocket. She hooked her arm in mine, linking us together. "Ready?"

I nodded, clasped my hands together to keep our connection, and closed my eyes, imagining the spot on the map. The center of my chest pulled, and Em's arm tightened around mine. One minute we stood on the road, and the next we were in unfamiliar terrain.

And we were sinking.

Cold water drifted over our heads, and I released Em and kicked, surfacing to catch a breath. Em popped up next to me, sputtering.

"Where did you dump us?" Her displeased tone carried across the water.

A plunk to our right startled me. My mind raced at the different predators that might be here. We didn't have any knowledge of this planet. It wasn't on the learning curriculum because the Director thought it was dead.

More plunks sounded from the right.

"We need to find land." Em started toward the noise.

My skin tingled. "Em, I don't think we should go that way."

Even though trees lined the distance beyond her, something was out there and hunting us. That empath part of me felt a basic, animalistic need approaching.

Whatever it was, it was close enough to transmit its feelings and make my heart stutter in my chest.

Em swam in front of me by a few paces, leading the way.

The water rippled to our left, and then Em screamed and vanished underneath the surface.

I unsheathed my knives and dove. A large reptile had Em's torso between its jaws. She pounded on its head, trying to get the thing to loosen its grip.

I plunged a knife into its scaled back. It released Em and turned its razor-filled mouth toward me, but it couldn't twist around enough to catch me in its jaws.

The beast was a hideous reptilian creature that reminded me of the makaras I studied from Elbeeon. It was similar to Earth's alligators and crocodiles but was far more deadly because of their claws and barbed tails.

I plunged my second knife into the middle of its back while pulling out the other, repeating the motions until I got to the back of its neck. That puncture hit something, and the creature stopped thrashing.

My lungs burned. I dislodged my knife and used the disgusting creature as a springboard to the surface. I gasped air in and headed toward shore, but my skin felt as if someone had raked nails from my ribs down to my knees. Still, I pushed myself, because my empathic abilities still brewed.

There were more of these predators in these waters.

I muttered a protective spell that would deflect the beasts away from me. I wasn't sure how accurate my enunciations were, though, so I led with my knives, sweeping them to the sides with each stroke, hoping to stave off another attack.

Em had gotten to shore but remained on her hands and knees, coughing out water. As I stumbled ashore, she turned, holding out her knife as if I were the beast that had attacked her.

She blinked up at me. "I thought that thing got you."

My knees buckled, and I dropped to the ground. "No such luck." I glanced backward at the rippling water. "But we aren't far enough away to be safe."

I moved closer to Em, threw her arm across my back, and forced both of us to our feet.

Em was in bad shape. Blood bubbled out of the punctures in her body every time she inhaled, but at least she was still breathing. We stumbled forward, and the soggy ground gave way to a harder surface. I muttered a spell to dry our clothing, and the wind whipped around us, making Em hiss as we pushed against it toward what I hoped was safety.

"You had to zap us right into a bog, didn't you?" Em coughed and sputtered through the words, but at least she wasn't stabbing me with the knife still clasped in her hand.

I didn't know if she even realized she held the weapon. I still had mine as well.

"Can you stand for a moment?" I asked as I halted.

She gave me a sigh and a nod.

I sheathed the knife that was in the hand I had around her and resumed my position, allowing her to lean on me. Both our outer hands were still armed with knives in case the forest was as daunting as the pond had been.

We stumbled into the unknown.

THE ELVREN ASSASSIN
CHAPTER SEVEN
Ren

I WORKED OUT. I ate. I paced the same patch on my rug by my window throughout the night.

Every time I closed my eyes, I could sense her, and I wished she were here. The more time passed, the more I was sure Eleka was not dead, and Avery would have to contend with Mya.

By the morning, my stomach was in knots, and I didn't think I got much more than a half hour of shut-eye.

Instead of going to the gym for another day of brutal routines meant to exhaust me, I headed to the cafeteria. I piled my plate with protein and sweets, bypassing healthy choices in favor of comfort foods.

I headed toward an empty table in the middle of the cafeteria, but I caught sight of one of the seasoned assassins I swore had gone to Eleka with Avery. His hair was a flaming orange that I had seen near the portal last night. I stopped a few steps beyond their table, where this asshat recounted his adventures to the others surrounding him, as if killing was worthy of a medal.

I sat in the extra seat, and the conversation stopped. All their gazes swiveled to me, and they stared as if I had grown a second head.

"You were saying?" I prompted the fae hybrid with what I hoped was not a challenging smile.

"This job was easier than anything I've ever done. They had no security at all, as if danger didn't exist in their realm." He grinned and shoveled a mouthful of food into his open maw. "Killed the queen, got her blood, and left an explosive in her and directions for the other assassins to detonate at the funeral."

He grinned like the psychopath he was.

"Eleka?" I asked.

He nodded.

"So, it's not a dead world like we were all taught."

The assassin snorted a laugh. "Nope."

"They sent Avery there, too. Did you see her?"

"I was in and out like that." He snapped his fingers. "But I think I saw her and one-twenty-two heading toward the market square while I headed toward the castle to get royal blood." He finally swallowed his food and narrowed his eyes at me. "My assignment wasn't locating Mya. Mine was to send a message if the realm indeed existed." He looked at his friends. "I think my message should be pretty clear in another day or so."

I leaned back in my seat, no longer hungry. From what I had studied, a royal funeral was quite the event. If they blew up the queen at such an event, that could end up hurting a lot of innocent people.

The psychopath cocked his head. "You worried about your little winged fae?"

"Avery will do just fine." I stood and took my tray to the trash, unwilling to engage in any further conversation.

The thought of defiling a corpse in such a way made my mouth sour and scratched at my empathy for the queen's family.

Without someone to train, my days were long and boring, so I went to the library and cracked open a book on Elvren traditions to get my mind off what would come to pass.

I hoped Avery wasn't anywhere near that bomb when it detonated.

THE ELVREN ASSASSIN
CHAPTER EIGHT
Avery

THE FOREST GAVE WAY to a field, and I squinted at a structure in the distance. I thanked whatever higher being was looking out for us because I wasn't sure I could remain moving, especially since I was fully supporting Em now.

"There's a building up ahead," I said, and my voice slurred with the exhaustion pummeling my muscles.

"We cannot be captured," Em muttered.

"If we do not get help, I'm not sure you will survive."

Em snorted. "This from someone whose back has been bleeding all over my arm this whole time?"

She raised an eyebrow at me, and then her head dropped to her chest again.

I would attend to my wounds the minute I got her patched up and fed. Once we ate and slept, we would be back to normal. But without those things, she probably wouldn't make it through the night. Between zapping halfway across a planet and being attacked by that bog monster, I was below zero on the energy scale.

No lights shone from inside the cottage.

My empath side registered nothing but Em's pain. "I'm not sure anyone is there."

"Good."

I saw her point. If no one was there to contend with, we could at least get patched up and rest. I hoped there some sort of food available. Otherwise, she'd take much longer to heal.

No one stirred, even when we stumbled up onto the quaint wraparound porch. I tried the handle on the front door, and it gave, opening the door wide.

"It has to be a trap," Em muttered.

"Why?" I was already moving her inside.

"Because no one leaves a furnished house unlocked. Especially one in the middle of nowhere." She waved toward the clean décor.

I couldn't argue with her logic. We even had locks at the complex, and none of us had furnishings like what this house had. But their queen was dead, and the occupants likely headed to the palace for the royal funeral.

"Maybe they were in a rush to get to the queen's funeral and just forgot to lock up. Besides, I don't feel anything. No emotions at all. If it were a trap, I'd at least have a sense of someone else besides you."

She grunted and nearly collapsed when I let her go to lock the door behind us. I grabbed her before she crumpled to the floor and maneuvered us to the couch lining the cozy cottage's far wall. She sank onto the soft cushions. I certainly hoped this wasn't a trap, but we did not have any other options. I was nearly tapped out, and Em was in the same condition.

I searched the cabinets and pressed on in my search for emergency supplies like bandages.

Otherwise, she'd end up bleeding out. I handed a box of pastries I found in the bread box to Em as I passed her and then resumed my search for first-aid kits.

I found what I was looking for in a closet that also housed towels. With my arms loaded with bandages and salve, I headed back into the main area.

"I need to bandage you up," I said as I dumped the supplies on the end of the couch.

"Let me do you first since I'm close to passing out already." She muttered a light spell, and the room brightened. "Turn around." She twirled her finger.

I gave her my back, and her tuneless whistle made me look over my shoulder at her. "That bad?"

My body had numbed since I'd gone into survival mode.

"Not punctures like mine, but gashes like a dozen knives slashed you from halfway between your shoulder blades down your right leg. Lose the clothing."

I stepped out of the pants, threw them into a bloody pile in front of me, and peeled my shirt off. The extent of damage to the fabric made me swallow, but the cool salve Em spread from the back of my knee all the way to the middle of my rib cage calmed the burn, beating the pain back into my subconscious. There were only a few places she covered with bandages; the rest she left open.

I eyed the pile of clothing. It needed more than a few stitches to make it whole. At least Em's wasn't a total loss. I'd have to scavenge the closets to see if there was anything I could wear as soon as I finished patching Em up.

The escape of air behind me made me turn. Em had slumped on the couch. I collected the garbage that she'd left while cleaning me up and threw it in the pail by the door. Afterwards, I peeled off her shirt, wincing at the number of punctures. It's a wonder her shirt was still in one piece, but at least closing it up would be easier than if it had been shredded. Her skin didn't look much better.

At least she had the forethought to lay a towel down on the couch, but I did not think it would be enough to save the fabric from bloodstains.

Em's breathing shallowed, and her pulse was thready enough to send my heart into overdrive. I went into triage mode.

Ren had taught me all the different triage methods over the years I'd trained with him. This was a situation where I had to be cautious about what I stitched up. In some cases, I'd have to clean the lesions by cutting contaminated tissue before trying to close the wound. The deepest punctures were above and below her left side, where the beast had initially chomped down. The other punctures weren't as horrifying, but they would need to be thoroughly sterilized.

While the DNA the Director mixed for us meant we had superior healing skills, it didn't mean injuries couldn't kill us. The fact she was bitten in that pond by a reptile meant the possibility of infection. At least the free flow of blood might have helped clean some bacteria out, but I had to work fast and stop the bleeding as best I could.

I got a tub of clean water and another bucket and started the painful process of cleaning each cut before I spread the salve over her wounds. By the time I finished, the night had given way to daylight, and the sun was high in the sky. Every rag in the house had been saturated with blood. The lesser cuts had already started stitching together, but the more serious wounds still wept, staining the bandages.

Her chest rose and fell in shallow breaths. I had done all I could do.

I laid a blanket over her, picked up the soaked rags, and set off in search of a place to clean up. The minute I stepped into the bathroom, I got a glimpse of myself in the mirror. My stomach clenched at the amount of blood covering me. I couldn't tell if any of it was mine or not, but I needed it all off. I did not care that my bandages would get wet.

I needed to clean the rags prior to cleaning the gore off my skin. I dumped the bucket of rags on the shower floor and turned the shower knob, fully expecting to be doused with frigid water, but I was rewarded with a marginally warm stream that heated quicker than I was used to. I dialed it back and went to work on the rags, soaping and rinsing until each one ran clear.

Then it was my turn, and I scrubbed my skin until no trace of blood in the water slipped down the drain. When I finished, my fingers and toes were wrinkled, and I felt truly waterlogged. I peeled the soaked bandages off and tossed them before gingerly drying off, taking care to not open any of the scabs that had formed over my injuries.

When I finished, I took some of the larger rags and wiped up the bloody trail from the bathroom to the living room, and then I stopped in the entry. The living room looked like there had been a massacre.

Em was still breathing. Eventually, I'd have to clean her up, but for now, I needed to clean this place before I addressed my lack of clothing and got some rest.

This time, the soiled rags went into the garbage, and I washed my hands in the kitchen sink before I went in search of clothes. I found a closet full of butter-soft leathers and slipped on a pair. They were loose enough for the material not to irritate my injuries, but not enough to slip down my body. The shirt I chose was easy to cut up the center so it would fall on either side of my wings. I barely got it buttoned up before I fell face-first on the bed next to the closet.

The last thought that flared in my mind was that I probably should pull the mattress into the living area to be with Em just in case she needed me, but my exhaustion was too big to worry about all the dangers that lurked around the corner.

THE ELVREN ASSASSIN
CHAPTER NINE
Avery

LIGHT SHONE IN MY eyes, and I blinked, trying to figure out where I was. I rolled, looked around me, and observed what was on me, none of which was familiar. Following that, the stiffness of being in one position too long hit like a punch from Ren.

I groaned as the fog cleared from my head. I had slept, but I did not know how long I had been out. It was bright out, like it had been when I'd slipped into unconsciousness. With how much I creaked as I got up, it had to have at least been a day I'd spent asleep. My first stop was the bathroom to relieve myself and check my wounds.

All that was left was a batch of scratches, as if someone had raked me with dull nails. I pulled the pants back up and latched them.

In the living room, Em still slept. Before I searched the kitchen for food, I first changed her bandages. Afterward, I rounded up something to eat.

She moaned as I cooked up some eggs like Ren had taught me, and then I brought the plate to Em.

Her eyes cracked open, and I offered her a sip of the juice I had found in the icebox. Its sweet taste soothed my throat, and from the way she closed her eyes as she sipped the drink, it did the same for her.

I fed her a few bites of the eggs before I took a taste. We traded off turns at eating until the plate was clean. I allowed her to finish the drink before I tidied up the kitchen.

Em's eyes closed again.

"What day is it?" she asked when I came back into the room.

"I have no clue how long we've been sleeping. I passed out too." I glanced at the door. "The good news is the door is still locked."

"Shit. I feel like I've been pummeled by the Director's goons."

I snorted a laugh. We had all survived the near-death beatings we probably shouldn't have had at the hands of the Director's elite guards. They liked to inflict pain. I think they were bred that way, and it always made me uncomfortable.

"It took me the rest of the night and into the day to patch you up. And the sun is brighter than it was when I finally finished cleaning this place up."

She punched a couple of buttons on her wristband, and her eyes widened. She swung her legs off the sofa and attempted to sit up but only groaned.

"I have been in the same place for over two days. Tonight, it will be three days, and I'm still not travel ready." She flopped back onto the couch and winced. "I usually heal faster than this," she muttered.

"There is a higher possibility of infection with those slimy beast bites." I chewed on my lip. I'd slept for more than a day? Now it made sense that all I had were scratches left. "And thankfully, you didn't die while I was passed out."

My mind wandered back to Ren. Over two days had passed, and we weren't back with news of Mya. I dreaded to think about what was happening to Ren and to Em's handler, Lo.

"Think you can help me into the bathroom?"

Her question pulled my attention back to her. Em's coloring became sallower the longer she remained upright.

"Are you going to get sick?" I approached her, thinking a bucket would be better, but she shook her head.

I supported her weight to the bathroom and left her there to do her business while I cleaned up the couch as best I could, stripping the covers and turning them so the stained sides faced downward.

I found a blanket and laid it over the cushions to give Em a clean, soft place to rest. The towel and cushion covers were as complete a loss as my clothing and joined the tattered material in the garbage.

I picked up her clothes and set them aside to clean and mend while she rested, assuming I could find mending thread and a needle in this cottage. Besides, I needed something to keep my mind off all the horrid thoughts of what was happening on Icarus that kept invading my brain.

"Avery," Em called, and I rushed back to the bathroom to help her return to the main room.

"You cleaned up," she said with a hint of surprise.

"Well, yes. If you're fighting an infection, lying on soiled fabric will not help the healing process." Once I helped her stretch out, I found another blanket in the bedroom and an oversized shirt for Em to wear and handed both to her when I returned.

"What am I supposed to do with this?" She waved the shirt at me.

"It's to cover you up while I clean and mend your clothing." I held up her shirt, showing her the number of holes in the fabric.

She grumbled and tossed the tunic I had gotten for her onto the chair, muttering about not wearing other people's clothing. She opted for the blanket instead and pulled it over herself.

"Can you get me some more of that juice?" she asked.

I brought her the entire container. She needed it more than I did, and she didn't hold back. When she finished sucking it dry, she let out a gargantuan burp, set the carton on the floor, and then closed her eyes again.

I searched for mending materials and finally found some in the back corner of a closet in the room across from where I'd slept. The blood had dried enough so I could flake it off the fabric by using a brush I found, and I stitched up the holes and set it aside. Her pants were even easier, and I was done before the last of the light faded.

I lit a candle and rummaged for more food. I scrambled up the rest of the eggs, and this time, I inhaled them without leaving any for Em. I had found some more pastries in the icebox and set them aside for when she woke, but my body craved protein for steady energy as opposed to the quick fix of sugar with a crash that would leave me useless.

I had a feeling Em would need at least another day to be in traveling condition. I chewed my lip at the possible opportunity here. I could leave her behind and try to find Mya on my own. That might at least give me a chance to warn her.

But if Em had a setback and died, I would never forgive myself. I shook my head. I couldn't leave her. If the homeowners came back, and she was all alone here, she could be hurt or killed, and I'd be just as culpable.

It was times like this that I cursed my soft nature. Honestly, if it had been me who'd been attacked by that beast, I was sure Em would have kept swimming and never looked back.

I wiped my hand down my face, almost hearing a sigh from Ren in my head. He did not like it when I pulled punches. He always told me not to hesitate when going for the kill, but I *always* hesitated. Ren said that instinct of mine would get me killed in the business of death agents.

Now that thoughts of Ren had invaded my mind, I couldn't help but wonder if he was alive, and if so, what he was doing. Had he been truly concerned about me, or was he just worried about what would happen to him if I failed?

I shifted in the seat and licked my lips at the thought of him. I dropped my hand to the place on my hips that his hands had gripped any time he had sex with me. He always left bruises, but it was the only place he truly touched me, and the way he held me made me wonder if there was something more under his cold exterior.

I wanted his hands on me, but I never asked for more than he offered. He said it was a lesson, not a declaration of emotion. He told me I needed to learn to move the right ways to take down a target. To leave them physically spent so they couldn't fight back when my blade pierced their chest.

I sighed, pushing him out of my head. I couldn't get lost in those thoughts, especially since the timeline the Director had laid out had already come and gone. I just hoped he would wait until he received word from us before he took his aggravation out on any of the handlers.

I kept vigilant watch until the wee hours of the morning when the predawn light lit up the sky. My eyelids drooped, too heavy to keep open. Forcing them to stay open was a losing battle and, eventually, I blinked out into the land of dreams and nightmares.

THE ELVREN ASSASSIN
CHAPTER TEN
Avery

EXHAUSTION HAS A WAY of sucking time. For us, it was at least another day because darkness shrouded the cabin.

Em's snore nearly made all the glass in the cottage rattle.

It took me a moment and a couple of blinks for my eyes to adjust. The front door stood open, and I lay face down on the floor rather than the chair I had been lounging in.

It wasn't Em's snore I heard. It was her growling and gasping as punches were exchanged between her and whoever had interrupted our sleep.

I struggled to get up, but a foot connected with my side. I rolled before a second kick landed and hopped to my feet.

"I know what you are," the female owner of the boot snarled at me and shook Em's outfit. "You defiled our queen."

"I most certainly did not," I barked back, parrying against a flying fist.

"Assassins wearing this blew up our queen. There were enough of you in this disgusting outfit for all of us to remember. Thankfully, the prince dropped them dead in their tracks." She threw the outfit on the ground before she struck again.

The fury among the three fae brushed over me like a tidal wave.

Out of the corner of my eye, I saw the glint of steel and parried again. A blade sliced into my forearm, and I hissed.

They would not stop until we both were dead.

My survival instinct kicked in, and I went on the offensive, hitting, kicking, and disabling my attacker as quickly as I could before she got another slice in.

Em defended herself against two male fae. She wasn't doing as well as I had against my now unconscious attacker.

I stepped in and peeled one man off Em. But that landed me a punch in the face that dazed me enough for the man to tackle me to the ground. Before he could land a second punch, he bowed back with a scream that turned into a bloody gurgle.

He collapsed on top of me, and his dead weight nearly crushed my chest. Em stood behind him with a bloody knife in her hand. Her other attacker lay dead on the floor, and the woman I'd knocked out made a noise like she was waking.

Em darted to where the woman had crumbled, rolled her on her back, and buried the knife in her chest, silencing her. She grabbed her clothing and slid it on while I rocked the dead man off my chest. Em limped toward the door and closed it before turning on me.

"You didn't give me any warning," she hissed while she lit a lamp near the kitchen. "They nearly killed me."

My head pounded at the sudden brightness the lamp projected. When she turned, I saw the bruising on her throat and along her face. They had pummeled her while I slept?

She crossed to the couch and started attaching her weapons to her suit. She handed me the healing salve.

"At least they didn't cut me," she muttered as she looked at my dripping arm.

Dizziness threatened to either drop me to the ground or unleash my stomach. I closed my eyes and slowly breathed, getting control of my roiling belly before I addressed my injury.

Her gaze locked on my forehead, and she sighed. "That's going to leave a nasty bruise."

I lifted my injured arm and touched my forehead. A knot the size of my fist met my fingers. I hadn't slept through the ordeal. I had been knocked unconscious.

But I had slept through them coming inside. So that was on me.

I grunted at Em, focusing back on my arm. I put a healthy amount of the cream on the cut, and she handed me a bandage to cover it.

"We have to get moving. We've been here for nearly five days."

"Are you in travel shape?" I asked.

While on her feet, she swayed enough for me to doubt her endurance.

Finally, her words sank in, and my heart lurched.

"What?" I asked.

"Whether or not I am isn't up for debate." She showed me her watch, and it did indeed state nearly five days since we'd arrived. "Our priority is to move, and we must do at least one zap to get us closer to the portal and the kingdom where Mya is." She opened the icebox and put eat-on-the-go type items on the counter. "See if you can find a bag. We need food to re-energize after our zap."

I was still stuck on the fact that we'd slept another day away in this place. I must have been more exhausted from the healing process than I thought. At least Em's cuts had scabbed over enough to move, but she was still sluggish, as if her body were fighting off infections from the beasts.

I stumbled toward the bedroom where I had slept the first night and slipped into the closet. I remembered a red pack that would hold an awful lot of groceries stowed in the back corner where I found the shirt I wore. It still leaned against the wall. Though it wasn't a color that would blend in, there was nothing else to choose from.

I brought it back into the kitchen. "Is this good?"

Em gave me a skeptical look but took the bag anyway. She packed in all that she had taken from the icebox and some dry goods from the cabinets. I opened the drawer under the counter where I had found an abundance of pastries. Em packed all of it and still had room for the healing salve, the first-aid kit, and extra bandages.

After hooking the pack onto her back, she spread the damp map out on top of the counter.

"We need to zap to a road that leads to the castle." She measured the last jump we did and shook her head. "I don't have the energy to do a jump that far right now."

I couldn't argue. I wasn't sure I'd make the jump with my head swirling. But at least I had more energy than Em seemed to have.

She traced her finger from our origin point along the road until it rested between where she had marked the portal and the bog where we'd landed and then tapped that spot. "We'll try for this spot right near this intersection of Cambridge Road and the North-South breezeway. But off the road enough to not make a scene while just popping in from nowhere. Hopefully, it won't be in another swamp."

I nodded, studying the names at the crossroads. "It's still quite a way to the kingdom."

"Yes. Probably a day's walk, if we're lucky. We'll have to eat while we move. No stopping once we get on that road." She took a breath and looked at her outfit. "You'll need to glamour us on our walk in case we run across people." Her gaze moved to the dead homeowners. "Especially if they recognize this outfit." She waved at the clothes she wore.

I would be overlooked, but she certainly wouldn't be.

"Okay." I wasn't sure how good my glamour would be, but I'd try my best. "But we might look like a couple of vagrants."

She laughed. "With how we look right now, that might not be a bad thing."

She had a point. She pocketed the map again and linked her elbow with mine. We locked our arms together, and she opened the door to a new day dawning. I focused on that spot on the map before we stepped forward into the pull of the zap.

We both stumbled on re-entry, but at least neither of us fell. The field we landed in lay next to a road full of groups traveling south on foot.

It was light enough to see their faces, and even without my empath powers, I could tell from their expressions that they were shot emotionally. They all carried the look of someone who had seen a ghost. Their emotions ran the gambit between confusion and anger. Sensations pelted me hard enough to mess with my concentration, and my glamour didn't solidify before those nearest to the field saw us.

"Assassin!" The yell broke through the air, and more than one of them had their fingers pointed in our direction.

"Shit," Em said and turned away from the road as people trampled behind us with murderous intent.

We lumbered toward the woods at least a hundred yards away. I doubted we could hide in the sparse forest, but if we could find a tree to climb, maybe Em would have enough mojo to make us both invisible.

Otherwise, we were dead meat.

THE ELVREN ASSASSIN
CHAPTER ELEVEN
Ren

THE AUDITORIUM HELD A dozen handlers peppered throughout the room. We never congregated anywhere together except the arena, so being summoned to the same room had us all on edge.

At least I wasn't alone in that fact. Their emotions flowed over me, scraping my skin and making my anxiety ratchet up higher.

Guards that I had never seen filtered into the room, and my stomach dropped like a lead pipe. These men looked almost feral. When the Director followed, his mood swept over me, and I clenched my teeth so they wouldn't click against his frigidly dark emotions.

He stopped at the front of the auditorium and glared at all of us. "Eleka is a dead planet." His words hissed like air let out of a tire. "And your wards are all dead."

"Excuse me?" It tumbled from my lips before I could stop it.

The Director's glare pinned on me.

Avery wasn't dead. If she were, I would know it. I would feel it in my heart.

"Your wards have failed." His blazing stare passed over all of us but lingered on me as if it was a personal triumph to see me squirm.

"How could they fail if you sent them to their deaths?" another handler said, and that earned her a pointed glare and a nod to his new goons.

They descended on her like a hungry pack of wolves priming us for what the next few hours would hold for all of us. Screams filled the auditorium, and the Director actually smiled at the viciousness of his guards.

They tore the handler's arm off when she tried to protect herself, and they beat her with her own limb until she lay still on the floor. I had no clue whether she died from blood loss or blunt trauma. It didn't matter. Her pain and horror were enough to clench my stomach.

"Does anyone else have any questions?"

I had at least a dozen, but I would not voice them here. Not with his fresh guards so blood frenzied.

"Those of you still with wards, I will give one of you a chance to survive. There will be a fight to the death in the arena tomorrow morning. If you do not show up, your remaining wards will be thrown in the ring in your place."

Silence fell over the room. The remaining handlers sized each other up before all eyes fell on me.

The Director stared me down. "As for you, Ren, your last chance at survival died with your only ward." He looked at the guards. "Take him to the arena right now. This will be a public beating." He smiled. "Everyone gets a strike."

I gulped. A Taser hit my chest, dropping me to the floor before I could flee. Guards grabbed me even as electricity buzzed in my ears, and they dragged me through the halls.

Assassins and handlers alike stopped to stare at the spectacle. Then an announcement came over the loudspeakers, beckoning everyone to the arena.

Once the guards secured my hands behind my back, and my wings so I couldn't use them to defend myself, they dislodged the Taser and dropped me onto my knees in the center of the dark arena.

The Director approached, his eyes glowing with malice.

He crouched in front of me. "Sixty-nine was never coming back from Eleka, even if they were successful. She was too soft, just like you. One-twenty-two had orders to kill her before they left."

He smiled at me, revealing his sharp vampire canines.

"You lied. Eleka is not dead," I snarled. "Your assassin who gathered the queen's blood for you told all his associates."

He delivered a punch to my nose that made my head jerk back, and stars twirled in front of my vision for a blink or two.

The Director leaned in. "That blabbermouth and his associates met with a nasty end." He straightened. "But at least their deaths were rather quick. I cannot say the same for yours."

The lights slowly came on as people started filtering into the arena, including those who had been in the amphitheater. When every seat was taken and the stragglers finally settled into their chairs, the doors slammed shut.

It only took probably fifteen minutes to a half an hour for the room to fill up. Just long enough for me to understand the volumes of pain I would experience.

I dropped my chin to my chest.

The Director grabbed a fistful of my dark hair and yanked my head back. "Ren's tenure in this organization ends today." He scanned the crowd. "By your hands. You each get your best shot. Whether that is a punch, a kick, a claw, or a bite, but that single action cannot be a death strike."

He yanked me to my feet. "I want him in agony and as close to death without crossing that line before I drop him in the wild for the scavengers to pick apart."

He sneered at me. "This is the price of failure. Remember this." He pointed at the crowd before he stepped away.

The guards opened the gates. In an instant, the room shifted from stillness to excitement, as if being involved in the act of killing aroused their bloodlust.

I knew at that moment I never belonged here. Neither did Avery. I just had to hang on long enough to escape to Eleka and find her before one-twenty-two killed her.

The crowd flooded the floor.

I closed my eyes, blocking the view of the people I had lived with for the last thirty years coming to take their pound of flesh from my bones.

I was sure the Director was not pleased that I made no noise. The only sound in the arena was the sound of flesh meeting flesh or the snap of bone.

When I could no longer hold my weight, kicks were added to the array of attacks. I couldn't cover my head, but I could at least curl up enough that my back and wings took the brunt of the pounding.

Not one part of my body was spared, and by the time the last punch landed, my mind was foggy enough for me to think that perhaps I had brain damage to go along with the horrific physical damage.

The guards took me under my arms and yanked me up. That was the only time any sound came out, and it was only a meek groan. I sagged in their grip, unable to hold weight on broken limbs.

"I hope the vultures pluck your eyes out first," the Director hissed in my ear.

I ignored him. I ignored the roars of the crowd as they dragged my half-dead body from the floor. I ignored the zap to the desert and the oppressive heat singing what was left of my wings. I even ignored the hot pain of a knife slicing into my side and the slam onto the hot sand of the desert floor.

What was important was keeping my heart pumping and my lungs sucking in even the slightest of air.

And keeping enough juice in me to zap me to that fucking portal.

"Come on, before those mangy beasts smell his blood. I would rather not be out here when they come to tear this shit apart," one guard said.

A boot hit me square in the face, and I nearly blacked out. After the stars cleared, I cracked open an eye, and the guards were gone.

But the hairless desert dogs stalked forward with drool sliding from their mouths.

Whatever had been holding my hands and wings in place had long since been destroyed in the arena, and I climbed to my feet by sheer force of will.

413

"Portal," I hissed and demanded the zap.

The sucking motion created sheer agony, but I clenched my teeth and took it.

I stumbled to the edge of the metal portal on the outside ledge where all the assassins jumped to different worlds. I swiped my bloody cheek on it.

"Eleka." The word wasn't even out all the way before the black smoke swallowed me.

All the lessons I taught Avery about portal transfers came back, and I focused on what little I could see of the dot in the distance. Every step had me almost falling as my broken bones scraped together. My legs would not carry me that far.

I spread my damaged wings and took flight. I flew right into a dark cave and almost crashed into the far wall of spikes across from the portal. My chest seized, and I banked, glimpsing the bodies littered on the barbs in the floor before I caught sight of an exit on the other side of the ledge that the portal sat on.

Magic nearly folded my wings, but I pushed through it, forcing myself through the door with a bellow of pain that sucked the rest of the air from my lungs.

Exhaustion and pain pummeled me as I darted through the outer cavern, racing against the cave's suffocating magic. Racing for air. Racing to save Avery. On some level, I knew I should be dead, but I wouldn't allow it. Not with Avery in danger.

A glow shimmered in the far corner, and I aimed for it, squinting as my lungs nearly imploded from lack of oxygen.

Darkness slammed into me, and I was unsure if this was an exit or if it was finally the end.

THE ELVREN ASSASSIN
CHAPTER TWELVE
Avery

WITH THE CROWD CHASING after us, we made it to the forest, dodging behind tree after tree until Em found one with branches low enough to climb without losing our linked elbows.

She closed her eyes, and both of us shimmered invisible before she pulled me up branch by branch until we towered above the ground. We settled onto the branch near the trunk and waited.

Thankfully, we had enough of a head start that no one saw us suddenly pop out of existence. Seconds later, the ground rumbled with the number of feet hitting it. The crowd blasted through the opening below us.

Calls of "where did they go?" echoed through the group. The galloping pace slowed to a stop, and the crowd retreated toward the road, grumbling that we must have transported somewhere else.

Still, neither Em nor I moved until the noise stopped. We waited until nothing reached our ears but the animal banter in the surrounding trees. Squirrels and birds argued as they scampered near us and retreated just as fast.

When we dared move, all my muscles were stiff, and my stomach grumbled loud enough to startle a couple of birds farther out on the branches.

Em blinked in and out of invisibility, and when she couldn't hold the magic any longer, we both popped into our physical shells.

"I need food." She swung her leg to the lower branch, climbing until she jumped to the ground.

I followed, and when I reached the forest floor, she had the backpack open and the contents of the pastry boxes nearly all eaten. I didn't think the woman even chewed. I grabbed the last pastry in the box and received a glare from her for touching her sweets, but I needed the sugar rush, especially if I was going to glamour us for the walk.

"It should take us about a day to get there, so eat up. I'm not bringing this pack with us. It's too heavy, and I can't really move freely with it strapped on my back. We can put the healing salve in one of our pockets along with the bandages, but that's all."

"Okay, so stuff our faces and then put the glamour on and start walking," I said, repeating her instructions, and she snorted confirmation.

"We'll head out after the sun sets. I don't want to chance another chase."

Neither did I. So, we settled on the ground, crossing our legs and munching on the food until the last bite was gone. The squirrels cleaned up the crumbs for us, and we left the pack hanging from a low limb as if it had been stripped off by the tree.

Once we cleared the woods, I had our glamour in place. The sun had already dipped below the horizon. The road still had travelers on it, but they paid us no mind as we headed north against the grain of traffic.

DAWN BROUGHT WITH IT an empty road ahead of us. Both Em and I were thankful. We had spoken little the prior evening because of the clusters of people passing by. But now that we were alone, I voiced some thoughts swirling in my head since we had left the cottage.

"Someone blew up the queen's body?"

"It sounded that way."

We had heard enough conversation on the road to confirm what that woman had said before she attacked me with the knife.

"You think it was one of ours?"

"Yes. It was probably a diversion to grab Mya, but it sounds like it failed." Her lips turned down at the edges. "And if the prince can kill with just a glare, do you think that's why Mya hasn't left? Because he threatened her?"

That seemed more of a possibility. "If his wrath scared her more than the Director's, then probably."

"The prince will never see me coming." Em grinned, and that glint in her eyes made me swallow hard.

I chewed my lip. "Do you think our handlers are still alive?"

Em startled at the question, and the look she shot me held enough trepidation to make me think that thought hadn't passed through her mind.

"It's been over forty-eight hours."

Em's cross look deepened, but then she shook her head. "We haven't failed like the others, so I think they'll be okay."

She didn't sound all that convincing. We continued in silence.

My mind wandered back to Mya. She hadn't seemed scared of the prince when I saw her outside the southern palace. She had appeared worried, but not like someone who was fearing for their life. She actually looked concerned for the prince, which made Em's statement settle as well as the compound's mystery meat in my stomach.

My thoughts festered, but I kept them to myself.

As night fell yet again, all the muscles in my legs and back declared mutiny. My feet burned from walking for so many miles uninterrupted, but at least my shoes didn't have holes in them yet.

The palace rose in the distance, illuminated by colored lights. It looked as majestic at night as it had in daylight. Although the resounding emotions riding the air still seethed with despair.

"I need food," Em muttered.

She steered us toward a lit area that wasn't far from the castle or the portal.

If we needed to make a quick escape, this was the perfect area to do that. My glamour still held, but it wasn't as solid as it had been when we started. We indeed looked like we had been traveling for a long time, so in that respect, I hoped she knew what she was doing.

I wasn't sure any self-respecting establishment would let us through the door. The last time we encountered any sort of crowd, we were chased into the woods like common criminals.

Neither one of us had the stamina to break into a run for any distance now that the food we had eaten a day ago had long since burned off.

But hunger trumped danger, and she kept us moving forward to the more populated area of town.

THE ELVREN ASSASSIN
CHAPTER THIRTEEN
Avery

MILLY'S TAVERN. THE SIGN loomed over us, and the delicious scents filling the air made my stomach growl. Em's belly made the same obnoxious sounds.

We traded a glance without a word because neither of us had money.

"Once I eat..." She sighed.

"You can do the invisible thing, and we can skip out without being caught," I finished and turned my attention to the tavern.

It might raise flags, especially since word of what happened at the queen's funeral reached the far corners of Eleka. People were much more cautious and on edge, and us skipping out on paying could be a problem.

"Yeah," she agreed.

Our stomachs made the choice for us. The zapping across the globe had tapped both of us, especially after the close calls we'd had.

We stepped into the crowded bar and made our way to a free table tucked in a corner.

Em picked up the small menu that stuck out of the holder in the center of the table and scanned the food choices before handing it to me.

I wanted everything even if I didn't know what half of it was, but I knew if we overdid it, it would bring scrutiny to us and our ragged appearance. The glamour was difficult to keep in place; it was about as bleary as I was.

"You choose," I said to Em.

She gave a nod and waved a server over to us. She spouted off at least a half-dozen dishes, water for our drinks, and smiled. While we would probably both like a little nectar, it most definitely would impact our minds. Maybe after we had food, we'd reconsider, but getting smashed right now would be dangerous.

Our drinks and food arrived, and I stared at all the finger foods on the table, unsure of what to attack first.

I picked a chip from the mound Em pillaged first. Spices filled my mouth and made my eyes water. I gulped down my drink and decided that was a little too fiery for my tastes.

I focused on the other items, none of which were spicy like the chips, and I indulged. We cleared the entire buffet in less than ten minutes and leaned back in our seats with our water in our hands. Our glamour solidified with the renewed energy filling me.

Before we could get up and disappear, the door opened, and I froze at the sight of the prince's entourage entering the tavern. Mya and the prince were in the center of the same guards we had seen leaving the beach palace earlier in the week.

I stared at them. Her with her enviable dark hair flowing over her shoulders and an outfit that screamed not to fuck with her, and the prince with his dark hair and sharp eyes that glowed blue, making the massive bruise on the side of his face even more noticeable.

But what struck me was the fact that Mya smiled as she took her seat. She did not look like she was being kept against her will at all.

Em slid from the chair as her eyes narrowed.

I grabbed her arm. "What are you doing?"

She glared at me and then moved her gaze toward the group. "Finishing our job."

She pulled out of my grip and slipped away, shimmering to invisible in the shadows.

I had to warn them somehow, but that could get me killed just as fast as Mya. My gaze jumped across the bar to Em's target and the shot of nectar in her hand.

I remembered the last time Mya drank nectar back on Icarus. It was not pretty, and she needed to be much more in tune with her surroundings right now.

The way she scanned the crowd scratched over my skin, and my wings fluttered. I almost lost my glamour as the magic caressed over me, but I held it with grim determination. I did not want to harm either of them.

I had never seen her smile before, and the way the prince looked at her was as if he treasured her. I imagined she flourished under that like a flower reaching for the sun. It threw me enough to think that perhaps she had found something here that I might have overlooked.

The guards surrounding her were as attractive as Ren. Maybe even more so. Especially the one with eyes the color of emeralds. His hair was the color of honey and wheat. He might give Ren a run for his money in the sparring ring, too. He certainly looked strong enough.

Mya set her drink down. Her lips moved, and I caught some words, even from this distance. It was a spell we all had learned in training. It ferrets out those who wish to do harm.

I shot my gaze to where I thought Em lurked, and so did Mya.

Both her and the prince's expressions soured as much as the food in my belly.

A disruption in the middle of the tavern caught my attention. Em's invisibility cloak failed, and she dropped to the floor.

People rushed toward Em but stopped short at the knife still clenched in her hand and the assassin's outfit that announced her to the crowd. The blade glared in the blinking colored lights.

Em didn't move, even when a large man near her kicked her knife away. If she had been awake, that man would have been filleted. He crouched, put his fingers on her throat, and then shook his head, confirming she was dead to those around her.

I had to force myself to sit still and count to ten to slow my roaring pulse. Witnessing such a stealth execution left a shivering cold deep in my bones. As much as Em had grown on me, I knew her end game wasn't the same as mine. If I went to her, I would be killed just as effortlessly.

Everyone's gazes darted to the prince and his entourage. No one moved as they scanned the room, looking for more danger.

The prince muttered something, but Mya shook her head, and he dropped his gaze to her. I was too far away to hear them, but he seemed to take her counsel without question. Then he took the shot glass and downed it before wrapping his hand around her arm.

I almost darted forward to intercept her, but she didn't look as though the touch was unwanted. Before she slid off the chair, the prince scanned the crowd.

"Spread the word. If there are any other assassins hiding in plain sight, they are stranded here. Their means to get home have been permanently blocked."

I nearly fell to my knees. If I couldn't get home, the Director would take it out on Ren.

I wasn't the only one accosted with panic and alarm. Most of the surrounding crowd held the same frantic expression I probably had.

"Are we not hidden, Your Highness?" one of the older patrons asked, his face a mask of horror at the thought.

"We are still hidden, Harrod," the prince said to the old man. "And the breach in security has been taken care of. Although there still may be a few who slipped through before I could fix the situation."

"Is that what happened?" He pointed to the prince's face.

The prince's stiff features softened, and he gave the older gentleman a nod. "If you notice any strangers who do not seem to know our traditions, please inform the king's guard. Do not take matters into your own hands."

He escorted Mya out of the tavern with the four guards surrounding them.

My heart thundered in my chest, and whatever adrenaline that had spiked at the sight of Mya and the prince syphoned out, leaving me exhausted and unsteady.

Patrons started filtering out, leaving Em on the floor as if she were nothing more than discarded garbage.

I slid off the seat and stepped into the crowd. A hand grasped my upper arm, yanking me back.

A big, burly man pointed at the check on the table. "You still need to settle your bill." His eyes narrowed as he stared at me, and in the next moment, his gaze jumped to Em. "You were with her."

The accusation was loud enough to pull the attention of the stragglers still in the bar. All eyes pivoted to me.

I scrambled for a reason I was with Em that wouldn't get me just as dead. "I met her on the road."

But my excuse didn't seem to penetrate the man's mounting fury.

He slung me into the center of the bar, and I tripped over Em's body, falling on my ass. Ren would be so disappointed in me. This was not how he'd taught me to fight.

But like the house and the crowd on the road, I wasn't ready to take a life as easily as Em had. Maybe I was defective, but I couldn't unsheathe my knives unless in a kill or be killed scenario.

I dodged a punch as I got to my feet. But by now, I was surrounded by over a dozen burly men with clenched fists. I took a breath, centering myself so when the next punch came, I maneuvered out of reach, but that put me within arm's length of another angry fae.

I wasn't sure how long I defended against their attack, but a few of the men lay unconscious. More seemed to join in, leaving me breathless and desperate for escape. I reached for my knives, giving in to the survival instinct dragging sharp nails across my skin, but that motion left me vulnerable.

A punch connected with my temple.

I shook the stars out of my head, but cold iron slid around my wrist, burning enough to capture my attention away from my attackers. The fight had moved me close enough to the bar for them to clasp my arm to the bar railing, locking me within range of these angry men.

I still had one free hand with a knife clasped in it, as well as my two legs, but it wasn't enough to deflect all of their punches. I got a few slashes in before they overpowered me and secured my other wrist to the railing, stretching my arms in opposite directions.

I screamed and kicked, connecting with many of the men, but not enough to save my torso and face from a beating that rivaled those that the Director's goons delivered.

"Enough!" A baritone voice shook the air.

The crowd parted, and a pair of royal guards stood in the doorway. The green-eyed one I had noticed before was there, and his chest rose and fell as if he had sprinted here. His glare was feral, as if he wanted to tear me limb from limb.

The absence of fists aimed at my body released all the stress holding me upright, and I sagged in the bindings, wincing at the pull of my shoulders.

Gorgeous green eyes crossed to stand before the bar where I was stretched out.

He glanced at the number of fae on the ground before turning his gaze back to me. "Feisty bitch."

I think I growled. I wasn't sure I could form words with how swollen my jaw was. It might have even been cracked, but I'd heal, given time. Just like I had in the past.

He reached into his pocket, pulled out a vial, and stepped within range of my kick. He didn't even flinch when my boot connected with his shin. His lips curved into a genuine smile before he gripped my jaw, prying my mouth open and pouring the contents of the vial into my mouth.

Before I could spit out the sweet-tasting drink, he clamped my mouth closed, his grip punishing and painful. I swallowed the elixir and growled my discontent.

Whatever he'd given me left a sweet citrus taste on my tongue as it sucked the energy from every muscle. My eyelids became so heavy that I couldn't keep them open.

Darkness slammed down on me, and I wondered if death had finally claimed me.

THE ELVREN ASSASSIN
CHAPTER FOURTEEN
Avery

I MOANED, AND EVERY muscle protested. My arms screamed as they held my weight, and I straightened my ankles so my feet press flat on the ground, taking the weight off my aching wrists.

I scanned my body with my mind, trying to decipher injury from stiffness. It seemed I had been out long enough for most of my injuries to fade. Angel blood sped up my healing, so while Em had taken days to heal from the makara attack in the bog, it had only taken me hours.

My first glimpse of the room left me confused. It wasn't a dungeon like I imagined. It was crisp and clean and had a single empty chair, as if someone planned on interrogating me.

When I dropped my gaze to my body, I startled enough to rattle the chains holding me in place. My borrowed clothes and all my weapons were gone, replaced by a slip that barely covered my body. It was less than I wore to bed back at the complex.

My heart thundered. Panic made my wings flutter.

The door opened, and the green-eyed guard walked in.

His eyebrow cocked as he studied my form. "I wasn't sure you'd even be alive this morning, never mind nearly healed."

His voice caressed me, but it didn't settle my panic at all. Especially since he stepped close enough for me to feel the heat from his body. His breath tickled my skin. He smelled like the decadent chocolate bar that Ren snuck back for me from one of his trips.

"What are you besides fae?" he asked, glancing at my fluttering wings before meeting my gaze again.

I shook my head.

"You don't know, or you won't tell me?" The backs of his fingers slid over my arm, and my skin pebbled in response.

"I need to speak to Mya," I said.

His half smile chilled me. "The prince and his mate will be along as soon as they wake. But I'm not sure you understand the wisdom of your request." His gaze hardened. "You will not be able to harm her while you are chained and drugged."

My eyes widened. My brain stalled on the word "mate," and I heard nothing more from this man. The prince was Mya's mate?

"Mate?" My eyelids fluttered as much as my wings.

"Yes." His fingers slid down my side, adding to the chill in the air. "And you cannot harm her."

"I'm not here to harm her."

He chuckled and stepped back, creating a distance that instantly pulled my body toward him. It was as if he had a magnetic field that left me tingling.

"You expect me to believe that?" he asked.

"Yes."

"And what of the tracker embedded in your back? Is that all a coincidence, too?"

"I will not hurt her." I clenched my teeth, frustrated by this man's inability to see the truth in my eyes.

"No. You just want to kill her and drag her body back to your precious Director. Don't you?" He crossed his arms.

I shook my head. "She's my...friend."

It was hard to choke out those words. Assassins didn't have any friends. Ren beat that into me, and Em solidified it. But in my heart, Mya was the one who saw me as a person, not a number like the rest of them.

"She named me," I said.

The guard blinked like a grain of sand had landed in his eye. "Named you?"

"Yes. She gave me the name Avery instead of calling me my assigned number."

His eyebrows rose, and he huffed a laugh. "I think I need to have a much longer conversation with the prince's cohort."

I batted my eyes and smiled. "Since I'm not a danger, can you let me out of these chains?"

He laughed a full, loud, and musical laugh, leaning back as it belted out of him. It actually tilted my lips into something resembling a smile. But my humor disappeared with the shake of his head.

"The only one who can let you out of these chains is the prince. And that is only after we've determined what your motives really are." He stepped closer, staring me down. "So, I'd start by answering my original question. What are you?"

"I'm a fae-angel hybrid."

"And what can you do?"

"Magic and fae glamour." I shrugged. "And I'm faster than most."

He cocked his head. "Faster?"

"Faster at healing. Faster at moving. Faster."

His gaze cascaded down my form, and he nodded. "What kind of magic?"

"Spells, potions. Nothing really special. Not like Em, who could become invisible." Envy laced its way into my voice, and I dropped my gaze.

He hooked his finger under my chin, lifting it. "Most women can't knock out a dozen burley men in a fight either," he said with a mixture of awe and snark.

His soft touch clouded my perception.

"Why aren't you obstinate like Mya?" he asked.

I blinked at him and narrowed my eyes. "Was it her choice to be the prince's mate?" My voice carried a harder edge, because if she were forced into it, I might rethink my charitable attitude.

"She is the prince's spirit mate."

That term meant nothing to me. I had heard of mates based on the Director's relationship with his bonded mate. But beyond that, the nuances of the additional term were lost on me.

"Do you know anything about spirit mates or mates in general?" he asked.

"Bonding with a mate is a serious crime in the league, punishable by death." Outside of the Director, there were no bonded mates allowed in the League of Assassins. Having a mate and being bonded were two different things.

"That sounds more like the type of organization Mya described."

"I find it hard to believe Mya revealed anything about the league to you." My ire came back full force. So was my strength and clarity.

He must have caught something in my gaze because he excused himself and came back a moment later with a pitcher and a glass. He poured half a cup and brought it to me. The citrus scent drifted up my nose, and my mouth watered.

I pulled my head away. "I don't want to drink anything you're offering. The last time you forced me to drink, I blacked out."

"You blacked out from your injuries, not from this." He gripped my chin and forced his fingers into my cheeks, prying my jaws open just enough to filter liquid through my lips.

An explosion of citrus danced over my tongue, and the guard released his fingers and pushed my chin up high so I couldn't spit out the liquid. I swallowed, and soon, warm heat spun from my stomach outward.

"Liar," I whispered as the room became blurry.

He leaned forward and wiped the edge of my lip with his thumb. "I don't lie," he whispered.

"Galen."

A sharp voice made both of us jump.

I turned my head, taking in the handsome prince I had seen in the tavern last night. The bruise on his face had faded to a sickly yellow. His sharp aqua eyes locked on me and narrowed.

"She was at the tavern last night?" he asked the guard.

"Yes. She entered with the assassin who died. At least, that's what the people in the tavern said when I arrived."

After the prince stepped into the room, Mya followed. Her eyes widened when they met mine.

"Why is she locked up like that?" Mya snapped.

Both the guard and the prince turned to her and waved at me like that explained my being bound this way.

"She has no ill intent. Otherwise, my spell would have ferreted her out at the tavern last night."

"We still need to remove her chip," the guard said.

Mya's face fell, and she gave a slow nod before turning to me. "It's better this way," she said, nodding toward the chains.

"Can I talk to you alone?" I asked, but my voice sounded too slow.

She cocked her head.

The guard pointed at the pitcher.

"Ah. Tastes like heaven, doesn't it?" She smiled. "But it plays havoc with your muscle control." She crossed and pushed the guard aside. "Give me a few minutes with her, please."

"But..." the prince started.

Mya lifted her hand and indicated the door. He relented, along with the guard. Mya poured another glass of the concoction and brought it to me.

"Is that what they did to you? Drugged you into compliance?" I nodded toward the glass.

Mya sighed and shook her head. "Tavin is my spirit mate. The other half of my soul. If I bleed, he bleeds."

She offered me the drink.

I gave her a side-eye.

"Drink, Avery. It will dull the pain when we dig out your chip. And believe me, you want that agony dulled."

I stalled with another question. "Are we really stuck here?"

She raised her palm. "See that scar?"

I nodded at the white line across her palm.

"That's a blood oath that I forced the Director into. To him and his associates, this was nothing but a dead world. He won't send any more assassins. We've sealed the cavern exit with the kiss of death, so anyone who comes through with more than fae blood will die on contact. Only Tavin and I can let people in or out of the caves."

My heart plummeted. "The Director will take my failure out on Ren."

Mya sighed and nodded. "I imagine all the handlers will be punished, but it might not be as severe as you think. Especially since the Director needs an entire guard staff to replace the one we killed." She met my gaze with a smile that sent a shiver down my spine. "So, Ren is probably safer than some of the other handlers."

"How did you kill so many?"

Mya's secret smile sent a rash of gooseflesh over my skin. "Drink."

She tipped the cup to my lips, and I did as she said, but this time, I allowed myself to enjoy the sweet tang.

"Maybe one of these days you and I will chill with a pitcher of this stuff and catch up," she muttered as she put the empty cup on the table. "It really is a great muscle relaxant."

"Better than nectar?"

She laughed but didn't answer me. "Galen," she called.

The green-eyed guard stuck his head in the door. "Yes, Your Highness?"

I snorted. "Your Highness?" I cocked an eyebrow at Mya.

Mya smirked at me. "Where is the chip?" she asked Galen as both he and the prince stepped back into the room.

He bit his lip and glanced at my wings before meeting Mya's gaze. "I believe it's burrowed under her wings." He scowled.

"And that is why I hate the Director," Mya snarled and looked at the prince. "Why didn't I let you kill him?"

Tavin chuckled. "Because we don't know if someone worse is pulling the strings. But I'll happily take another trip with you and rectify that mistake."

"Oh, I see why you like him," I slurred, and my head bobbed.

When I looked up again, the prince's underlying melancholy hit as if seeing me was a reminder of all he had lost. His mother had died at the hands of an assassin. Sorrow bit at my insides.

"I'm sorry about your mother," I said in almost a whisper.

My eyes closed, and my head dipped.

"She's an empath," Mya muttered from behind me. "The Director would have killed her eventually for not conforming to the emotionless husks he wants us all to be."

She spoke as if I wasn't in the room. And she wasn't the only one who'd told me that hideous truth.

The world swam in and out of focus until pain gripped my back, causing everything to come roaring into stark clarity. I screamed, trying to move away from the pain, but with how I was stretched out, there was nowhere to go.

"Galen, distract her," Mya snarled.

"How?"

"I don't know. Think of something that would capture her attention and do it."

Galen stepped into my field of vision, and he caressed my cheek, trying to distract me from the pain ripping through my entire form. His thumbs wiped the tears off my cheeks. He searched my gaze as if my pain was his and, in the next moment, breached the distance, pressing his lips to mine in a searing kiss that quieted my scream.

When his tongue explored my mouth in an exquisite quest, my scream turned into a whimper. Pain still clouded my mind, but this sweet sensation tempered it.

When the burning in my back released, I gasped and pulled away from him.

Mya came around in front with her eyebrow cocked and her fingers coated in blood. "That's certainly one way to distract her." Her lips toyed with a smile as she dropped my chip into my empty glass and drowned it in the nectar she had given me. "Think you can put that miracle salve on her wound?"

Galen nodded and grabbed a container off the table in the corner before slipping behind me. Coolness spread from the point of pain, dulling it under the healing butter he spread on my back. Afterwards, he passed the container to Mya and released my ankles and wrists.

My legs wobbled, and I took a step, but my knees wouldn't support my weight.

Galen swept me off my feet and looked at the prince for direction.

"Lock her up until I have a chance to inform my father of this development." He traded a glance with Mya, and she nodded.

"The cells are more comfortable than our rooms back at the complex," Mya said to me and then she turned to Galen. "Be sure you give her enough blankets to keep warm. And a pillow. I don't want her to suffer any more than she already has. Understand?"

Galen looked at the prince. When he said nothing to contradict Mya, Galen nodded and carried me from the room.

Mya was correct. The cells were indeed bigger than the private rooms back at the complex, but there was no privacy. Galen set me gently on the cot on my side and stepped away for a moment before he returned with blankets and a pillow. He tucked me in and brushed a lock of my hair out of my face with a wistful look on his face, as if he didn't understand his actions.

"I'll see that you are brought food," he said.

In an instant, he disappeared, leaving me alone in the cell. Silence settled, and any time I shifted, my back protested. My drugged brain attempted to process all I had learned since I woke this morning, and it simply couldn't reconcile that I was stuck here.

The only reprieve from the mounting panic inside was Galen's kiss. It had nearly made me forget I was being mercilessly butchered.

Now the Director would assume I was dead, too, and Ren would be beaten to a hair's breadth from death because I failed.

My heart sank at the thought.

I prayed Ren would be spared.

THE ELVREN ASSASSIN
CHAPTER FIFTEEN
Ren

"HOW THE HELL IS he even alive?" The voice sounded vaguely familiar.

Pain gripped my back, and my throat vibrated with a sound I did not recognize. I could not get away from the fire branding between my shoulders.

Heat trickled down my cheeks, and something sweet entered my mouth before I swallowed, and the pain subsided enough to grant me a reprieve.

"I don't know. I don't understand how he got through the caverns, and I certainly have no clue how he didn't die from the outer cage. I set that to kill."

"He wasn't touching the metal," that familiar female voice said.

A yank in my back pulled a yelp from me, and I slipped into the black.

My eyes fluttered open, and my first thought produced a huffing laugh. I could see, so the vultures didn't get my eyes.

I blinked and assessed my surroundings.

Bars.

I was in a dungeon of some sort, but it was cleaner than most of the rooms in the complex. It reminded me of a medical bay, but one for criminals. Where the hell was I?

My brain was not firing on all cylinders, and I tried to move, but pain flared through every muscle. Slowly, the entire ordeal came back with a vengeance.

Surprise raked fine nails over my skin. I hadn't died from the beatings. Nor had I died from my flight through the portal and those air-sucking caverns.

If I didn't fuck up at the portal, I was on Eleka, and it certainly was not dead.

Avery.

Her name blared in my mind.

She was still in danger.

I tried to push myself up, but agony overrode all my senses, yanking me back into oblivion.

THE ELVREN ASSASSIN
CHAPTER SIXTEEN
Avery

GRUNTS AND THE CLANG of a cell door pulled me from my stupor, but the jail I was in was shrouded in shadows.

I barely made out human shapes a few cells down, but someone was dropped on the cot. That person was heavy enough to make the cot groan.

"Tell the prince the prisoner has been secured," a voice said before the clang of metal on metal resounded.

The only thing I could distinguish in the dark were green eyes as they shifted my way, and right after, they vanished with the creak of a door. Feet shuffled outside my cell, passing by, and a light blinded me before a door across the hall closed.

I shut my eyes and sighed, lulled into a stupor by the soft sounds of running water, making me drift down into a fitful sleep.

A hand threaded through my hair, and soft cooing telling me to shush snapped my eyes open.

Green eyes stared at me so close I could feel his breath. "You were having a nightmare."

I blinked and glanced around, trying to get my bearings. My mind slowly gave up the hazy cloud hanging over it, but when my vision cleared, I cocked my eyebrow.

Galen crouched on the side of the cot in only a towel. His wet hair dripped onto his skin, sending glistening paths of water down his cut chest.

"What?" I whispered, buying some time as everything slammed home in my mind.

None of the guidance Ren gave me addressed this overwhelming need accosting me with Galen so close to me. Oh, Ren had taught me what men wanted and what I would have to do to get close enough to kill once the Director sent me on my first assignment, but I had never felt an overwhelming attraction at this level during those private lessons.

And Ren never looked at me the way Galen was right now.

His lips tilted at my breathy question, and he removed his hand from my cheek. "You were calling out in your sleep, and I was compelled to come soothe your fright." He laughed and glanced at the floor. "I'm not sure what possessed me to do that."

He stood.

I sat up too fast, and my head spun in a dizzy swirl. I gripped the edges of the cot to steady myself, and the use of my back muscles sent a wrenching pain through me, yanking a gasp from my throat.

Galen crouched again. His hands gripped my shoulders gently. "You shouldn't make sudden moves like that until your back is fully healed."

The concern in his eyes, along with his soft touch, caressed that part of me that always craved something more. It was the same part of me that made me strong enough to withstand the attempted brainwashing from the Director and his goons.

"I know what you want," I said.

Ren told me what men wanted. He'd made sure I mastered all my moves since I had no other special abilities like Em's invisibility and Mya's energy-syphoning gifts. He told me this would be my special ability to render men defenseless.

"What is it you think I want?" He slid back on his heels, letting go of my shoulders.

"Sex." I dropped my gaze.

Galen snorted a laugh. "You are injured. And just because I kissed you doesn't mean I want to fuck you."

He stood and crossed his arms, looking down at me with a hard stare.

"All men want sex."

He rolled his eyes and gave me a slight nod. "Sex isn't necessarily the goal of all men. Sometimes we want someone to listen to us, to make us feel special but not by using sexual favors. And sometimes we want to be the hero and ride in to save the fair maiden."

He grinned with a faraway look in his eyes that warmed my soul, but soon after, his whimsical smile faded.

"So, sex isn't all men want?"

"No. Who the hell told you that is all we wanted from women?"

"My handler. He said I had to learn how to seduce a man to get close enough to kill them. So, he taught me things."

His body flexed as he tightened his arms together. "What did your handler teach you?" His voice carried a sharp edge to it.

I reached for the towel clasped around his waist to show him one of the more powerful things I'd learned from Ren.

Galen grabbed my wrist. "Am I one of your targets?"

His gaze narrowed as he stared down at me and he licked his lips.

I shook my head. With him, I was compelled to do the things Ren taught me, likely the same way Galen felt obligated to soothe my nightmares.

He released me and stepped back. "Why don't I believe that?"

I blinked and stared at the floor. His confusion and want kept splashing over me in waves. "I'm an empath. I can sense your desire."

"You're an assassin who will use anything, including your body, to get to your mark. Mya warned us about your kind. She explained the psychological warfare the Director and his handlers rained down on the assassins throughout their upbringing, and the constant threat of physical harm after you are let out into the field."

"It never worked for me."

"What never worked for you?"

"Their programming. Which is why Ren taught me things that were forbidden. I don't think he believed I could kill based on an order." I looked up at Galen. "And he's probably right. I am not sure I could take a life without it being self-defense."

He sighed and closed his eyes, pinching the bridge of his nose. "Mya said you were different. I witnessed your formidable fighting ability, which she confirmed you were scrappy as hell when she sparred with you. And yet you did not kill any of those men attacking you at the tavern."

"I've never taken Mya down," I mumbled, because I wasn't sure I could articulate why I didn't kill those who were attacking me. It just didn't settle right with me. It was the same with the woman in the cabin.

"Neither have I," Galen said. "But that's beside the point. I cannot take the chance that you would coerce me in such a way that I'd let my guard down, and then you'd escape and go after Mya. It's a fatal mistake, and I will not make it. It will put my kingdom in jeopardy."

"But you do desire me?" I asked, because that was the primary emotion from him as he caressed me with his gaze.

"Any man in his right mind would. But you're a prisoner here, and it is wrong to take advantage of you in this setting. Just as it was wrong of your handler to take advantage of you while masking it as training," he growled and then stormed out of my cell, slamming the door closed before he stalked toward the main area of the jail.

I blinked as his harsh words crawled under my skin.

Ren had taken advantage of me?

THE ELVREN ASSASSIN
CHAPTER SEVENTEEN
Avery

LIGHTS BLINDED ME, AND I rolled onto my
stomach, burying my face in my pillow. My
back ached, but it wasn't as much pain as when
I'd gone to sleep.

I turned my head toward the front of the
building where they had dumped someone into
one of the cells, but a black privacy curtain
blocked my view of the rest of the jail.

Galen padded quietly to my cell and put his finger to his lips. He let himself in and took a seat on the edge of my bed.

I opened my mouth, but he shook his head, sending me a warning glare.

The door to the jail forcefully swung open, followed by the sound of chairs scraping on the floor. Galen blocked my view of who had entered the building, but I saw the door latch closed behind whoever it was.

"I know you're awake." Mya's voice rang through the small space.

A groan sounded from the cell behind the curtain.

A wave of anguish swept through me, and I looked at Galen. Whoever they had locked up was in terrible shape, both physically and mentally.

Galen leaned close. "Do not say a word. Understand?"

His breath tickled my ear, and his sharp gaze made me nod.

"Did the Director send you?" Mya asked.

"No," a voice rasped, so low I almost didn't catch it.

"And you expect me to believe you?" Mya laughed, but the tone held no humor.

It sounded cold enough to make me shiver.

"Just let me kill him," the prince's impatient tone rang through the jail cells.

The stoic way Galen sat next to me with his hands clenched into tight fists made me wonder who it was they were questioning.

"No. He didn't trigger the gate." Mya's tone gave no chance for an argument.

I imagined the prince crossing his arms and frowning at her, and it made me smile.

Until the man in the cell spoke clearly enough for my heart to stall.

"You killed all of them?" The accusation rang through the room in a voice I would recognize anywhere.

I had heard that beautiful timbre almost every day for the last twelve years of my life. And the man who owned that lyrical voice haunted my dreams for just as long.

I sat up, but Galen's arm snaked around me, yanking me to his side. His other hand covered my mouth, the warning in his eyes clear. He would not let me tip Mya's hand.

"Yes," the prince confirmed. "Every dirty assassin sent here with the intent to harm my family has been put down."

The prince's words were true. I did not fall into that category, which was why I was still breathing and not dead on the tavern floor like Em. But Ren didn't know that. I wanted to speak. To tell him I was here and fine, but Galen's head still shook, and his eyes carried an unyielding warning.

"You had better kill me because I'm making it my life's mission to rip your head off." The flare of rage Ren transmitted hit harder than his despair.

"You're assuming you will live long enough to get out of that cell," Mya said. "You were in rough shape when we pulled you out of the cave. That wasn't anything the magic in there does. Do you want to tell me what happened and why the hell you would come here of all places if the Director didn't send you?"

Devastation filled me, and I sagged against Galen. My eyes filled with tears at the weight of the emotions filling me. They weren't mine. They were Ren's.

"The Director said they all failed. That Eleka was indeed a dead planet. But that did not match what number five-three-seven said when he came back a few days earlier. He said he had killed the queen and sent the message the

466

Director instructed." Ren groaned, and the creak of the cot sounded. "Three-five-seven told me the last time he saw Avery was when she and one-twenty-two were headed toward the market."

"That still doesn't explain your injuries." Mya's growl equaled the impatience I felt from both her and the prince.

"I made the grave mistake of arguing with the Director in a public forum."

"You still haven't told me why you came here." Mya's voice hardened.

"Because if Avery died, I would have known."

"Bullshit."

Ren laughed his dry, humorless laugh. "Before the Director had every member of the league beat me to within a breath of death for failing again, he had the audacity to tell me that if one-twenty-two was successful, her directive was to kill Avery before she came back to Icarus."

I jerked in Galen's grip, and he tightened his hold on me. Galen's thumb made small circles on my side to soothe the shock of everything Ren was spilling.

"So, again, why Eleka?" Mya sighed the question. She was losing patience.

"I was dead anyway. So why not go to the place the Director proclaimed as off-limits?"

"That's easy. To kill me," Mya said. "At the Director's orders with this bullshit story to cover his ass."

"No. I'd never try to kill you, Mya. You were Avery's only real friend."

"There are no such things as friends on Icarus," Mya said.

Her voice carried a bitter tone that I understood all too well, and after hearing of Em's duplicity, I understood how different I was from everyone else, including Mya.

"Would you have killed her if you had been given the order?" Ren asked.

Silence filled the space, and Ren scoffed.

"I wouldn't have," he growled low.

"Oh, but you'd gladly take advantage of her any time you pleased?"

"Excuse me?" Ren actually sounded put off by Mya's question. "I taught her how to survive."

Mya's snort followed. "Yeah. Right. And you got nothing out of it at all."

"Don't give me that judgmental bullshit. I did what was necessary to protect her. I taught her skills that she would need if she was ever sent out for a job. One-twenty-two could become invisible and get close to her targets. You have that kiss of death thing. Avery is an empath. She has no special skills that can render a target defenseless. So, I gave her the instruction she needed to come within range to deliver a fatal blow."

"And crossed the Director's hard line by engaging in forbidden acts with your protégé."

"Yes."

"Why?" Mya's exasperation snapped in the air. "Why not just let the Director terminate her for being defective?"

We had seen that happen a few times over the years. Someone who didn't obey or was too skittish to knock out a fellow assassin. If they didn't have the kill response, they were put to death. I always wondered why I was spared because I did not have that automatic kill response. Far from it.

"Because I've been in love with that girl for years and protected her from the Director, trying to stall the inevitable." Ren's voice cracked. "Avery wasn't like the rest of us. She actually had some heavenly grace left in her angel blood." He took a breath. "And as to why I came to

Eleka...if Em was still alive and hunting you, I had a chance to protect Avery."

My eyes widened, and my heart squeezed with his words.

"Does the Director know where you went?"

"No. I was dumped outside to die, but I had enough energy left to zap to the portal and imagine Eleka. Blood wasn't a problem, as you saw. Once I was in the portal, I flew." He laughed. "I nearly crashed into the wall across from the portal before banking and seeing the exit. Then I pushed my limits, flying as fast as I could through the gate into the outer cavern. I thought my lungs were going to explode when I saw the outer exit. I aimed for it, and that's all I remember until I woke here."

"And you were ready to take our army to Icarus and wipe them all out," Mya scolded.

It took me a moment to realize her jab was at the prince, not Ren.

"You believe him?" the prince asked, his tone as incredulous as Ren's story.

"The Director can track me here, though," Ren said. "So, I wouldn't put that idea away just yet."

"We took care of that," Mya said. "He cannot trace where you are now that we removed your chip. So, unless he figures out you didn't die where they dropped you, he'll believe you are dead. If he thinks you came here, he will also assume you are dead because all the others sent after the queen's funeral died when they touched the outer gate. My kiss of death magic is infused into the bars. So, anyone trying to get to Eleka or anyone with more than fae blood trying to leave will turn to dust when they touch that gate. But removing your chip wasn't without damage."

Her tone changed, almost reflecting the regret I felt dancing around her feelings.

"What do you mean?" Ren's tentative question made me suck in air.

"Your chip was wrapped in the muscles that control your wings. We were able to remove it, but I had to go deep and severed muscles and tendons to get to it."

The curtain separating us fell, and my eyes widened at his blackened wings. Wings that drooped as if there was nothing supporting them. His torso was so bruised it looked as if his coloring was purple instead of the naturally tan skin he usually sported, and the number of lacerations brought tears to my eyes.

"And?"

"And I'm not sure you'll ever fly again."

Ren's shoulders sagged, and his head dropped forward.

Mya nodded in our direction, and Galen removed his hand from over my lips, but he did not leave my side.

"Ren?"

His head shot up, and he turned fast enough to hiss in pain at the motion. His face and chest were as scarred and beaten as his back.

"Avery?"

I covered my mouth as hot tears leaked from my eyes. I nodded.

Ren turned back to Mya and the prince sitting outside his cell. "You said you killed all the assassins."

"We said we killed all those with nefarious intent," Mya answered with a wry smile. "Which I should inform you right now, if you even think of laying a finger on Tavin in some misguided attempt at retribution,"—she threaded her fingers through the prince's hand—"I will kill you myself. Harming him harms me."

Ren gasped. "Bonded?"

"Spirit mates," Tavin corrected. "We share a soul and have access to each other's powers."

Ren shifted his gaze between the floor and me. He blinked, focusing on Galen's protective hold on me.

"Why is he touching you?" he snarled.

"Because I knew as an empath, this conversation would be hard on her, and she would need the support," Galen said, his voice challenging Ren.

"The conversation is over," Ren said. "I suggest you get your hands off her right this minute."

Galen did not move his hand away from me. "You are lucky you're locked in that cage because I'm about a second away from pounding you into the hereafter for what you've done to Avery."

I gasped and looked up at Galen. His jaw was so tight I thought he'd fracture all his teeth. The hostility radiating from him matched his glare aimed at Ren. His gaze slipped to mine, and his tension eased.

"He took advantage of you. I cannot abide that sort of behavior," he explained.

Although he did not need to. His protectiveness over my feelings and my honor was endearing.

"But he's my handler." Even though I was angry with Ren, I couldn't let Galen hurt him.

"No. Not here he isn't. He is just a man who has wronged you in the most heinous of ways. He took your innocence for his own selfish purposes." Galen cupped the back of my head and kissed my forehead before he got up and left me alone in the cell.

Mya and Tavin stood as Galen walked past them and out the door.

"We'll talk later," Mya said, looking at me before she turned, and she and the prince followed Galen out of the jail, leaving me with only Ren's out-of-control emotions to contend with.

Ren put his head in his hands. "I thought you were in danger, and I wanted to be here to protect you."

My insides jumbled with emotions, and I didn't know which ones were mine and which were his.

But I knew one thing. My handler had lied to me.

"Years?" My anger bloomed with that one word.

I was sure Ren felt it as acutely as I did. He had always been better at ignoring his empathic side, but he could read me better than I could read myself sometimes.

He nodded without looking at me.

"You've lied to me for years?" My voice rose at his non-answer.

He stiffened and turned. "I never lied."

"No. You just omitted one massive truth." I wouldn't bring up what he'd told me about all men. Perhaps that was only his narrow perception, given his upbringing in the league.

His gaze turned into a glare. "And how would that have gone over on Icarus? Huh? I was protecting you."

I stretched out on the cot, facing him, chewing my bottom lip before letting the words tumble out. "Protecting me while you beat the shit out of me in the sparring ring and brought me back to your room to patch me up, only to teach me things the Director would kill us for?" I huffed. "Right."

Galen could have easily let me do those things for the pleasure he would have gained from it. But he couldn't. He had principles, much like I had.

Ren didn't. Ren was more of the programmed beast the Director wanted than I was.

"Rest so you can heal, and after that, I'm going to kick your ass," I said and winced as I rolled to give him my back.

He grunted then muttered, "In your dreams."

Little did he know, my dreams tonight did not center on him. They were singularly focused on my green-eyed guard, who wanted to be the hero.

THE ELVREN ASSASSIN
CHAPTER EIGHTEEN
Ren

WHAT THE FUCK JUST happened?

I lay back on the cot, wincing as I tried to roll. At least most of my bones had mended while I was unconscious. But I was still a long way from a sparring session.

My brain combed over everything. Mya thought I took advantage of Avery, and she was right. I totally used my position to get her into a compromising one. I never liked what I saw in the mirror back at the complex. I loathed myself for causing Avery physical harm and for callously shattering her innocence.

The alternative was seeing Avery subjected to the type of beating I had received. And I didn't know if she was strong enough to survive something that destructive.

Besides, the Director would have made me watch the beatings and witness the scavengers ripping her skin from her bones until there was nothing left. That was not an option.

I would go through it a hundred times over to spare her that type of physical anguish.

I compartmentalized things; she didn't.

Now she looked at me with something close to contempt. My stomach soured at the reality of possibly losing her because I was such a self-serving prick.

I tried to flex my wings, but that left me with crippling pain racing through my back as if I were being stabbed with a thousand knives.

I was a master at healing, and even with all the beatings I had endured, I had never lost control over my wings. But now, I couldn't even get them to open.

It was as disheartening as seeing Avery's glare.

THE ELVREN ASSASSIN
CHAPTER NINETEEN
Avery

I WOKE TO THE rattle of keys and rolled, staring at a young female fae who brought in a tray of food.

"Galen said you might like a privacy screen for the toilet." First, she put the tray on the cot, and next, she dragged in a prettily decorated screen and placed it around the toilet.

She left the cell door open while she retrieved the screen, which meant they didn't think I was dangerous. On one hand, it was a relief, but on a more basic level, it annoyed me. Everyone always underestimated me.

Instead of making a big deal of it, I offered my thanks as she left and clasped the door closed, and then I dug into my meal, ignoring the eyes boring into me from a couple of cells away.

The girl slipped his tray through the opening at the foot of Ren's cot. Once she left the building, I studied his profile as he ate. His bruises and cuts had faded a little since his conversation with Mya and the prince. But his wings still drooped.

"What will you do if your wings never work again?" I asked as I studied the blackened, molted mess attached to his back.

They were a stark contrast to his pristine white wings I had seen before I left Icarus.

He glared at me. "Does it really matter to you whether I fly or crawl?"

His vitriol had me moving back against the far bars behind me.

"Excuse me for caring," I muttered and focused on my food.

Before he could launch into a tirade at me, the door to the jail opened. Guards filed in, securing the area before the king himself entered. His son took after him, except the king had a ruthless edge that I didn't get from Tavin. He bypassed Ren and came to stand before my cell.

I stood and curtsied in the manner I had been taught to honor fae royalty. It was drilled into us to gain favor and get closer to our royal targets. I also averted my eyes.

"Look at me, girl," the king commanded.

I jumped my gaze to his.

"You are part Elvren. Correct?"

"Yes, Your Majesty."

"And part angel, from what Mya tells me?"

"Yes. I have fallen angel DNA."

He rubbed his chin. "And you have been bred and raised in the League of Supernatural Assassins."

He'd not phrased his statement as a question, but I answered him anyway. "Yes, Your Majesty."

He cocked his head and narrowed his eyes. "You seem more resigned rather than proud."

"Correct, Your Majesty."

"I am not sure what to do with you."

I pushed down the need to make excuses for my associates. There really were no excuses for the things they did. So, I kept my mouth closed and waited for my sentence to be rendered.

"You seem to have charmed Mya and my son enough for them to advocate for your release. However, I cannot have an assassin from Icarus given free rein in my country. For both my kingdom's safety and yours. Do you understand?"

I didn't really, but I nodded anyway.

He nodded to his guards, and they opened the cell and took me by the arm.

"Do not harm her." Despite his injuries, Ren jumped to his feet and leaped toward the bars even before we passed by his cell.

"Ah. The assassin who risked starting a war because he disregarded orders." The king's tone was one of disdain, and his glare toward Ren carried the same contempt. "What we do with her is none of your concern. If I were you, I would be more worried about *your* punishment than hers."

The guards led me toward the door.

"I swear..." Ren started what I imagined would be a tirade that included threats of some kind that would not bode well for him.

"Ren, stop," I interrupted and glared over my shoulder. He actually heeded my warning. "I can take care of myself, despite what you think."

The guards led me out the door with the king following our little procession.

The king kept pace behind us and did not speak until we were inside the castle proper.

I gawked at the atrium. I had never seen such opulence before. When I finally had my fill of the magnificent art and beautiful tapestries, I turned my gaze to the king.

His soft smile startled me.

"Mya said you were innocent in ways that she could never articulate properly." He glanced around at the castle. "You've never been inside a castle?"

"I've never been away from Icarus, Your Majesty."

"How old are you?" he asked, seeming perplexed.

"I'm nineteen, Your Majesty."

He grunted. "Still a child." He turned to the guards. "Take her to the servants' quarters. Galen, set up a room for her there." He faced me again. "The room is charmed so you cannot come and go as you please until I am satisfied that you are not here to harm Mya or my son. A guard will be available to take you wherever you would like to go inside the palace, in our gardens, or to the market."

"Yes, Your Majesty." I executed another curtsey and followed the guards to a room that was significantly larger than any space I had ever had alone. It was almost as big as the ten-person dorms.

I gawked at the fourposter bed on the far wall and the sitting area near the door.

"Is this not acceptable?" Galen asked as he stepped in and waved the guards away.

I spun around and stared at him. "It's huge."

A smile toyed on his lips for a moment. "It is one of the more spacious rooms in the servant quarters, but it is small compared to the compound for the guards and their families."

He walked over to one of the two doors to the right of the bed. "This is your bathroom." He swung the door open, showing me a space that was roughly the size of the cell I had been in, and then moved to the other door. "And this is your closet. Mya conjured you some clothes

486

since she didn't think you had anything else to wear. She also said there are personal items for you in the bathroom and in your drawers. I believe she covered all the essentials and more, but if you prefer to go to the market and select your own items, I can accompany you."

"Aren't you the prince's guard?"

"Yes, but he lets me out on my own every now and again." He winked at me.

I widened my eyes.

"Seriously, I do not usually work every day all day. I get time off. And if you are not averse to it, I'd like to spend some of my free time with you." He glanced at the ground, and his cheeks reddened.

I stared at him, blinking fast as his words sank in. This good-looking guard wanted to spend his free time with me? I did not know what to say to that.

"I could show you the palace." He waved to the doorway.

I glanced down at my soiled clothing. "Um. I'd like to clean up since I haven't in days."

Even the slip they'd put me in was marred with dried blood.

"Oh. Okay, maybe another time." He backed away, and the red in his cheeks deepened.

Disappointment raked over me. *His* disappointment. I didn't mean to offend Galen.

"If you'd like to wait, I'll be glad to take a tour of the castle and the grounds with you," I blurted before he got past whatever charms held me prisoner in the room.

Galen paused briefly before a gorgeous smile appeared on his lips. He took a seat on the couch and waved toward the bathroom. "By all means. I'll just wait for you here."

I went to the dresser and opened the top drawer. There indeed were "personal items," as Galen had put it. I grabbed a pair and then stopped in the closet to see what Mya had conjured.

I had no idea how much time I spent staring at the dichotomy of the flowing dresses next to the leather pants and shirts tailored for my wings. It humbled me, and I did not know what to choose.

Galen stepped into the closet with me and reached past me to pull a dress off the hanger. "That would be appropriate for a walk in the castle garden."

"Thank you." I glanced at the rest and then focused on his bright-green eyes that crinkled at the outer edges when he smiled. "It's overwhelming."

He retreated with a nod, and I headed into the bathroom and the shower that was too big for one person. Mya had set me up with some fine citrus wash and towels that were so soft, I almost wanted to wear them. I combed out the knots in my wet hair and shook my wings before drying the rest of me and putting on the undergarments and the dress Galen chose.

It complemented the blues in my wings, and the buttery-soft fabric flowed around my knees as I crossed back into the room. It was exactly the kind of dress I had seen women in the market wearing, and though I had initially scoffed at wearing something this impractical, it felt divine against my skin.

Galen scanned me and grinned. "There are shoes in the closet, too. I'd suggest flats. They're better suited for walking."

I slipped on the ones that looked like they would be the most comfortable, and I was not disappointed. It was like walking on clouds.

Galen took my hand, and I stared at our clasped fingers.

"I can hold your hand or your arm. But in order to get you out of this room, there needs to be physical contact. As soon as we are out of here, you can choose to let go."

I followed him out the door, and once we were in the hall, I walked by his side, my hand still in his. His light grip warmed me, and my heart fluttered. My mind wandered back to that kiss when I'd been in such pain.

"Why did you kiss me?"

He slowed to a stop and ran his free hand through his hair. "I am drawn to you, Avery. And it was all I could think of to distract you from the pain." He chewed on his bottom lip as he resumed our stroll. "Did it work?"

He glanced sideways at me as if he were afraid of the answer.

"It worked." Oh, how it worked. It lit something inside me that made even this innocent contact heat me from the center of my being all the way to my toes.

It was something I wanted to explore more.

Galen turned to the right at the atrium where we had entered the castle and led me into a room he called the grand ballroom. Glistening marble tables lined the walls, and the burgundy with gold trim chairs accented the sconces on the walls. The stained-glass windows painted the floor with colored light. It looked magnificent.

Instead of leading me through the ballroom, he retraced his steps to a door on the opposite side of the atrium.

He touched the door but didn't open it. "This is the throne room, where the king hears the people's grievances or passes judgement on criminals."

He led me away, but I pulled him back at the intensity of emotions emanating from the room.

"I'd like to see it." I had never actually seen a throne. Sure, we'd read about them and were taught this was likely the best place to impress a target. But I wanted to see the reality. I wanted to understand the feelings pelting me.

Galen looked at the door and opened his mouth.

"Please," I added before he could deny my request.

He unclasped his hand from mine and put his arm around my back, pulling me to his side before he opened the door to lead me into a packed throne room.

No wonder anger suffocated me. The place was packed, and the mood was one of vengeance. Then agony draped over me just before a cry that voiced the emotion shattered the still air.

I moved toward the pain before Galen could stop me. He followed close behind, but the emotions of the crowd pummeled me with murderous thoughts, overriding the anguish.

When I finally breached the crowd, I stopped at the sight before me. My heart wrenched in my chest hard enough for me to gasp.

Ren knelt with his arms stretched out in chains so tight that every muscle in his arms and back stood out. Blood coated his back. His blackened, molted wings lay on the ground, doused in the blood running freely from where they'd been severed.

Galen's hand clasped around my arm. I'm not sure if he was trying to stop me or console me, but I twisted away from his grip when the executioner approached, ready to deliver the final blow.

I was mad at Ren, but I most certainly did not want him dead.

I darted across the distance, muttering a protection spell that surrounded Ren, and slid into the space between him and the executioner's blade.

"No," I whispered, splaying my hands out.

The executioner's eyes hardened, and he brought the blade back to strike us both down. I prayed my protection spell would survive even after my death.

I closed my eyes, waiting for the whistle of the blade.

THE ELVREN ASSASSIN
CHAPTER TWENTY
Avery

"STOP!" MYA YELLED, AND the executioner pulled the blade back before it bit into my skin.

He took a step away from us.

Galen was halfway to me when he stopped, blinking. His expression was unreadable, and his gaze darted to Mya and the prince flanking the king's throne.

"Ren does not deserve a death sentence. He did not come here to harm any of you. He came after *me*. To save my life." I remained in place between Ren and the man tasked with taking his life, but I directed my plea to the only one in the room who could have ordered this. "Your Highness, I beg of you. Do not condemn him for one of his few noble acts." I glanced at Galen. "Do not condemn him for his upbringing." I pointed at Mya, including her in my attempt to stop this madness. "*Our* upbringing."

"Let it go, Avery," Ren said with enough pain in his voice to give me pause. "Don't damn yourself for me."

My wings fluttered, and I turned to face the king and dropped to my knee, bowing my head. "Please, my king. I ask for your mercy and time to prove ourselves to this kingdom."

"I refuse to gamble the lives of those in my kingdom." The king's hard voice penetrated me like a dozen bullets. "Not for a man who has no honor."

"Make him my responsibility," Galen said from behind me. "I will not allow him to harm a single citizen of this kingdom. And I will not hesitate to put him down if he attempts to."

I slowly straightened and climbed to my feet, shocked at Galen's offer. Especially since I knew he wanted to do irreparable harm to Ren.

"And what of her?" The king jutted his chin at me.

"I will vouch for Avery," Mya said. "She is not a danger to Eleka."

"And what about *you*?" someone from the crowd yelled.

The prince stepped forward, glaring at the crowd. "I vouch for my spirit mate and your future queen."

His voice chilled me.

The king pursed his lips. He did not appear pleased by any of this. "Leave us."

His voice echoed over the crowd, and they filtered out. When it was only us, the royal family, and their personal guards, the king walked down the steps to Galen.

"I do not appreciate your stepping in, Galen." He crossed his arms.

"I know, Your Majesty. But she put herself between an executioner's blade and this wretch." Galen closed his mouth and lowered his gaze.

The king's half growl and glare back in his son's direction gave me a fragment of hope. But that died when he said, "Put him in the dungeon."

"No. He needs medical attention. Put him in my room." The words tumbled out of my mouth before I had the good sense to stop them. But since I had already started, I pointed at his back. "You had him butchered. At least let me patch him up before you lock him up somewhere that isn't sanitary."

The king stepped close to invade my space, and instead of cowering at his terse glare, I stood tall and looked him in the eye.

"Please," I added in a soft plea.

The king's jaw tightened as he stared me down. "You need to learn your place in my kingdom." He glanced at Galen. "Be sure to educate her in the ways of the court."

"I will, Your Majesty." Galen bowed his head before stepping forward, taking my arm in a tight grip. "And what shall I have done with him?"

The king's nostrils flared as he looked at me. "Bring him to her quarters until his back is healed. Once he is out of danger, you better find a suitable spot for him that is as equally warded as her room."

Galen's eyes darkened, but he nodded.

The chains holding Ren released, and he fell to his knees with a yelp of pain.

The guards grabbed Ren in a not-so-gentle hold and dragged him to my quarters, with Galen and me following close behind.

"Wait," Galen said as they dragged Ren to the side of my bed.

He disappeared into the bathroom, came out with one of the plush, oversized towels, and laid it on the bed before nodding.

The guards dropped Ren face-first on the towel and left the room.

"Do you have any of that nectar you gave me in the jail before Mya took out my chip?" I asked Galen.

He met my gaze and pressed his lips together as if he wanted to refuse. He closed his eyes, inhaled deeply, and nodded before he headed toward the door.

"And some of that healing salve?" I called after him.

Ren needed all the help he could get, and that gel worked fast. Faster than our natural healing abilities.

I climbed onto the bed on the far side of Ren and stared at his butchered back. Sorrow bit at my insides. I'd never get to see Ren fly. I'd seen him rise in the arena, but not truly fly, and now I never would.

He turned his head and glanced up at me. "They cut off my wings."

A single tear slipped down his nose before he closed his eyes and buried his face in the towel.

The shock of his tears rocked me to the core, and all I wanted to do was wrap my arms around him and ease his pain. Instead, I gently squeezed his shoulder to offer my support, even though it was not nearly enough to compensate for being butchered.

I couldn't say how I'd feel if they cut off my wings.

Galen stepped into the room with a pitcher, a cup, and a jar of salve. He put them on the nightstand and stood over us like a lost sentry. His awkwardness with the situation rubbed on my nerves.

"You don't need to stay. I've got this." I smiled at him, even though I wasn't sure I had this at all.

My stomach felt like a metal ball pinging chaotically around the inside, pulverizing everything in its path.

Trails of blood seeped down Ren's sides, and the rawness of where his wings had been sliced tightened my chest.

"You sure?" Galen asked.

"Yes. I've triaged worse." I went to the bathroom, grabbed a bucket I found under the sink, and filled it with clean water before taking a few of the hand and face towels.

When I returned, Galen was gone. Ren's gaze tracked me as I pulled over a straight-back chair and sat next to him.

Before I started working on his back, I poured a cup of the nectar and glanced at him. "Think you can prop up on your arms or roll on your side because you can't drink this without wearing most of it in that position."

He slowly moved his arms to his sides and pushed up on his forearms.

Agony pelted me, and I ignored the sensations flowing from Ren. I brought the full cup to his lips and helped him drink until he consumed the last drop.

He fell back onto the bed with a groan. "What is that stuff?"

"I'm not sure, but it didn't stop the pain when they dug out my chip. At least you were unconscious for that. Be thankful I'm only cleaning and putting the salve on your wounds."

I dipped the face cloth into the water and gently swiped his back.

He winced but remained still.

"I know. It hurts," I whispered as I worked on disinfecting the wound.

Infection could slam him back into mortal danger.

It took me a solid hour to clean the dirt and grime from his exposed wounds and put the salve on. I continued to wash the grime off him from his prior beating and subsequent flight through the portal and time in the cell. After applying a second coat of the miracle healing gel on his back, I went to the bathroom to clean up.

I returned and climbed on the opposite side of the bed, curling next to him. He turned his head my way.

"Thank you," he slurred, and a rare, genuine smile tilted his lips.

"Mmm." I was still angry with all his duplicity back at the complex, but seeing him helpless and a little goofy from the drink was certainly endearing enough to set my heart thumping. "Sleep."

His eyes slipped closed, and I wondered if having him here in my room was prudent. It certainly left me open to many things going wrong.

Ren wasn't patient on his best day, and when he finally noticed the way Galen looked at me, there would be hell to pay.

THE ELVREN ASSASSIN
CHAPTER TWENTY-ONE
Ren

I CLOSED MY EYES, and while sleep would have been a blessing, having her this near to me left all my senses tingling with want.

She had intervened. I guess I never expected anyone to sacrifice themselves for me, especially Avery. After all, it had been my job to beat her into submission on Icarus.

When her breathing evened out to that of sleep, I opened my eyes and studied her. Strands of her purple hair fell across her face, and I had the urge to tuck them behind her ear. I kept my hands to myself, though. Her wings complemented her hair, just like her eyes. All that purple and blue accented by her alabaster skin stirred the need I hid from the world.

I turned away before I did something I'd hate myself for in the light of day. Avery was my weakness. I'd walk through the fires of hell for her, but I had never told her how deep my feelings ran.

The drink she had given me was wearing off, and every ache and pain in my body became like an acute stab of discomfort, which probably meant a sleepless night. And I needed sleep to heal.

I rolled onto my side, and my back screamed with razor-sharp agony. I clenched my teeth against making a sound. If I could reach the damn pitcher, I'd drink the rest of that nectar and hopefully drop into a drunk stupor.

Anything to avoid the devastation lurking in the dark shadows. The reality that my wings had been severed would kick my ass if I let it. My wings defined me. They were what made me an angel and not just a man. Without them, I was lost in the abyss with little hope of ever surfacing again. Despair creeped into my mind, clouding it in darkness.

How I wished Avery had let them kill me. Then I wouldn't have to feel. I wouldn't have to face my failures. I didn't want to see that look of disgust on her face, like the way she'd looked at me this morning when she realized I had taken advantage of her on Icarus.

She had every right to be pissed at me, and yet she'd put herself between me and the executioner's blade.

I glanced at her again, sensing she wasn't really sleeping. "Why?" I whispered.

"Why what?" she asked with her eyes closed.

"Why'd you save me?"

She sighed and opened her eyes. "Because what is between us is complicated and messy and wrong on so many levels, but it's mine. And I have precious little that's ever been mine, so I've always held what we have dear to my heart."

"I beat the shit out of you regularly in the sparring ring."

"You bested me."

"No, Avery. I assaulted you because I was commanded to treat you that way. I was ordered to beat your angel tendencies out of you. Otherwise, you would be terminated." I tried to roll toward her, but the minute my back hit the bed's surface, it was as if it had been doused with gasoline and set on fire.

Air sucked into my lungs and stayed in place as my entire body tensed, making the pain transcend to a blackout state.

Light taps on my cheeks brought me back into a world of pain. It hadn't hurt this much when they'd cut my wings off. Either that or I was already in shock from the rest of my injuries to the point of being numb.

I blinked my eyes open to Avery's concerned gaze.

"You passed out."

No shit. At least I kept that thought to myself. "They cut off my wings. What the hell did you expect?"

She recoiled.

That came out harsher than I meant, but I was not myself right now. I was angrier than I had been on Icarus, but I knew that stemmed from this unmanageable agony gripping my back.

Avery poured another cup of the sweet nectar and offered it to me. She still played the role of a nursemaid.

I gazed at the drink then at her.

"It will take the edge off and allow you to get some rest. And you need rest to heal, Ren."

"Fine." I pushed up on one arm, wincing as the muscles in my back shifted.

I downed the cup she handed me, and after a minute, warmth spread through me. I dropped onto my stomach and hugged the pillow, wondering if I'd ever truly recover from the loss of my wings.

THE ELVREN ASSASSIN
CHAPTER TWENTY-TWO
Avery

MORNING CAME FAST, BUT Ren was still unconscious. His coloring had improved enough so I couldn't see the bruising from the Director's beating, but his bandages were marred with dark spots, as if our natural healing abilities had no impact on where his wings were severed.

I sighed and changed his dressings before heading to the shower to clean up. The water felt heavenly against my tired skin. The last few days had been filled with emotional trials, and I don't ever remember feeling this strung out. Showering breathed a bit of energy into my fogged brain, and I dried off and wrapped the towel around me before I headed into the main room to figure out clothes.

I stopped at the sight of Galen inside my room. He wasn't wearing his usual guard attire. Today he wore a simple tunic that complemented his eyes and a pair of leathers that hugged the muscles in his legs and sent my mind into a tailspin.

His eyes widened, and he turned his back to me as if seeing me nearly naked was some sort of sin.

I dropped the towel and slid on a pair of underwear. "What's wrong?"

"You're not dressed." He glanced over his shoulder at me and swiveled his gaze away just as quickly.

My lips curved into a smile. Ren never shied away from me when I dressed in front of him. He also didn't hide watching me, but the difference was Ren didn't have the same longing in his eyes as Galen had right now.

Instead of teasing him, I slid into the closet and chose another flowing dress and a fresh pair of shoes since the flats I had on yesterday were soaked with Ren's blood.

I dressed and then stepped back into the room. The door clicked as I closed it, and Galen stole another glance. This time, he turned toward me with interest sparkling in his eyes.

"I figured I'd see if you wanted to resume the tour of the castle," he said and shuffled his feet.

I looked at Ren and sighed, torn by the responsibility I felt toward him and the need for a non-eventful day. I needed light conversation and motion since I had been delegated to a cell for a couple of days. I also needed something to distract me from the worry winding its way through my nerves.

"As long as you promise me a calm, uneventful tour." I smirked. "I don't think I could take another challenging situation after the last few days."

Galen chuckled and nodded. "I will do my best to make this as calm a day as possible with no surprises."

He held his hand out for me to take. I stepped closer, threading my fingers through his, and let him lead me out into the hallway. I closed the door to buffer the hustle of the castle from Ren. He needed more rest for his back to heal.

"Is he going to be okay?" Galen asked as he led me away from my room.

That he asked about Ren when he disliked the man made my legs feel gooey, like they were made of rubber instead of skin and bones.

I shook the swoon away and focused. "Physically, yes. But I'm not sure what the psychological effects of losing his wings will do to him. I can't even fathom it. And his wings were really something to behold."

I sighed, feeling the slam of loss in the center of my being.

"Yours are as well." Galen scanned the wings on my back.

"They are just fancy ornaments. Ren could fly."

Galen sighed. "I know I asked after him, but I would prefer not to discuss the fallen angel today, if you don't mind." Galen's gaze flicked to mine and then forward again. "Besides, it's a beautiful day to stroll through the royal gardens. I'd rather not bring clouds into our sunny day."

I rolled my eyes at his poorly framed metaphor but nodded my assent. I didn't want to discuss Ren. Everything to do with him was complicated, and I craved simplicity.

When Galen opened the ornate stained-glass doors in the ballroom, all thoughts of Ren and our complex relationship disappeared.

I gasped at the plethora of colors and sweet scents just outside the grand doorway. Every spectrum of color dotted the landscape. Just like the first time I stepped out of the portal cave, the visual sensations overloaded me, especially when met with the assault on my senses.

Galen kept his hand in mine as we strolled through the paths between flower beds. He explained what each different breed of flower was and showed me the good herbs and flowers as opposed to the ones that were beautiful but deadly.

When we reached the far side of the garden, he pointed out a special crop of herbs near the servants' wing of the castle.

"That's where I get what I need for my healing salve. The buttermilk weed provides mystical properties that make it work better than most salves." He brought me to the small patch of purple-tinted flowers and crouched down, plucking one from the ground. When he stood, he tucked it behind my ear.

I leaned into his touch, and his eyes sparkled just before he dipped in and pressed his lips to mine. Without the pain vying for my attention, his kiss weakened my knees. I pressed against him, with my palm over his pounding heart, while twirling my tongue with his in a lazy dance that jump-started my desire.

He pulled away and pressed his forehead to mine. "Damn."

His chest rose and fell the same way mine did, as if we had sprinted across the garden instead of our leisurely walk. I ran my palm up his chest to his cheek and snaked my fingers around his neck, pulling him back to my lips.

Galen had been my first kiss, and the second lit a fire in me. I did not want this bliss to end.

He groaned, and this time, his kiss was more fevered and frantic, as if I had awakened the same need in him I felt in my soul.

One minute I was in his arms, and the next, he stepped back far enough for me to feel the sting of rejection, even with his yearning caressing every inch of my skin.

"Avery, this isn't right. I'm responsible for you. I cannot take advantage of you like this." He put his palms out and then wiped his face.

I nodded and straightened my back against my disappointment. "I need to get back to check on Ren."

I turned toward the castle and nearly sprinted away from him, but his hand grasped my arm and forced me to face him.

"I won't be responsible for you forever. But until you've earned your freedom..." He inhaled and glanced beyond me as he schooled his features, reminding me more of Ren than the soulful guard I had been accustomed to. "I can't cross that line."

Damn sense of honor. It irked me enough to want to take him down in the sparring ring.

"Do you think we can spar a little later?" I blurted as I envisioned him rolling over my hip and onto his back on the mat.

If I couldn't sleep with the man, I'd beat the crap out of him.

Galen's stoic face broke out in a smile. "You want to spar with me?"

"Yes. Throwing you on the mat might be a fun way to get this pent-up aggression out." I smiled as sweetly as possible.

"Pent-up aggression?" Galen laughed, a full one that stopped my breath in my lungs. "That's a good way to describe it."

I grinned. "So that's a yes?"

"Sure."

THE ELVREN ASSASSIN
CHAPTER TWENTY-THREE
Avery

I CROSSED THE THRESHOLD with Galen by my side and halted at the empty bed. I scanned the room and found Ren sitting on the couch. His white shirt hung open, giving me a full view of his chiseled chest.

I flushed, especially with his dark hair dripping wet, leaving see-through drops on the shirt. He looked like a tragically lost, but stunningly beautiful, angel. I didn't think I'd ever realized how good-looking Ren was until this moment. He was perfection incarnate in a sinfully delicious, ripped package.

He stood and glared at Galen's hand on my back. "Do you have to touch her?" Even his tone issued a challenge.

"Actually, I do to get her through the barrier. Just like I'll unfortunately have to touch you to get you out of this room."

"You're inside her room. Now remove your hand from her back."

All my warm thoughts about his physical appearance iced over at his possessive tone. "Ren. Stop. Galen has been nothing but a gentleman these last few days."

Ren's eyes narrowed at me. "The last few days?"

"You've been passed out for days, Ren."

"And my back hasn't healed yet?" He dropped the shirt from his shoulders and turned, showing me his scars. Scars that I'd been applying the healing salve to every day and re-bandaging.

I knew his healing was slow, but at least it had scabbed over and wasn't weeping blood and pus any longer.

"It's healing," I assured him.

He slid the shirt back over his broad shoulders and plunked himself down on the couch again. "Days?"

I nodded and turned to Galen. "We can spar later."

I shooed him toward the door, but he didn't budge.

"I will take him to his room now." His tone was as unyielding as Ren's glare.

Ren cocked his head and slowly stood. "You can come and go into this room as you please?"

His hands curled into fists, his hostility radiating outward.

Galen grinned in a way that irritated me, as if he were purposely needling Ren, and he nodded.

This was not the man I had gotten to know over the past few days. The one who'd walked through the gardens and knew the name of all the flora and fauna we passed. The man who looked at me like I was a gift sent to this world.

But that man now had as much hostility flowing from his muscles as Ren.

Ren growled. He actually growled. "I don't like that."

"I don't give a damn what you think," Galen said. "And I'd be more than happy to drag your unconscious ass out of here."

"Do I look like I'm unconscious?" Ren stalked forward.

"Galen, he's still healing." I stepped between the building tensions and put my palm on Galen's chest.

My actions only upped the testosterone in the room.

"Do not touch him."

Ren's voice held a deadly warning, and I went to pull my hand away, but Galen's hand captured mine, pressing it to his chest.

"She can touch whoever the fuck she wants," Galen spit out. "Except you," he added as an afterthought.

I ripped my hand out from under his. "Get out! Both of you!"

I pointed toward the door. I didn't need this right now, and I certainly didn't want to have Ren's wounds split open and have to patch him up after he was acting like such an ass.

Both of them stared at me with their mouths parted in shock.

Before hostilities could escalate again, the prince and Mya strolled into the room.

Tavin waved toward the hallway and leveled a hard gaze at Ren. "I understand your room is ready," he said without missing a beat. "Mya has agreed to take you to it since I would rather have seen your head on a post."

"He's not a criminal," I snapped.

"He's an assassin," Tavin slung back.

"No. He's a handler." I couldn't let them think the worst of Ren. I might have been angry with him, but I didn't like that they were all against him.

"Fine." Ren got to his feet.

"I'll go with them to ensure her safety," Galen said before Ren could say any more.

"I can defend myself, or didn't you learn when I schooled your ass?" Mya grabbed Ren's arm, leading him out the door without waiting for either Tavin or Galen to follow.

"Where is she taking him?" I asked.

"Diagonally across the hall," Galen said. "It's not nearly the size of your space, but it's what was available."

I hoped Ren did nothing stupid in the few steps between here and his room. Otherwise, Mya would wipe the floor with him.

THE ELVREN ASSASSIN
CHAPTER TWENTY-FOUR
Ren

MYA LED ME ACROSS the hall and into a room that was probably the size of the one I had back on Icarus. It wasn't fancy like Avery's, with only a single bed, a dresser, a closet, and a small bathroom.

She let go of my arm once we were inside. "For the record, I don't trust you."

"Same," I replied.

She cocked her head.

"Is this a long game for you?" I twirled my finger.

Her lips pressed together, and hostility bloomed inside her. "I could ask the same about you."

I laughed. "I would think you would recognize a beating meant to kill from something meant for discipline."

Mya blinked and stepped back.

She and her precious prince had been the ones to pull me out of the portal cage, and she had mutilated my wings to get that damned chip out.

"If you thought I was here to harm you or your prince, why did you save me? Why take my chip out?"

"Because people could get hurt if the Director detonated that fucking chip. It isn't pretty, and anyone near you could have been harmed or killed. I wouldn't put it past the Director to do that if he somehow figured out you survived."

That was a new and chilling fact that I didn't know about. I thought the chips were just for tracking.

"How do you know that?" I asked.

"The Director once illustrated it to me by exploding a subpar assassin. And I'm pretty sure that's what they put in the queen and waited for the funeral to blow her to bits. I think they hoped I would be close enough to the explosion for it to kill me."

"Why would he do that instead of beating us to a pulp and leaving us to the scavengers?"

"Because he's a sick fuck."

I couldn't argue with Mya's assessment. She was right.

"You've got the same deal here that Avery has. Until you prove yourself, you'll need an escort in and out of your room. If you try to leave, you'll be shocked and thrown across the room from the impact. It isn't pleasant."

"You've experienced that?"

She tilted her lips in confirmation, and I chuckled.

"I'm not a threat to you or the throne. I came here for Avery."

"To save her." She snorted.

I nodded and glanced at the floor. When I arrived, I was in no condition to go against one of the more seasoned assassins.

"And to save *my* life. If I hadn't done something extreme, I would be just another set of bones picked clean by the scavengers."

Mya seemed to consider that. "When you're healed, we'll get you back into the training ring."

"Why?"

"Because it's always good to be sharp. You never know what dangers lurk around the corners."

That was exactly the kind of answer I expected from Mya. She was never complacent. She always dove into everything she did. I realized she was going to make one hell of a queen if Tavin ever made their bond legal with marriage.

I certainly never wanted to be on this girl's bad side. She was brutal with frightening efficiency. Which was why she was at the top of the assassin list and why the Director went ballistic when she didn't come back from this realm.

I avoided her as much as possible because her demon side agitated my inner angel. We were natural enemies bred to destroy each other.

She glanced behind her and then looked back at me. "Can I ask you a question?"

"Go for it."

"What else are you?" She shifted on her feet and gazed at the ground. "I mean, we all heard the rumors. But they didn't make sense to any of us. You had to have some other DNA mixed in, right?"

I shook my head. "I'm the only one I'm aware of with singular DNA. I mean, there could have been others before I was created, but I don't know."

"I've always had an aversion to be anywhere near you."

I chuckled. "Yeah. We're natural enemies."

She cocked her head.

"Angels and demons. As far away on the spectrum as you can get. I'm not fond of being near you either."

She snorted a laugh.

"I mean, you've been decent to Avery throughout the years, so it's not that I dislike you," I said. "It's a cellular reaction. But it doesn't mean I want to harm you. In that respect, I'm like Avery. With all that said, I don't want to hang out with you."

Her snort turned into a succession of snorting, and her eyes sparkled with humor.

I smiled and spread my arms in a wide shrug.

When she wound down from laughing, she said, "Well, one other piece of advice. Galen's a good guy. If you hurt him, I'll have to hurt you."

"If he touches Avery, I will kill him."

Her smile faded away, and a scowl of irritation replaced it. "Don't make us regret letting you live."

She turned and marched out of the room. I crossed the space until the air vibrated with danger. The barrier was set between the outer edge of the doorjamb. I leaned on the inside edge and gazed at Avery's room. She stood at the door with her arms folded and a frown marring her beautiful features.

Our eyes met, and I silently cursed the barrier.

IT TOOK ANOTHER TWO days for my back to heal to nothing more than skin discoloration.

I was going stir crazy being relegated to this space. At least on Icarus, I had the freedom to roam the halls or go to the gym or the sparring ring. And, of course, the cafeteria for meals. But being locked in a room felt more restricting than the complex.

I decided to test the boundaries. I threw myself against the barrier and was indeed thrown back. The shock reverberated all the way into my teeth. I stood and brushed myself off and did it again and again, each time clenching my teeth in anticipation of the prickling shock.

Galen slid to a stop before my door, his gaze hard and angry as his chest puffed in and out with each breath. He reached in and yanked me into the hall by my upper arm. His grip was nearly as strong as a vise as he dragged me along.

We were nearly matched in height, and I could have broken the grip and tried to run, but the architecture of the castle distracted me.

It was not like the sterile white walls of the complex. The rich tapestries on the walls made me want to stop and study the art, but Galen didn't slow down until we were in the gym.

He threw me toward the center of the mat. I stumbled and caught myself, spinning to face him.

I stopped when my gaze landed on Avery. I hadn't seen her since I was dragged from her room, and my heart leaped into my throat. Relief washed over me, but it was short-lived as Galen blocked my view of her.

"What is your problem?" he bellowed at me.

I took a deep breath, falling back on all I had learned through the years and all I had taught Avery. Emotions in the ring would get you hurt, so I struggled to push them all down into the box in the center of my being.

"Being locked up like a common criminal." I set my stance and kept my arms loose. I was in the mood to whoop some ass. Bonus points if I put this jackass in the grave. I waved him in. "Let's see what you've got."

I had to give him credit. He didn't barrel into me like his violent emotions suggested. He approached warily.

My mind snapped back to Mya's conversation with him. If she'd beat him, he knew to be wary around us.

Avery's anxiety pelted me almost to the point that I missed Galen's first strike, but I got my arm up fast enough to parry and spin out of the way of his counter move. My arm stung where we'd connected.

I was a little off kilter without my wings, so when I turned back, I wasn't as steady. I caught Galen's punch in my shoulder, nearly dislocating the fucker.

But in doing that, he was in range of my punch. I lifted him off the ground with the force of it. But he blocked my second hit and pushed me backwards. I caught myself before I fell.

He jumped and spun with his foot aimed at my head. I ducked with a kick of my own and hit the side of Galen's supporting leg at the knee. The satisfying snap echoed through the room, and he hit the mat.

Before I had the chance to gloat, he swept my feet out from under me. I landed on my back. Sharp pain ripped through my spine, and my lungs seized, refusing to allow air in or out. I rolled onto my stomach and pushed onto my knees.

"Stop!" Avery's voice rang out as Galen's foot connected with my ribs.

I hardly felt the kick. I was too preoccupied with opening my lungs back up as the burning in my back hit a new level. I clamped my eyes closed and pressed my forehead to the mat.

Avery fell on her knees next to me. "Breathe, Ren," she whispered in my ear. "Get me more healing salve," she barked at Galen.

She ripped my shirt, and it fell over my sides to the floor. Red tinged the edges of the white fabric.

"You idiot. You ripped open your wounds."

I couldn't argue with her. Hell, I couldn't fucking breathe.

Coolness spread over my back, and I forced air into my lungs at the relief.

"That's it. Breathe."

I took at least a dozen long breaths before I finally looked up at her. "Disappointed that you won't be able to kick my ass?"

Her lips twitched. "All I need to do is knock you on your back, and you're out for the count. That's not a worthy sparring partner."

"Fuck you, Avery." I put my head back on the mat.

She was right. This injury made me weak and easily beatable.

"You need to figure out your balance, too."

I turned my head and glared at her. "No fucking shit."

"No need to get snippy." She screwed the cap onto the salve and handed me the jar. "I'm just telling you what I'm seeing."

I narrowed my eyes into slits. As much as I wanted to be pissed at her, she was right. And she enjoyed being the one giving out pointers while I nearly writhed on the mat.

I took a breath. "How would you suggest I figure out my balance?"

Her smugness faded, and she tilted her head in confusion. I had never once been open to advice on fighting form. Whenever she had tried to offer it to me on Icarus, I beat her because questioning your handler was not done. Not without consequences, even when your ward was right. It always burned me that they made us such uncompromising hard-asses.

"I have never fought without wings. How do you suggest I compensate?" I pushed back onto my knees, blinking away the spin in the room.

Galen paced near the door with a noticeable limp. His hands rested on his hips, and irritation flowed from him in waves.

I wanted to be with Avery as long as possible. If I was an asshole about all this, I'd get tossed back into my room, and who knows how long I'd be locked up this time?

"You seriously want my advice?"

I gave her a tired sigh. "Yes. We aren't on Icarus anymore. I can hear you out without retribution. You have the right to correct me here."

"Oh." She looked at her hands. "I don't know."

"So, you were just being a wiseass?" I cracked a grin.

Her cheeks burst with color. "Yeah."

"It is something I have to figure out because I am off balance." I wiped my face. "He got a hit in." I rubbed the front of my shoulder where Galen's fist had connected.

"That surprised me. I've never seen you taken down before."

"It's been a long time since I've been taken down in a fair fight." I shut my eyes briefly and laughed. "I think Mya was the last one to take me down." I glanced at Avery's wide eyes. "That was before I became your handler."

"Well, you still knocked Galen down first. I haven't been able to do that yet, and he's even pulling his punches on me."

My building good mood crashed.

"Hey," I called out.

Galen turned toward us with a scathing glare.

"Why are you pulling punches on Avery? She'll never learn to be a better fighter that way."

His lips pressed together. "I'm not an asshole like you are."

I climbed to my feet, ignoring the flare of a burn in my back. Avery stood next to me, and I swept her feet out from under her and dropped next to her, clamping my hand around her throat.

"Get out of this," I ordered.

She clawed at my hand, and I eased up enough for her to get air and not pass out. But I knew my grip still hurt and would leave a bruise. She knew the moves, but I saw hesitation in her gaze.

"You cannot worry about doing harm to your attacker." I clamped harder and glared at her. "Get out of this."

Out of the corner of my eye, I saw Galen charging towards us. She must have also witnessed it because that determined resolve emerged. She performed the move I'd instructed, breaking my grip and subsequently flipping me onto my back beside her. She stood and backed away as Galen skidded to a halt next to her.

"Are you okay?" he asked her.

"I'm fine," she snapped while keeping eye contact with me.

I remained on my back, forcing myself to breathe through the stun of renewed pain.

"You did good," I said and then hardened my gaze at Galen. "If you want to teach her to defend herself in all situations, do not pull your punches. If you can't find it in yourself to hit her, allow me to train her the right way."

"She could get hurt."

"She *will* get hurt. So will you." I slowly pushed into a sitting position. "But wouldn't you rather her get hurt here than out there where there is no mercy?"

"This is Eleka. There is no danger out there except you crazy assassins who broke into our world."

"There's always danger." I climbed to my feet. "There's always someone who wants what you have."

That dig was intentional, and Galen glared at me.

"Teach her properly," I said. "Or let someone else do it."

"He's right." Mya's voice rang out from the gym's doorway. "When have you ever seen Tavin go easy on me?"

"Yeah, but..." Galen waved at me.

Avery shifted her weight. "Protecting me doesn't help anyone. I am the fighter I am today because Ren worked with me and challenged me. He never pulled a punch. Would I have preferred him not to land any of his brutal hits?

Of course, just like I bet he would prefer I hadn't slammed him on his back."

"I could have done without that," I admitted.

"Turn around," Mya barked.

I showed her my back.

"You let him spar before he was totally healed?" Mya pinned her gaze on Galen.

"He kept throwing himself against the barrier in his room."

"No sparring for you for a few more days, and I need to give the go-ahead. Understand?"

Mya's bark of authority surprised me, but it still didn't stop me from challenging her.

"Am I a prisoner in your castle?" If I had to deal with another couple of days cooped up in my room, I'd go bonkers.

"No. But you also do not have free rein to wander around either. With an escort, you are welcome to explore the castle." She looked at Galen. "See that a guard is available in the event Ren wants to see more than the four walls of his room."

"Yes, Your Highness," Galen muttered.

"Now go. Tavin and I are due for our weekly sparring session." She waved us out the door.

Galen grabbed my arm and threaded his free hand through Avery's.

The simple action turned my blood to lava. All I wanted to do was punch him again.

THE ELVREN ASSASSIN
CHAPTER TWENTY-FIVE
Avery

REN'S AGGRAVATION AT SEEING Galen hold my hand as we walked back toward our rooms raked across my skin like a handful of blades.

He said nothing, and Galen basically shoved him through the barrier before bringing me to my door.

"The king said you didn't need this anymore." He waved his hand over my door as he whispered my name. The magic sparkled before it faded. He let go of my hand. "Go ahead."

I glanced at my doorway and then over my shoulder at Ren's room. Ren stood inside with his arms crossed and a glare aimed at us.

I slipped inside and then jumped back outside without issue. I grinned at Galen and went back into my room. When I turned to close the door, I was surprised to find him standing inside.

"I wanted to apologize." He shifted his weight and glanced out the door before looking at me. "I didn't, um, mean to upset you."

"I'm not upset, Galen. I'm frustrated that you don't think I can take you giving your all in the sparring ring. Especially with how you found me." I took a seat on the couch and waved to the chair next to me, inviting him to stay and talk for a while.

He took a seat and leaned his elbows on his knees. "I don't know that I can, Avery. I keep seeing you beat to shit from those men who were still standing as opposed to the ones you knocked out." His sincere green eyes locked on mine. "Maybe I should let Ren continue to train you instead."

I stared at him and then nodded. "But not until his back heals."

Galen inhaled and leaned back before he exhaled. "Okay. But I'll be there because there's no way I'm leaving you alone with him."

His possessive protectiveness made me smile. "Okay. As long as you do not interrupt the sparring, even if you think he's hurting me."

He grumbled, but he eventually nodded. "Did you want to go to the market today? I need to get a few things and thought you might like to accompany me."

I had not been off the castle grounds since they'd brought me in, and the idea of going to the market and actually being able to enjoy it appealed to me. "I don't have any money."

"If you see anything that you fancy, I can lend you the money until you have established yourself here."

"Established myself?"

"Figured out what you want to do to earn money."

I blinked at him. "Like what?"

I was trained to kill. That skill didn't seem to be of any use here on Eleka.

"You are pretty good at triage. Have you thought about being a medic?"

I scoffed. "How often does anyone here find themselves brutally cut or beaten?"

Galen laughed. "More than you can imagine. Most of the cuts are kitchen accidents, but we have some industrial accidents, too. Now and then there are fights that break out where one or more participants find themselves in need of medical attention."

It was something to think about. But for the moment, I was still fixated on the market.

"When are you going to the market?" I asked.

"After I clean up." He stood and headed to the door. "I'll be back in a little while, and we can go."

Galen left, and I cleaned up, changing into one of the flowy dresses in my closet that reminded me of the women I had seen at the market when Em and I had first walked through.

Instead of waiting inside my quarters, I stepped out into the hall, and the thrill of freedom tingled down my spine. I glanced toward Ren's room and startled at him staring at me. He leaned against the doorjamb, inches from the barrier. The hard look in his gaze was enough to make me want to cover up.

"Where are you going?" he asked in that accusatory tone I was starting to hate.

"The market. Can I get you anything while I'm there?"

"A knife so I can bury it in his chest." He nodded to a point beyond me, and I turned to see Galen approaching.

I rolled my eyes at him and headed toward Galen without responding. Ren's jealousy was off the charts.

Someday, he'd snap.

THE ELVREN ASSASSIN
CHAPTER TWENTY-SIX
Ren

AVERY STEPPED OUT OF her room, looking like a damn goddess.

The fact that she was free to come and go irked me because I wouldn't know where she was now. Before, I had the comfort of knowing she was either in her room or with Galen. As much as Galen irritated me, I knew she would not be harmed in his presence.

But right now, with how she looked, I wanted to kill that bastard, especially when he offered her his elbow, and she so easily slipped her hand through his arm.

She had to know he wanted her. She had to feel his attraction. I could feel it even from this distance, and it burned as much as my healing back.

"Hey, what about me?" I yelled after them.

"I'll send a guard." Galen's reply echoed in the hall.

"Yeah, right," I muttered and flexed my back against the near constant itch of healing.

I wanted to scratch it before I lost my mind, but that would make the healing process rather difficult, especially if I ripped the scabs.

I turned away and paused at the sound of footsteps. A moment later, a guard stepped into the room. His face was pinched, as if he were trying his best not to sneer at me. This guard was shorter than I was and lean enough to be considered skinny. I could probably snap his neck once outside this room if I wanted, but he hadn't done anything to me that warranted an attack.

"You wish to see the castle?"

I could have been difficult and said something sarcastic, but I didn't think that would breed trust. I needed to be trusted because I needed my freedom, even if it was limited to the castle.

"Yes."

"What would you like to see?"

I blinked. "All of it. And if you know this realm's history, I'd love to hear it."

I excelled in history and civilizations while training on Icarus.

"We have a library that has many books on our history."

I lit up at the idea of a library, but I wanted time to study the architecture and the tapestries. Galen had dragged me by too quickly to get a solid impression.

"That's good to know. But today, I'd like a tour if you wouldn't mind."

He grabbed my arm and led me into the hallway, turning in the direction that Galen and Avery had headed before he dropped his hold.

"What's back there?" I pointed behind me.

"The rest of the servants' quarters and the kitchen." The guard glanced at me. "I can show you on the way back."

"What's your name?"

"Zaos."

"Thank you, Zaos." As we approached the ornate tapestries, I slowed, taking the time to study the mural. "This is quite beautiful."

Zaos smiled and looked up at the pictures in the weaved yarn. "The queen made that."

"Really?"

Zaos nodded. "All the tapestries in the castle were the queen's creation. She was a talented weaver. She said it calmed her from the chaos of ruling."

It sounded like someone I would have liked to meet. Anyone who created such beauty had to have a good soul.

"You like my wife's work?"

I glanced over my shoulder at the king.

Zaos bowed so deep I thought he was inspecting a spot on the floor. The king waved him off.

I returned my gaze to the tapestry. "She was very talented, Your Highness."

The king stepped next to me and studied the work as if he had never seen it before. "She was."

His sadness draped over my shoulders. I did not acknowledge it. I was too lost in the intricate designs before me.

"Did she paint, too?" I asked.

"Yes. I have hung some of her paintings in the library. But these were so stunning that I lined the main hallway with them. I wanted the world to see her art."

I smiled, warmed by the love he projected for his wife. That was a rarity according to the textbooks we had access to on Icarus.

"It might take me years to study all her work." I stared at the exquisite craftmanship. "Each piece requires full attention to see all the nuances she weaved in. Like the child in the hay pile." I pointed at the haystack in the tapestry. "Or the puppy hiding behind the wheel."

I wanted to run my hand over the fabric to see if I could actually feel the queen's love for creating such things, but I refrained.

The king sighed. "She always has a hidden gem in the tapestry. Enjoy your tour."

He walked away leaving me with a frazzled Zaos.

I stared at the fabric as if I could get the queen's story right from the stitches themselves. I guess I stood there for quite a while because footsteps approached and then stopped.

I turned, thinking that maybe the king had come back to say something else, but Galen and Avery stood a few feet away, staring at me.

I ignored Galen and waved at the tapestry. "Have you studied these yet?"

Avery stared at me, blinking like she didn't know what to make of me studying the tapestries. "No."

"It's an incredible piece of art. The queen made it."

Galen's eyebrows rose, and he looked at Zaos for an explanation.

"He was interested in the history of our realm and wanted to stop and study these." He pointed at the wall hangings.

"Art has always spoken to me," I said, returning my gaze to the hanging yarn spun with care and craft that stole my breath, like Avery always did.

"When you're all healed, you'll be training me," Avery said, capturing my full attention.

The thought of hitting her always made me feel physically ill. But I've ignored that for so long that it was no longer a problem.

The idea of rolling around on a mat with her sweaty body against mine pulled a grin to the surface. "I look forward to it."

IT TOOK THREE DAYS to tour the entire castle and absorb all the tapestries and various pieces of art. By that time, my back had healed so well that the scars had faded so they weren't noticeable in the bathroom mirror.

Mya gave me permission to resume training.

Zaos appeared like clockwork and escorted me to the gym. The door was cracked open, and Zaos nodded toward it, taking his station next to the opening like a programed sentry.

I went to step in and froze. Galen's mouth was on Avery's. He was kissing her, and she was actually returning the kiss. I stepped back, blinking as fury raked across my entire body, clenching my muscles.

That asshole touched my girl.

Galen pulled away from the kiss. "Ren should be here any minute, but I have to check in with Tavin. I'll be back before you two can get into it, okay?"

She nodded, and her smile beamed.

I closed the door and took a breath before opening it as if I had just arrived. I attempted to school my features into something neutral, but I wasn't sure I achieved it until Galen pushed past me with a nod.

I gave him a tight smile belying the hellish storm brewing beneath the surface.

The minute the door shut behind me, I caught Avery in my sharp gaze and walked straight to her, stripping my shirt and discarding it on the floor. I didn't wait for her to get centered. I grabbed her throat and walked her backwards until she hit the wall.

Rage shook my entire being, and all I saw in my head were her lips on his. I squeezed hard enough to cut off her airway.

Hard enough to crush her as she had crushed me.

THE ELVREN ASSASSIN
CHAPTER TWENTY-SEVEN
Avery

REN SLAMMED ME AGAINST the wall with his hand around my throat. His eyes broadcast his frustration with his whole situation.

"Why?" he growled.

That's when I knew he'd seen what had happened with Galen.

I pulled at his fingers, trying to get some air beyond his powerful hold. He didn't want an answer as to why I'd kissed Galen. He wanted to beat me for what he viewed as a betrayal. Ren thought he owned me, and my building relationship with Galen aggravated him to the point of brutality.

My vision warbled, and lightheadedness set in. If I didn't break his hold, I was going to pass out.

I jerked my knee up, aiming for his crotch, but his free hand grabbed my knee, stopping me. I lifted my arm and started to twist to try to break his hold like Galen had taught me, but Ren anticipated my counter and pressed his entire body against me, closing the distance I needed to execute the move.

He released my throat, grabbed my wrist, and slammed it above my head. I went to claw him with my free hand, but it ended up in his other hand's grip against the wall.

"What else have you let that asshole do to you?" His steel eyes bore into me like he could pry an answer from me by his will alone.

"What I have and haven't done with Galen is none of your concern." The only thing Galen had ever done was kiss me, despite my growing desire for more.

But he was still responsible for us, so he would not take advantage of me. At least that was what he kept telling me when the kissing grew hot.

"It *is* my concern. You are mine." His lips crushed over mine, and he plundered the depths of my mouth with his tongue. His strokes were demanding and claiming and as brutal as his sparring.

It stirred something inside me. Ren had never kissed me before. Sure, he'd let me suck him off and bent me over his bed to take my innocence. But he'd never once claimed my mouth.

One minute he pressed against me, and the next he was thrown across the mat by Galen. I had never seen that shade of rage on Galen before, nor had I felt his emotion so acutely. He wanted to end Ren.

From the look on Ren's face, he would gladly kill Galen. It took half a dozen blows from each of them for me to get my wits and tap into my own emotions instead of their overwhelming fury.

I had to do something, or one or both would end up dead today.

I saw an opening and darted between the two of them.

"Stop!" I bellowed and pressed my palms over each of their hearts.

"Move, Avery." Galen's snarling command left me with no other alternative.

"No." It was all I could articulate as I pushed out my will, my claim on the men who represented both halves of me. Angel and fae.

The air swirled around us, and energy snaked out, branding both of them with my rune. A breeze tickled the skin behind my ears before the air settled.

"Did you just fucking bond with him?" Ren snapped, staring at my neck.

Galen cocked his head, and he caught me in his glare. "What have you done, Avery?" he asked with a voice full of warning.

I dropped my hands from their chests, where my bonding rune had blazed into their skin—a pair of wings, one fae, one angel, wrapped in a golden braid right over their hearts. I stepped back from between them so they could see the matching sigils.

"What the actual fuck?" Ren growled.

I took a deep breath. "Now, if either of you succeed in killing one another, all of us die."

"Are you out of your fucking mind?" Ren yelled.

Zaos, who had been stationed outside the door, stepped inside.

"I can't deal with this right now." Ren put his hand up and stalked off.

He still didn't have the freedom to move about the castle unescorted like I had earned.

Galen pointed his chin at Ren, and Zaos nodded and turned to escort Ren back to his room.

Ren stopped at the door. "Don't you fucking touch her, or I will kill you, despite the consequences."

He pointed at Galen and slammed the door to the gym.

The echo chilled me. I turned toward Galen, still feeling the brunt of both their fury.

Galen took a breath , his sharp glare pinned on me, seizing my lungs. "What in the bloody hell did you think you were doing?"

I didn't expect the leg sweep and ended up on the ground with Galen on top of me. His anger mixed with something dangerous, something I'd never seen in him.

"You bonded with me without my permission," he snarled. "Without the bonding ritual."

He crushed my lips with his. This wasn't Galen's tender kiss.

"How did you do that?" he asked when he came up for air.

"I willed it."

He cocked his head. "You willed it?" He tilted my head from one side to the other, studying my neck. "You willed my rune on your skin?" He traced it with his fingertips. "As well as his rune?"

That one, he flicked with his fingers, as if touching it would taint him.

"Yes." I licked my lips. "I care for you both, and I have had enough of the hostilities between you. If I didn't step in today, you would have killed each other."

I shook my head.

"And what of our choice in all this?"

I took a deep breath at the thought of either of them not wanting to bond with me. "You did not wish to bond with me?"

His eyes sparkled with both his anger and his lust. After narrowing his eyes in contemplation, he dipped his lips to my throat, where I was sure Ren had left bruises with how hard he had squeezed. Galen brushed his tongue against my neck, sending gooseflesh over my exposed skin. Then he moved lower to my breasts, shocking me.

"What are you doing?"

He looked up at me. "Showing you how shortsighted you were to bond with both of us." He tore my shirt open, exposing my chest. "I expect you to answer every one of my fucking questions, understand?" His hands caressed my breasts with such reverence that I gasped. "I need to know what you have and haven't done with that asshole." His mouth captured my nipple, creating heat throughout my body. "Has he done that?"

I stared into his emerald eyes. "He hasn't even kissed me until today."

Galen stopped, and anger brushed his cheeks red. "But..."

"He showed me what to do to distract a man." I reached down and rubbed him through his pants, and damn if he wasn't as hard as rock. "With my mouth, and then he bent me over the bed and..."

I sighed.

Galen closed his eyes, and when he opened them again, an impish grin surfaced. "So, he never pleasured you?"

I didn't even know what to make of his question.

"He never touched your breasts?"

"No."

He purred and continued down my body, kissing my bruises and licking my skin like I was one of the fruity pastries the cook delivered to the room once a week. He paused when he reached my pants.

"Nothing like this?" He lowered the edge of my pants and licked a line across my belly.

I shook my head and glanced at the door as he tugged on my pants. "Um, someone might come in."

"I don't care. I am claiming my bonded since she already marked me." He stripped my pants, and I expected him to turn me onto my hands and knees and plunge inside me like Ren used to do, but he lowered his mouth to the apex of my thighs.

The sensations sent me into space. I moaned and threaded my hands through his hair. I had never been loud with Ren. He and I had been doing something that could have gotten us killed, and if he had done what Galen was doing to me with his mouth and his hands, Ren and I would have been publicly executed.

I reached nirvana, crying out Galen's name as I had my first orgasm ever. It roared through me with enough force to curl my toes and nearly roll my eyes back in my head. I panted as my body shuddered with each fresh sensation. Galen kissed his way back to my lips and slid inside me slowly as his gaze locked on mine.

His lips curved into a smile that all but melted my insides, and his eyes glowed greener than I'd ever seen them. He ground his hips in a symphony of slow motion that shoved me over another cliff's edge. This bliss was nothing like what I'd experienced with Ren.

While it had been pleasant with Ren, my body didn't react like it was taken to a different realm, one full of heavenly sensations that made me peak over and over again.

Galen was a stunning man and sexy as sin itself. And when he looked at me, it made me feel like I was the most cherished being in the world.

"Being inside you is even better than I imagined." He dipped his lips to mine, kissing me softly at the same pace as his slowly grinding hips.

But it soon transcended into a frenzy of motion and moans. Our hips slammed together, creating a delicious friction that shot me over the hurdle again as Galen arched his back and groaned my name while he rolled through his own wave of bliss.

His eyes closed, and his head lowered so his chin hit his chest. I reached out, tracing the outline of my rune over his heart. He trembled under my touch, and he glanced down at my fingers against his skin.

He dropped to his elbows, settling on top of me, and smiled. "I am moving you to my chambers."

That was not what I expected to tumble out of his mouth.

"I've gotten used to having my own space." I wasn't ready to give that up, especially after never having it before.

"This is not negotiable, Avery. Ren is going to take out his aggravation on you, and I will not be a party to that."

"He won't hurt me."

Galen scoffed and uncoupled from me. He dressed while I shuffled my pants back up from around my ankles.

"He was assaulting you when I came in here." He held out his hand to help me from the floor.

As soon as I was on my feet, I picked up my tattered shirt. "This is a dead giveaway." I flicked the fabric the same way he'd flicked the rune from Ren.

Galen reached down, grabbed a discarded T-shirt off the ground, and offered it to me. I wasn't sure if Galen realized it was Ren's shirt. Ren had peeled it off before he clamped his hand around my throat. I slid it on and inhaled Ren's scent. Guilt bit at the edges of my heart.

"I need to face him sooner rather than later. And not with you by my side, Galen. I bonded with both you and Ren, and he deserves my time just as much as you do." I dropped my torn shirt in the nearest receptacle and put my hand up before Galen started to argue with me. "You both have my heart, but in different ways. I know you don't get what I did, but if I lost either of you, it would shatter me."

I lifted on my toes and kissed him. What I meant to be just a peck became more at his insistence.

"I don't like this," he muttered when the kiss broke, but he relented then dropped me off at my room before he walked away.

I waited until he was out of sight before I sighed and entered my quarters. The minute my door closed behind me, I found myself plastered face-first against the wood.

"You branded me without my consent," Ren growled as he tore at my clothing.

I elbowed him hard enough for him to fall back a step.

"You 'taught' me things without *my* consent," I said with finger quotes. I took a deep breath and ran my hands through my hair. "Without being honest with me," I amended, because he hadn't forced anything on me.

He stared at my shirt, and a crease appeared between his eyes. He pointed at it without asking in so many words.

"My shirt was ripped."

He crossed his arms. "It was not ripped when I left."

"Why are you even in my room?" I asked, avoiding the comment completely.

"Because I felt like an ass for the way I treated you and convinced Zaos to let me in here so I could apologize. But the longer I sat here waiting for you, the angrier I got at this." He waved at his bare chest where my rune glowed on his skin. "I eventually would have dealt with it if you had only bonded with me, but you forced your rune onto both of us."

"You never would have stopped trying to kill each other!" I yelled, clenching my fists. "I did it to protect both of you!"

He darted forward, his hand clasping my neck like he had in the gym, and he uttered the same question. "Why?"

"Because I love you both, you asshole," I hissed.

His eyelashes batted like I'd short-circuited him, and his grip on my throat released so I could breathe.

For the first time, his gaze softened to a point that I could see below the shield he put up for everyone else. The shield that had hidden his adoration for years. But it was there. Just not as openly displayed as Galen's.

"I'm still angry with you, but that doesn't negate all the complicated feelings I've had for you for years. But I did not understand it quite as well as you did. I thought it was respect for teaching me to defend myself. For pushing me when I had nothing left. It was a psychological game, and the Director played on every one of us in the same manner. Our handlers would reap the punishment if we failed. It was a powerful threat." I chuckled at his raised eyebrow. "It did not work on everyone. Some assassins hated their handlers."

"But you didn't."

I shook my head. "No. Far from it. I would have come back to you. Even if I had failed, I would have come back and thrown myself at the Director's mercy to save you the beating." I licked my lips. "But the prince closed the portal, so I was stuck here with zero options for saving you."

"If you had come back, the Director would have killed you on the spot." Ren palmed my cheek. "He told me if you ever show your face on Icarus, you would face the same death sentence as me. That is, if Em hadn't already killed you."

The fact that Em was tasked to kill me when our job was over still burned, especially since I had saved her ass with the water beast.

I leaned into his palm. "Why didn't you ever kiss me before?"

"Because you'd see too much of my soul." He stepped closer and brushed his lips against mine. "And I wouldn't have been able to keep pretending well enough to fool everyone around us."

His lips captured mine, and his hand threaded into my hair, keeping me in place while his tongue plundered my mouth.

He wrapped his arm around my waist and pulled me flush against him as he maneuvered us toward the bed. Halfway across the room, the door banged open.

We separated and looked at Galen in the doorway with a book in his hand. He stared at us with daggers in his gaze.

"Only a twin flame can force a bond rune." He slammed the book closed and tossed it toward us.

Ren caught the tome and stared at the title. "*The Art of Bonding*?"

"And twin flames normally only have one partner, not two." He glared at Ren and then at me. "This defies everything that book outlines."

"What is a twin flame?" I asked.

"It's rarer than a fated mate or soulmate. But not as rare as a spirit mate." He pointed at the tome in Ren's hand. "All you need to know about these things is in that book. I suggest both of you read it." He turned to leave. "And I am moving Avery to my quarters," he added before he shut the door behind him.

Ren gazed at the door then at the book and finally to me, his expression growing more intense. All the soft edges he had shown me had vanished, replaced by unreasonable fury. "You slept with him, didn't you?"

THE ELVREN ASSASSIN
CHAPTER TWENTY-EIGHT
Avery

REN DROPPED THE BOOK on the floor and seized me, tossing me toward the bed. "You fucked him in the gym?"

I scrambled back on the bed, but he was faster. He grabbed for me and only got a fistful of the fabric of my pants. They ripped when he yanked me to the edge of the bed. I rolled onto my stomach to get away, but he gripped my hips, pulling me back to the position I was used to on Icarus.

His fingers slipped inside me and pulled out just as fast. "You fucking did."

He slapped my ass hard, and I yelped at the sting. A moment later, he spread my cheeks and slammed his hard member inside my ass.

I cried out at the pain of his penetration.

This time, when the door opened, it was accompanied by a growl.

Ren threaded his arms under my knees and picked me up, leaning my back against his chest.

I grabbed his wrists, trying to get some control over him, but his thrusts were brutal.

He turned toward the door with my pussy wide open for Galen to see.

"You already had her. It's my turn." Ren bit down on my shoulder as he maneuvered me up and down his shaft in punishing thrusts.

The burn of it left me breathless.

Galen stared at my open legs and then looked into my eyes. His cheeks reddened.

Ren laughed. "He looks like he wants to join in," he whispered in my ear. "Would you like that?"

One of Ren's hands moved to the space between my legs. He toyed with the spot that Galen had licked before dipping his fingers inside me. The fullness of having him in my ass with his touch deep within me pulled a moan to the surface. Ren's fingers were more skilled than I gave him credit for, and he had me panting as much as Galen had with a few swipes of his thumb.

"If I had my wings, we would be flying." The longing in his voice made me cry out, and he kept up the brutal pace as he played with me. "Now come for me, Avery. Scream my name."

His whisper was as demanding as his pace, and I did. My trembling cry punctuated the wet sounds his fingers made as they slammed in and out with the same bravado as he was taking me with.

"Fuck yes." He kissed my neck, pulled his fingers out, and lifted them to my mouth. "Suck," he whispered in my ear.

I complied, still staring at Galen as he watched, while I sucked my own juices mixed with Galen's cum from Ren's fingers. Galen's breath came in quick, shallow bursts.

His pants tented with how turned on he was by watching this, and that made me even more needy.

"Galen, fill her. Now," Ren ordered.

Galen sucked his lower lip between his teeth, hesitating. But that lasted for the length of a heartbeat before he moved across the room and pressed against my front, wrapping my legs around his waist as his member slid inside.

I cried out at the fullness, and the two men moved as one with brutal thrusts that claimed my body.

"You bonded with us both. This is your penance," Ren whispered in my ear before he bit down on my lobe, grunting as he spilled his seed inside me.

Galen pumped once more before losing control. Then he stumbled back and zipped himself up as his cheeks turned crimson.

Ren pulled out and dumped me onto the bed before he sauntered into the bathroom and closed the door.

My chest heaved, and my body felt as if I had been through a dozen back-to-back sparring sessions.

"Fuck, that was hot." Galen ran his hand through his hair.

I lay spent on the bed. My mind had gone numb from the experience.

"Have you ever..." I asked with a breathy quality in my voice I didn't recognize.

He laughed and shook his head. "No."

Galen's previous parting words finally surfaced in my mind, pulling my attention away from his endearing grin.

"I'm not moving without Ren," I whispered.

Galen's smile faded, and he put his hands on his hips and looked at the floor, waging a silent debate with himself. "Fine, but you are in my bedroom with me. He gets the guest room that I originally had set aside for you." He picked up the book and put it on the end of the bed. "And you both need to read this to understand what this means for the three of us."

He turned to leave.

"Galen?"

He stopped with his hand on the doorknob.

"Thank you."

He cocked an eyebrow at me. "Don't thank me yet. I'm sure between the two of us, you might find it hard to walk in a day or two." His lips tilted into a sly smile. "He was right. This is your penance."

THE ELVREN ASSASSIN
CHAPTER TWENTY-NINE
Ren

I STARED AT MY reflection in the mirror, and my gaze dropped to Avery's rune carved in my chest. I had stared at it before she came back from the gym, but now it seemed to glow, creating a warm blanket around my heart.

I did not deserve the celestial creature in the other room.

With a sigh, I turned on the water and washed my face, wondering when I became this selfish, self-serving prick. What I did was not out of love. It was not out of adoration. That was an assault on Avery stemming from my anger.

Granted, being bonded without my permission set this off, but the thought of another lying with Avery made me lose my fucking mind. Yes, I was her first at everything, but I wanted to be her last and only. Not just another man in her life, which was where I'd been delegated to now.

The door opened, and Avery stepped inside, looking wrecked and satiated at the same time. I gripped the edges of the counter to keep myself in place, waiting for her admonishment.

She bypassed me and stepped into the shower. She took her time washing herself, and I turned and leaned on the counter, watching her through the glass. The smile she sent me nearly took me out at the knees.

"Do you want to join?"

I pointed to my chest, shocked by her question.

"Who else?" She rolled her eyes at me.

"I don't know. Maybe Galen?"

"No. Ren. You."

I was a certifiable idiot for questioning her the first time, but my clothing nearly shredded as I ripped it off and stepped under the blessedly hot stream of water. But it wasn't the idea of showering with her that moved me so fast. It was the impish light dancing in her eyes.

She took my hand in hers and kissed my fingers like they were made of gold. "I didn't think you knew how to do that."

Her cheeks flared red.

"Can you imagine the chaos that would have caused had I done all the things I've ever dreamed of to you at the complex?" I stepped closer, framing her face in my palms. "And I have dreamed of so many things."

I leaned in and captured her lips in a gentle kiss. I slid my hands from her face, down her throat, to her chest. I cupped her breasts and ran my thumbs over her nipples, grinning as they hardened from the light touch.

"You should be worshipped." I met her violet gaze and lowered to my knees in front of her.

I followed the flow of my hands with my lips, caressing her with every ounce of adoration I'd held close to my heart for so long. She trembled under my touch, and I maneuvered her so she had the wall to lean on.

"Ren," she whispered in a way that made me pause.

I glanced up at her.

"Don't you dare stop," she scolded.

I smiled, and she beamed like my grin gave her a boost, and then I lifted her leg over my shoulder, licked along the inside of her thigh, and stopped. "Stop what?"

She turned a different shade of red and threaded her hand into my soaked locks, guiding me to where she wanted my mouth.

I flicked my tongue over her sensitive bud. "Right there?"

I could not help teasing her. I ran my fingers over her, and she jolted when they passed the same area I had swiped with my tongue.

"Yes," she whimpered.

The water rolled down her hardened nipples, splashing on my cheeks as if baptizing me with her pleasure.

I slowly licked her from her entrance to the spot she wanted me to focus on, playing with her like I'd never done before. Oh, I'd wanted to touch her, to work her into a frenzy. I wanted to hear the little noises she made that led her to an orgasm.

But if I had done this on Icarus, I could never hide my heart, no matter how much I wanted to protect her.

I focused on all the pent-up passion I had locked away for years and gently played with her with my fingers and my mouth until she catapulted over the hurdle with a throaty moan of my name. I did not stop until she begged me for a break.

I sat back on my heels and looked up at her, worshiping the glow on her skin and the blotchy pink on her cheeks that went so well with the purple tones in her hair and eyes.

She held on to the wall as her chest rose and fell in satiated pants. Her head remained tilted back against the wall, and her eyes were at half mast, glazed with satisfaction.

When she finally looked down at me, she chuckled. "Yeah, that would have gotten us dead."

I stood, and she wrapped her hand around my hard member and started to drop to her knees.

I grabbed her shoulders and shook my head. "You don't need to…"

She put her fingers over my mouth, shutting off my words as she searched my gaze. "You don't want me to suck you?"

"I did not do that for something in return. It wasn't a quid pro quo, Avery. Besides, I've become very adept with my own hand." My libido balked at the words tumbling from my mouth. It conflicted with the very core of my wants.

"Do you want me to or not?" She pushed me against the wall.

I swept a wet piece of hair that stuck to her cheek away and then met her gaze. "You already know the answer to the question. But if you are doing this because of a sense of obligation, in that event, no. I can tend to my own needs."

"And if I'm doing it to see you become just as undone as you made me?" She leaned forward and sucked my lower lip between her teeth before releasing it.

Her mouth moved to my throat, following the line down to my chest. A low groan rumbled in my throat.

"Avery," I whispered as she lowered to her knees, and at that moment, words ceased when her lips slid over my tip.

Back at the complex, I usually sat and never watched what she was doing for the same reasons I never touched her more than necessary.

But here, worlds away from that prison, I kept her gaze as she started her slow creep down my cock. Her tongue rolled around me, licking all the sensitive places I'd told her about. She opened her mouth and nearly swallowed me before her lips molded around my shaft.

"Holy fuck," I whispered and threaded my hands into her hair, keeping it from falling into her face.

She slowly retracted, sucking hard enough for her cheeks to hollow out, and then repeated the action, nearly driving me insane with her leisurely pace.

My hands trembled, and I resisted the urge to take control. This was more intimate, more special than any other time she'd had me in her mouth. This was exactly what I had dreamed of when I made her get on her knees on Icarus that first time.

"Avery," I said, forcing the word out of my tight throat. Everything I ever wanted to say was fueled into that one word, and she smiled around my member. "You don't...have to finish."

I groaned as she sucked harder, pulling me deeper into her heavenly mouth.

She slid her lips to my tip and sucked gently, tickling me with her tongue.

"I know," she said and picked up the pace with both her hands and her mouth until I thought I was going to burst at the seams.

I tightened my hands in her hair, and while I wanted to close my eyes and tilt my head against the tile behind me, I kept eye contact with her. That impish light dancing in her irises left me as breathless as her mouth.

My muscles contracted, and I pushed my hips forward. I had no clue what nonsense was spilling out of my lips, except that it included her name as I lost control.

Avery sucked and swallowed every drop of my cum until I let go of her hair. I leaned my head back on the shower wall, wondering how my legs still supported me.

Avery stood and snaked her hand into my hair, pulling me to her lips.

When she broke the kiss, she stared into my eyes. "I think I get it."

I cocked an eyebrow, trying to figure out where those words came from or what they even meant. My brain was totally fried at the moment.

"Get what?"

"Why you acted the way you did on Icarus." She shuffled under the water and ran the soap over herself before handing it to me, finishing the shower we'd started ages ago.

After I shut the water off, I took the towel she offered me. "What's your point?"

"Neither of us is quiet." She winked at me and headed back into her room to find clothing.

I snorted a laugh and reached for my clothes, still piled where I'd left them. I dressed, thankful I hadn't ruined anything in my mad dash to get undressed.

I sauntered back into her bedroom, hand combing my wet hair out of my face. "Was that your first...um..."

I snapped my mouth closed on the rest of the question. I didn't want to know. I didn't want to kill this happy buzz I felt right now.

Her smile faded, stomping my buzz out anyway. When she slowly shook her head, that wall inside me slammed back into place.

I swiped the book off the end of the bed and took a seat on her couch.

"You were my first in everything else," she said.

I glared at her. "I wasn't the first to kiss you, either."

THE ELVREN ASSASSIN
CHAPTER THIRTY
Avery

A KNOCK ON THE door interrupted my packing. I crossed and opened it to stare into Mya's furious eyes.

She stepped into the room. "You forced a bond?"

"She did," Ren answered from the couch as he turned another page in the book Galen insisted we read.

"What are you doing in Avery's room?" Mya snapped.

Ren glanced up briefly and pointed to the rune visible on his chest. He hadn't bothered to button up his shirt since he came out of the bathroom.

Mya gasped. "I thought..."

"I bonded with them so they wouldn't kill each other."

"Galen is a royal guard. Did you ever think about that in this insanity of yours?"

I cocked my head.

"If someone goes after Tavin, who do you think they have to go through?"

I blinked. My mind wandered to the night at the tavern and how the guard had surrounded them in a protective barrier. "Oh."

"Yeah, and if something happens to Galen, it's bad enough, but then I'd lose you as well."

Ren snorted. "If she hadn't, I would have eventually killed Galen." He looked up from the book. "And I'm still considering that option."

He flipped another page and tilted his head at me as if silently daring me to challenge his comment.

Mya's eyes grew bigger with each revelation. "And you're allowing him to live under the same roof as Galen?"

"Galen insisted on bringing me to his quarters, and I insisted I wouldn't go without Ren."

Mya pinched the bridge of her nose. "Ren, can I have a moment with Avery alone?"

"No, you may not." He didn't even look up at her.

"I could just yank your soul," she muttered.

"I'm curious. Did you have that power before, or is that something you inherited from the prince?" Ren turned another page before looking up at her.

"It's my power, not the prince's."

His eyes narrowed. "Then why the fuck didn't you yank that bastard's soul out of him when you were at the complex?" He tossed the book on the coffee table and stood, prowling toward us. "Why didn't you take the Director down?" he snarled.

"Because I didn't realize I could do that until fairly recently." She crossed her arms.

He pointed to the ground with a cocked eyebrow.

"No. Ireland. A bunch of thugs were chasing me, and I got desperate."

He kept his sharp stare pinned on her. "And you still didn't take that fucker down?"

Mya sent her own seething glare at him. "I was as brainwashed as the next assassin, and fear played a big part in why I didn't lash out at him." She invaded his space and speared her finger into his chest. "You know the mind games they play. You played right along with the Director."

"No, I did not." Ren stepped back.

"You ran her into the ground." Mya pointed at me.

"I trained her." He jutted his chin out.

"How come she was the only assassin you handled? Other handlers had at least a half dozen, sometimes more."

"Because she was my last shot. If I failed with her, I'd be beaten to death, like my original handler was."

Mya jerked back, and my eyes widened.

He shifted his focus to mine. "Empathy fucked my chances of ever going out into the field again." His jaw muscles jumped. "I failed as an assassin. I could not kill in cold blood, but because I was fast and strong and one of the Director's special fucking experiments, he offered me a chance to be redeemed by smashing the empathy out of you." He laughed and returned his gaze to Mya. "I hated that bastard with every fiber of my being, because at every goddamned turn, he threatened her life to keep me in line, and he had no intention of letting her live anyway."

"You still crossed the line with her, though?"

Ren nodded. "I did what I had to in order to help her understand what vile pigs men are. If she believed the lies I fed her, it would be easier for her to put her bleeding fucking heart aside and do the job I never could."

Mya digested his words faster than I did. "And yet you're so sure you would have killed Galen."

His lips curved into a terrifying smile. "That's different. He touched what is mine."

"You don't own her," Mya said before I could object myself.

"And you wouldn't do the same if someone touched your precious prince?" He raised a challenging eyebrow.

Mya blinked, and her mouth popped open and then closed as she looked at the floor. Her cheeks reddened.

"Point taken," she muttered.

"I'm possessive as fuck. So, her forcing the bond on me wouldn't have been a big deal once I wrapped my head around it. But her bonding with both of us? I can't deal with that." Ren headed back to the couch and flopped onto the cushion, picking up the book again. But then he paused. "What can Galen do?"

"He can glamour like Avery, but nowhere near the scale Tavin can. And he can create a healing salve like no other in this kingdom. Plus, he's almost as good a fighter as the prince and I. And the thing that saved your life..." She pointed at Ren. "Galen can talk sense into both the king and my prince when no one else can."

Ren snorted as if the last thing hadn't been spoken aloud. "The only person who ever took you down was Treya."

"Tavin could best Treya." She flicked her hair over her shoulder.

"Is that how he got you?"

She smiled. "Sort of. The spirit mate thing kind of made it impossible for me to leave." Mya glanced at me and back at Ren. "I don't know if you're really the asshole you project, but a word of warning. Don't screw up and make the king change his mind about you. The fact that you three are bonded means nothing to him, and he'd sacrifice Galen to see you headless if you cross any of us."

Ren tensed. "How come Avery isn't being spoken to this way?"

"Because she has fae blood, and you don't."

"I'm full-blooded angel. I'm not a mixture of DNA like every other experiment the Director ever launched. Doesn't that count for anything?"

"No. Only fae blood counts here." She met my gaze, and then Mya left us alone.

I had learned more about Ren in the last five minutes than I had in the last twelve years as my handler.

He had been one of the younger handlers. Most of the others were seasoned assassins, but Ren was barely legal when he was assigned to me. I had recently come out of the children's ward and into the assassin training and education stage in the complex.

Ren always seemed stoic to me, like he did not have any scope of emotions. The only one that ever surfaced was anger.

"Why didn't you ever tell me any of this?" I asked.

Ren looked up from the book. "Because I didn't want to see the look of pity on your face."

I crossed toward him, kneeled in front of him, and took the book from him before taking his hands in mine. "Look closer."

I knew he had empathic tendencies even though he suppressed them.

He closed his eyes and hung his head.

"You don't have to hide who you are, Ren. We aren't under the Director's thumb anymore."

"I wasn't a saint, Avery. I was brought up with the same teachings that you were."

I cocked an eyebrow, and he chuckled.

"Okay, maybe not the same teachings as you." A smile toyed on his lips. "But the same principles were beaten into me. But like you, I couldn't buy into the bullshit they were burying us in. I had the same bright-eyed view of the world that you have and saw the innate goodness in others. It's part of our DNA. It's part of having angel blood pumping in our veins. And it's why we continually fail as assassins." He took a breath. "It's only when it's tainted with other, more questionable DNA that we become moldable against our base nature."

I squeezed his hands, and he stared into my eyes, softening enough so I could see underneath this iron wall he put around himself.

"You want me to be me? I don't have a clue who I really am outside of what I've been conditioned to believe and project." He pulled one hand away and wiped his face. "I'm possessive to a fault. That's something I know, and that wasn't conditioned." He stared at me and sighed. "Avery, I'm thirty, and I have no idea who the fuck I am." His hand dropped to his chest, and he traced the rune. "With one exception. I know I belong to you."

I didn't know what to do with Ren to break through the wall he had put back in place after our shower. Today was a small win, a tiny crack in that façade of his, but I knew there was far more underneath that he had yet to share with me.

Ren buried himself in the book Galen had left. He had read some passages aloud relating to bonding and the link the three of us now shared as I packed up my items into boxes I found in the closet.

Galen hadn't come back yet. Restlessness gripped me, and Ren couldn't leave without a guard in place. No one was outside my quarters today, and my nerves pinged like a silent warning.

"I'm going to go see what's taking Galen so long."

"He probably has court duty or whatever royal guards do," Ren said, his nose in the book.

"Do you mind if I go?"

He looked up and pointed to the book. "I'm content to read. It's pretty enlightening."

Ren always had a thirst for knowledge, and he threw himself into it to buffer himself from the truths he'd learned today.

I lingered at the door nibbling on a hangnail, unsure of whether to leave him. But my gut was twisting and I didn't know if it was Ren's emotions or something else.

"Stop procrastinating. Go find our fearless chaperone." He waved me away.

I smiled at his description of Galen and slipped out the door. I scanned the hallway with that warning sense pinging around in my gut. A couple of servants headed towards this area, which wasn't unusual considering this was the servants' wing, and the kitchen was off to my right. I turned in their direction and received nods as I passed by.

The two of them spun toward me so quickly that I didn't have time to react before one of them covered my nose and mouth with a cloth. The smell of it overwhelmed me.

I breathed in to scream, but before I could make a sound, whatever they soaked the cloth in yanked me into the darkness.

THE ELVREN ASSASSIN
CHAPTER THIRTY-ONE
Ren

FEAR FILLED ME BUT vanished as quickly as it had slammed into me. I shot to my feet and rushed to the door, but I couldn't get past the barrier like Avery could. It knocked me back a few feet.

Avery was nowhere in sight, but I was sure it was her fear that had accosted me.

I didn't feel emotions at the same level when it was someone else.

I reached out with my mind to locate her. It was one of my talents I never disclosed to anyone. I always could feel her when I tried, but right now, I couldn't. It was like a black hole. When I had told Mya I knew she was alive, this was how I could tell, and it worked unless she was unconscious.

Oh. Fuck.

"Galen!" I bellowed and ran at the barrier again.

This time, it threw me halfway across the room. He'd feel me trying to break out. At least he had the last time I tried from my room. It was his magic that created this fucking thing.

"Anyone! Help!" I kept running at the door and being thrown, yelling like a maniac as every second created a burning panic in my bloodstream.

It must have taken close to an hour of slinging myself against the barrier before Galen appeared at the entry. He looked just as harried as I felt.

"What the fuck is wrong with you?" he snarled.

"Avery's gone." I ran my shaking hands through my hair. "She went to find you, and then I felt her fear, and then nothing."

I knew how ridiculous it sounded, but my heart doubled down with anxiety. It was worse than it had been on Icarus when the Director said all the assassins who he had sent to Eleka were dead.

Galen blinked, and in the next instant, his gaze darted around like he was going to lose it.

"Let me out of here so we can go find her," I demanded.

Galen didn't hesitate. He waved his hand, whispering my name, and the barrier dissolved.

I rushed out the door, but I didn't know which way to go. My heart thundered in my ears as I glared at him. "What the fuck took you so long?"

"A threat was delivered to the king, so we were in the situation room trying to decipher whether it came from your realm or from someone in the kingdom. The threat mentioned the unwelcomed guests staying in the castle. We surmised the targets were all three of you, and Mya should be protected at all costs because of the danger to the prince. I was ordered to keep them safe." He raked his hand through his hair. "When you kept repeatedly hitting the barrier, I knew something was wrong, but I couldn't leave until Tavin cleared me."

Speaking of the devil, both Mya and Tavin rounded the corner as if the castle were on fire.

Mya's gaze bounced between the two of us and darted toward Avery's room. "Where's Avery?"

"You tell me. How easy is it to infiltrate the castle?" I couldn't help my condescending tone.

"Before Icarus's assassins came, it was easy, but since my mother's funeral, and the subsequent attacks, this place is warded, so anyone with ill will toward the crown cannot pass through the doors."

"Based on the threats Galen said you received, you might want to extend that to include your spirit mate." I turned toward Galen. "Is there a record of who was in the castle the last few hours?"

Galen glared at me as if my barking orders were out of line.

"Avery could be lost somewhere on the grounds," Tavin said.

Both Galen and I turned to him as if he had gravely insulted us.

"Avery was afraid just before I lost her connection," I said.

Mya paled.

"How do you know that?" Tavin asked.

I lost Tavin's question in the sudden flare of pain across my back, and immediately after, the connection went silent again. My back even bowed from it enough so that Mya's eyes widened.

"You felt her?" she asked.

"I've always felt Avery, and now that she's my bonded mate, it's more pronounced. When she's awake."

Her gaze swung to Galen. "Did you?"

"Not like he does, but yes, something surfaced in me and disappeared just as quickly. It was like her fear earlier. But I didn't recognize it the way Ren did."

I nodded. "At least we are still alive, so that means she is as well, but that could be temporary."

I reached out and grabbed Galen's wrist and closed my eyes.

"What are you doing?" Galen asked.

"Leveraging our connection with her to see if we can get her to open her eyes and show us where she is."

Mya scoffed.

I glared at her. "Angels have a little bit more than speed, strength, and empathy."

I shut my eyes again and concentrated, drawing on both our bonded connections to Avery.

"Come on, baby. Open your eyes for a second. Let me see where you are," I whispered and focused on the cord between us and Avery. I pulled on it until I felt her surfacing. "That's it. Just a quick look, and then you can go back to where the pain is dulled."

My voice hitched, and Galen's breath sucked in.

"They hurt her," Galen said.

"They're still hurting her," I amended as my side bloomed in pain. "Just concentrate. We've only got one chance to figure out where they have her."

Tavin reached out and put his hand on Galen's shoulder. I sent a sideways glance at Mya and closed my eyes again, concentrating. I'm sure we looked like four idiots in the middle of the hallway, but I did not give a damn.

"Come on, Avery. I know you can hear me. Open your goddamned eyes right this minute." I used the same tone I used to on Icarus to get her to give a little more. It was the tone I knew she hated, and I could almost feel her jaw tighten in response.

But damned if it didn't work.

I got a glimpse of the room. And Avery's gaze landed on something that burned the blood in my veins.

THE ELVREN ASSASSIN
CHAPTER THIRTY-TWO
Avery

A PUNCH TO MY side pulled me out of my stupor, and I winced. Rope circled my wrists in a tight bond that hung from a hook above me, high enough so my toes barely scraped the floor.

I kicked out, connecting with someone's shin. That earned me a punch in the face that made me see stars.

My vision cleared, but the hits kept coming, pulling gasps from my split lips.

"She's awake." A woman's voice cut through the crowd. It seemed to pause the beating. "I want her suffering to be long and drawn out."

She glared at all those around me and then at me.

I blinked and shook the cobwebs from my head. A blonde fae approached me with a face so pinched in disgust she must consider me worse than a piece of dung on her shoe.

"I'm sure the prince's cohort will send out a rescue team in due time, but until then, my friends here will break every bone in your body for the sheer fun of it."

She reached out and drew her nails down my cheek so hard I was sure she drew blood.

"We would have preferred to capture her, but she is never alone in that castle. You were the next best thing. I'm sure she will send the royal army to rescue one of her little assassin friends. It would be even more of a bonus if she came herself. Either way, anyone who comes for you will die."

"And if no one comes?" I asked.

"Then we'll attack the palace, overthrow the king, and execute that witch and the angel assassin, who you had the audacity to save." She straightened her back. "Those royal bastards have been in power long enough."

She turned to a seamstress sewing an elaborate dress. "I'd like those on my wedding dress." She pointed at my wings and then turned to me with a feral smile. "The prince is mine. He'll marry me, or he will die. He needs to be with someone who isn't an absolute disgrace to this kingdom."

I snorted a laugh. "Like you aren't a disgrace? Organizing an attack on the palace makes you and everyone in this room traitors."

If she killed Mya, her prince would die, too, but if I revealed that, they might storm the castle right now.

Besides, she put way too much credence in my relationship with Mya to think she'd organize the guards to come find me.

Ren was more likely to barrel into this losing situation. I scanned the room, and the crowd was big enough to make me shiver. If he still had his wings, he might get to me, but without them, he wouldn't have a prayer.

My task was to stay alive. Keep my lungs working and my heart beating until I had a chance to get free. I wasn't the only one who would die if I couldn't.

The blonde threw a right hook that hit me square in the jaw and made my head ring. Then she stabbed me in the side, but not deep enough to hit a major organ, just enough to cut my intestines and provide a horribly slow and painful death.

She tossed the knife to someone else, announced she was going to get some work done, and gave the seamstress a nod on her way out.

The crowd descended with fists more brutal than Ren had ever been in the ring. I blacked out, but a fiery burn in my back pulled me into an arching scream. It was worse than when Mya dug the chip out of my back.

I was glad when a fist connected with my temple, dropping me back into the land between life and death.

THE ELVREN ASSASSIN
CHAPTER THIRTY-THREE
Ren

GALEN AND TAVIN JERKED away, their eyes flying wide open along with mine.

There were far too many people in that room for only Galen and me to take on alone. They were planning on staging an uprising, but that wasn't what boiled my blood.

The image of a seamstress sewing Avery's stunning wings onto what looked like a wedding dress surprised both Avery and me. I was sure Galen felt that stinging shock just as well.

Those bastards had cut off her wings.

"Tell me you know where that is," I said through clenched teeth.

"There are too many for us to fight," Galen said. "Can you assemble the army?" he asked Tavin.

"We don't have time for that. Besides, I have a better idea." I turned to Mya. "Can I borrow some of your soul-sucking power? I will give it back when we return."

"What?" she asked.

"No," Tavin said at the same time.

"Can I borrow some of your powers? If I don't, it will not be much longer before we are dead, along with Avery. I will return it to you just as soon as we get back. You have my word."

"Your word means nothing," Tavin said, but Mya raised her hand.

"Do you swear on Avery's life you will return it?"

I nodded. "And if I die, you will know because it will return to you anyway."

Mya nodded, and I stepped close to her.

I put my hand over her heart and my other on her back to steady her. "Concentrate only on that piece of your power."

I shut my eyes and followed her mental concentration to that single point where the light of her soul shone brightly. Her power snaked around my reach until I coaxed it to flow across my palm. I closed my fist and yanked.

She whined, and I stepped away from her as light shone between my fingers. I held on to it, but it came close to overwhelming me. This was a demon's power, and it burned. I clenched my teeth and held tight.

I opened my eyes and met her wide-eyed stare. "Thank you. You gave us the ability to get her out without getting mortally wounded. And it will still keep you and the prince safe behind these walls as long as he fixes the damn charms."

I gave the prince a pointed look.

"Are you sure you'll be able to use it?" Mya asked.

I nodded. "These aren't innocents. And they will feel the full wrath of an angry angel." I moved my gaze to the prince and waited for him to give us the go-ahead. If he didn't, he'd lose his best guard. "You saw. You know they aren't just planning on killing Avery."

He gave me a curt nod.

I grabbed Galen's wrist with my free hand. "Lead the way, Galen."

He stepped forward, and a wind tunnel engulfed both of us as he zapped us to where he believed Avery was. Thankfully, where we appeared was cast in shadows, but it gave us a clear view of the inside of a warehouse.

I squeezed Galen's wrist hard enough to feel bones shift, but he didn't react. His glare focused on the assholes surrounding Avery, punching her unconscious form. The sound of flesh giving filled the room, along with the cackle of the seamstress.

I sealed my eyes closed and tapped into the power in my palm, casting my mind out like an invisible net over every living being within the entire building. Before I used this awful power, I muttered an incantation to protect the innocent. I opened my eyes and did not see any halos except for the ones encompassing Avery and Galen.

Satisfied, I yanked with vicious intent. Bodies dropped where they stood. The infusion of souls into my palm burned nearly enough for me to let go of the piece of Mya's power.

I blinked and released Galen. "Go get her."

I had to contain Mya's power before it got loose. I crossed the warehouse slowly, scanning the bloodless carnage. I stopped by the seamstress and growled, crushing the overwhelming need to stomp her head into a pulp. Instead, I unclasped the dress that had Avery's wings sewn into the back and draped it over my arm.

The only one in this realm ever to adorn her wings would be Avery.

Galen crossed with Avery in his arms. His eyes held so much trepidation that it gave me pause.

"Bring us to your chambers and tell Tavin to bring Mya." I shifted the dress to the arm that I held Mya's power in and grabbed Galen's elbow before he zapped us back.

"I can't fix her. She needs medical attention," Galen said as we reappeared in the castle, inside his quarters, which were easily three times the size Avery's room had been.

"I can as soon as Mya gets here and I give her this." I held up my glowing hand and clenched my teeth.

I dropped the dress on the back of a chair and concentrated on breathing and controlling the power in my palm.

The door burst open, and Tavin stormed in with Mya at his heels.

"The entire factory dropped dead," he snarled, as if that made any difference at all.

"Innocents in that factory were protected." Without waiting for permission or even dignifying him with a more sarcastic response beyond my simple answer, I crossed to Mya and slammed my palm to her chest, pushing that dark poison back to where it belonged.

My entire being sagged with relief, and I turned away from the seething prince to concentrate on Avery.

She had never been this bad when I carried her into my room at the complex. She was nearly in the state I was in when the guards dropped me in the desert.

Galen laid her out on his bed, and I traded a glance with him as I climbed up next to her on my knees. His frown broadcast little of the turmoil clanging around his form.

My judgement of him had been harsh. The man loved this girl as much as I did, and he'd only been exposed to her for less than a month. I had been her mentor since I was eighteen.

My entire life revolved around Avery, and if she died, I would gladly join her. There was no life without her in it. Not for me, and from the emotions I got from Galen, he was walking the same road.

I stared at the devastated body before me. So many of the wounds were catastrophic that I didn't know where to start. It was a miracle her lungs still drew in air and her heart still pumped blood. I didn't know how she'd survived this. Too many bones were smashed and shattered. Bruises covered her face and abdomen, but it was the steady flow of blood that worried me the most.

I swallowed hard and gazed at her other bonded. "Help me roll her onto her stomach. The open wounds need addressing first."

"How can you sound so calm?" he asked as he helped gently roll her.

The bedding had already absorbed enough blood to stain through to the mattress.

"Panicking has done no one any favors." I took a calming breath, centering myself and digging deep within me for every ounce of energy I could tap. "Get me some food, please. I'm going to need it."

I spread my hands over Avery's butchered back, where they'd hacked her wings out. At least mine had been cleanly cut. Hers looked like they'd used a dull knife—or worse, a serrated knife—and sawed at the muscles.

Light spilled from my palms. My entire form tensed with what I knew would come next. But I forced myself to remain vigilant. Her suffering pummeled every muscle, and every sensation she had endured hit me tenfold. If I lost consciousness, she would die.

This was so much more brutal than anything I had ever done in the past, and her agony was now mine. I clenched my teeth against crying out as every shattered bone, every plunge of a blade, every punch and hit and cut assaulted me.

Avery's skin began mending, and her bones scraped back together.

Tears blurred my eyes, and I kept pushing my power out from the epicenter of my soul.

A hand landed on my shoulder, fracturing my attention for a millisecond. I flicked my gaze to the owner.

Galen kneeled beside me on the bed, offering whatever strength flowed through him to me.

The bond we had with Avery allowed me access to his fae strength. Which was a damn good thing because I was almost tapped out, and Avery needed so much more to have a fighting chance.

I returned my focus to Avery, and the light flared again.

When she finally stirred and turned her head in my direction, I trembled with pain and exhaustion. But she was conscious now and not a screaming, writhing mass of agony under my hands.

Light faded from my palms, and the room spun into darkness.

THE ELVREN ASSASSIN
CHAPTER THIRTY-FOUR
Avery

R EN'S EYES ROLLED BACK in his head, and he collapsed next to me on the bed.

I popped up to my elbows, but my body protested, dropping me back face-first onto the mattress. Memories surfaced of the horrific ordeal, and I cried out at the one that Ren made me see. My wings being sewn onto that woman's wedding dress.

"It's okay," Galen's soft voice cooed.

The bed squeaked, and then he stood at the bedside behind Ren, reaching for a pitcher and a glass with a straw. The familiar citrus scent filled the air, and he came around to the other side of the bed, next to where my head lay.

He crouched down and offered me the straw. "Drink."

I didn't hesitate; I hurt everywhere. I'd hung on through the beatings because I knew if I succumbed to death, both Ren and Galen would be struck down, too.

"I heard Ren in my head," I said. "He made me wake up long enough to see what they did."

A tear escaped.

"He made you wake up so we could figure out where the hell you were." Galen wiped my cheek gently.

I expected his touch to hurt like hell, but there was no pain. My cheeks and jaw had been smashed, but they weren't now.

I blinked, and my stomach dropped as I pushed up on my arms again. This time I was able to support my weight, and I inspected Ren, searching for signs of trauma.

It was more like him to have broken into that warehouse to save my ass, but everyone there had expected some sort of rescue mission. Ren had no special abilities that could wage a war like that.

"What did he do?" I looked back at Galen.

His half-tilted smile shocked me.

"Did he drag Mya and the prince there?" My voice rose.

The rebels were hoping for that, or for the royal army at the very least.

"No. Ren and I came to get you."

My eyes widened, and I turned my head to take in Ren's unconscious form before I looked back at Galen. He had to be wrong. Neither of them could topple that many armed men, and neither of them showed signs of injury.

"How long have I been out?" I asked.

"I think we've been back about an hour?" He didn't seem that certain, but the timeframe made little sense to me at all.

Neither of them possessed the power to be invisible, either.

"How?"

"Did you know Ren could borrow powers from others with their permission?"

His tone caught my attention first. It carried admiration, not disgust. And in that instant, his words sank in.

"He what?"

"He borrowed a piece of Mya's soul-yanking power. And before we left, he got that dress for you." Galen glanced over my shoulder at Ren.

"Ren killed?"

"Ren leveled everyone in that building," Galen said. "And then when we got here, he healed you."

I knew about Ren's healing abilities, but he suffered when he used them. He had taken my pain so many times that I'd refused to allow him to do it anymore. Especially if all I needed was some food and rest to heal. But today, I was shattered inside and hanging on by a thread. The thought of what he'd had to endure brought hot tears to my eyes.

"No." I put my hand over my mouth to stifle the sob that threatened. "When he does that, he takes my pain."

Galen blinked and looked beyond me again as he sat back on his heels. It was his turn to say, "He what?"

"In order for Ren to heal, he has to absorb the pain. He has to feel the agony of the injury before he can make it go away." I turned toward his passed-out form and put my hand on his cheek. "Damn it, Ren," I muttered.

"I don't think you would have made it if he hadn't done what he did."

I turned to Galen. "I would have lived, but I'm not sure how long it would have taken me to heal to the point I could move." My brain registered something else Galen had said. "He borrowed Mya's power?"

"I gather from your question you didn't know he could do that."

I laughed and shook my head.

"What else can your elusive angel do?" Tavin's voice fell over the room.

He stood with a tray of food in one hand and a pitcher of nectar in the other. Mya followed with another tray filled with the pastries she had once told me were to die for.

"I don't know." I really didn't. I only knew the things he'd revealed to me, like the healing power and his strength and speed, and when he had wings, he could fly. "But I can tell you for certain he didn't borrow anyone's power on Icarus."

Mya snorted. "That's for sure," she said and set her tray down on the bedside table nearest Ren.

"He will have to answer for what he did when he wakes," Tavin said.

Galen stretched to his towering height. "He spelled the place to protect the innocent before he struck." He looked at Mya. "It was the opposite of your spell to ferret out those who would do harm. No one but Avery lit up." His eyes narrowed. "Did your father's guard collect the papers that were strewn about in the room where they held Avery?"

Tavin's jaw muscle jumped. "They all dropped dead."

Galen blinked. "Your father's guard dropped dead?"

Tavin pinched the bridge of his nose. "No. They found everyone dead. They did not say they found any papers supporting cause for mass murder."

I pushed myself up into a sitting position and pulled the pillow in front of me to cover my unclothed form. My muscles ached enough to know I had been close to death, but there were no bruises, only echoes of pain.

Tavin cocked his head as he scanned me. "You should not be that..." He waved at my form.

"Ren healed her and then passed out." Galen's voice carried a warning.

Tavin's gaze jumped to his. "You are defending that asshole?"

"Yes. He did what you would have done in the same situation. What *I* would have done had I been able to do that kind of devastation like she can." He pointed at Mya. "So yes. I am defending him, because if he hadn't freaked the fuck out and alerted us to Avery being missing, you would be burying the three of us, and you would never have known about the insurgents."

"Even if we died," I said, "they would have come after Mya. That dress the witch was sewing my wings on was meant for a bride for the prince who wasn't a disgrace to this kingdom. Their words, not mine." I raised my hands against their sour expressions.

Tavin ran his hand down his face and traded a glance with Mya. "The building was burned down."

"When?" Galen asked.

"The fire started while the guards were inside. It's a miracle they got out."

Galen took a deep breath. "I stand by what Ren did. And the fact there was a fire tells me there were more than just those in the building vying for your father's downfall."

Tavin grunted and put his hand out for Mya's. The minute she took it, they blinked out, probably teleporting to the king to inform him of this new information.

"Can you get me some of those pastries?" I pointed to the platter next to where Ren was still out for the count. "And then help me get Ren to a clean bed?" I gazed at the bloody blankets and surveyed the enormous bedroom. "Where are we?"

My brain kept pinging through all the information I had been fed in the building, where at least a hundred people had landed punches or sliced me after I woke from my initial blackout.

Galen started with the pastries, handing me the platter, and then he hauled Ren over his shoulder and disappeared from the bedroom.

When he came back, he said, "This is my bedroom in my quarters."

"Oh," I said with my mouth full of pastries.

Mya was right. These were the most delicious things I had ever eaten.

"Let's get you cleaned up, and then I'll let you get some rest while I clean up this room for later."

"Rest where?"

"The guestroom. With Ren. I think he deserves to wake with you by his side after all he did today. He didn't relish killing those people, and he struggled with the dark nature of Mya's powers the entire time." He escorted me into the bathroom.

"What about you?"

"I transported us there and then carried you back here. Ren did everything else. We owe our lives to him, and as much as I hate to admit it, I think I understand why you protect him the way you do."

"Are you warming up to Ren?" I teased as I stood on wobbly legs at the edge of the shower stall.

His lips tilted at the edges. "What do you think?"

THE ELVREN ASSASSIN
CHAPTER THIRTY-FIVE
Avery

I CAME OUT IN the towel to an empty bedroom and a stripped bed. The side closest to the bathroom was stained so badly that Galen would need a new mattress.

He'd hung a slip on one of the drawer handles on his dresser for me. I put it on, folded the towel, and returned it to the towel rack.

My chest cramped, and I gasped. I stumbled into the main living area. Galen lay on the floor, clutching his chest.

He reached for the other bedroom, pointing.

Ren.

I forced my body to move, my heart to keep beating and my lungs to draw air, despite my need to drop to the floor like Galen.

"Keep breathing," I hissed and moved into the bedroom.

Ren's pallor was almost as white as the sheet folded neatly over him. His chest didn't move at all.

"Damn it," I muttered and climbed onto the bed. "Don't you die on me. You hear me, Ren?" I yelled in his pale face.

I pinched his nose, tilted his head back, and I covered his mouth with mine, pushing air into his lungs as he had taught me. All his first-aid drills came back like a blast of lightning. I breathed a second time into his mouth and then straddled him and started chest compressions.

"If you die, I will find you in the afterlife and kick your ass for all of eternity. Do you hear me?" Tears blurred my vision, and I ignored the cramping trying to bow me over.

"You okay out there?" I called out to Galen.

My heart faltered with every second he didn't answer. If Galen died, saving Ren would be in vain.

"Hurts," Galen's raspy voice answered, the sound closer than I expected.

I glanced over my shoulder. Galen sat with his back against the doorjamb, rubbing his chest in a similar spot to where I was doing chest compressions on Ren. His breaths were shallow and labored, but at least he was breathing.

I got to the thirty count and breathed into Ren's mouth before starting the cycle over again, ignoring the lightheadedness threatening to overcome me.

A thump on the floor behind me ripped the top off the well of my panic. Galen.

I screamed wordlessly and slammed my fist down on Ren's chest, willing his heart to start.

A flash of white light filled the room, and pain ripped through my back.

Ren's eyes flew wide open as he gasped a large gulp of air into his lungs.

Coughing behind me eased the stress in my limbs, but I still delivered a hefty slap to Ren.

629

"Don't you ever do that to me again, understand?" My voice shook with the hysterics gripping every muscle.

Losing him for even a fraction of a second was too much for me to handle.

Ren cupped his cheek where my hand had connected. "Ouch."

Color reappeared in his skin, especially red in the shape of my handprint.

I collapsed on him, and tears started as if someone had turned on a faucet. I swatted his shoulder and sobbed as his arms encircled me. "You jackass. You nearly killed yourself fixing me."

THE ELVREN ASSASSIN
CHAPTER THIRTY-SIX
Ren

GALEN CLIMBED TO HIS feet and gripped the door as if he were the one who had the heart attack. His paleness revealed how close I really was to pulling all of us into death's grip. But his wide eyes staring at Avery also told me I was not hallucinating.

Either that or all three of us were indeed dead.

Iridescent angel wings protruded from Avery's back. Soft down draped over me, and I ran my knuckles against them, not trusting what I was seeing.

"I'm sorry," I whispered in her ear and kissed her cheek, tasting the salty sweetness of her tears. "I didn't consider the consequences of pushing myself beyond my limits." I let out a soft laugh. "Or pushing you beyond yours."

She lifted her head and sniffled with the cutest crinkle of confusion between her eyes.

I reached beyond her shoulder and ran my hand over the crest of her wing, and her eyes rolled back in ecstasy. I knew that feeling. She'd once run her fingers over mine, and I nearly dropped to my knees from the powerful sensation it caused through my entire being.

But the reaction was limited to Avery's touch. Others had touched them, and nothing impacted me like her touch. That was when I realized she was my heart and soul, and I'd do whatever I could to make sure she survived. Even if it meant my demise.

Even though every muscle hurt with the echoes of Avery's agony, I still took delight in the fact that my touch did the same to her.

"You like me touching your wings?" I teased, but my voice didn't hold its usual strength. I sounded like I had been at death's door.

Her eyes snapped wide, and she glanced over her shoulder. "Oh my god!" Her hand fluttered to her mouth, and her wings trembled and extended. "Can I fly?" Her eyes sparkled with all the possibilities written in her expression.

I studied her wingspan and nodded. "I think so. They look strong enough."

But I wouldn't be able to soar into the clouds with her. I ran my finger along the edge of one wing and then dropped my hand.

"I wish you could teach me." Her gaze carried the same sadness blanketing me.

I looked beyond her at Galen. "Did they ever bring food?"

Avery popped off of me and landed on her feet, darting toward the door. "They brought the most heavenly pastries."

"Wings!" I barked before she crashed into the door with her newly gained appendages.

I still remembered that lesson, but I had been a toddler. Catching a wing on a doorframe usually meant spinning out of control and landing on your face.

Avery halted and flexed her back. The wings tucked in nicely, and she sent me an awkward smile.

The minute she cleared the door, I pinned my gaze on Galen. "What happened?"

"You passed out after healing her, and I brought you in here so I could try to salvage my bed."

"And Avery?"

"She took a shower."

My brain still couldn't wrap around my heart stopping, but the ache in my chest told me it had truly happened. Avery had been in nearly the same condition I had been when I arrived in this realm, except she'd had her wings brutally hacked off and bled more than me.

Sheer force of will had kept me alive then, and it seemed it kept her alive through her ordeal. I just hadn't been smart. I was too preoccupied with saving her, and I'd gone too damned far.

Avery stepped into the room with a platter of pastries, and she shoved them into her mouth like the little kids at the complex when the cooks made a rare, tasty dessert. As she passed by Galen, he grabbed a couple as well.

They both looked like they had entered nirvana at the taste, and I picked one off the platter when she offered it to me.

One bite and I understood the bliss carved in their features. Citrus explosion. That was the only way to describe the crème inside the airlike pastry. I pushed up on my elbow, moving aside so Avery could sit on the edge of the bed.

I was pretty sure I sucked down half that platter in a matter of seconds, and when I went to grab the last pastry, Avery slapped my hand.

"Come on. I died for you. I deserve the last pastry." Okay, perhaps I was being a bit dramatic, but damn, these things were good.

She rolled her eyes, set the tray on the bedside table, and split the pastry in half, offering one part for me while she plopped the other half in her mouth with a grin. I took the pastry between my teeth with a grumble, but at least I got part of the tasty treat. She could have eaten the whole thing to spite me.

With a food coma threatening, I stretched out on my side and ran my fingers over the wing nearest to me.

Avery responded with a purr of delight.

Galen hadn't moved from his station near the door. He watched us interact as if he weren't a part of this merry, cursed band of ours. He remained rooted to his spot, as if entering the room fully would somehow agitate me.

"You don't have to stand so far from us," Avery said, almost echoing my inner monologue.

Galen's gaze moved to mine as if looking for approval. But I was not the center of our universe. She had already rolled out the welcome mat, and I was oddly not bothered by it. I guessed our adventures in saving Avery had changed my perspective. Or maybe I didn't feel threatened by him anymore.

"Do you mind?" Galen asked.

"I'm sure you are as curious as I was about her wings."

I felt every second of my almost death, and the food made me sluggish enough to want to close my eyes. But this was only temporary. As soon as the food hit my bloodstream, I'd have as much energy as an over-sugared child.

The way Avery moaned when Galen stroked her wing did more for my vigor than the food. But she had been through physical trauma, and I didn't want to assume she wanted more than only a wing stroke.

We kept playing with her new wings, enjoying her unique sounds. Galen traded a look with me and tilted his eyebrow.

"You want to tag team her now?" I asked.

His cheeks turned red, and Avery scowled at me.

"I'm already lying down." I grinned. "And I could be convinced to let her ride me into oblivion." I met her sharp gaze. "But only if she's up for it. She's had a hell of a day." I took her hand and kissed her palm. "It's your choice."

Avery pouted. "What if I just want to be spoiled?"

"I'm not sure my heart can handle that yet." I slipped her finger into my mouth and twirled my tongue around it, tasting remnants of the pastries.

"Oh, but you could go for a ride?" She pulled her hand away.

"That requires minimal movement on my part." I shrugged a shoulder. "Besides, I'm sure Galen would be happy to oblige."

Her head tilted to the side a fraction. "You wouldn't go into a rant?"

I shook my head.

Her gaze bounced between the two of us before settling back on me. "What exactly happened between you two while I was having the shit beat out of me?"

I chewed my lower lip, trying to put it all into words. Galen had believed me when he finally came down to the room and did not beat me to a pulp for interrupting something so serious. Nor was my change in attitude related to the insight I got from him when I allowed him into my head while I coaxed Avery to open her eyes. And it wasn't his willingness to blaze into a hostile situation to get Avery out of that warehouse before the unthinkable happened.

His lending me strength while I healed Avery helped, despite what it ended up doing to me. But my change in attitude stemmed from something more basic than any of those things.

I finally locked on to what had flipped my switch and then met Avery's questioning gaze. "He trusted me."

Avery's eyebrows arched, and then they lowered like she understood my reasoning. "Yeah. Galen's easy to trust." She turned to him. "Why are you suddenly so accommodating?"

Galen shrugged. "He did what was necessary, without hesitation, as I would have if I'd had any power."

"And will this mutual respect last?" She eyed the two of us.

Before either of us could answer, a knock on Galen's door interrupted us. Galen stiffened when it opened, and Tavin and the king stepped in, followed by what looked like the entirety of the royal guard.

Where I lay, I could see the front door and the procession. But even without the view, the number of footfalls indicated a good-sized crowd.

Galen stepped away from Avery and squared himself between the door and us as if he were readying himself for battle.

Tavin stepped into full view, with the king beyond his shoulder. His face seemed pinched, as if he did not wish to follow whatever orders his father had issued. He looked exactly like he had when he read off my initial death sentence. But this time, Mya wasn't with him, and Avery wouldn't get the chance to be my white knight again.

He startled at the sight of Avery and her stunning wings. His mouth opened and abruptly snapped closed as if he'd remembered his place. He sighed and met Galen's hostile glare.

"He needs to come with us." Tavin pointed at me like I was a common thief.

Galen crossed his arms and stayed in place. "No."

Before this escalated and blood spilled, I cleared my throat and swung my legs over the side of the bed. The room spun, and I gripped the mattress while I blinked the dizziness away.

"Tell me you at least fortified the spell around this castle," I said as the room continued a slow and sickening twirl.

"What is wrong with you?" Tavin asked.

"Did you fucking fortify the castle?" I glared and almost puked on the floor.

Avery gripped my arm, and whatever spinning motion had captured me halted as if she were my ground wire.

"He used all his energy on healing me and ended up having a cardiac arrest." Avery jutted her chin out in defiance.

I had seen that look a thousand times, and it always brought a smile to the surface.

Tavin's gaze shot to Galen, and he nodded confirmation.

"Avery withstood the heart attack and brought him back. He was not breathing, and his heart wasn't beating. If she had lingered in the shower for any longer, we'd all be dead, and you wouldn't have a chance to seal our graves," Galen growled, with enough venom in his voice that I waited for the first strike to hit him.

But Tavin only stared at him, blinking as he processed the fact that his best friend might have died once already today. I certainly did, but I guessed I'd evaded death yet again.

But based on the king's hard expression, it looked like my dodging days were done.

"We got a sealed message that stated he took great delight in the deaths at the factory," the king said, "kicking the bodies as they fell and laughing like the devil possessed him."

"A message." Galen rubbed his chin and stared down at his friend. "And you believe someone's written message over your oldest friend?" He gazed beyond Tavin. "Where's your other half?"

Tavin stared at the floor. "She did not agree with our decision."

"And what is your decision?" Galen asked.

"A public execution," the king said. "That will appease the call for blood, and it will stop this rebellion before it's even started."

Avery stood and flexed her wings, blocking me from their view. "You cannot have Ren."

She was so blissfully naïve. The king wanted me dead the day he first laid eyes on me. Nothing had changed in his mind. But at least Tavin had the sense to look sick about the decision.

"Stand down, Avery," I said and forced myself to my feet. "No sense in all of us losing our heads."

The glare I got from her nearly made me laugh. It was a poor joke, but Galen snorted and sent an unapproving look my way.

I took Avery in my arms and delivered the type of kiss that would see me through to the other side. I pulled her flush against me and willed her to free herself from my fate.

If she could force a bond, I could break it.

THE ELVREN ASSASSIN
CHAPTER THIRTY-SEVEN
Avery

I WHINED UNDER HIS kiss. Pain pulled at the center of my being, and Ren deepened the kiss right before he pulled away from my lips and pressed his forehead to mine.

"I love you, Avery." His voice sounded hollow.

I gasped. "Ren. No."

Things with him had always been complicated and messy. I loved the man despite our rocky history. And this was his goodbye.

"I think I've always loved you, Ren." My vision blurred as he stepped away.

Our fate loomed like a dark cloud, but there was no life I wanted to remain in that didn't include Ren.

Galen put his arm out, stopping Ren. "We all die if you die."

Ren glanced at me then back at Galen. "Take care of her."

His directive iced my veins. I rubbed my neck where his mark was. But I couldn't feel the small relief map of his rune. My eyes widened in understanding.

"What did you do?" Galen grabbed Ren and ripped his shirt open, revealing his perfectly chiseled, rune-free chest. "God damn it, don't you realize this will ruin her?" he bellowed.

I couldn't speak. My chest constricted painfully, as if Ren had reached in and tore my heart out with his bare hand.

I shouldn't have revived him. I should have just wrapped my arms around him and died in his arms.

I ran toward Ren, but Galen snagged me in his arms.

Ren turned before he stepped out the door. "Please come. I want to see you in that dress."

He nodded toward the chair, where the dress the seamstress had sewn my fae wings onto sat. Then he walked out with an army of guards surrounding him.

GALEN WALKED NEXT TO me in his street clothing as I stared ahead, not giving away any of the turmoil churning under my skin. This time, the execution was not in the throne room, but in the town square at the bottom of the castle's grand entry.

I stalled on the top step, and Galen paused as well.

Ren kneeled with his head on a wooden stump and his hands clasped behind his back as the townspeople gathered. Tavin, Mya, and the king were surrounded by royal guards, and the other guards stood in the back of the crowd. It looked like every royal guard in the kingdom except Galen was present.

Mya dipped her head, and her lips moved, but I didn't catch the spell. But I felt it as it filtered over my skin. It felt familiar, but movement drew my gaze back to Ren as the executioner stepped into place with his glistening instrument of death leaning casually on his shoulder. The arced blade refracted shards of light over the crowd.

The guards parted, and the king stepped forward.

"I received word that there were witnesses to the deaths at the factory. And this man was said to be responsible." He pointed at Ren. "Before I enact his execution, I would like those witnesses to step forward and recount his heinous acts so the people of Eleka will not question my judgement."

I glanced at Galen, but his gaze locked on Tavin.

"Galen," I whispered as half a dozen people stepped forward, led by a woman with golden hair.

"Shush." He shook his head and even glared at me sharp enough for me to almost pull away.

The woman turned toward Ren with a sneer on her face, and then she curtseyed to the king. "Your Majesty, this man broke into the factory armed with swords and cut down everyone, all so he could get to his dead whore. And when he realized she was already dead, he set the building on fire to cover his tracks. I barely made it out alive, sir."

The king's eyebrow rose. "And where were you when this massacre took place?"

"Hiding in the shadows, Your Majesty." She grasped her throat. "It was terrifying." Her voice shook. "*He* was terrifying." Her shaking hand pointed toward Ren.

The king moved his gaze to those who surrounded the woman. Two women and four men. "And were you also there to witness this heinous act?"

The men nodded, but the women were slower to concur. It took them a few seconds to nod.

"Were you also hidden in the shadows?"

One woman shook her head. "No. I was outside, and I saw him fleeing toward the castle covered in blood." She pointed at Ren.

The king's nostrils flared, and he looked over the crowd and gave a curt nod. The executioner stepped into place as the guards moved in, blocking the pathway to the dais where Ren knelt.

"No!" I cried as the executioner raised his blade, waiting for the signal from the king.

Ren's gaze shot to mine. His lips tilted in a smile that drove all logic from my mind. They were going to kill him based on lies. I could not let this happen.

I launched into the air. My angel wings shredded the dress, leaving swaths of fabric on the stairs and me only in a silk slip.

"That's my dress," the woman who'd damned Ren cried as the fabric fell from my body.

I landed in front of Ren and dropped to my knees, surrounding him with my wings.

I would not allow them to kill him. I would die before I let that happen.

THE ELVREN ASSASSIN
CHAPTER THIRTY-EIGHT
Avery

I OPENLY GLARED AT the king from my protective position around Ren. The bastard had the audacity to wink at me.

With another nod, the guards grabbed the six witnesses.

"So, you admit to torturing this poor girl and hacking off her wings for your own personal use?" the king asked in a dangerous tone.

The woman's mouth opened and closed like a guppy out of water.

Galen ambled down the stairs like there were no time constraints.

My heart clanged in my chest as I glanced over my shoulder at the executioner. The blade still hung in the air while he waited for the judgement to be rendered.

Galen approached the woman struggling in the guard's grip. "Your recollection of events is pure fiction."

"How would you know?" she growled.

He cocked his head. I imagined he wore that condescending smile he used to aim at Ren.

"Because I was there," he said. "I brought Ren to the factory to save Avery. I saw what your rebels did to her. You were not among those inside that building. Otherwise, you would have died with the rest of the people in there who held malice toward the royal family and the refugees from Icarus."

"Refugees? They are scum and not worthy of the prince's attention," she spit at Galen.

"Ren never took a life before the factory. Avery has never taken a life, period. But I have." He took his knife out and slammed it into the woman's chest. "That is for harming my mate. And for plotting to overthrow the royal family."

Gasps filtered through those closest in the crowd, followed by whispers as the information spread to the rest of the people.

One of them sneered at Galen. "Why would we believe you?"

"Because I am a member of the royal guard. I have been protecting Tavin and his family since long before you were born."

"Why don't you come up here and tell the people what really happened, Galen?" the king said and waved to the center of the stage.

Ren kissed my cheek softly from under the down cover of my wings, and I looked down at him.

"You knew?" I whispered.

"No. Not until they brought me out here. Outside of the castle's charms."

Galen cleared his throat, and we looked at him as he reached down to take my arms and help me to my feet. He then freed Ren's arms and moved him away from the chopping block.

The crowd murmured.

Ren rubbed his wrists and gave Galen a nod of thanks.

"Do you know what pure of heart means?" Galen asked the crowd and turned to the king, waiting for anyone to answer.

"Avery is pure of heart." The king nodded toward me.

"It was easy to see in her, but not as easy to see in Ren. He hid it behind sarcasm and steel eyes that gave away nothing." Galen glanced at Mya. "I don't know how they maintained it in your world, but they did. And despite some of his more questionable acts, Ren does not deserve a death sentence for what happened. There were plans to overthrow the king and make Tavin marry that."

He pointed at the dead woman the guards still held. "There was no blood. No terror. I don't think the people in that factory even knew they died. The power Ren used was borrowed. He did a spell to protect the innocent. Those who did not have nefarious intent toward the crown or Avery were not intended to be harmed." His gaze pinned on Mya. "If anyone in that building were innocent, they would be standing here."

"You and Avery were innocent," Ren said. "I didn't see anyone else on the floor where Avery was tied up."

"I ran," a youthful voice within the gathering called out. "People around me at the machinery dropped, and it scared me, so I ran."

Another hand raised among the audience and another until a dozen young adults and a few children stood with their arms high.

Ren's chin sank to his chest, and he trembled in my grip. Gratitude scraped over me, and then he inhaled and picked his head back up. His face turned back into the neutral mask I was used to from our years at the complex.

"Was there any screaming as these people indicated?" the king asked, pointing toward the liars in our midst.

"No, sir. He is right. One minute they were working, and the next they collapsed on the ground."

"No blood?" he clarified.

"No, sir."

"Did you know they were beating her on the ground floor?"

The survivors shook their heads. "That area of the building is off-limits. They hold private meetings in there that we are not allowed to attend."

The king turned a glare onto the six survivors. "Mya, are there any others present?"

"Yes," Tavin answered for her.

"How many?"

"It looks like twenty more souls who want us dead," Tavin said as he scanned the crowd.

"Show me."

Mya sucked in a stream of air, and twenty others in the crowd beyond the six already detained swayed. I could pick them out now, since she'd sucked most of their energy out, leaving them exhausted husks. A couple of them tried to flee, but they collapsed on the ground from Mya's magic.

She inhaled again, and those still on their feet dropped to their knees.

"Collect them, please," the king said.

His guardsmen dispersed into the crowd and dragged them all to the stage, including the six who'd lied in an effort to kill Ren.

The king turned to the crowd. "Galen put the right term to these three new citizens of our realm. Avery, Ren, and Mya are refugees seeking asylum here. Much like we originally sought this realm for asylum against tyranny. If we had stayed on Elbeeon, we would have been slaughtered. Avery and Ren faced that on Icarus." He glanced at Mya. "And Mya is my son's spirit mate, so while you may not like what she was, you must respect who she has become."

"And as far as these citizens..." He waved at the twenty-six men and women huddled together on the platform. "Their crimes include abducting and nearly killing a refugee, organizing a rebellion, and lying to send an innocent man to the gallows. What is your punishment for such crimes?"

Shocked silence filtered across the crowd. It was a shrewd move to give the people the responsibility for the punishment. This way, they could not label him a tyrant.

Someone yelled, "Death!"

They all chimed in unanimously, chanting it over and over.

"Punishment has been decided." He turned to his son and waved to the gathered criminals, who were now one mass of terrified limbs that shook enough so I could feel their tremors in the wood we stood on.

With a tilt of his head, the convicted clan instantly collapsed, dead by Tavin and Mya's shared magic.

"That about does it." The king headed down the stairs, and the crowd parted, letting him through to the palace steps.

Tavin waved us forward. Ren took one of my hands, and Galen took the other. We followed the king, with Tavin and Mya behind us, as the guard filled in the gaps around our procession.

The minute the doors of the palace closed behind us, Tavin and Mya started toward their wing of the castle, but the king spun around and glared at me.

"You still do not know your place, young lady," he said.

I dropped my gaze. "I could not let you kill Ren, even if I had to die to make my point."

The king huffed and turned to Ren. "I had no intention of killing you. You were the bait we needed to flush out the rest of the rebels." His eyes narrowed as he studied Ren. "I have never seen anyone break a bond by will alone and survive." He crossed his arms. "Why would you even attempt it?"

"I thought my time was up, and I refused to be responsible for her death, too." Ren raised his shoulder and let it drop. "And I figured Galen deserved a happily ever after with Avery."

The king stared at him for a long moment. "Mya tells me you are almost as accomplished a fighter as she is. And I have seen her and Tavin spar."

"Mya was the last one who brought me down before Galen did the other day."

"After you took me to the mat," Galen corrected.

The king slowly nodded, as if he had more on his mind than Ren's fighting abilities. When the king looked at Galen, he asked, "Do you feel he is adept enough to be a member of the royal guard?"

Galen's jaw dropped as quickly as mine.

"No offense, Your Majesty, but I'm not royal guard material," Ren said. "I just got my pass to freedom, and I would very much like to see your realm and find out what I am passionate about beyond Avery. Right now, I need to figure out who the hell I am before I commit my life to the throne."

The king's eyebrows arched as he studied Ren. I gulped the sudden swell of fear that the king would lash out at Ren. After all, any dissent or refusal of any kind on Icarus was met with a swift and severe beating.

But the king just gave a curt nod, swiveled on his heel, and marched away.

THE ELVREN ASSASSIN
EPILOGUE
Ren

"Happily ever after?" Galen snorted after he closed the door to his suite behind us. He cocked a single eyebrow. "You really think she'd ever have a happily ever after if you died?"

"She has you, so, yeah." I turned to Avery. "I'm sure she'd miss being filled, but there are toys for that."

My lips twitched into a grin.

She swatted my arm for another inappropriate joke. I moved like lightning, slamming her into the nearest wall as all my restraint evaporated. My hunger for her plowed into me while my tongue plundered the depths of her mouth.

I tore at her clothing as furiously as she ripped at mine. I guessed thinking I was going to die and then handed a reprieve sparked my libido beyond anything else. I needed to be inside her, to feel her come for me. I needed that connection, especially since I had severed it to save her.

Fabric shredded, and I lifted her legs, wrapping them around my waist. I was already hard, and my god, she was already wet when I plunged inside her. I groaned at the bliss she instilled in me, and I reached up, running my fingers over her wing.

Damn if she didn't grip me tighter. Her throaty moan nearly blinded me with lust. I wanted to live in this heaven forever.

And I wasn't alone. Galen's want filled the room, and I turned my head to look at him and the rune still carved in his chest.

I gripped Avery's thighs and started toward the bedroom but stalled at the disappointment filling the air.

I glanced behind me. "You coming?"

Galen's eyes widened, and then he moved as if I had said the room were on fire.

I grinned at Avery. I was ready to cash in on the offer from before. The pastries we had eaten and thinking I was going to die and never feel her skin against mine ever again fueled every cell. I dropped backwards onto the bed, letting her ride me and leaving her backside open for Galen to explore.

Avery palmed my cheek and looked at me with those soulful eyes of hers. "I love you."

Her words warmed my soul. She was mine, and everyone would know it after tonight.

"Yeah, well, you might curse me after tonight."

Before she could ask why, Galen settled behind her. The pressure of him breaching her ass nearly undid me. Avery's throaty moan had me pushing myself all the way inside her. My eyes nearly rolled back from the sensation.

"You might not want to talk to either of us when this night is through." Galen slammed home at the same time I brought my hips up, filling Avery so completely that she cried out.

I guided her hips up and down my shaft while Galen snaked his arm around her waist to plunge into her so hard and fast that the friction threw me into orbit. Avery's pussy was so wet and slick and hot and tight, my mind nearly blanked.

But I wanted her screaming my name. Galen probably wanted the same because he started caressing her wings, and Avery tightened in a supreme orgasm that milked my cock to the point of near explosion.

I sat up, changing the angle of my thrusts, and took her breast into my mouth, sucking her hard nipples, and licked my way up her throat to her ear. I wanted her to hear my words when I marked her as mine. I nibbled on her lobe, and she squealed.

I glanced at Galen, and he was as lost in this heaven as I was. As tempted as I was to force a break in their bond, I couldn't do that to either of them. So, I framed my oath carefully so he was not excluded.

"I take you as mine," I whispered in her ear, and then leaned forward to lick Galen's rune before I trailed kisses to her mouth. "Mine to love." I gently caressed her lips and pulled away enough to look into her wildly sexy eyes. "Mine to fuck."

Her mouth tilted into a smile as she softly exhaled my name.

"Mine to share." My gaze flicked to Galen and back to Avery before I kissed her with every ounce of the love and passion she'd bred in me.

Our tongues rolled together in an exquisitely slow dance that had her panting when I pulled away from her lips.

"Mine," I growled and pushed inside her as deeply as I could, willing my mark to claim her. To show the world she belonged to me.

Galen moaned behind her as his pace increased.

My magic manifested in a ring around her throat like a choke chain emblazoned on her skin. A braided gold link entwined with all three of our runes.

My throat blazed as well, as if the same mark was surfacing there, and this claiming was mutual. One look at Galen showed the same golden braid and runes that marked Avery. I wondered if her original rune on his chest would remain.

She was too consumed with bliss to notice. Our names bled into one long moan as her next orgasm hit with the force of a tsunami.

Both Galen and I slammed our lengths inside her holes, and my orgasm ripped through every muscle, fueled with the knowledge that we were all equally bound together.

Avery's scream of ecstasy echoed off the walls, and both she and Galen collapsed on top of me. Thankfully, Galen rolled off to the side of the bed, answering my curiosity. His chest was bare.

I remained coupled with Avery, and I caressed her wings, feeling every one of her aftershocks. I smiled as I stared at the ceiling. I didn't think I'd ever feel this level of satisfaction. It took me a second to recognize the emotion filling my soul.

This was what happiness felt like. I was fucking happy.

I let out a huff of a laugh, and Avery lifted her head.

She stared at my throat and blinked like her brain couldn't quite understand what she was seeing. Her fingers traced it before her attention shifted to my gaze.

I grinned. "My rune trumps yours."

Avery

HIS WORDS DIDN'T COMPUTE at first. My gaze shot to Galen, stretched out beside us. My rune was no longer on his chest. It was like Ren had erased it, and for a moment, devastation claimed my heart.

After I glanced at Galen's throat, my gaze darted back to Ren. His shit-eating grin told me all I needed to know.

Ren had bound the three of us together with the same marking. An explicit statement that we all belonged to one another, instead of my possessive mark. His rune was not hidden, like mine had been. It was an announcement to the world of his acceptance of our situation.

And the mark was beautiful. Like heaven had reached through him and crafted a necklace made from the gods. It was humbling and endearing, and my eyes heated with misty tears.

Galen's gaze caught on my throat and widened before jumping to Ren's. "You bonded with her?"

Ren's answer was a wider grin. He was still inside me, twitching back to life.

"I warned that you might not like me after tonight. But I wanted my own happily ever after." He glanced at Galen. "Even if that includes you."

"You're more of a sappy shit than I thought," Galen said and looked down at his chest. He shot up to a sitting position as his hand brushed his non-marked chest, looking every bit as frantic as what had flowed through me before I'd seen his throat.

"He marked you, too." I ran my finger along the ornate rune Ren had rendered for the three of us.

Galen's gaze shot to Ren with wide eyes, like he didn't understand why Ren would do that when he so obviously had the power to break bonds.

He looked at my throat again. "The rune is as stunning as her wings. I'm humbled to be included in your happily ever after."

My heart soared.

The End

Thank you for reading. If you enjoyed ELEKA: THE HIDDEN KINGDOM, please consider leaving a review and check out the other stories set in the same League of Supernatural Assassins world!

LEAGUE OF SUPERNATURAL ASSASSINS

When given a target, an assassin takes the shot ...

... or suffers the consequences.

Genetically created as predators and raised to be assassins, they were trained to fight, obey orders, and kill. Those who didn't disappeared.

So, when the League's top assassin escapes, it leads to questions. How did she pull it off, and how long before she's caught?

But when Treya returns with a soulmate and threatens the life of their creator if he doesn't leave her alone, everyone is shocked.

Could they gain their freedom as well?

Where would they go? More importantly, is there a soulmate out there for them?

Get it now and discover how these assassins navigate the bloody waters of their life, their dreams, and their desires.

https://www.sheri-lynnmarean.com/league-of-supernatural-assassins-shared-world/

About J.E. Taylor

J.E. Taylor is a USA Today bestselling author, a publisher, an editor, a manuscript formatter, a mother, a wife, a business analyst, and a Supernatural fangirl. Not necessarily in that order. She first sat down to seriously write in February of 2007 after her daughter asked:

"Mom, if you could do anything, what would you do?"

From that moment on, she hasn't looked back.

Besides being co-owner of Novel Concept Publishing, Ms. Taylor also moonlights as a Senior Editor of Allegory E-zine, an online venue for Science Fiction, Fantasy, and Horror, and co-host of the popular YouTube talk show Spilling Ink.

She lives in New Hampshire with her husband and during the summer months enjoys her weekends on the shore in southern Maine.

Visit her at www.jetaylor75.com to check out her other titles.

If you liked ELEKA: THE HIDDEN KINGDOM, check out J.E. Taylor's other fantasy romance titles:

THE FALLEN VALKYRIE DUET

A fallen Valkyrie. A Fae-Wraith hybrid.

Enemies become allies to survive a god's wrath.

Odin's Order to reap an innocent soul from Earth makes me question everything I have ever known as a Valkyrie. Protecting the innocent is our basis for existing, and now I must decide. Do I blindly follow his order?

If I don't, I will be just another casualty in Odin and Thor's destruction of the realms. Anyone who challenges their rule dies a very public death, regardless of their origins. And now they have enslaved Earth.

Reyfyre, a fae-wraith hybrid, and one of Asgard's enemies, has been hiding in this realm his entire life. When he finds me, he offers asylum as long as I help him kill Odin and Thor.

With everything they have done, how can I refuse?

When a bounty is placed on my head, we make the decision to leave Reyfyre's mountain sanctuary and head to New York to get lost in the city of millions. But the trek across the Canadian wilderness brings us face to face with hidden refugees, predators, and thieves.

There's no other option but to survive.

If we die, then there will be no one left to stop the callous gods before they destroy the only realm left.

But are we strong enough to take down a god?

If you like dark twists on Norse Mythology, you will love the Fallen Valkyrie duet.

A FRACTURED FAIRY TALE

BOOKS 1-10

Little Red Riding Hood, Cinderella, Brave, Rapunzel, Frozen, Snow White, Sleeping Beauty, Aladdin, Beauty and the Beast and Peter Pan— all fairy tales you know and love, but twisted, fractured into something new.

Shifters and magic claw through the pages of these fractured fairy tales, giving you a thrilling take on an old tale.

Will the heroine survive whatever the evil villain has in store? Or will Love conquer all?

Grab your hard cover copy of A Fractured Fairy Tale—books 1-10 and find out!

A Fractured Fairy Tale books 1-10 includes

Red, Cinder, Brave, Tangled, Frozen, Snow, Spindle, Jasmine, Belle, Hook

Find these titles and other fantasy and suspense titles on J.E. Taylor's website!

www.JETaylor75.com

Milton Keynes UK
Ingram Content Group UK Ltd.
UKHW020621230424
441593UK00006B/258